PRAISE FOR

NEVER ANYONE BUT YOU

"Gorgeous and heartrending."

—*The Observer*, Best Books of the Year

"A beautiful and extraordinary book, strange and moving and (as always with Rupert Thomson) quite unlike anything else . . . It's a long time since I read a love story quite so convincing and truthful, and the background of the artistic avant-garde in the twenties and thirties is brilliantly evoked. But the fragrance (I can only think of it as a fragrance, like some old perfume such as Mitsouko) of the love affair emerges from the pages as if the very paper is suffused with it . . . A great novel."

—Philip Pullman, author of the bestselling
His Dark Materials trilogy

"In prose so sharp it glitters, Rupert Thomson reveals in fiction what inevitably remains hidden in nonfiction—lived experience. Through the measured but incisive voice of Suzanne Malherbe, the reader enters the intimate world of two lifelong lovers, artistic collaborators, and anti-Nazi rebels who left behind a haunting photographic legacy. After I finished this acute and tender book, I felt that two fascinating ghosts had become real."

—Siri Hustvedt, author of *The Blazing World*

"In this novel about Claude Cahun and Marcel Moore, Rupert Thomson tells the thrilling story of how, fusing love and art, one of the great collaborative partnerships of the twentieth century mounted an unthinkably brave, largely unsung campaign of political witness and resistance. The voice Thomson gives Marcel is a brilliant invention: flashes of poetry trouble the patina of its self-control, intimations of the wildness and terror of genius."

—Garth Greenwell, author of *What Belongs to You*

"Hands down, Rupert Thomson is one of my favorite writers of all time. I impatiently wait for his new novels, and he never disappoints. The atmospheric *Never Anyone But You* is exquisitely crafted and pulls you deep into the love affair of two extraordinary women. Magnificent. As always."

—Andrea Wulf, author of *The Invention of Nature*

"*Never Anyone But You* puts a hidden piece of history into its long-overdue place in the spotlight. Rupert Thomson deftly weaves a story that spans several decades—the Paris Surrealists, Nazi-occupied Jersey, heroic acts of resistance, and intense and enduring (and forbidden) love—into one seamless whole. Nail-bitingly tense and incredibly moving."   —Monica Ali, author of *Brick Lane*

"Riveting . . . With skill and verve, Thomson relates the largely untold story of two unsung heroines . . . One of the reasons they come so thrillingly alive on the page is because he successfully portrays them in many different guises—as artists, socialites, iconoclasts, and resistance fighters . . . [a] remarkable novel."   —*Minneapolis Star Tribune*

"Beautiful . . . *Never Anyone But You* probably contains some of the most elegant writing of any novel published so far this year."

—*The Times* (UK)

NEVER ANYONE

BUT YOU

NEVER
ANYONE

BUT
YOU

RUPERT THOMSON

OTHER PRESS / NEW YORK

First softcover edition 2020
ISBN 978-1-63542-001-2

Copyright © 2018 Rupert Thomson

First epigraph on page vii from *Collected Poems in English
and French*, copyright © 1977 by Samuel Beckett.
Used by permission of Grove/Atlantic, Inc. Any third party
use of this material, outside of this publication, is prohibited.

Second epigraph on page vii from "X" in *Pigeon*,
copyright © 2009 by Karen Solie, reprinted by permission
of House of Anansi Press, Inc, Toronto. www.houseofanansi.com

Photos of Lucy Schwob (top) and Suzanne Malherbe (bottom)
on page 347 courtesy of the Jersey Heritage Collections.

Production editor: Yvonne E. Cárdenas
Text designer: Jennifer Daddio
This book was set in Horley Old Style by
Alpha Design & Composition of Pittsfield, NH

10 9 8 7 6 5 4 3 2 1

Library of Congress Cataloging-in-Publication Data
Names: Thomson, Rupert, author.
Title: Never anyone but you / Rupert Thomson.
Description: First American edition. | New York : Other Press, 2018
Identifiers: LCCN 2017030118 | ISBN 9781590519134 (hardcover) |
    ISBN 9781590519141 (ebook)
Subjects: LCSH: Malherbe, Suzanne, 1892-1972—Fiction. | Cahun, Claude,
    1894-1954—Fiction. | Women artists—Fiction. | Lesbians—Fiction. |
    GSAFD: Biographical fiction. | Historical fiction. | Love stories.
Classification: LCC PR6070.H685 N49 2018 | DDC 823/.914—dc23
    LC record available at https://lccn.loc.gov/2017030118

ROBERT LUCIEN WOKLER

1942–2006

if you do not love me I shall not be loved
if I do not love you I shall not love

—SAMUEL BECKETT

In the fact of your absence,
you are in some way here

—KAREN SOLIE

AN EVENING SWIM

1940

I was in the sea when the first bomb fell. Some way out, and floating on my back. Staring up into a cloudless sky. It was a Friday evening towards the end of June. As one of the planes banked to the south, over Mont Fiquet, I could make out stark black shapes on its wings. Swastikas. Fear swerved through me, dark and resonant, like a swarm of bees spilling from a hive. Upright suddenly, I trod water, my breathing rapid, panicky. Like everybody on the island, I had been dreading this moment. Now it had come. There were several planes, and they were flying high up, as if wary of anti-aircraft fire. Didn't they know that all our troops had been evacuated and only civilians remained? A wave caught me, and I went under. The ocean seemed to shudder. When I came up again a column of smoke was rising, treacle black, above the headland to the east.

I began to swim back to the shore. My limbs felt weak and uncoordinated, and even though the tide was going in it seemed to take a long time to make any progress. A knot of people huddled on the beach. Others were running towards the road. One of them tripped and fell, but nobody waited or even noticed. Claude had swum earlier. She would be upstairs, smoothing cream into her arms and legs. Edna, our housekeeper, would be preparing supper, a tumbler of neat whiskey on the windowsill above the sink. Our cat would be sprawled on the terrace, the flagstones still warm from the sun—or perhaps, like me, he had been alarmed by the explosions, and had darted back into the house. It seemed wrong that the waves paid no attention to what was happening, but kept rolling shorewards, unrushed, almost lazy.

I was wading through the shallows when I heard another distant thump. It sounded halfhearted, but a fluttering had started in my stomach. Normally, I would dry myself on the beach, savoring the chill on my skin, the last of the light, the peace. Instead, I gathered up my shoes and my towel and hurried back towards the house, feeling clumsy, nauseous.

As I reached the slipway, two more planes swooped over the bay, much lower now, their engines throbbing, hoarse. I cowered beside an upturned rowing boat. The chatter of machine guns, splashes lifting into the air like a row of white weeds. I felt embarrassed, though, a forty-seven-year-old woman behaving like a child, and stood up quickly. I entered our garden through the side door. Claude was standing on the grass bank that overlooked the beach. The hose lay on the lawn behind her, water rushing from the nozzle. Dressed in a white bathing suit, she had one hand on her hip. In the other she held a lighted cigarette. She had the air of a general surveying a battlefield. They might have been her planes, her bombs.

"Were you in the sea?" she asked.

I nodded. "Yes."

"I thought you were upstairs."

"No."

"So you saw them?"

I nodded again.

"I saw everything," she said. "I even saw the faces of the pilots."

Her voice was calm, and she was giving off a kind of radiance. I had seen the look before, but couldn't remember where or when. I stood below her on the lawn, my hair dripping. The short grass prickled between my toes.

"I have a strange feeling, something like elation." She faced east, towards Noirmont. Smoke dirtied the pure blue sky. "I think it's because we're going to be tested."

"You don't think we've been tested enough?"

"Not like this."

Earlier that month, we had heard rumors that Churchill was prepared to abandon the Channel Islands—they were too close to mainland France, too hard to defend—but there had been no mention of any such decision on the BBC. The news bulletins were full of bluster. The Nazis had reached the Seine, we were told, but "our boys" would be waiting on the other side, and they would "give as good as they got." The next thing we knew, Nazi motorcyclists were spotted on the Normandy coast, near Granville, and "our boys" had retreated to Dunkirk. In mid-June, once the troops stationed on Jersey and Guernsey had been shipped back to England, the civilian population was offered the chance to evacuate. Long queues formed outside the Town Hall, and the telephone lines jammed as islanders asked each other for advice. It was a time for drastic measures. Two dogs and a macaw were found shot dead in a back garden in St. Helier. A man arrived at the airport with a painting by Picasso under his arm. His wife was wearing a sable coat, even though the temperature was in the upper seventies. They had no other luggage. Half the population put their names down for evacuation—more than twenty thousand people—but the Bailiff, Alexander Coutanche, declared that he was staying, come what may, and in the end only six or seven thousand left. There followed a week when things seemed to return to normal. The sense of calm was abrupt and eerie—you could almost hear the grass growing on the lawns of all the empty houses—but we knew it wouldn't last, and now the Nazis had bombed the island it was clear the occupation was only days away, or even hours.

"Perhaps you were right," I said. "Perhaps it would have been more sensible to leave . . ."

Claude shook her head. "We already had that discussion—and anyway, it's too late now. There aren't any boats."

"I know. It's just—"

She stepped down off the grass bank. "Come here." She took the towel and began to rub me dry. "You're trembling."

"It's probably just shock," I said. "I was in the sea when they came over."

She wrapped the towel round my shoulders and led me back across the lawn. Once inside, she poured me a cognac. I swallowed it in one. Afterwards, we went out to the road and looked towards

St. Helier, but there was nothing to see except the black smoke drifting southwards on the summer breeze. The planes had gone. The skies were quiet.

Later, while we were having supper, the push and pull of the waves could be heard through the open window, and it was possible to believe that nothing had happened. Still, we sent Edna home early, telling her not to bother with the dishes.

A MARRIAGE
OF CONVENIENCE

Our first meeting of any consequence was in the spring of 1909, in Nantes. She was still called Lucie then. She was fourteen and a half. Her father, Maurice Schwob, was Jewish, and he owned and edited *Le Phare de la Loire*, the biggest newspaper in western France. Her mother was a Catholic. Madame Schwob was often ill, and spent most of her life in clinics. On the morning my mother took me to their apartment, on Place du Commerce, a reason was given for Madame Schwob's absence, but it sounded unconvincing, even to me, only drawing attention to the shame it was intended to conceal.

A maid showed us into a parlor cluttered with the ornate, ungainly furniture so favored by bourgeois society at the time. It was still raining—it had rained all night—and the corners of the room lay in deep shadow; the space in which we stood felt rounded and bleary, like a crystal ball that was no longer being used. Lucie had been attending a school in England, my mother told me, but she was back now, and perhaps I could be a friend to her. Outside, trees gleamed black beneath a somber sky.

The door opened, and Lucie stepped into the room, followed by her father, a solid man with an affable, lined face. Shorter than me, and slighter, Lucie seemed removed and ethereal, as if she existed in a different dimension from the rest of us, and yet I felt a jolt as our eyes met, the strong but subtle click of recognition. Words came with it, words that whispered inside my head. *Ah yes. Of course.* Lucie and I had played together as young children, but I had only the sketchiest memory of that. Some moments are so dazzling that they obliterate everything that came before. This new Lucie had a pale, almost luminous complexion and wavy, dark-brown hair, and on her cheek, halfway between her provocative, determined mouth and the delicate curl of her left ear, was a smear of red that looked like jam. I imagined I could taste that jam, and her cheek beneath it, the raspberries picked during the summer and simmered in sugar, her skin creamy and cool. I couldn't remember having such thoughts before, even about boys, and I found myself blushing, but the light in the room was so dim that I don't think anybody noticed.

Lucie came forwards and spoke to me in English. "How do you do, Suzanne?"

We shook hands.

Her father sighed, then turned to my mother. "I'm afraid Lucie has become something of an Anglophile."

"Father," Lucie said, "I always was."

She let go of my hand, but her eyes, which sloped downwards at the outer edges, remained fixed on mine. What did she see in me? I'm not sure. I was quiet. A little shy. My hair fell past my shoulders and was parted in the middle. There were ink stains on my fingers. Later that morning, she told me I looked like a statue. No, not a statue. A caryatid. I was monumental, she said, unable to resist the play on words. Thinking I might be offended, perhaps, she hastened to add that she was paying me a compliment. There were more than two years between us—I was nearly seventeen—but I was aware of no difference in age. If anything, I felt younger. She had a kind of authority, even then—the extended hand, the steady gaze. I had never met anyone like her. Henri Michaux, who later became a friend of ours, put it best. In his collection of prose poems *Un certain Plume*, the headwaiter places a lamb cutlet in front of the protagonist and, bending close to him, speaks in a voice that is mysterious and deep. That which you have on your plate, he says, does *not* appear on the menu.

The room darkened.

Over by the window, my mother was talking to Monsieur Schwob, a murmured conversation in which I thought I over-heard the word "therapeutic." Beyond them, in the square, the fierce, gravelly crashing of the rain. I was still staring at Lucie. I couldn't take my eyes off her. My mouth was dry and my heart was jumping. Later, Lucie would claim that she had felt the same. She said it was the first great moment of our lives.

Lucie attended the lycée, as I did, though she didn't take many courses. She spent most of her time studying at home, under the supervision of a teacher hired by her father. Even so, she would often be waiting outside the entrance when school finished for the day. Back then, Nantes was known as the Venice of the West, and we wandered the streets for hours, losing ourselves in the maze of canals and waterways the city was famous for. We would stop at a small *buvette* or taproom on Quai Duguay-Trouin, which overlooked the point where the Erdre emptied into the Loire. The walls were dark brown to shoulder height and yellow higher up, and the iron-bound barrels behind the bar gave off the musky smell of oak and crushed grapes. The proprietor had a large placid face that seemed out of keeping with her sharp tongue and her sullen disposition. Here come the troublemakers, she would say when we walked in, though all we ever did was sit in the corner, drinking *café noir*. Maybe she had sensed what lay ahead.

On one of our first afternoons alone together, Lucie asked me how I saw my future. I told her my passion was drawing, and that I was planning to study at the École des Beaux-Arts. Lucie's ambition was to write.

"My uncle Marcel was a writer," she told me. "I was very close to him. He died five years ago."

"I'm sorry."

Her eyes drifted away from me, towards the window.

The curve of her throat, the slope of her nose. Something leapt inside me, like a flame.

"He was a pervert." She looked at me sidelong. "Sometimes he dressed in women's clothes."

I already knew that Lucie liked to shock. The way to impress her, I thought, was to appear not to be impressed.

"I'm descended from a poet," I told her.

"Really?"

"Yes. His name was François de Malherbe."

She sat back. "Never heard of him."

"Well, I'd never heard of your uncle either," I said, "not until just now."

"That's hard to believe."

"Why?"

"He was friends with Oscar Wilde and Colette," she said. "He even wrote a play for Sarah Bernhardt."

"I've heard of *them*."

Lucie looked at me, eyes glittering. "You're very funny."

No one had ever told me I was funny before. It's difficult to convey quite how intoxicating that was.

It was autumn before I summoned up the courage to show Lucie my work. She stood beside me in my bedroom as I opened my portfolio and began to turn the pages. There were pencil sketches of half-naked female dancers and ink drawings of the skeletons of leaves and fish, and also of mythical figures such as mermen, sirens, and Egyptian gods.

She touched my arm. "Slow down. You're going too fast."

I stepped back and let her look.

"They have confidence and grace," she said at last, "and there's a natural feeling for design—a kind of stark simplicity." She turned to face me. "You know who they remind me of? Aubrey Beardsley."

My heart seemed to expand. "I've always loved his work."

"You're good, Suzanne. You're really good."

"You sound surprised."

"It's relief," she said. "You're much better than I thought you'd be."

She had a suggestion, she went on. As I probably knew, Beardsley had worked with Oscar Wilde, providing the illustrations for several of his books. What if we were to form a kind of partnership? Her words, my images. She would soon be starting work on something she was calling "Vues et visions," which would be incomplete, she now realized, without my drawings. I would be delighted to collaborate with her, I told her, but then I would have agreed to anything that might bring us closer.

Just then, we were distracted by loud voices in the corridor. My brother Jean appeared with Patrice, a friend from medical school. Two years older than me, Jean had dark eyes and a face that was pale and serene. He took after my mother, his looks more Spanish than French. Patrice was tall and spindly, all knuckles and elbows, with sticking-up red-blond hair.

"Ah, my artistic sister," Jean said, "and Lucie, her unusual friend . . ." As always when he talked to me, his tone of voice was affectionate but condescending.

Patrice asked if I would be coming to the dance at the weekend. I told him I wasn't sure.

Jean spoke to Lucie. "Patrice has taken a fancy to Suzanne. I think he wants to marry her."

"Shut up, Jean, for God's sake." Patrice was blushing.

"Maybe Suzanne has other plans," Lucie said.

Jean smiled. "Like what?"

But Lucie had already turned away, and was seemingly engrossed in my work.

Later, Lucie and I put on coats and scarves and left the house. The streets were cold and still, the sky a soft yielding gray that seemed to promise snow. As a rule, Lucie did most of the talking. That afternoon, however, she stared at the ground, two frown lines between her eyebrows, as if she had been set a riddle she couldn't solve. We crossed the railway tracks near the Gare de la Bourse and sat on a bench under the lime trees, overlooking the slow-moving river.

"What do you think of Patrice?" she said eventually.

"He's all right. I don't know him very well." I paused. "Why do you ask?"

She shook her head. "No reason."

"So what are these other plans," I said a few moments later, "that I'm supposed to have?"

Lucie reached down and tied her shoelace.

"All in good time," she said.

Spring came again. We cycled south, over the bridges and out of the city. Fog had rolled in from the coast, and a stealthy silence enveloped us. The creak of Lucie's back wheel, the crunch of our tires in the dust and grit. My breathing. Sometimes a house loomed out of the murk—the sharp angle of a roof, the low, mournful barking of a dog. We passed a row of poplars—elegant gray shapes, barely suggested. The landscape was subtle and elusive as a Japanese watercolor.

After riding for two hours, we left our bicycles in a ditch, and I followed Lucie along a track that curved between two hedgerows. Sometimes she glanced at me over her shoulder, and there was tension in her face, and also a kind of wonder. A dark wood rose ahead of us. She found a path that led off into the trees. A new silence, even stealthier. The floor of the wood was ankle-deep in mauve-blue flowers, their bitter, milky smell so strong that it brought me to a standstill.

"The first time I saw bluebells was in England," Lucie said. "After Easter, they were everywhere. In France, they're much more rare."

"I've never seen them before." I knelt down and touched one of the flowers. Its thick green stalk, its cluster of bells. "There are so many. It's as if the ground's covered with smoke."

Lucie smiled.

We sat under a tree, our backs against the trunk. I asked her what England was like.

"I love the English," she said. "They're so tolerant. They allowed me to be myself." She gazed up into the foliage. "I think they have more imagination than the French."

"Are you sorry to be back?"

Her eyes slid sideways, finding mine. "Not any more."

It was hard to know how to interpret what she had said. I was aware of her presence, like a sort of heat.

Later, as we moved deeper into the wood, she told me she had decided to change her name. From now on, she would be called Claude. She hadn't told her father. It would only worry him. There wasn't much, she said, that didn't worry him.

"Claude," I said, looking at her.

"You don't like it."

"I do. It's just—"

"It sounds like a man."

"Well—yes."

"That's the whole idea. It's important to challenge people's preconceptions."

The fog had thinned, but the light was fading. The scent of bluebells, already dense, seemed to have intensified.

Your identity should not be imposed on you, Lucie told me as we walked back through the trees. You have to create it yourself. Her cheeks had flushed, and her hands made star shapes in the darkening air. You have to *make* yourself, she said. You can't let anyone else make you, least of all your family.

"But they *did* make you," I said.

"That"—and she had a triumphant air, as if I had just fallen into a trap she had prepared for me—"is the savage irony of our predicament. That is the great paradox."

She had a new surname as well, she went on—Courlis, like the bird—but she wasn't happy with it. She would need another one. She would choose it soon. Stopping in her tracks, she looked at me. It might be good if I thought of a new name too, she said. Something that came from inside. Something I could properly inhabit. Something genuine.

We climbed onto our bicycles and set out for the city. The evening felt still. Becalmed. Lucie's hair streamed behind her as she rode, brown against the deep green of the trees.

As we approached the outskirts of Nantes, a woman in a black dress rushed out of the gloom towards us. I pedaled faster, but she ran after me and gave me such a shove that I lost my balance and fell onto the road, my bicycle landing on top of me. I called out to Lucie, but she kept going. I watched, astonished, as she disappeared into the dark. The woman stood over me and laughed. It was peculiar laughter, like a series of inhalations. Beneath her dress, her feet were bare.

A man came up and took the woman by the arm. She offered no resistance. He said he was sorry, then asked if I was hurt. There were lines of worry round his eyes, and I knew this wasn't the first time the woman had run out into the road.

I stood with my bicycle between us, like a barrier. One of my knees was grazed, the stocking torn, and my dress was covered with dust.

He apologized again, then spoke quietly to the woman and led her away.

Though shaken, I mounted my bicycle and rode on. I caught up with Lucie a few minutes later. She was sitting on a grass verge, hugging her knees.

"You could have waited," I said.

She looked past me, down the road. "I'm sorry. I was frightened."

"So was I."

"You don't understand," she said. "I thought it was my mother."

On a warm summer afternoon, Claude took me to Place du Bouffay, and we stood exactly where the guillotine had stood. During the Revolution, more than five thousand people had been executed in the square. Though the sun was pressing on our heads and shoulders, we shivered a little at the thought. An interesting fact about the guillotine, Claude said. The authorities had it painted red in an attempt to render the bloodshed less disturbing for those who came to watch. She spun in a slow circle, arms outspread. Three hundred years earlier, she went on, Gilles de Rais had been hanged and burned in the very same place. Gilles de Rais, otherwise known as Bluebeard—guilty of the mutilation, rape, and murder of one hundred and fifty children. A small bone stood out on her wrist, and her left eye flickered. Her neck was like a stalk. I asked if she had lost weight, and she said she had.

"I've been starving myself," she told me.

"What?"

"I've not been eating." Her chin tilted upwards a little. "I like the feeling. Also, it helps me with my writing."

I felt as if somebody had taken hold of my heart and squeezed. I hadn't known Claude for much longer than a year, but to me she looked ill.

Later, in a dark corner of our favorite *buvette*, I asked if her father knew.

"He hasn't noticed," she said. "He's too busy, with the newspaper. But I think he smelled ether on me the other day. I've been inhaling ether." Her pupils dilated so suddenly that I seemed to be off balance and rushing towards her. "Have you ever done that?"

I shook my head.

"I think I might be an etheromaniac. Isn't that a wonderful word?" She laughed one of her small, dry laughs. "The trouble is, it's not very good for you, and your breath smells afterwards, sometimes for days." She made a face. "Paracelsus used it on chickens, apparently, as an anesthetic."

I glanced sideways, through the window. A black barge heaped with sand slid past. The barge had a name, but I couldn't make it out. Gulls jostled in its wake.

"You want to know what it's like, Suzanne?" she went on. "You float backwards, out of yourself—not smoothly, but jerkily, as if you've become mechanical. I saw my body from the outside. It looked like a doll that wasn't being played with, a doll that someone had thrown down. All the life was with me, where I was. And that was all I was—pure energy.

"Then I was adrift on a dark sea. The water was thick, like oil, and the waves were luxurious, hypnotic. Not waves at all, really, but undulations, like a sheet shaken out over a bed, or a curtain billowing, and there were waves inside me too, a welling of contentment, all my troubles gone . . ."

I brought my eyes back from the window.

"Sometimes you pass out." Claude reached for my hand. "Do you want to try?"

"I don't know," I said. "Perhaps."

When she took her hand away I could feel the imprint of her, a warm shape cooling.

"My father keeps looking at me," she said. "Staring—"

The words flew out of her, one sentence tumbling over another. I worried she would spin out of control and break apart. I wasn't supposed to worry, though. She hadn't come to me for that. She had come to me for something else, something her family couldn't give her.

But she was still talking.

"—afraid I had to exaggerate—you know, about how sensible you are. I had to make you sound—well—a bit boring, actually—"

"Thanks very much."

She grinned. "It's not what I *think*. It's just for him. I told him you steady me. Keep me level. I said that you were my salvation." She gave me an anxious look. "I hope I didn't go too far."

"Salvation," I said. "It's a big word."

"When it comes to you, no word is big enough." Her face acquired a sudden, strange nobility, as if she were about to sacrifice herself on my behalf. "There's no world unless you're in it."

I didn't speak, but a thought rose into my head, as hard to miss as a full moon. *That's how I feel too. About you.* Sitting by the window, I seemed to experience Claude's ether dream. I was cast loose on dark waters, powerful and unafraid. I floated free. And then, in a finger snap, my new name came to me, the name that would be mentioned in the same breath as hers, and it flew straight from my brain into my mouth and out into the air.

"Marcel Moore."

"What?" Claude too, it seemed, had been in something of a trance.

I repeated what I had said. Marcel, after her uncle. I had never met him, but I admired him, both as a writer and as a spirit. And there was another factor. Marcel was a man's name, and yet it sounded feminine. I liked the way it loitered between the genders, as if it couldn't quite make up its mind.

Claude was nodding. "And Moore?"

"It's an English name."

"You wanted to set yourself apart . . ."

"Yes." Though the truth was, I had chosen the name to appeal to the Anglophile in her. Also, she claimed she was related to George Moore, the Irish novelist.

"How did you think of it?"

"I don't know. It just arrived."

Claude leaned her elbows on the table, her slender forearms upright, and considered me. "Marcel Moore," she said. "That sounds like someone I could love."

Claude's family owned several properties, one of which was on the Atlantic coast, in Le Croisic. A traditional Breton house, with solid stone walls and pale-blue shutters, it stood on the quayside, overlooking the harbor. From the wrought-iron balcony on the first floor you could watch the sardine fishermen unloading their catch or mending nets. In 1910, Claude and I went to Le Croisic on holiday. My brother Jean had been in the same class as Claude's brother, Georges—their friendship was the reason our two families had become so close—but they chose not to come with us. Jean was intent on following my father into the medical profession, and he was busy studying. As for Georges, he had often cared for Claude when she was young—he had been like a mother to her, she told me, when their mother first fell ill—but he was about to be married, and no longer had much time for her. Their absence was a blessing. In Le Croisic, Claude and I could be alone together. If the sky was cloudy, I drew or painted at the kitchen table, while Claude curled up in a chair with books about Buddhism, or practiced yoga on a reed mat in the yard. I tried to prepare food that she would eat. I cooked pale omelets, using the whites of three eggs and only half a yolk. I steamed spears of asparagus. I made cups of hot chocolate, sweetened with muscovado sugar. When the weather was fine, we spent whole days sunbathing on secluded beaches. We turned a deep, dark gold. As I stretched out on the sand, the world shrank to a fragment of itself. All I was aware of was Claude beside me, her right hand resting on the hollow of her belly. The delicate mole near her armpit. A twist of wet brown hair . . . One afternoon, as I lay next to her, I turned my head until my lips almost touched her shoulder. Was she asleep, or was she only pretending, waiting to see what I would do? I longed to go further, but didn't dare. Instead, I drew the smell of her skin into my lungs. I breathed her in. My heart rocked like a small boat caught in the wake of a larger one.

———

That winter, after days of heavy rain, the Loire burst its banks. Nantes had always been at the mercy of the river—there had been flooding in 1904, when I was eleven—but according to my father it felt more destructive than usual. A bridge was swept away, and since many of the city's streets were underwater the tram service had to be suspended. A drowned goat washed up on a neighbor's doorstep. This was proof, my grandmother Olympe remarked, if proof were needed. The devil was at large. My father, a man of science, looked at me and rolled his eyes.

One Sunday in December, Claude picked me up from my house and we walked south, towards Quai de la Fosse. On Île Feydeau, we had to use the rickety wooden walkways that had been erected as temporary pavements. She was in one of her heightened moods. Wild, vivid talk spilled out of her. She had been writing all night, she said. She'd hardly slept. In the middle of Pont Maudit, we stopped and leaned on the parapet. Bending round the stone stanchions of the bridge, the brown, swollen river bristled with snapped-off branches and other debris. As I watched, a table floated past, legs in the air.

"I almost died the other day," Claude said. "Our housekeeper found me on the bathroom floor."

My breath caught in my throat. "What happened?"

"I put some drops of ether in a glass of Château d'Yquem," she said, still staring at the swirling water. "I took too much." She gave me a look that was defiant and accusing. "It was deliberate."

"You tried to kill yourself?" I found it hard to say the words. She nodded. "Yes."

"But why?"

"There's not enough to keep me here."

Turning away, she moved on across the bridge, towards Île Gloriette. I remained motionless for a few moments, then I ran after her.

"You've got so much to look forward to," I said. "All your dreams—"

"If only it was that simple."

Île Gloriette was an industrial zone, its narrow high-sided streets lined with warehouses and factories built from smoke-blackened brick. There was floodwater here too, but fewer walkways. Sometimes they gave out, and we were forced to double back. On rue Pélisson we came across a rowing boat tethered by a frayed rope to an iron ring in the wall. Claude looked both ways to see if there was anyone about, then stepped down into the boat. It tilted sharply, and she nearly overbalanced. Small waves fled towards the row of houses opposite.

She beckoned to me. "What are you waiting for?"

I hesitated.

"Don't worry," she said. "We'll bring it back."

I untied the rope and climbed in.

We rowed east, Claude sitting in the stern. When we spoke, our voices seemed to fill the empty streets, amplified by the water that surrounded us. Sometimes I saw a face in an upstairs window, pale as a lily trapped under a bell jar. The island felt abandoned, sinister.

We passed a sign that said rue Monteil. Up ahead was the Lefèvre factory, where the famous biscuits—Petit-Beurre—were made, and the air was heavy with the sweet smell of wheat flour and evaporated milk. I wanted to know more about what Claude had told me. I wanted to believe she had been exaggerating, and that the whole thing had been an accident. I couldn't find a way of asking, though. Instead, I resorted to a question that ran parallel.

"What's wrong with your mother?"

Claude squinted at the tapering brick chimneys of the factory. "They think she's schizophrenic."

I had never heard the word, even though my father was a doctor. Claude said it was relatively new. First used in a lecture by a Swiss psychiatrist called Eugen Bleuler, she said, "schizophrenia" was derived from the Greek words for "to split" and "mind." If she understood the condition correctly, schizophrenics were people whose thinking had become fragmented, and who tended to suffer from severe delusions and hallucinations.

"Is it curable?" I asked.

"I'm not sure." She flung a fast, anxious glance in my direction. "You don't think I'm like that, do you?"

I pulled on the oars. The water was black, and light from the setting sun broke up on the surface, like bits of a smashed red plate.

"No," I said. "Of course not."

"Good."

There was a whirr and clatter of wings as a pigeon flew low over our heads. We ducked down, our hands around our ears, then we looked at each other and laughed.

Some months later, when summer came, Claude and I took a train down to the Côte d'Azur. Claude's grandmother, Madame Courbebaisse, lived in a village a few miles outside Toulon, and Claude had written to her, suggesting that we visit. Anything to get out of Nantes, she told me, what with her father constantly worrying about her, and Georges having moved into their apartment with his pregnant wife. I would like Le Pradet, she said. The house stood on five hectares of terraced land that was planted with oaks and pines, and the beach was only a short walk away.

"And you'll meet Toinette," she added casually.

"Toinette?"

"My mother."

Something lurched inside me. Something tumbled. I wasn't sure if I'd been hoping to meet Madame Schwob, or dreading it.

"I thought she was in a clinic," I said.

Claude shrugged. "Sometimes they let her out. She's staying in a rest home nearby."

We arrived late in the evening, the trees motionless and black in a sky dense with stars, the air loud with the grating of cicadas. The next morning I woke early. I was in the drawing room, waiting for Claude to come downstairs, when I heard ponderous footsteps in the passageway outside. I stayed where I was, by the window, my back to the garden. I tried to tell myself it was just Claude's grandmother, but I already knew that she was light on her feet and fidgety as a bat.

At last a woman appeared, large enough to fill the open doorway, and dressed in dark-blue taffeta. Beneath her wide-brimmed hat, her jaw was bullish, determined.

"Lucie?"

I ought to have stood up and introduced myself, but I couldn't speak, or even move. If I was ill-mannered, though, Madame Schwob didn't seem to notice. Instead, she slowly advanced across the room, her feet and body at an angle to me, as if she were inching along a narrow ledge. I had no idea what was in her mind; it was possible that she viewed me as something unpleasant, even dangerous—a spider, for example, or a snake.

When she was within touching distance, she bent down and peered at me. I still hadn't moved.

"You're not Lucie," she said.

"I'm Suzanne," I said. "Lucie's friend."

Her gaze was attentive but veiled, and though I knew I was being scrutinized I also felt, oddly, as if I had not been seen.

She stepped back and glanced down at her hands. Frowning, she began to remove her gloves.

"Can you sing?" she asked.

I nodded. "Yes."

"Sing for me."

She settled on a green divan, her gloves in her lap, and looked at me expectantly.

I was on my feet and about to begin when Madame Courbebaisse walked in. She spoke to her daughter in a low voice and took hold of her arm. Shaking her off, Madame Schwob started shouting abuse. I slipped out of the room.

Though Madame Schwob only appeared at the house towards the end of each day, there were many quarrels and altercations— Madame Courbebaisse seemed tormented by her daughter, who she referred to as "the lunatic"—and in an attempt to lighten the atmosphere Claude and I dreamed up a series of entertainments. One evening, we put on a play Claude had written. We took the male leads and cast girls from the village in the female roles. On another night, I sang songs made famous by Paul Delmet in the 1890s—"Petit chagrin," "Les deux tulipes" . . . Once the concert was over, Madame Schwob clapped with her fingers separated, like a child. Her eyes were glistening with tears. Was it happiness she was feeling, or regret, or was she nostalgic for a part of her life that there was no returning to, before the madness wrapped her in its folds?

1912. A spring afternoon in Nantes, the weather unseasonably hot. Claude and I sat in the Café de l'Europe, three doors down from where she lived. We had ordered a second iced coffee—or was it a third? As always, we were putting off the moment when we would have to say goodbye. Outside, the square was bleached white with sunlight, but the interior of the café was dark and cool. According to the newspapers, the attempts by Great Britain and Germany to reach an agreement about naval spending had foundered once again. The arms race was out of control.

"The British will never back down." Claude pushed a lock of hair out of her eyes. "My father thinks there will be war."

All the light from beyond the window seemed to have collected on Claude's face. Her skin had its usual flawless pallor, and I could see the gold crazing in her irises. She looked at me and took a breath. She bit her bottom lip.

"What is it?" I asked.

"I just realized something. I'm not sure how to say it, though."

I smiled. "That can't possibly be true. You always know how to say things."

"It's going to sound strange."

"Tell me."

"I don't feel that I exist unless you look at me." She seemed astonished then, as if what she had just said was some kind of revelation, one of those truths you only become fully aware of when you find the words for it. "When you're not looking, it's almost as if I disappear."

I wondered if I could say what it was in my mind to say. I decided that I could. "In that case, I'll never take my eyes off you."

Her face held quite still. A single tiny movement, and the moment would evaporate. "Is that a promise?"

"Yes."

She lowered her eyes and smiled. Then she stood up. "There's a place I want to show you."

We left the café and walked to the offices of her father's newspaper, *Le Phare de la Loire*. In the downstairs lobby, we met a young boy who told Claude that he had very much admired her recent theater review. She thanked him, but didn't stop to talk. As we climbed the stairs, I asked her who he was. Jacques Viot, she said. He wasn't even fourteen yet, but he had real talent. She thought he would soon be writing for the paper.

On the first floor, we passed through a set of double doors.

"The library," she said.

The air had a sweet, pungent smell. The glue used in the binding of books must have softened in the heat. In the distance, I heard the muffled tapping of a typewriter.

"I come here to read," Claude told me. "Late at night, when all the editors have gone home."

I followed her down the aisles between the stacks. From the back of the library, it was possible to look into the empty apartment opposite. The wallpaper was the same in every room—a tangle of orange roses with black stems. The street was so narrow that I could almost have stepped from one building into the other. Light filtered down from a sky that could not be seen.

We were surrounded by scientific periodicals and mono-graphs, all highly specialized, their pages musty, foxed. Claude read the titles out loud, one after the other, the language so obscure and technical that it sounded like an incantation or a spell, and then she knocked into me, almost clumsily, as if she had lost her footing. It seemed involuntary. An accident. But suddenly her mouth was close to mine, and my arms were round her waist, her small, urgent body pressed against me, her lips tasting of coffee.

"I have longed for you," she murmured, "night after night. My longing poisoned me. It was like tetanus or septicemia. It got into my blood and made me ill. I was like someone who was dying—slowly dying." She reached out and touched the window, her forefinger leaving a faint print on the glass. "I never realized that something that wasn't there could kill me. I didn't know that could happen."

"I was dying too," I said.

"Were you? Really? I thought you had no interest in me. I thought I was the only one who felt something."

"No *interest* in you?" I laughed softly.

I told her what I remembered of our meeting three years before—the dim light in the room, the rain, the smear of jam.

"I had jam on my face?" she said.

"Yes. Just here." I touched the place. "I felt the same thing you were feeling. Didn't you notice?" I stood back and looked at her. "You didn't see me blushing?"

"I thought I was making you uncomfortable. Because I was younger."

My face burned, as before. "It wasn't that."

"What was it, then?"

Before I could answer, she pressed her lips against my lips. I felt her tongue. Long, whirling moments. Our bodies seemed to want to merge. Incorporate each other.

The door to the library opened. I tensed, my mouth still close to hers.

Footsteps approached. Claude's father appeared at the end of the aisle. He looked startled.

"I'm showing Suzanne the library," Claude told him.

"I thought someone had broken in," he said. "An intruder . . ."

She smiled. "No, father. It's just us."

Just us. That summer I thought about Claude all the time. I lost my appetite, and found it hard to sleep. When darkness fell, I walked along the quays for hours, past freighters loading and unloading. I often ended up under the pylon that supported the north end of the transporter bridge, leaning against the metal stanchion and listening to it creak and tick as it cooled after the thick heat of the day. A decade later, a Polish daredevil would die attempting a leap from the middle of the bridge into the river. His photograph appeared in all the newspapers—his tense, hopeful face, his wiry hair, a white skull and crossbones on the front of his black leotard. On those warm nights, there was a queasy, prickling sensation around my heart, like pins and needles, as if it had been numb and was coming back to life. But perhaps it had never been alive—not until then. If I looked at myself in the mirror, my eyes seemed to glitter with a hectic, otherworldly light. My mother was so concerned about me that she spoke to my father, and he summoned me to his office for an examination. Though my father still practiced as a histopathologist, specializing in the study of disease in human tissues, he was also director of the École de Médecine. After conducting several tests, he satisfied himself that there was nothing wrong with me, but my brother had his own ideas.

"I think she's in love," Jean said one day, at breakfast.

I stared at my plate, my heart beating in my throat. How did he know? *What* did he know?

"There's a friend of mine," he went on, "who sends her poems . . ."

My father's eyebrows lifted. "No daughter of mine is going to marry a poet. We already had one of them in the family. It was a disaster." But he was smiling.

"He's not a poet," Jean said. "He's a doctor."

"That changes everything," my father said.

"Which friend?" my mother asked.

Jean shrugged. "Ask her."

"I'm not in love with Patrice," I said, "if that's who you're referring to."

My family exchanged knowing looks. They thought I was lying.

From that moment on, Patrice became my alibi.

Every time I left the house, no matter what my destination was, I made Place du Commerce part of my route, hoping for a glimpse of Claude. Once, as I passed through on a tram, I saw her leaving the Café de la Bourse, on the southeast corner of the square. She was wearing a sailor's outfit, the trousers dark and loose, the blue-and-white collar on the tunic as wide as her shoulders, and she had a folded newspaper in her hand. Something shifted or dropped inside me, like a picture slipping in its frame. By then, we had already spent time in the bluebell wood again, this second visit far less chaste. Another time, we fell asleep in a field of ripe wheat. I had woken with Claude's arm across my belly, a light rain falling miraculously from a sky that didn't have a cloud in it.

The following spring, while exploring the countryside to the northwest of the city, we happened to cycle along a track that led to a disused quarry. Nearby was a small two-story house with a garden so overgrown that the ground floor was hardly visible. Trees crowded in behind, making it feel overlooked but safe. We climbed in through a broken window and crept from room to room, but found no evidence of human habitation, only mouse droppings, bird lime, and a smell so dry and peppery that Claude began to sneeze. The stairs had rotted. Some of the floorboards too. Hanging from the ceiling in the room by the front door was a black metal chandelier with frosted green glass panes. Like something from a pirate ship, I thought. We made a bed of grass and weeds under the window and covered it with a pair of torn velvet curtains. Though we felt less exposed than we had in the woods or the field, there was still the fear that somebody might come, and we pulled a wardrobe across the door as a barricade. Claude christened the place La Maison sans Nom—the House without a Name. It became our refuge, a kind of home.

One afternoon, as we lay side by side in the green gloom, Claude asked if I would ever marry.

"I suppose so," I said, "at some point. Doesn't everyone?"

"I don't think my father wants me to."

"Why not?"

"He's worried I might have children and pass on my mother's illness." One arm behind her head, she stared up at the chandelier. "He has never actually said so, but I know that's what he's thinking."

"That's terrible, Claude."

"Not necessarily. A husband, children—maybe it's not what I want. Maybe the whole thing's a blessing in disguise—" She broke off, then she said something strange. "Will you give me a year?"

"What do you mean?"

"Don't do anything for a year. Don't make any big decisions."

Though I wasn't sure what I was agreeing to, I nodded. "All right. But this has to remain a secret."

"This." She was mocking me gently. "Actually, there's a part of me that wants people to know about us. I mean, I'm not ashamed. Are you ashamed?"

"Of course not. But that's not the point."

"So what is the point?"

I sighed. "Imagine what our parents would do if they found out."

"They'd probably send us to Bondy-la-Forêt or Amélie-les-Bains." Claude was grinning. But these were places where her mother had spent time.

"That's not funny." I stood up and began to straighten my clothes. "You have to be discreet. Can you do that?" I looked at her across one shoulder. She was still sprawling on our makeshift bed, her shirt unbuttoned, the shallow slope of one breast showing.

"Shut up and kiss me," she said.

Claude's announcement in the Café de l'Europe had startled me—touched me too—but in a wider sense it amounted to a kind of provocation. She had implied that she didn't need men in order to exist. All she needed was me. In the world in which we lived, though, women didn't exist *except in relation to men*. If a woman stepped outside the confines of the behavior assigned to her gender, it could be seen as a symptom of madness. Any subsequent efforts on the part of that woman to appear rational could be viewed as dissimulation—which was also, of course, a symptom of madness. If, in other words, she tried to prove she was sane, it would be taken as evidence that she was not. She would be locked up, and stay locked up. Psychiatric practice served a system that was overtly patriarchal, a system that Claude, a natural iconoclast, longed to overturn. The fact that she wasn't allowed to articulate or even acknowledge her feelings frustrated her, and her mood would veer from one of reckless defiance to the deepest melancholy and despair.

One September evening I called at the apartment on Place du Commerce with a copy of Dostoyevsky's *The Possessed* that Claude had lent me. I hadn't finished with the book; I just needed an excuse to see her. The front door opened to reveal Claude talking to her father in the entrance to his study. When she noticed me, she broke off in midsentence, ran down the hall, and launched herself at me. In her enthusiasm, she seemed to take flight, and though she weighed almost nothing I staggered backwards, into the stairwell.

"Lucie!" her father called out. "You'll knock poor Suzanne off her feet."

But Claude was whispering, her warm breath in my ear. "I love you, I love you, I love you . . ."

Over her shoulder, I could see her father watching. I made a face to let him know I was embarrassed by Claude's show of affection, but also powerless. He shook his head and disappeared into his study.

Claude was always testing the border between what could be expressed and what had to be concealed. She liked to exploit the fact that our feelings for each other lay beyond most people's imaginations. This is Nantes, she said once. A sexual liaison between two women is unthinkable. She chuckled. It might be ironic, she went on, and it was certainly paradoxical, but there was a sense in which we were actually *protected* by convention. We were safer than we realized.

I wasn't so sure.

"Take a picture of me."

We were upstairs in the little house in Le Croisic. It was a spring afternoon, and gold light from the harbor rippled across the ceiling. Claude lay on her back in bed, the sheet pulled up to just below her chin. She reminded me of someone who had been imprisoned or restrained. Was she thinking of Toinette? I picked up the Kodak camera she had borrowed from her father and opened it and stood beside the bed.

"Not like that," she said.

I looked up from the viewfinder. "How then?"

"You should be looking straight down from above. As if you were on the ceiling."

I glanced at the ceiling.

She let out an exasperated sigh. "Stand on the bed and look down at me."

I did as she said, my feet on either side of her.

"How does it look?" she asked.

"Strong."

"Good. Take a picture. No, wait." She reached up and pulled her hair away from her face, arranging it in such a way that it fanned out on the pillow, all around her head, like a halo, like foliage. Like strange, dark flames.

I peered at her through the viewfinder, her head and shoulders trapped in the small tight frame. "That looks astonishing."

"You can take the picture now."

She stared up at me, her eyes wide open, her lips slightly parted. Light fell across the right side of her face. The left side was in shadow. She managed to look both receptive and wary, but also undaunted, as if she was about to undergo an ordeal that might challenge her, but would never defeat her. I understood that the expression on her face didn't necessarily have anything to do with me. It was a performance. At the same time, she told me that the photographs wouldn't work if I were not behind the camera. My gaze had an impact on her, she said, like sun on skin. She seemed to flower under it. Then she smiled and said, "Or do I mean *deflower?*"

That year, Claude became so thin that even her father noticed. At his insistence, she saw a doctor, who viewed her weight loss as an illness, or even as an instance of deviant behavior.

Not long afterwards, I was summoned to Monsieur Schwob's office on Place du Commerce. When I knocked on the door and entered, he glanced up from the letter he was writing and asked me to take a seat. His manner was somber, but not unkind.

He held up a copy of his own newspaper. "Have you read any of Lucie's articles?"

"I've read them all," I said. "They're excellent."

Claude's pieces on fashion and the performing arts were just like her—original and charming, every word salted with a mischievous and sometimes caustic wit.

"In May, the *Mercure de France* will be running extracts from 'Vues et visions,'" Monsieur Schwob said.

I nodded. "I'm hoping to provide her with illustrations at some point."

"I look forward to that. Your drawings are exquisite."

I thanked him.

"But that isn't why I asked to see you." He put the paper down. "You spend a lot of time with Lucie, don't you."

"Yes."

"Do you believe she's in good health?"

I hesitated, choosing my words carefully. "She's not like other people," I said. "She has always been delicate."

"I'm extremely concerned about her, Suzanne." Monsieur Schwob tugged at his mustache. "Sometimes I think the only answer is to put her in a *maison de santé* . . ."

He looked at me steadily, the wood-paneled walls of his office seemed to close around me. The window behind his head was watery, pale with the day.

"I'm not sure she would benefit," I said at last.

He leaned forwards, one hand folded over the other, white cuffs protruding from dark sleeves. The clock on the wall ticked uncertainly but heavily, like an ancient heart.

"There is one alternative," he said.

I stared at him until his amiable, creased face began to blur. I hardly dared to breathe.

"I could send her away for a month or two," he said, "to a place where she could regain her strength. But she's stubborn. I don't think she would agree to go by herself.

"She needs someone to travel with her," he went on, "and make sure she does what she's supposed to do. Someone she trusts. Would you be prepared to take on such a role?"

"Yes, of course."

He frowned. I had answered too quickly.

"It's a lot to ask, I know. You're older than Lucie, but not by much—and after all you have your own life to think of."

I mentioned other trips that Lucie and I had taken—to Le Croisic, the Côte d'Azur. I reminded him that we had known each other all our lives. Not entirely true, but still. As families, the Schwobs and the Malherbes had always been close, I said, so close that they might almost be viewed as a single entity.

He gave me a penetrating look, as if I had stumbled on something I wasn't supposed to know about.

"Nevertheless," he said, "I'd like you to give the matter serious consideration. This isn't something to rush into."

I glanced down at my hands, which lay clasped in my lap. "Lucie is my dearest friend. You of all people, Monsieur Schwob, must be aware of that. Nobody cares about her well-being more than I do."

"Your father said something similar." Monsieur Schwob paused. "In fact, this whole thing was his idea."

I waited.

Still looking at me, he nodded slowly, and there was a shift in his eyes, a softening.

"Very well," he said. "Good."

When summer came, Claude and I traveled to Switzerland. Her father had arranged that she should spend a few weeks at a sanatorium called La Colline, where she was expected to eat regular meals and to take part in activities such as hiking, swimming, and canoeing. Every so often I sent him a telegram, reporting on her progress. By the end of the month, I was able to tell him she had put on several kilos.

After the rest cure was completed, we took two rooms in a grand hotel on the shores of Lake Léman. The water was so calm and flat that it mirrored the blue sky with absolute precision. To the north, the Alps were visible; in the heat haze, their snow-capped peaks looked lacy, one-dimensional. Sitting in the hotel bar on our first evening, we felt a heady sense of release. Away from Nantes, and from La Colline, we could finally relax—or, as Claude put it, *It's only among strangers that we can be ourselves.* I was twenty-two, Claude still only nineteen.

One night, when she was in my room, lying face down on the bed, I ran my fingers over a number of small scars on the backs of her legs, so small they almost looked like pockmarks. I had noticed them before, in Le Croisic, and in La Maison sans Nom—they showed more clearly when she was tanned—but I had been too shy to mention them. Here, though, in Switzerland, I felt I could ask.

"What happened here?"

She looked up at me, through her hair. "Don't talk," she murmured. "Just touch me. Keep touching me."

The French windows behind her thrown wide open, the vast black stillness of the lake beyond . . .

The next day, on the private beach that belonged to the hotel, she caught me staring at the scars again.

"You really want to know?" she asked.

I nodded. "Yes."

"Do you remember the Dreyfus affair?"

"Vaguely."

She gave me a disapproving look. She expected me to be informed, as she was.

Dreyfus's only crime, she said, was that he had been born a Jew. Those were words that Dreyfus himself had used. He was an army officer who was accused of having passed state secrets to the Germans in a note. When the handwriting was shown not to match his own, high-ranking military and government personnel claimed that he had disguised it in order to deceive them. It would have been funny, she said, if it hadn't had such horrific consequences. Dreyfus was tried, found guilty, and transported across the Atlantic in a steel cage, exposed at first to gale-force winds and rain, and then, once the ship entered the tropics, to blistering sun. On his arrival in Guiana, he was placed in solitary confinement. For four years, he didn't see or talk to anyone, not even his jailers.

Claude spoke about the concept of the scapegoat, and about hypocrisy and prejudice, and about how those in authority will do anything to safeguard their position, even if it involves a violation of the very principles they were appointed to uphold. She listed the main offenders. She knew their names. Fabre, Henry, Sandherr, Mercier, Du Paty de Clam—and Drumont too, editor of the openly anti-Semitic newspaper *La Libre Parole*. Drumont had written a "disgusting book," in which he recorded the wealth and influence of all the Jews in France. His aim was to incite envy and hatred. It was so easy, wasn't it, she said, to cast the first stone.

She was five when Dreyfus returned to France. During the trials, convictions, and appeals that followed, the anti-Semitic feeling that had been so virulent in the early 1890s began to surface once again. Pale and fragile, with a nose that sloped down at the end, just like her father's, Claude became a target. It didn't

help that her name was Schwob. At school, she was subjected to
all manner of abuse. She would often hide in the broom cupboard
during break to avoid being bullied. Once, she fell asleep and
missed most of a lesson.

"Do you know the story about Franz Kafka?" she asked.

I shook my head.

One sunlit morning, Kafka had been walking in the botanical
gardens in Prague when a beautiful young woman waved and
called out to him. Though he didn't recognize her, he smiled and
waved back. How good the world could be sometimes, he thought
to himself. How kind. It was only later that he realized what she
had been saying. *Dirty Jew.*

"That's what they called me too," Claude said. "A dirty Jew.
They called me a traitor too. They even called me Judas."

After school one day, some children from her class used a
skipping rope to tie her to a tree. When they taunted her for being
Jewish, she didn't attempt to deny it. Quite the opposite. I'm the
granddaughter of a rabbi from Frankfurt, she told them proudly.
They pelted her with gravel. She got home later than usual, her
uniform mud-stained, crumpled. Her father lost his temper. Do
you have no self-respect? Thinking to show him what had happened, she began to take off her skirt. He tried to stop her. What
are you *doing*? But when he saw the cuts and scratches on her legs,
his eyes misted over, and the creases curving past his mouth grew
deeper. It's all right, father, she said. I'm not hurt. He demanded
to know who was responsible. If I tell you that, she said, they'll
have even more reason to despise me. When he informed her,
a week or two later, that she would be leaving the school—the
country too—she didn't want to go. She thought it would be seen
as a sign of weakness. As a defeat. But it was a relief to arrive at

Parsons Mead in Surrey, and to have the opportunity to re-create herself. The English didn't see her as a Jew. To them, she was just a foreigner.

"You weren't homesick?" I asked.

"Not really." She yawned and stretched. "I loved it there." Removing her dark glasses, she jumped to her feet. "Come on. Let's swim."

On our last night in Montreux we ate at a bistro on the water-front. In among the mountains, on the south side of the lake, low-voltage lightning flared and flickered. At the next table was a Swiss family—a father, a mother, and two little girls. The younger of the two had something of Claude's alertness. Something of her impatience too, as if the world wasn't quick enough, and she was always waiting for it to catch up. Prompted by the similarity, perhaps, I asked Claude about her early life.

She lit an English cigarette and began to describe what it had been like to grow up in the apartment on rue du Calvaire, which was where her family had lived before the move to Place du Commerce. Her mother's outbursts would often be preceded by an intense, insistent tenderness. She would stroke Claude's hair over and over. *Mon petit crochon*, she would say—a mingling of the words *crouton* and *cochon*. But it wouldn't be long before she started finding fault. *You're too short to be elegant, and your nose isn't Greek enough.* Later, there would be screaming and breakages. Claude recalled a night when her mother bent down and seized her by the wrist. Sentences came sizzling towards her. *I don't know who you are. Who are you?* The inside of her mother's head was scorched and blackened, like a pan of water that had boiled dry. Another time, her mother chased her along the corridor and kicked her in the back. She fell over, crying. She could only have been three or four. Her mother knelt in front of her. Begged to be forgiven. She found the pleading even more disturbing than the violence.

I looked out over Lake Léman, its surface scuffed and dark. I hadn't expected anything so detailed, or so distressing.

Following an outburst, Claude went on, her mother would always disappear, but the silence in the apartment would feel tense, provisional. It would be days before the air relaxed. She was a disappointment to her mother. She had made her angry. Driven her away. Worse still, her mother hid from her—or was hidden. The places had abstract, complicated names that seemed designed to baffle and exclude. *Sanatorium, clinic. Spa.* She missed her mother—she *loved* her—but when she asked if she could see her she was told that visits weren't allowed. Why? she would cry, her small hands knotted into fists. Why can't I see her? People appeared unable to explain. All they would say was they were sorry, and it was for the best.

"Who looked after you?" I asked.

At first, she was sent to her aunt Maggy, she told me, but Maggy was in love with a married man—a musician—and her father thought she set a poor example. After a few weeks, he moved her to her grandmother Mathilde's apartment in the Cours Cambronne, with its bandstand, its lime trees, and its statue of the general. Mathilde had been beautiful when she was young, eyes a blend of green and brown and gold, hair falling to her waist, and she had lived an exotic life, eight years of it in Egypt, where her husband had worked as an adviser to Cherif Pacha, the minister of foreign affairs. By the time Claude arrived she was almost blind and rarely left the apartment, but she fed Claude on a diet of books and talked to her about the Bible and Greek mythology and the death of Socrates. She saw something in Claude, and insisted that she give expression to it. She did her best to make up for the failings of Claude's mother.

"So you never had much contact with your mother?" I said.

"Almost none."

"And now?"

"There was that time with you, in Le Pradet—"

"But apart from that?"

"The doctors are always talking about the 'therapeutic value of isolation.' They think that if she's to find any equilibrium or peace she should avoid things that remind her of the past. That includes me, unfortunately . . ." She finished her whiskey and ordered another. "She came to visit once, when I was six or seven. The room was dark, and people were talking in hushed voices. I couldn't see her properly.

"My father stood behind me, one hand on my shoulder. He pushed me towards her. Told me to kiss her. Her skin smelled bad, like the water in a vase when all the flowers have died—"

Claude's mouth crumpled, and she blinked back the tears. She took a drink, then wiped at her face carelessly, almost savagely. She didn't want to cry in front of me. She didn't even want to seem to be moved.

"She peered at me as if I wasn't fully realized," she went on. "As if I was only a sketch of a child. Or as if I was someone she had heard about, but never actually met. Someone she was only vaguely interested in, and wouldn't remember afterwards.

"There was no feeling coming from her. She wasn't even curious . . ."

My love for Claude burst out of me, like a rope thrown across an abyss, but she was deep in her own thoughts, eyes lowered. The love I felt for her fell short.

I looked around. The Swiss family had gone. We were the last people in the place.

I signaled for the bill.

The path that led to the hotel ran along the edge of the lake. The lightning had come closer. No forks, just weak, sickly flashes. Thunder muttered in the back of the sky, and the air was warm and damp. There was no storm, no rain. Only a kind of tension. Claude was unsteady on her feet, and had to lean against me.

When we reached her room, I helped her onto the bed, then I went back downstairs. It was nearly midnight, and the dining room was closed. As I stood there, a flash of silver through the window showed me crisp tablecloths, clean cutlery—everything laid out for breakfast. Passing between the tables, I pushed on the swing door that led into the kitchen. Though the lights were on, I thought at first that the large, high-ceilinged room was empty, but then I noticed a door at the far end that was open to the night. A man in a white jacket leaned against the frame, one hand in his trouser pocket, smoking.

"Excuse me," I said.

He looked over his shoulder. He was in his forties, with slick black hair and gaunt cheeks. He had long, prehensile fingers, which made the smoking of a cigarette appear exotic, and slightly sinister.

I asked if he could make some coffee.

"The kitchen's closed," he said.

"It's my friend. She drank too much."

He shook his head. "You Parisians."

"We're from Nantes."

We stared at each other for a few moments, then he flicked his cigarette stub into the darkness and walked over to the stove, rubbing his hands lightly, one against the other, as though removing dust or dirt. "It should be strong, yes?"

"Yes. Thank you."

"And black?"

"Yes."

While he brewed the coffee, his back to me, I stood where he had been standing, looking out. The night was irritable with lightning.

"Will there be a storm tonight?" I asked.

There was a brief silence before he answered. "In the mountains, maybe. Not here."

He handed me a tray with a small pot of coffee and two cups. I asked him what I owed him.

"Nothing," he said.

I thanked him again.

As I moved away, towards the door, he spoke into the space behind me. "Your friendship is very close."

I stopped and looked at him. "I'm sorry?"

"It's very intimate, your friendship. I have watched you together. On the beach."

What had he seen? It was impossible to know. But it seemed Claude and I had not been as free from scrutiny as we had thought.

He scratched his cheek. It was so quiet in the kitchen that I could hear the rasp of fingernails on stubble, like someone striking a match.

"You're lucky to have found her," he said.

I sensed that he had guessed the truth about us, and that he didn't disapprove. It occurred to me that he might also be a homosexual.

"I'd better go," I said, "or the coffee will get cold."

I moved on into the darkened restaurant, the door to the kitchen swinging shut behind me.

The next day, I woke just after dawn. After looking in on Claude—she was still asleep—I went downstairs and sat on the terrace, under a blue-and-white-striped parasol. It was already hot. I opened my sketchbook and began to draw the old English couple at the next table. As I worked, I was aware of the glitter of the lake to my right, like a field of silver foil, and the chink and clatter of cutlery on fine bone china. From somewhere behind me came the plump sound of a tennis ball being stroked this way and that.

Claude appeared an hour later, in dark glasses and a headscarf. I closed my sketchbook and put it to one side.

"Did you sleep?"

She lowered herself onto the chair opposite me. "I think so."

"I can't stop thinking about what you told me."

"I drank too much. You mustn't let me drink so much." She glanced towards the lake and shuddered. "I feel dreadful. Look." She held her hand out over the table, palm facing down. All the fingers trembled.

"Are you sorry you told me?" I said.

"No. But I don't want to talk about it any more."

She rarely went into detail about her mother, but the story was always with her. Some shadows don't fade, not even when the sun goes in.

The waiter from the night before approached our table. In the daylight he looked less sure of himself. His cheeks and chin were gray-blue. In his long fingers was the local newspaper.

He spoke to Claude. "How are you feeling this morning, Mademoiselle?"

She gave him a pale smile. "Was it you who made the coffee?"

He nodded.

"That was kind of you," she said.

"Have you heard the news?" He showed us the front page of the paper.

Germany had declared war on France.

On a colorless October morning I was out in the garden, raking the dead leaves, when my brother Jean appeared. He came and stood beside me, but looked off into the trees. He had volunteered to serve in the ambulance corps, and was wearing his new uniform.

"You're up early," I said.

He looked at his boots. "I have to leave today."

"I'm sorry you're going. You'll be careful, won't you."

Still looking down, he smiled. "I'm not sure it will make much difference if I'm careful."

I knew what he was thinking. He would have very little control over what happened to him. His survival would depend on chance—the path of a bullet, the trajectory of a shell or a grenade.

"All the same," I said stubbornly, "it can't do any harm."

He appeared to consider this.

"We're not so unalike, you and I," he said eventually. "We're self-sufficient, and don't give much away, and people find that difficult." He fiddled with a loose button on his tunic. "Now I'm being posted to the front, our parents are bound to worry. You should be aware of that, and tell them everything's going to be all right." He looked me in the eyes for the first and only time that morning. "You should keep telling them that, even if you don't believe it."

"All right," I said. "I will."

He nodded. "Good."

I had spoken automatically, without thinking. Inside, I was still examining his unexpected declaration. *We're not so unalike, you and I.* This was as close to *I love you* as Jean could get, and I longed to throw my arms around him, but the distance in him prevented me. Instead, I watched him nod again, this time to himself, then move back towards the house, his boots leaving black imprints in the dew.

In the spring of 1915, Claude's father found her unconscious on her bedroom floor. Though she assured him it was a fainting fit—it was always happening, she said—he suspected there might be more to it than that and insisted that she remain at home, and under observation. The alienist he brought in to oversee her convalescence had strict rules. There were to be no visits. Claude managed to persuade their housekeeper to deliver a letter to me without anybody knowing. She had lied to her father, she said. Plagued by what she called *mal du Loire,* her own personal euphemism for suicidal thoughts, she had ingested ether and opium. She was sorry if she had worried me. Claude being Claude, though, she couldn't help but revel in the drama. *Apparently, my lips were blue!* Apart from that jaunty, smuggled note, I didn't hear from her at all.

While she was recovering, I saw her only once, and the minutes I spent with her did nothing to lessen my anxiety. I sat on a hard chair next to the bed while the alienist stood by the door, his arms folded, the air whistling in and out of his high, pinched nostrils. Intimidated by his presence, I was uncertain as to what I might or might not say. After mouthing a few platitudes, the kind of remarks that Claude would, as a rule, have ridiculed me for, I lapsed into an awkward silence.

Towards the end of my visit, the alienist was called out of the room. The moment he left, I took Claude's hand.

"You have to get better," I said.

She seemed listless, almost bored. Had she been given some kind of sleeping draft?

"You're not listening to me," I said in a fierce whisper. "This is what they can do to us, if we don't watch out. They can stop us being together. Is that what you want?"

She still hadn't spoken, but I thought she was listening.

"You asked me to give you a year," I went on. "I've already done that. If you want more, you have to get well."

"Blackmail," she whispered. But she had a faint smile on her face.

"Do what I say," I told her, "and I'll give you my whole life."

Her eyes found mine.

"If you can't actually *be* well, assume the *appearance* of being well." I tightened my grip on her hand. "Defer to their superiority. Be submissive. Whatever you do, don't tell them there's nothing wrong with you. They won't believe you. Demonstrate it through your actions." I paused. "Above all, don't criticize your father."

She nodded. "All right."

"Fool them, Claude. You're cleverer than they are. All you have to do is pretend—"

I had been so focused on her that I hadn't heard the alienist returning. "What do you mean 'pretend'?"

How much had he heard? I didn't know.

"It's nothing important, Monsieur," I said. "I was just talking about a project we've been working on."

He consulted his pocket watch. "I think it's probably time you left."

I leaned over Claude's bed. "Remember what I told you," I whispered as I kissed her on the forehead.

Outside, in the square, a raw wind blew, and the air smelled of drains. There was a part of Claude that didn't believe she deserved to live. It frightened me to think it might be the strongest part of her. If that was the case, they would never let her leave. Our love was over. I sank down onto a bench and cried so hard a woman stopped and asked me what was wrong.

"Everything," I said.

That autumn, only a few weeks after I began my studies at the École des Beaux-Arts, my father died suddenly. A colleague found him slumped over his desk. He had just returned from a nearby brasserie, where he had enjoyed half a bottle of Fleurie and a *menu du jour.* The cause of death was a heart attack. He was seventy years old.

You might expect somebody who studied disease to be morbid, but nothing could have been further from the truth. Despite working long hours and shouldering heavy responsibilities, my father was always playful. At Christmas once, we invited a few friends to our house for a game of charades. When it was my father's turn, he appeared in a hat with a lamp attached to it and a white ankle-length garment that resembled a djellaba.

What am I? he said. Nobody could guess. It turned out he was pretending to be Monsieur Schwob's newspaper, *The Lighthouse of the Loire*. Monsieur Schwob laughed so hard that a button flew off his waistcoat and struck the side of my mother's wineglass. She was shaking her head. She thought my father's sense of humor inappropriate in a man of his age and social standing. I wouldn't have changed anything about him, though I did sometimes have the curious feeling that he was younger than I was. Years later, long after we had left Nantes, Claude observed that my father was surreal before the word had even been invented.

My mother grieved stoically, her complexion paler than ever, dark smudges beneath her eyes. As a widow, she appeared to grow more beautiful. She had a stark, moonlit coloring I had seen in paintings by El Greco. It was his remarkable *Madonna of Charity* she most resembled. I was less graceful, less discreet. I shut myself away. Drew tombstones, coffins. Men laid out on marble slabs, their eyes weighed down with coins. When I emerged I spoke in monosyllables. There was a lavish funeral—my father had been a public figure, popular with everyone he met—but I found it difficult to believe that he was dead. At night, at home, I kept expecting him to walk in through the door, joking about a patient's bizarre behavior or going into raptures about his favorite *Nantaise* speciality, glass eels. How was I supposed to adapt to his absence? What happened to that unique and fluctuating space, the space he used to occupy? I remembered Claude describing her mother as hiding, or being hidden. That was how it felt. If I looked hard enough I would find him. In a cupboard, behind a curtain. Under the stairs.

———

The following summer Claude and I couldn't holiday in Le Croisic, since the area had been commandeered by the army. Instead, we traveled to Saint-Malo and caught a boat to the Channel Islands. Jersey lay only a few miles from mainland France, and most of its towns and streets had French names, but Claude was charmed by what she called its "English atmosphere"—the policemen in their dark-blue helmets, the gingerbread for sale in the shops. The island was famous for its beaches, though the difference between high and low tide was as much as a mile and a half in some places, which could make swimming hazardous; we thought we could feel the pull of the distant Atlantic, even in the most sheltered of the bays. On the rare days when the sun didn't shine, we rented bicycles and rode inland, quickly finding ourselves in country lanes, between high hedgerows, or plunging down steep hills into narrow, concealed valleys, where we saw red squirrels. Trees closed over our heads, and the gardens surprised us with their exotic plants—date palms, evergreen oaks, and even sugarcane. We came across mansions built in the Victorian style, with pillared porches and snaking gravel drives, proof that great fortunes could be made in farming, but also, possibly, hinting at darker activities, like piracy and smuggling.

We stayed at the St. Brelade's Bay Hotel, in the southwest of the island, since it overlooked a wide, unspoiled beach. Though it was our first visit, the proprietors, Mr. Harden and his eldest daughter Helen, sent a horse and cart to collect us from the docks in St. Helier, and when we arrived they welcomed us like the old friends that we would, in time, become. Beyond the hotel, next to a slipway, was a Norman church and a fishermen's chapel. Most days, we climbed up through the trees behind the graveyard. There was a path that led over the headland to a small hidden treasure of a cove called Beauport. Sometimes we sunbathed naked in the field of bracken that grew on the low cliff above the beach, or sometimes we climbed down the wooden steps and spread our towels on the stones, the deep blue and green of the English Channel punctuated by oddly shaped rocks, one of which resembled an old man's head.

One afternoon, we caught the bus to Bonne Nuit in the north of the island and set out along the coastal path. When we reached Sorel, we rested in the long grass, close to the cliff edge. The island of Sark lay to the northwest, a long low slab of darkest blue, its outline blurred in the heat haze, and seeming to hover just above the sea. It looked like a lost kingdom, half there, half not. During the walk, Claude had been talking about how she saw our relationship, and as we lay side by side beneath a cloudless sky she took up where she had left off.

"I don't think of us as lesbian," she said. "We're just people—people who happen to love each other."

"We're *women* who happen to love each other," I said.

"Gender's irrelevant. I would love you whatever you were. Man, woman—hermaphrodite . . ." She smiled.

"What's gender, anyway?" she went on after a moment. "It's just a matter of organs and cycles and—what do you call them?—hormones. I refuse to allow myself to be defined by a few biological characteristics. When I stand in a room by myself, I'm not standing there as a woman. I'm a consciousness. An intelligence. Everything else is secondary."

When Claude was in full flow, it was hard to disagree with her. "Masculine, feminine," she said. "I can do all that. But neuter—that's where I feel comfortable. I'm not going to be typecast or put in a box. Not ever. I'm always going to have a choice."

The smell of warm grass, the distant airy murmur of the waves . . .

I think I might have dozed.

When I opened my eyes again, Claude was lying on her back, gazing up into the sky.

"If life was always like this," she said, "it wouldn't be so bad, would it?"

On a dark wet day during the third year of the war I was standing near the front door, shaking the rain from my umbrella, when my mother approached, saying she wanted to have a word with me. Her eyebrows were raised, and her mouth, usually so generous, had tightened or shrunk, which I took for signs of disapproval. Since Claude's recovery, we had been careful, making love while on holiday, or in out-of-the-way places, or in the apartment on Place du Commerce, when nobody was home. Even so, the idea that we might be caught often preyed on us, especially on Claude, who was more thin-skinned than I was, and more prone to feelings of persecution. As I followed my mother down the corridor, my mind flooded with fear and dread. Had she found out about us? If so, how?

She led me into the drawing room. Once seated, she spent a few moments arranging the folds in her dress. With its velvet wall hangings and its somber furniture, the room seemed designed to complement her Spanish looks. Outside, the rain grew heavier.

She looked me full in the face. "I don't know quite how to say this."

I held my breath. I was prepared to deny everything, even if she had evidence.

"Monsieur Schwob has asked me to marry him."

A laugh burst out of me. Though it only lasted an instant, it was abrupt and loud, and it hung on in the room, like a shape punched in the air. The blood drained from my mother's face. Her black hair looked blacker still.

"Have I said something amusing?" Her voice was cold and curt, but also injured.

"No, no. Sorry—"

I remembered my mother taking me to the Schwobs' apartment in 1909. It had been raining, as it was now, and she and Monsieur Schwob had stood by the window, their heads close together, their voices hushed. I remembered overhearing the word "therapeutic," and realized they must have been talking about his wife. I remembered the time my father dressed up as a lighthouse, and how one of Monsieur Schwob's buttons flew across the table and bounced off my mother's glass. I remembered how they looked at each other. There was nothing in their faces. It was just the fact that the look had happened. And I remembered how solicitous Monsieur Schwob had been since my father's death. He had called on us most days, and never arrived without a gift—tickets for the theater, oysters from Cancale . . .

I tried to focus on the proposition my mother had laid before me. "What about Madame Schwob?" I said.

"He has divorced her." Glancing down, my mother brushed something invisible from her skirts. "Monsieur Schwob couldn't live with her. No one could. He spoke with her doctors, and they agreed—

"If the idea upsets you," she went on, looking away from me, into the room, " if you feel it's too soon, or somehow inappropriate, I won't go through with it . . ."

I was only half listening. Now my fears of being found out had been dispelled, I was beginning to wonder what effect the marriage might have on my relationship with Claude. Thoughts my mother couldn't possibly have imagined were whirling through my head, and I realized I was blushing. In an attempt to stop her noticing, I said the first thing that came into my mind. "I just want you to be happy."

In the meantime, my mother had regained some of her equanimity. She was also, it seemed, relieved—though for different reasons. "That's very thoughtful of you, dear, but your happiness comes first—yours, and that of your brother."

My brother.

In 1915, when our father died, Jean had come home on leave. He had been stationed in marshy woodland in Alsace, and his skin was soggy, gray. He would stand in front of windows, staring out. His face would empty in the middle of a conversation. The only time he was able to rouse himself was when I mentioned I might volunteer for the medical corps. *No, don't,* he said. *They get no sleep. Their hearts give out.* Only the week before, he had buried a nurse who was the same age as I was. *Stay here. Our mother needs you.* Six months later, when he returned from the front, he was lying on a stretcher in an ambulance. I spent hours by his bedside, holding his hand, something that would have been impossible before. He was weak and feverish, and shouted in his sleep. Though his doctors suspected he might have contracted some sort of blood disease, they had been unable to suggest an effective course of treatment, or even a convincing diagnosis. He was in and out of hospital all the time, but his condition didn't seem to be improving.

I asked my mother what Jean had said.

"He didn't say anything. He just grunted and turned away from me." She sighed. "I feel a gap has opened up between us. I never know what he's thinking."

"He probably has more important things on his mind." I turned to my mother quickly. "I'm sorry. I didn't mean to be rude—"

She patted my hand. "It's all right. I know."

"I think it's a good idea, the marriage."

"Really?" She looked hopeful suddenly, and much younger.

"I've always found Monsieur Schwob to be a kind and decent man," I said, "and I would very much like to have Claude as a sister."

"Claude?"

"Lucie. She has changed her name to Claude."

"That's a pen name, isn't it?"

I thought it wise not to add that Claude would soon be taking her grandmother Mathilde's maiden name, Cahun. In fact, it was possible I had already said too much, since my mother's gaze rested on me for longer than was usual or necessary, but then something in her seemed to resolve itself, and she stood up and moved towards the window. She had more energy, more purpose. Perhaps she felt a weight had lifted.

"This rain," she said brightly. "Will it never stop?"

Since both the bride and the groom had been married before, their wedding was a discreet affair. Only immediate family and a few close friends were present. Claude's brother, Georges, attended with Madeleine, his wife, but he had vehemently objected to his father's divorce—he had sided with Toinette—and he made no attempt to conceal how he felt about the marriage. After the ceremony, he refused to shake hands with the newlyweds, and when he spoke to me at the wedding party his voice was strangled. The whole thing was a travesty, he said. A farce.

His face, with its brooding eyebrows, loomed in front of mine. "You're not in favor of it, are you?"

I had just as good a reason to feel betrayed, since it was possible that my mother and his father had become involved even before my father's death, but Georges's self-righteousness and self-absorption annoyed me so much that I found myself speaking in their defense.

"What if they love each other?" I said.

"*Love.*" He looked around, full lips twisting in horror and disgust. "This isn't love, it's lack of principle. It's weakness." He turned his back on me and went in search of Madeleine.

The couple took their leave soon afterwards.

"Has Georges left?" Monsieur Schwob asked me when I walked up to him.

I nodded. "I think so."

"He's so busy these days." Beneath Monsieur Schwob's mustache, his smile was small and brave.

When I offered him my congratulations, he took both my hands in his. "You're a dear girl, Suzanne," he said, "and I'm delighted you're now part of the family." He beamed at me. "Well, perhaps you always were. I'm only sorry Jean couldn't be here. How is he?"

"No better, I'm afraid."

He shook his head. "This wretched war."

Among the guests that day was the actor Édouard de Max. He had arrived with an American woman called Constant

Lounsbery, who was a playwright, Claude told me, and a Buddhist. They had both been close friends of Marcel Schwob, her favorite uncle. In his late forties, and a leading man at the Comédie-Française, de Max was at the pinnacle of his fame. His black hair had the purple glint of a crow's wing, and his leather gloves were an ostentatious yellow. Though Claude had assured me that he was homosexual, he spent his entire time talking to the female guests, and there came a moment, inevitably, when he turned his gaze on me.

"Maurice tells me that you're quite an artist." His voice was smooth as honey poured over the back of a spoon.

I told him I was studying at the École des Beaux-Arts, and that drawing was my passion.

"Not your only one, I hope," he said with a smile that was at once provocative and playful. "Would you perhaps consider drawing me?"

"It would be an honor."

Constant came over and took de Max's arm. "Terrorizing the ladies," she said, "as always."

"I don't think this young woman is frightened of anyone." De Max pushed a stray lock of hair back off his forehead.

"Really?" Constant considered me, her eyes a stringent green, like gooseberries. "And what about romance, Suzanne? Will we be hearing wedding bells again before too long?"

De Max was also watching me.

"There must be a young man," Constant said, "surely—a lovely girl like you . . ."

Just then, the speeches began, and I saw that the playwright had taken my discomfort for coyness. Of course there was a young man. There always is.

Later, champagne was served, and Claude, who seldom drank anything but whiskey, swallowed three glasses in quick succession. In front of everyone, she put an arm around my waist and tried to kiss me, her hot breath in my ear.

"Lovers first," she said in a loud whisper. "Now sisters!"

Luckily, nobody seemed to hear.

I ushered her outside, into the garden. Dusk was coming down. Warm yellow lamps hung from the trees.

She couldn't believe how convenient the marriage of our parents was, and how unlikely. It was as if they had entered into a conspiracy on our behalf. She saw them as naive, almost childlike, since our knowledge exceeded theirs, but perhaps that is always the way, she said, when you're in possession of a secret.

She walked through a flower bed, her new dress catching on a rose and tearing. Then she was noisily sick behind a tree.

Later still, when we were in a carriage, traveling back to the Schwobs' family home, she took my arm and drew me close. "You know what I think, Marcel? I think we made this happen."

"Being sisters, you mean?"

She nodded. "We're powerful, you and I, and the world has woken up and taken notice. It has molded itself to our desires." She looked out at the dark streets of the town. "Our parents' love will make our own invisible. It's the disguise that we've been looking for." She smiled. "It's our painted guillotine."

A few weeks after the wedding, Monsieur Schwob suggested we take over the apartment on the fourth floor of the building on Place du Commerce. We had always dreamed of living together, and Monsieur Schwob seemed once again to be unconsciously colluding with us. Only later did it occur to me that his offer might not be as altruistic as it appeared to be. Perhaps the newly-weds wanted to have the second-floor apartment to themselves. If Claude no longer lived with them, they would be spared any embarrassment or awkwardness. Moreover, if Claude and I shared lodgings, it would be easier for me to discharge my duty of care. Monsieur Schwob might even be hoping that I would keep him informed on the state of her health. A photograph taken not long after we moved in was revealing about our mood. Claude's face was half turned away, but her eyes were locked on the camera, as if it was a predator and she was cornered, unable to defend herself. Though I tried, as always, to cook food she liked, she had started eating less, and the weight loss showed in her cheeks, which were hollow, pinched. As for me, I had a look of grim determination. I was worried Claude might once again fall seriously ill, and that her father would carry out his threat to have her incarcerated. It's for the best, Suzanne, he would say in his reasonable voice. He would be persuasive. He would be firm. As a woman, I would lack the power to stand up to him, and Claude and I would be separated again, for longer this time. Perhaps even forever.

But the threat came from a different quarter, one I hadn't had the foresight to anticipate. Early one morning, during our second summer on Jersey, Claude returned from a walk in a state of excited agitation. She had met a man, she said. He had been mending nets at the foot of the slipway, below the church. His name was Robert Steel, and he was a fisherman, though he also worked on his family's tomato farm in the hills above the bay.

"He has the body of a statue," she told me, over breakfast.

"You said that about me once—" The moment the words left my mouth I wished I hadn't spoken, but Claude only smiled.

"This is different," she said.

With me, she had been talking about my presence. It was my air of stillness and gravity, apparently, that made me statuelike. But Bob—she called him Bob—conformed to a physical archetype, a kind of erotic ideal. The statue he reminded her of was that of Antinous. Did I know it? I shook my head. Antinous was a Greek youth who had been the lover of Emperor Hadrian, she told me. He had wide shoulders and a narrow waist. Long thighs. After his death, a cult had been established in his name.

"Bob also has something of Rimbaud about him," Claude added.

"Really?" I poured myself more coffee. "Does he write poetry as well as grow tomatoes?"

Claude sighed. "The Rimbaud who gave up writing when he was twenty-one. The Rimbaud who became an adventurer." She reached for a bread roll and began to butter it. She had an appetite that morning, something that was almost unheard of. "Bob dreams of going to America—or Canada."

"Will you go with him?" I asked.

"Of course not. I have to complete my studies." She looked at me across the table. "You're in a funny mood this morning."

That summer, she saw Bob nearly every day. Inevitably, I came to know him too. He was patient and well-meaning. He would be loyal. He was like the ground on which you might choose to build a house.

Once, when I was left alone with him, he told me Claude was a mystery to him. He couldn't make her out.

"You're nineteen," I said.

He was bouncing a small gray pebble on the palm of his hand. "What's that got to do with it?"

We were sitting in the shadow of the cemetery wall, on an upended rowing boat. It was low tide, and Claude was over by the rocks, collecting strands of seaweed for a photograph she wanted me to take. The seaweed, she had told me, was all that she'd be wearing.

"Do you think she likes me?" Bob said.

"You're asking the wrong person."

"You're her sister."

I sighed. "Who knows what she thinks? She lives in a world of her own."

"Sometimes I think she does. Like me, I mean." He flung the stone in the direction of the sea, then pushed his hair out of his eyes and grinned. He seemed to find Claude amusing. It didn't bother him that he didn't understand her. It wasn't relevant.

I worried that Bob might take her away from me. I worried that I only appealed to the tortured Claude, the Claude who had been twisted out of shape. I suspected—no, feared—that there might be another Claude who longed to be conventional. It was an incarnation that had been buried deep, but it could be unearthed. The love of a straightforward person like Bob might undo all the harm that had been done to her, restore her to how she was supposed to be. Was my love capable of that? I wasn't sure. In any case, I wanted her to remain the odd, skewed girl who I had fallen for. I wished she had never met Bob Steel. I wanted him gone. I fantasized about him lying at the foot of a cliff with a broken neck. I fantasized about him drowning. He would be hauled to the surface, tangled like a fish in one of his own nets. If he were to die, I thought, he could have a cult.

Like Antinous.

———

July 1918. An ordinary weekday morning in our apartment in Nantes. I went to the box-room I used as a studio, and was about to start work on a fashion illustration when Claude appeared in the doorway.

"This came in the post," she said.

She handed me a letter.

Earlier that month, she had been rejected by an American university, since she lacked the necessary qualifications, but as I scanned the letter she had given me I saw that she had enrolled instead at the Sorbonne, where she would study philosophy and literature. As I stared at the matter-of-fact, typewritten lines, she told me she would be moving to Paris in September. Her father had agreed to give her a modest allowance, and she would be staying with friends of the family, in their apartment on avenue de Suffren. My mind had jammed. I couldn't speak.

"I thought you'd be proud of me," she said.

"I am proud of you," I said. "But I'm still at art school, and I don't finish for another eighteen months."

"I know. The only option is to live apart—for now."

To live apart. After we had fought so hard to be together.

"I'm going to miss you terribly," she went on. "We can visit each other, though, and we can write. It's not that long."

"Eighteen months . . ." I stared at my hands. They were stained with ink, just as they had been on that dark rainy morning nine years before.

Claude said something about our love being too strong to be destroyed by something as petty and mundane as distance. My patience came apart like wet paper.

"Is that what you tell Bob as well?"

Her mouth tightened. She disapproved of jealousy—on ideological grounds. She thought it was bourgeois, demeaning. Primitive. She seemed to have forgotten that she had also once been
jealous.

"Will you still see him?" I asked.

She shrugged. "Probably. From time to time."

"He's so unlike you. He isn't interested in any of the things
you're interested in." I grappled for something I could use against
him. "He doesn't even read."

"Actually," she said, "I find that quite refreshing."

I had been mean-spirited, and she had outwitted me—she
nearly always got the better of me in arguments—but I found
out later that my remarks had had an effect. While in Paris, she
sent Bob at least one parcel of books. Along with the collected
works of Oscar Wilde, she included something by her uncle—and
Rimbaud's poetry, of course . . .

Paris. We had already visited the city several times. During the
early years of the war it had felt feverish, unreal. The restaurants
and cafés were crowded, and the women were arrayed in all the
latest dropped-waist dresses and cardigan suits, but sometimes,
if you looked up, a huge, ghostly zeppelin slid past the rooftops,
and if you left your bedroom window open at night you could hear
shells exploding on the battlefields to the north and east. Once,
in Le Dôme, we sat next to Apollinaire, the poet who had coined
the word "surrealism." Wearing a sky-blue army uniform, he was
dark under the eyes and his shoulders sloped, but a smile flickered
at the edge of his small mouth, barely visible, like a lit match in a

shaft of sun. He had been wounded in the head while fighting in the trenches, and Claude wondered whether he was taking opium for the pain. It would explain his distracted air, she said. It would explain that smile. He died two years later, just days before the Armistice, but at least we had caught a glimpse of him.

When I stayed with Claude in the spring of 1919, the first place she took me to was a bookshop and lending library on rue de l'Odéon called La Maison des Amis des Livres. She had become friends with the owner, Adrienne Monnier, a witty, voluptuous blond woman who dressed in waistcoats, silk blouses, and skirts that were ankle-length and full. Adrienne's clothes were always gray and white, the same color as her shop. Claude couldn't decide if she looked like a peasant or a nun. She lived with a stick-thin, stylish American called Sylvia. Between them, they knew everyone.

That night, after the reading, Adrienne introduced us to a slender, mercurial figure, eyes glittering beneath the brim of his black trilby.

"This is Philippe Soupault," she said. "He's working on a book with André Breton."

Claude stared at him. "You know Breton?"

He nodded casually. "I met him two years ago, at the Café de Flore."

"Claude writes," Adrienne said.

Soupault looked at Claude, a lit cigarette slanting from his lip. "Would you consider contributing to my magazine? It's called *Littérature*. I just launched it."

Claude frowned and stared at the floor. "I'm not sure I've got anything to say."

"That's the kind of writing that interests me most." Grinning, Soupault pushed his hat to the back of his head.

But Claude only murmured something about her own incompetence.

Later, as we waited for a tram to take us back to avenue de Suffren, I asked Claude who André Breton was. She gave a little shrug. She had heard the name, she said. She thought he might be influential.

"And the man we met—Soupault—he works with Breton?"

She lit a cigarette. "So it would seem."

"Why didn't you agree to write for him? I thought you wanted to become part of literary Paris."

A tram approached, brakes grinding, but it was going in the wrong direction.

"I don't feel ready," she said.

She was adamant, but also furious with herself. She smoked one cigarette after another, and tore a fingernail with her teeth.

I told her not to worry. There would be other opportunities.

"You think?" The look she gave me was scathing, but also desperate. Her cigarette was trembling between her fingers.

"You only just got here," I said.

One sultry Friday afternoon, my time at the École des Beaux-Arts almost at an end, I climbed the stairs to the apartment on Place du Commerce. On reaching the fourth floor, I saw that the door was open. A bag that looked familiar lay in the hall.

"Claude?" I called out.

I found her in the bedroom, packing clothes into a suitcase. She was wearing a simple black vest and a pair of pinstripe trousers, and she had cut off all her hair again. She had cut it for the first time the year before, in Jersey. Mr. Harden and his daughter

Helen had noticed—who could fail to notice?—but they had been too discreet to mention it. They probably think I've become a Buddhist, Claude said. Or you've got lice, I said. I remembered how Claude had laughed at that. Why was she taking her things, though? I leaned my portfolio against the wall. My mouth was dry and my legs felt shaky. I had believed her when she told me that our love couldn't be destroyed by distance. I had been naive. Complacent. She was leaving me, as I had feared. Backing away, I walked into the kitchen and drank a glass of water. For a few moments that was all I was aware of, that thin cascade of liquid dropping through my body, clear and cool.

Claude came up behind me. "Are you all right, my love?"

"I'm hot, that's all."

"Aren't you happy to see me?"

I turned to face her. "Why are you packing?"

"We're moving to Paris," she said, "both of us." She kissed my cheek, then swung away from me. "We're original, unique. We need to live in a place that recognizes that."

"Both of us?"

I followed her into the living room. She opened the window and leaned on the sill, looking out. I stood next to her. It was evening, the river a creased silver, the barges black. She wasn't leaving me. The knot inside my body loosened.

"I found us a studio," Claude said. "In Montparnasse. It's only small, but it will do for the time being."

I remembered something Adrienne had said to us when I last visited. "You know what Apollinaire called Montparnasse?" She didn't wait for a reply. "The eccentrics' district." She looked at Claude and then at me and laughed. "Perfect for you two."

Claude touched my shoulder. "You haven't said anything about my hair."

I turned to her and smiled. "What hair?"

"Do you like it?"

I ran a hand over her head. Almost nothing there. Just bristles. It was like stroking an animal, though I couldn't think what kind.

"You do, don't you," she murmured. "I can tell." She took my hand and brought it to her lips. "So will you come to Paris with me?"

"How's Bob these days?" I asked.

"I think he finds me impossible." She shook her head. "What about you? Do you find me impossible?"

"Of course." Looking into her eyes, I felt my own eyes fill with light. "When do we leave?"

THE KISS OF
UTTER INDIFFERENCE

By the time Claude and I moved into our studio on rue de Grenelle in 1920, Philippe Soupault and André Breton had joined the Dadaists. More of an ethos than a movement, Dada delighted in the illogical and the absurd, often using nonsense to promote the belief that nothing had any meaning. Dada is anti-Dada, as Tristan Tzara, its leader, stated early on. Most of those involved in its proclamations and performances had direct experience of the Great War. Breton had worked as a military doctor, in psychiatric wards. So had the poet Louis Aragon. Paul Éluard, also a poet, had been the victim of a gas attack while serving as a medical orderly. Soupault had volunteered for the infantry, and had been wounded. Dada seemed rooted in a disgust with the attitudes that had brought about the carnage, and was also, in some sense, a genuine response to trauma. As a result, it felt necessary and valid, though it was hard to know where it would lead.

In the meantime, the war had had some radical side effects. Since women had been drafted into the workforce, occupying roles that would once have been the sole preserve of men, we had acquired a degree of freedom and independence that would have been unthinkable a decade earlier. All of a sudden we had jobs. We drove cars. We even wore men's clothes. What's more, Coco Chanel had created a sensation known as *la mode garçonne*. For many, this new look represented an assault on traditional values, since it appeared to blur the boundaries between the sexes. Some saw it as a threat to society itself. In a village to the south of Paris, a father killed his daughter for daring to cut her hair in the style of Joan of Arc. Claude, of course, had already gone much further.

One night, as we walked home after a dinner at Adrienne's apartment, we passed a *bal-musette*. Through the steamed-up window, we saw a man with a red accordion strapped to his chest and a woman bent over a violin, her hip-length brown hair swaying like a pendulum. The music was jaunty and relentless, and couples whirled beneath the stark electric lights, some in tuxedos and evening gowns, others dressed in ordinary, hard-wearing clothes, as if they had just that minute finished work. As we hesitated, the door opened and two men in white tie and tails stepped out onto the pavement. "No knickers," one of them was saying, "not even in the winter—" Slipping past them, Claude and I pushed through the crowd and began to dance.

Claude put her mouth close to my ear. "I think they were talking about Alice Prin."

"Who's she?"

"An artist's model and a singer. They call her Kiki of Montparnasse."

"She doesn't wear knickers?"

"Never."

Later, when we were thirsty, we went up to the bar and ordered beer.

A man with a head of tight ginger curls was leaning against the wall with a cigar. Finally, he spoke to me. "He's a bit young for you, isn't he?"

It was Claude who reacted first. "I'm older than I look."

"How old?"

"None of your business."

The man laughed.

"Don't mind him," said a woman in a low-cut silver dress. "He's probably just jealous."

The man wandered away, though he glanced at us from time to time, across one shoulder. We finished our drinks. The music had become faster and giddier, and we danced until our feet were sore, then we spilled out onto the street. By then it was after midnight, and a woman was singing somewhere, her voice unsteady, slurred.

The wince and rumble of a passing tram.

The black wind on the quays.

On our way back to rue de Grenelle, Claude repeated what the man had said. She took it as a compliment. A seal of approval. She was delighted to have escaped the prison of her gender, the tight cage of her sex. In years to come, she would sometimes use the words when we were in bed together. *You don't think I'm a bit young for you?* she'd murmur. But her eyes would be glowing in the darkness, and her skin would be hot to the touch.

———

Early one morning, only a few weeks after moving to Paris, the telephone rang as I was in the middle of a dream. Leaving Claude asleep, I went out to the hall and picked up the receiver.

"Suzanne? Is that you?" My mother sounded uncertain, faint. Unlike herself.

"Is something wrong, *maman?*" I said.

"It's Jean—"

My brother was dead.

I stood by the front door, in the half-dark. At the far end of the narrow hall, the door to the drawing room was open. The room had a window that overlooked the street, and natural light poured into the hallway, making the polished floorboards gleam like steel. That summer, while Claude had been in Jersey, learning how to catch fish with Bob, I had stayed behind in Nantes. For two months, I had spent part of each day in the hospital, at Jean's bedside, but he was always either asleep or delirious, and I had been certain he would not recover. The disease had taken too much out of him. Sometimes I told him stories. Sometimes I sang to him, songs I knew he liked—Tino Rossi's "Reviens" . . .

"Suzanne?"

"Sorry. I was just—"

Before he left for the trenches, Jean had asked me to tell our parents that everything would be all right, but I think we both knew it was a nonsense. I remembered a photograph Claude had taken. Jean was sitting in our garden with his legs crossed, his thumbs tucked into the pockets of his waistcoat, his face tilted skywards. He looked so confident, almost complacent. If you looked closely, though, you could see a cat crouching under his chair, and the fact that he was unaware of it made him seem gull-ible, naive. It was his mystery illness, I thought, that the photo-graph had been alluding to. It was his brief, grim future. Jean was dead, aged only thirty.

"I'm glad your father's not here," my mother said. "This would have destroyed him."

I couldn't imagine how my father would have reacted. What would have become of all his playfulness and humor? There would have been no place for them. But if the qualities that made him who he was were crumpled up and tossed aside, like old newspa-per, what would be left? A man who was no longer recognizable, not even to himself. My mother was right. It was lucky he was gone, and none the wiser.

"What about you, *maman?*" I said. "How are you?"

"How do you think?"

Grief had cracked her heart, she told me later. At the same time, though, I knew she had the toughness of a stoic. I once heard her say that happiness needs a dark setting if it is to shine. Also, she had Monsieur Schwob, and he would console her.

I returned to Nantes, and Claude traveled with me. During the quiet, empty days that followed, I kept thinking about the moments Jean and I had spent in the garden after he was called up. The rake in my hands, the dead leaves heaped nearby. No hint of a sun. Something had driven him outside to talk to me on that October morning. Perhaps he had known, at some deep level, that he would not return—or that if he did it would be as someone altered, someone else. He had wanted to let me know he cared for me before that happened. It was just that he couldn't put it into words.

We're not unalike, you and I.

At the funeral I saw Patrice. His hair was neater, but he had the same awkward, hopeful look. He was married, he told me, though he didn't have children yet.

"You were a good friend to Jean," I said. "He was very fond of you."

"He was such a mischief-maker."

I didn't recognize this as a description of my brother, but I nodded anyway.

Patrice looked down, shuffling his feet. "It was true what he said, though—about my interest in you . . ."

I smiled. "But you're happy now."

"Yes."

As Patrice stood in front of me, I wondered what it would have been like to be his wife. There was a flutter in my stomach, like the pages of a book turned over by a gust of wind. I didn't think it was regret. The nervousness or apprehension I was feeling didn't have anything to do with the life Patrice could have offered me, since that life was predictable and safe. I knew that life. It had been all around me when I was growing up, and it was still here, in Nantes, whenever I returned. No, it was the life I was living that unnerved me. The path I had chosen was the one that I could not imagine.

In the summer of 1921 Claude and I traveled to Jersey again, and this time we treated ourselves to seven weeks. As always, we stayed at the St. Brelade's Bay Hotel. We swam before breakfast and then again in the late afternoon. We sunbathed naked in the bracken above Beauport beach, and in among the split, clay-colored rocks near Grosse Tête. At Claude's insistence, I took roll after roll of film—Claude striking poses on the wall outside the hotel, Claude reclining in the shallows at low tide, Claude pressed against a lightning-blasted tree. She claimed the photographs helped her to think about herself, the many possibilities that lay before her. Who she could be.

After lunch one day I cycled to Ghost Hill, which lay to the east of St. Brelade. Claude stayed behind. She was working on *Heroines*, a series of prose poems in which she took famous women such as Salomé and Helen of Troy and gave their stories a new and often unexpected twist. While out, I stopped at the tobacconist in St. Aubin and bought two packets of Craven A, an English cigarette Claude liked. By the time I approached St. Brelade, there was only an hour of daylight left. Set back against the ridge that enclosed the bay was a white château bristling with turrets and crenellations. People said it had been built by a French general who had subsequently lost his mind. Everything below me was sunk in soft mauve shadow, though the sea beyond the headland was still lit by the sun. I freewheeled down the road, dog roses clouding the air with their creamy scent. A rush of happiness. A family sitting on the wall outside a café waved at me as I sped past.

I climbed the stairs to our room. The French windows were open, and a sheet of paper stuck out of the typewriter—*Cinderella*, it said along the top—but Claude wasn't there. She wasn't in the bar either, or on the terrace. In reception I came across Vera, a young Englishwoman we had met on a previous visit to the island. Claude objected to the way Vera had latched onto us—like a spaniel, she said—and though I was also wearied by her company I tried not to be too rude. I asked Vera if she knew where Claude might be. She nodded eagerly. She had seen Claude leave the hotel at six o'clock. I looked at my watch. It was almost eight.

After checking the room again, I crossed the road and stood above the beach. The light was fading fast, but so far as I could tell nobody was swimming. I took off my shoes and began to walk. The sand was cool. As I neared the west end of the beach I heard a woman's voice, and then a man's. At the foot of the slipway, under the churchyard wall, Claude and Bob were sitting on an upturned rowing boat. It was dark by now, and the whites of their eyes stood out in their tanned faces. Claude was wearing her new navy-blue bathing costume, the white star over her left breast ringed by dozens of smaller stars.

I told her I'd been looking for her everywhere.

"Well, here I am," she said.

Bob laughed.

His laughter wasn't spiteful or mocking. He didn't seem capable of even one uncharitable thought. Somehow that made it worse. The unfettered joy that had flowed through me when I was freewheeling down the hill into the bay was gone.

"I bought you some cigarettes." I showed Claude the packets of Craven A.

"I've been smoking Bob's," she said.

"How are you, Bob?" I said. "I haven't seen you in a while."

He looked at Claude, as if the answer to my question was something they might need to confer on. It was the kind of deference you see in people who are infatuated with each other, people for whom there is no other world. Sickened, I glanced out to sea. A swollen orange moon had risen above the jetty. Claude murmured something in English, and Bob laughed again.

"Are you still thinking of going to Canada?" I asked.

I longed for him to carry out his dream—though, in truth, I wasn't sure that Canada was far enough. That moon above the jetty might be a better proposition.

"I don't think I can," he said. "I'm needed on the farm."

"They can't manage without you?"

Claude gave me an inquiring look—she had picked up on my acerbic tone—but Bob remained oblivious.

"It's a lot of work," he said.

I spoke to Claude. "I'm going to have dinner. Are you coming?"

"In a while."

I put the cigarettes beside her, on the keel of the boat, then turned and hurried up the slipway, back to the road. I ate alone that night. My teeth grated on the tines of the fork. Everything grated. There was a moment when my eyes were so hot that I thought I might set fire to the dining room just by looking at it.

Later, Claude found me wandering in the hotel gardens. I had calmed down by then, my mind just cinders. She joined me on the gravel path and lit one of the Craven A's I had bought for her.

"You should leave me," I said.

I wasn't bluffing. I meant it. And it felt like a relief to have the words out in the open.

Claude, meanwhile, had come to a standstill on the path. She held her cigarette near her face, but didn't put it to her lips.

"Bob makes you happy," I told her. "It's obvious that you should be with him." A star dashed across the sky. It was as if someone had drawn a quick chalk line high up in the dark. What did it signify, a shooting star? Good luck? I smiled bitterly. "I don't want to hold you back," I went on, "or get in the way. I want the best for you. I always have."

Still Claude didn't speak.

I moved on along the path. There was no wind, and the air was cool on my bare arms. I listened to the crisp sound of my shoes on the gravel.

"You mustn't think you're indispensable to me," I said.. "You're not. I'm sure I'll manage."

This was a lie. I couldn't bear the thought that she might go. But I'd had enough of seeing her with Bob. Of having to appear not to care.

She dropped her cigarette on the path and stepped on it. "Are you asking me to choose between you?"

I wanted to say yes, but I didn't dare, and she noticed me not daring. I could never hide my moments of weakness from her. She was too perceptive. Her face had softened, though. I didn't think that she would take advantage.

"You *know* who I'd choose," she said.

I stopped and looked at her. Light silvering the slope of her nose, her teeth like tiny cubes of ice. Just then, I loved her more than ever. More than I thought possible. It was as if something had reached into my guts and pulled.

"You fool," she said. "I'm not leaving."

I never knew—I still don't know—what passed between them. I never saw them kiss. I saw them holding hands once, as they walked along the beach, but they looked less like lovers than young children or old friends. Years later, when Claude published *Disavowals*, she tried to defuse the apparently intimate and autobiographical nature of the book by claiming that one of her principal aims was to challenge or to undermine the whole idea of the self as an authority. Hence the title, which inferred that her confessions, if that indeed was what they were, could not be relied upon. What, then, to make of the fact that she put Bob's initials—R.C.S.—on the title page of the first chapter, a chapter in which she appeared to be describing a passionate affair? *Fast and good. Short but sweet. Our bodies met from knees to shoulders.* Elsewhere, though, I came across these words: *I want him . . . He won't have me.* Could it be true that Bob had, at some level, rejected her? Or was she covering for herself? Because this is how the paragraph went on: *Do I really want him? Yes? No?—I don't know for sure.* Perhaps there was something in her that prevented her from taking things too far. Either way, she continued to seek him out and spend time with him, and I was left to stew in my jealousy and my exasperation.

Not long after arriving back in Paris, Claude went missing. At first I didn't worry, but as the hours went by and she failed to appear I began to wonder if she'd had an accident. In the back of my mind, also, shapeless and still, was the fear that she might have killed herself. There had already been at least two attempts. Suicide wasn't a whim or a game for Claude. She had felt its seductive pull for as long as she could remember. Death was a fisherman who cast his intricately feathered lures onto the water, she had told me once, and she could never find the strength to resist. Before she knew it she was lying on a grassy bank, gills fluttering, a barbed hook in her lip. If she was unlucky, death would throw her back—and so far she had been unlucky.

Not sure what to do, I spent most of the day pretending that nothing had happened—with Claude, I had become accustomed to ailments and crises, or perhaps even anesthetized—but when darkness fell and she still had not returned a sudden flurry of panic drove me out onto the streets. We had recently moved to an apartment on rue Notre-Dame-des-Champs, and Claude's aunt, Marguerite Moreno, lived a few doors down. I tried her first. There was nothing she could tell me. Next, I went to Adrienne's bookshop, but she hadn't seen Claude for days. Nor had Sylvia. Constant Lounsbery hadn't seen her either. I telephoned Charles-Henri Barbier, a friend Claude had made not long after leaving the Sorbonne. He offered to help me look for her. I thanked him, but said I would be better on my own. I called on everyone I could think of. Nobody had any idea where she might be. I even knocked on Gertrude Stein's door, only to be told by her melancholy lover, the one with the drooping eyelids and the weighty metal earrings, that Gertrude was working, and couldn't be disturbed.

I wandered the streets without a plan, feeling increasingly desperate. I felt stupid. There was something I wasn't seeing, something I had failed to imagine. Try as I might, though, I couldn't think of an explanation that wasn't catastrophic. Either she was dead or she had left me. I walked into the Cyrano on Place Blanche and took a table by the window. I ordered a pastis. It was ten o'clock by then. Some people I recognized from La Maison des Amis des Livres were sitting by the far wall. Philippe Soupault, with his hat pulled down low over his eyes. Aragon in a black leather coat. Paul Éluard and his Russian wife, Gala. Soupault stopped at my table and spoke to me. He had not forgotten that Claude had turned him down. Maybe, in time, he said, she could be persuaded to reconsider. Maybe, I said. I drank a second pastis, and then a third. The cloudy, milky liquid burned my throat. Soupault passed my table again and asked if I wanted to come to Breton's apartment. An event was taking place, he said. It was close by. He pointed through the window, across the square.

"What kind of event?" I asked.

"Do you know Desnos?"

I shook my head.

"He's a poet. A good friend of Breton's. He goes into trances and speaks directly from his unconscious. Breton calls it 'taking subversive action through language.'"

We walked through light rain to rue Fontaine. Breton lived at number 40, above a cabaret called Heaven and Hell. Once inside the building, I followed Soupault up the stairs. My forehead felt warm and clammy. I saw Claude sprawled awkwardly on a pavement, one leg twisted under her. An open window high above, pale curtains drifting . . .

As we stood outside Breton's door, Soupault was looking at me. "Are you nervous?"

"Perhaps. Just a little."

"Don't be."

On the floor, where a doormat would traditionally be found, was a book by Anatole France, an author Breton was known to despise—in his novels, France celebrated the sort of blind, unthinking patriotism that had led to the Great War, and to the futile sacrifice of so many lives, including that of my brother—and Soupault and I both wiped our feet on its already torn and tattered pages before we rang the bell.

Inside the apartment it was dark, and people stood about in the shadows, talking in hushed voices. The mood was one of expectation, and also of self-importance. André Breton was younger than I imagined he would be, but he had the appearance of great substance and authority. I thought this might have something to do with the size of his head, which was out of proportion to the rest of him and topped with hair that was swept back, almost leonine.

I moved into a room that overlooked the street. On boulevard Clichy the nightclub signs flashed on and off, and the room glowed pink, then blue, then pink again. The tribal masks and fetish dolls that hung on the walls jumped out at me. Jumped back. Breton's new wife, Simone, serene as a high priestess, was serving glasses of mandarin-flavored curaçao.

"Shall we begin?" Breton said.

Several people took their seats at a round table. Those of us who couldn't find a chair stood behind them, in a circle. A young man with curious, oyster-colored eyes achieved a state of auto-hypnosis that lasted more than an hour. This was Robert Des-nos, the poet Soupault had spoken of. I wasn't sure if the trance was real, and there was a sense in which it didn't matter; in the context of the evening, authenticity had many forms. Desnos talked fluently, translating the random, disconcerting emanations of his unconscious into lucid images and words. He juxtaposed his dreams and fears with a number of mundane concerns. One moment he was a seer. The next, a fool. Eventually, he became violent, threatening the man sitting next to him, and Breton had to step in and wake him up.

Later, I found myself standing in front of Desnos. Something of his performance remained—a certain distance, an aura, a kind of afterglow.

"That was remarkable," I said.

His smile was sleepy, dreamy, his heavy eyelids lowering over those extraordinary eyes. "I don't remember a thing."

It was after midnight when I walked back down the stairs. When I said goodbye to Soupault, he asked if I had enjoyed myself. I told him that I had. In truth, I didn't know what to make of the event. It had somehow managed to be at once compelling and ridiculous. I shook my head. Claude, though . . . Where could she be? The alcohol was wearing off, and I felt blurred and numb, but also frantic. If I pictured the inside of my head, I saw forked lightning flickering at the base of a huge black sky.

I hurried back to rue Notre-Dame-des-Champs. The apartment was dark and silent. I stood at the window, looking out. A tree shook in the wind.

When I woke the next morning, Claude still had not come home. I did the things I always did—I bought bread, made coffee, swept and mopped the floors—but I moved in a kind of stupor. I was desolate. From now on, I would live alone. It was the first day of a new gray life.

Charles-Henri Barbier appeared at the door.

"Any sign of her?" he asked.

I shook my head.

Still only twenty-one, Charles-Henri had a strong nose, like a warrior, and eyes that always looked concerned. He had studied at the Sorbonne, as Claude had, and belonged to a group of young intellectuals who produced *Philosophies*, a magazine to which Claude had contributed. That morning, he talked about Claude's spontaneity. It was an attribute he approved of, he said, one he wished he had himself. He was still with me when a key turned in the lock and Claude walked in with two sunflowers wrapped in brown paper and a bag of avocados. She was wearing a pale-blue cotton shirt and a pair of baggy trousers that were spattered with mud. There were traces of gold paint in her eyebrows and inside her ears.

Charles-Henri greeted her, telling her we had been worried about her, then tactfully withdrew. When the door had closed behind him, Claude put her arms around me.

"Poor Marcel. I wasn't thinking." She started, as if she had discovered a truth. "But that's how we should live, isn't it—instinctively, and without restraints."

"There's no such thing as should," I muttered.

She stroked my hair. "You're right."

"Where were you?"

The previous morning she had woken at five, she told me, a kind of shiver at the edges of her field of vision. She was seeing in too much detail—the jeweled bubbles in a glass of water on the bedside table, the shadow between each page of a closed book. I was fast asleep, and she envied me that sleep, so untroubled and oblivious. She decided to go out. The click of the front door closing was neat as a full stop—but an end is also a beginning. She walked east, towards Île Saint-Louis.

Half an hour later, she was descending a flight of steps that led down to the river when a voice called out.

"*Garçon?*"

The word was unexpected, and yet completely in tune with her shifting, fluid sense of herself. It was almost as if her thoughts had become audible. Looking round, she saw an African woman seated on a bench. The woman wore a faded coffee-colored dress, dusty black ankle boots, and a pair of sunglasses with oval lenses.

"Can you help me?" She spoke French with a heavy, sugary accent.

Claude walked over. This was hardly the first time she had been mistaken for a young man or a boy, but she felt a thrill nonetheless.

"My eyes are not so good," the woman said.

She explained that she had wandered far from her people, and that she needed some assistance in finding her way back.

She spoke with a grandness that implied the journey would be long and dramatic, and Claude pictured wooden market stalls on cracked red earth and distant, wind-carved dunes that rose and fell like waves.

"I'd be happy to guide you," she said. "But where are they, your people?"

"The Zone."

This was a derelict space on the outskirts of the city, the dwelling place of gypsies, ragpickers, and other dubious itinerants. Not another country, then, but still a good few miles away.

She asked the woman's name.

"I'm Soulef. And you?"

"Claude."

How could she explain the feeling of exhilaration as Soulef took her arm and they began to walk? Was it the sense of purpose that only a coincidence can offer?

They crossed the river by way of the Pont Neuf and moved north, towards Porte Saint-Denis. Soulef murmured to herself constantly. Her mysterious, explosive exclamations—*Mais oui!* or *Voilà!*—didn't appear to be prompted by anything that happened on the street but rather by events or revelations that were taking place inside her head. She smelled marvelously of rose petals and molasses. A little pale blue stole into the sky, but the air was still cool. It seemed unlikely it would rain.

After perhaps an hour Soulef came to a halt. They stood at the junction of rue d'Hauteville and rue de Paradis, the streets high and narrow, almost gorgelike, with shops and bars occupying the ground floors of many of the buildings.

She lifted her head. "We should have a drink—something to fortify ourselves."

"I don't usually drink," Claude said. "Not in the morning, anyhow."

"Usually is not a word that applies today," Soulef said.

They entered a bar on the corner, and a young woman put two glasses of calvados in front of them. Like Soulef, the young woman looked African, though her skin was darker. Swallowing the drink in a single gulp, Soulef banged the glass down on the counter, wiped her mouth on her sleeve, and turned away. The young woman watched her go, her face undisturbed, like a pond that absorbs a thrown pebble without producing any ripples. When Claude asked to pay, the young woman shook her head and made a quick, sharp sound against the roof of her mouth with her tongue.

Out on the pavement, Soulef reached for Claude's arm and they set off once more.

"That young woman in the bar," Claude said. "She didn't want any money."

"She's my daughter," Soulef said.

Claude glanced over her shoulder. Though she was shocked—puzzled too—she couldn't think of anything to say.

As they journeyed north, they drew comments from several people on the street. One man with a ladder balanced on his shoulder stood in front of them and pointed to the east. That way for Salpêtrière, he said. Salpêtrière, as Claude was well aware, was the city's most notorious asylum.

Soulef adjusted her dark glasses. "The third rung from the top is rather weak," she said. "Beware of accidents."

The man gaped at her as she moved on.

When Claude asked how she knew about the ladder, she dismissed the question with a wave of the hand. "The ladder has no relevance."

A few minutes later, she said, "You can always make things happen if you articulate with sufficient confidence and power."

By the time they arrived at Porte de Clignancourt it was nearly dark. They pushed through the flea market and on into the Zone, an area of wasteland between a railway line and a canal. A derelict factory stood on the mud, its doors hanging off their hinges, most of its windows broken.

A fire burned near the entrance, old chairs and carriage wheels sticking up out of the flames. A few people huddled in a small group, talking and smoking. One of them was bald, and had a drum strapped to his chest. On seeing Soulef, there was a flash of gold and a watery hiss as a tattooed woman brought two cymbals together.

"My people," Soulef said.

That evening, a banquet was held on the top floor of the building. There were rabbits roasted on skewers, tomatoes salvaged from the gutters in the market, and clay jugs of rough red wine. Afterwards, when the table was a mess of spillages and bones, Claude asked Soulef about her family.

"I found them, just as I found you." She gave Claude a strange, fierce smile, her mouth shiny with meat juices. "If you wish, you could be one of us. You'd be most welcome."

Claude couldn't think how to answer.

"Though I suspect," Soulef added, "that you have another path."

Towards midnight, a man played the accordion, and a young couple danced. Drizzle fell from a gritty, granite sky. Later, a woman painted Claude's face gold, like a Buddha. Later still, Claude stripped off her clothes and swam in the cold canal. As she dried herself next to the fire, a man walked towards her on his hands, his legs bent at the knee, the heels of his boots dangling just above his forehead.

"You know, of course," he said, looking sideways and upwards at her, "that Soulef is a fortune-teller of great repute."

"I had no idea," Claude said. "She didn't mention it."

"That's because she's modest."

"You think she would tell my fortune?"

"How would I know?" he said. "I'm not the one who can see into the future." Still on his hands, he walked away.

Claude broke off and looked at me. "You know something, Suzanne? If I went back to the Zone, I don't think there would be any trace of their presence."

"You're sure they were really there?"

Claude shrugged. "Even if I imagined the whole thing, it would be no less valid."

"And that woman," I said. "Did she tell your fortune, in the end?"

Claude looked at me, her expression delicate, but fully inhabited, complete, like a glass of water filled right to the brim. "Yes."

"What did she say?"

"She said, 'You've found your soul's companion. The other you.'"

"Did you say anything?"

"I smiled and said, 'I know.'"

André Breton, Robert Desnos, Philippe Soupault . . . It was only later that I understood the significance of what I had witnessed that night—not the birth of Surrealism, perhaps, but a glimpse of the movement in its infancy. Back then, in the days before the first manifesto, the emphasis was on words rather than images. Inspired by Freud, the Surrealists used automatic writing and trancelike states to unearth the truths hidden in language and in themselves. They were trying to capture the actual functioning of thought. They wanted to replicate the kind of instinctive, irrational awareness that was found in dreams, and could also be induced by games and activities, most famously, *déambulation*, as Breton called it later, a random drifting or wandering through the city that left the walker open to chance encounters and discoveries. We didn't realize it at the time, but in her spontaneous meeting with Soulef, and her apparent willingness to go wherever Soulef went, Claude had acted just like the Surrealists. In fact, her behavior had preceded theirs. But we made no attempt to join them. While we shared many of their sympathies and their objectives—the rejection of traditional structures like religion and the family, the opening of a dialogue between reality and dream, the determination to re-enchant a disenchanted world—and while we subscribed to a romantic version of Marxism, as Breton did, we saw the movement as one that was dominated by men who seemed unwilling or unable to take women seriously, and who regarded homosexuality with wariness, if not disgust. Also, we had no real interest in affiliation. We were too private. Too particular.

As for my visit to rue Fontaine, I didn't mention it to Claude. I'm not sure why. It might have been because I didn't want to appear to be competing with her. She thought she was the one who had had an adventure. It didn't occur to her that I might have had one too. Or perhaps my attending that event in Breton's apartment seemed at odds with the impression I had given—namely that, in her absence, I had been consumed with anxiety and fear. As the weeks went by, it became more and more difficult to bring the subject up—there was never a right moment—and in the end, almost by default, it turned into a secret.

St. Brelade's Bay, sometime in the early twenties. The kind of afternoon that doesn't feel hot until the wind drops. By now, Helen Colley and her son Bob were running the hotel, and since they thought of us as regulars—we had holidayed in Jersey every summer for the past few years—they had given us a room with a south-facing terrace and a panoramic view of the beach. Claude was sitting by the French window, her legs in the sun, the rest of her body in the shade. She was reading an issue of *Inversions*, an underground homosexual magazine to which she had contributed, and which, some months later, would be seized by the police and banned. From outside came the muted cries of gulls and children.

That morning I had traveled into St. Helier to collect several rolls of film from Sennett & Spears, the local developers, and I had spread some of the photographs out on the bed.

"Damn," I said.

I was looking at an image of Claude in her bathing suit, an attempt to replicate a picture I had taken a few years before. Perched on the rocks and sitting sideways-on to the camera, she had drawn her knees up to her chest. Her hands were looped around her ankles. At first glance, she looked like a child, but the expression on her face was self-possessed and challenging, almost fierce. It would have been a good picture had there not been a shadow in the bottom right-hand corner.

"Damn," I said again.

This time Claude looked round. "What's the matter?"

When I told her about the shadow, she stood up and walked over.

I pointed to the corner of the image. "It's my head and shoulders. At least, I think that's what it is."

"I like it," she said.

"But it's a mistake."

"It's a good mistake." She paused. "There are all sorts of ways in which the shadow completes the picture."

I shook my head. "I'm a terrible photographer."

"You're not."

"I'm going out for a while."

On leaving the hotel, I took the path that climbed through the trees behind the church. If I walked fast, I thought to myself, I would be able to watch the sun setting from the rocky outcrop west of Beauport.

That evening, over dinner, Claude returned to the subject of our earlier conversation. What I had succeeded in doing—and she used the word advisedly, she said, since the picture was without doubt a success—was to create a portrait of our relationship. I stood between her and any other viewer, my presence binding as a signature, a ring. I was watching over her, she told me. We couldn't be separated, not even in a photograph.

"Is that all I am to you?" I said glumly. "A shadow?"

"Don't be absurd." She sipped her whiskey. "It even works aesthetically. Didn't you notice how the rounded shadow of your head offsets the triangle of shadow between my ankles and my thighs?"

"That's unintentional—"

But "unintentional" was a word we tried not to use. It was a word people hid behind. *I didn't mean to. It was an accident.* There was no such thing. Every accident contained an element of the deliberate. This was the principle that lay behind André Breton's concept of *déambulation*: you had to accept—or even own—that which you came across by chance. Was it also Breton who had insisted that one should always leave a window open for the visitations of the unconscious and the unexpected?

I took out Claude's camera and turned it in my hands. A Kodak Type 3 Folding Pocket model with red bellows and a spirit level, it had belonged to her father, though he had never used it with any great enthusiasm. There were very few pictures of Claude as a child. "You don't think it's time we invested in a new model?"

"What's wrong with that one?" Claude asked.

"It's twenty years old—at least."

She gave me a swift, sly look. "You're not blaming the camera, are you?"

I didn't answer.

"Don't worry about the shadows," she said. "They're hard to avoid if the light's behind you—"

"I forgot to tell you," I said. "Something happened—on my walk."

While I was on the headland, between Beauport and Fiquet, clouds surged up from the northwest, and a strong wind that smelled of rust tugged at my clothes. The light faded rapidly. That was when I saw him, in the long grass next to the path. At first I took him for a child, since his head was no higher than my shoulder. As I drew nearer, though, I realized it was a man on his knees. He had his back to me, and his right elbow was moving rhythmically. His head turned when he sensed my presence. We were close enough to speak to each other, despite the wind, but he said nothing. He just watched me, over his shoulder. His right arm had fallen still. Somehow I couldn't bring myself to move.

At last, he rose to his feet. He was huge, with hands that hung against his thighs like tools. Since he stood with his back to the setting sun his face was in shadow, and when he finally spoke he used Jèrriais, a language I had seldom come across, and didn't know.

"You have no place here, not alone."

That was what I thought he said, though I couldn't be sure. Did he think the darkness would envelop me and I would lose my way? Did he think I might fall to my death? Or was he warning me against himself—what he was capable of, what he might do?

"I was about to turn around." I gestured behind me. "I'm staying at the hotel. Over there."

He still hadn't moved.

"Go back," he said.

I obeyed.

"It sounds like one of the Raymond brothers," Claude said.

She told me there were three or four of them, and that they were all enormous men. Though they couldn't read or write, they were astonishingly good with numbers. She had watched them once, playing darts in the hotel bar. They would come down from the hills to drink.

"Where was I?" I asked.

She shrugged. "I think it was the summer you were nursing your brother."

"You must have been with Bob." I knew he liked a few pints after work.

"Maybe," she said. "I don't remember."

She talked about inbreeding on the island. There was a mental hospital in St. Helier, she claimed, where the products of all the incestuous relationships ended up. She was looking past me, into the night.

"This is a wild place," she said.

"May I join you?"

We looked round. It was Vera, the Englishwoman.

Claude pushed her chair back. "We were just going to bed," she said. "We're very tired."

It wasn't true. We hadn't even ordered coffee.

"Oh." Vera looked at the floor.

"I'm sorry, Vera," I said. "Perhaps tomorrow."

Like the Raymond brothers, Bob's family were island people. They had never had anything to do with artists or intellectuals— or with anyone from Paris, for that matter. That was not their world. Once or twice, I caught Bob's relatives laughing at Claude behind her back, and though it hurt me to see them mocking her I couldn't help but find it reassuring. They didn't approve of Bob's interest in Claude. They saw no future in it.

If Bob's mother began to confide in me, it was perhaps because I seemed capable and solid—more like one of her own, in other words—and since I viewed her as an ally when it came to Bob and Claude, sensing that she might be against the relationship, I tended to encourage her. One morning, we visited the Steel family's farm up on La Moye. Bob had told Claude that he wanted to show her the greenhouses where they grew tomatoes. As I had no particular interest in greenhouses, I offered to help Mrs. Steel with her chores. We were seated at the kitchen table, shelling peas, when she suddenly asked me why my sister's hair was so short.

"I think it suits her," I said. "Don't you like it?"

Mrs. Steel's mouth widened and narrowed, and she shook her head. "She looks like a man. It isn't right."

I remembered the young woman whose father had killed her because she'd cut her hair in the style of Joan of Arc.

"She's not like the rest of us, is she," Mrs. Steel said.

She leaned towards me, and a smell came off her, rancid as butter left in the sun. She seemed avaricious, as if the information she was seeking might provide her with some form of nourishment.

"What do you mean?" I asked, though I could see all the questions circling inside her.

"Was she ever—you know—*put away?*"

This was the moment I had been waiting for. You might even say I had engineered it. I hesitated, as if unsure whether I should speak. But I was sure. I'd never been more sure.

"No." Eyes lowered, I split a pod open and used my thumb to send the peas tumbling into the bowl that stood between us. "Her mother was, though."

"I knew it." There was a coarse, almost sensual thrill to Mrs. Steel's voice.

"Please don't say anything to Claude," I said, "or to your son."

If Claude found out, she would never forgive me for revealing her family secret, or for interfering in her life.

"Don't you worry," Mrs. Steel said. "I won't breathe a word."

But she knew what I had done. I saw a shrewd light in her eyes, and also, I thought, a glimmer of respect. I had showed myself to be ruthless, as she was. If I wanted something I would fight for it, and I would use whatever ammunition came to hand.

Some months later, back in Paris, I went to see Édouard de Max in Georges Rivollet's *Les Phéniciennes.* Since meeting de Max at the wedding, I had made many drawings of him, one of which

I had given him as a fiftieth birthday present. More recently, I had designed posters for several of his productions. I admired his work, both in the theater and in film. He was one of the great actors of his age.

That night, he was playing Créon, a role ideally suited to his powerful and brooding presence, and once the curtain had fallen I went backstage. After a show, he was generally surrounded by admirers, and I would have to push my way through the crowd just to offer a few words of congratulation, but when I walked into his dressing room I was surprised to find him alone. His satin robe was half undone, revealing gray chest hair. He had yet to remove his makeup. His eyes were rimmed in black.

"Suzanne," he said in his rich, doomed voice. "How very good of you to come. Is Claude here too?"

"She sends her apologies. She's not well." I had left her at home, complaining of stomach pains.

"I'm sorry to hear that," de Max said.

His performance had been a tour de force, I told him, as always.

"*As always.*" He let out a morbid, fatalistic laugh. "That's precisely the feeling I had this evening. I'm just repeating myself, over and over. Everything I do, I've done before. There's nothing new."

"That's not what I meant."

"Forgive me, Suzanne. I'm not myself."

"Are you ill?"

"No, no. Just weary . . ." He paused. "I'm fifty-three. Can you imagine?"

Sweat had mingled with his makeup, tiny white grains lodging in the lines that fanned out from the corners of his eyes. He was beginning to detach himself from the role he had played that evening. It was eerie, and slightly disturbing, like watching a snake cast off its skin; there was the actor, and then there was the man. I felt the transformation was sacred, and shouldn't be witnessed, but he didn't seem to care.

"Would you join me in a drink?"

Without waiting for an answer, he reached for the bottle on his dressing table and poured me a glass of something clear.

"Schnapps," he said. "A present from a German critic." He shrugged, then gulped from his glass.

I sipped from mine. "Do you mind if I draw you while we're talking?"

"Oh Christ. Do you have to? I'm a complete wreck."

"I like wrecks."

"Suzanne," he said, "you have no mercy."

"There's nothing to be afraid of." I reminded him of the lithograph I had given him.

"Ah yes. On the occasion of my unmentionable birthday." He let out a sigh. "So very kind of you."

I remembered how he had held my picture away from his body, his head cocked. My God, he had said, I look as if I'm about to pounce on something and devour it. It was true. I had portrayed him in bloody crimsons and inky blacks, his face distorted as he glanced over his shoulder, his upper body hidden by a swirling cloak. I look oddly *hungry*, he added, and it was clear that he was pleased. He liked to think of himself as dangerous.

He pushed his hair back from his forehead and nodded gloomily. "You have a real gift. I should be honored to be drawn by you."

"You don't object, then?"

"Not so long as I can drink." When he had refilled his glass, he held the bottle out to me.

I shook my head. "No, thank you."

"I hear Claude's been acting . . ."

"She has, yes."

Since our move to Paris, Claude had taken part in a number of experimental productions. She had grown up surrounded by actors—Marguerite Moreno, Constant Lounsbery, and de Max himself, of course—and it was inevitable, perhaps, that she would be drawn to the theater.

De Max began to reminisce about Claude's uncle, and how Marcel had once adapted a play for him and Sarah Bernhardt. *Francesca da Rimini* was the title. He had taken the role of Francesca's lover, Paolo, who was caught in a hurricane made up of the souls of the dead. It had been a sensation—an absolute sensation. This was in 1906, before Bernhardt's leg was amputated. She was a remarkable woman, he told me. Impossible too. A monster, really. While on tour, she slept in a coffin lined with satin. Her evening gowns had dead bats pinned to them. Her pet alligator drank champagne. Once, she decided to have a tiger's tail grafted onto the base of her spine, and found a surgeon willing to perform the operation. Her friends talked her out of it. So many stories. Marcel knew Bernhardt, of course. That was why she had agreed to appear in the play.

"Poor Marcel," de Max went on. "I saw him two days before he died, in his apartment on Île Saint-Louis." He poured himself another schnapps. "It was freezing outside, Paris all white and frosted, like a cake. He was in bed with pneumonia, and his tiny red dog—I think it was Japanese—was sitting on his head. And Marcel fighting for air, but weak, so weak . . ." He sighed again. "It tore me apart to lose him. He was only thirty-six."

Though my eyes moved constantly between de Max's face and the sketchpad on my knee, I was careful to nod or to murmur a few words every now and then, since it was important that he kept talking. I wanted to prolong his transition from actor into man. I wanted to try and capture the moment when he hovered between the two, transparent, spent.

And then, suddenly, I noticed that his voice had altered.

"I'm sorry," I said. "What was that?"

"Put down your pencil."

"Why?"

"You know why." He gave me his most seductive look, his chin and eyelids lowered, his black hair falling across his forehead. "I've always admired you, Suzanne. You have a certain—nobility . . ."

If this hadn't reminded me of something Claude might say, I might have laughed, but my thoughtful reaction, which took longer than laughter and was less dismissive, must have led him to believe that I was not entirely unreceptive to his admiration, for he moved nearer, his robe gaping open. He took hold of my head, his hands closing over my ears. I felt, oddly, as if I were under the sea. Looking into my eyes, he covered my mouth with his. His tongue, which was hot and acrid, forced its way between my lips. My drawing pad slipped off my knees. As I struggled for breath, a deep note resonated inside him, and one of the lightbulbs that framed his dressing table mirror winked, then blew. Still clutching my pencil, I placed my free hand on his bare chest and pushed back hard. The legs of my chair screeched on the wood floor. I stood up abruptly.

"I should go," I said.

De Max gazed at the floor, grinning foolishly, then turned towards the mirror. His huge, dramatic face was blank, almost astonished. He reached for his glass of schnapps. Was he even aware of what he had done? And if so, would he remember?

As I backed out of his dressing room he was still staring into the mirror, though he didn't appear to be looking at himself. I thanked him for the drink. Either he didn't hear me or he chose not to respond. I found myself in an unlit passageway behind the stage. My lips were stinging. Worried that he might pursue me, I glanced over my shoulder. His dressing room door stood half open, a wedge of bright yellow in the dark, and a stillness seemed to emerge from within, the resonating stillness of a tomb, and him inside, like a rare black beetle trapped in amber. Groping my way to the stage door, I slipped out into the night.

Once in the cobbled alley that ran down the side of the theater, I wrapped my arms around myself as if I were cold. Nothing had happened, I told myself. Not really. Then it occurred to me that he too might leave by the stage door. I moved out of the alley and onto the street. A black cat ran past, its tail vertical. Should I avoid him from now on? No, that might arouse suspicion. It would be more elegant if I feigned amnesia. Kiss? What kiss? He had drunk most of the bottle. It seemed unlikely he would remember his momentary indiscretion. He might not even remember that I had visited his dressing room. He would let his heavy head rest on his arm, and when he woke an hour or two later, stiff-limbed and cold, he would think he had dreamt about me. Because no one had come to see him after the show. No one cared. He was finished as an actor. Finished.

I walked fast. By the time I was halfway home I was sorry I hadn't been calmer, more understanding. I could have teased de Max affectionately. I could have blamed it on the schnapps. Those Germans, I could have said. If this is what they drink, no wonder they thought they could conquer Europe. But I had been too dull-witted, too slow.

Soon I was turning the corner into rue Notre-Dame-des-Champs. As I pushed through the gate I looked up at our apartment. The lights were all still on. I opened the front door.

"Claude?"

There was no reply.

In the drawing room, a single small lamp burned. The room was crowded with shadows, and I thought I saw de Max over by the window, his broad back hunched, his face turned towards me. As I stared with more intensity into the gloom, my body motionless, my breath jolted by the beating of my heart, the image broke up into familiar components—a partially drawn curtain, a wing-backed chair, a lacquer vase . . . I remembered the graze of his whiskers, and the pepper smell of his dried sweat. I remembered his fiery tongue. How would it have been, I wondered, if he had taken things more slowly? How would I have felt if he had courted me? If I had been his lover—

A weak voice called my name. I hurried down the corridor and into the bathroom. Claude was sitting on the tiled floor, against the wall. She looked at me, her face white and strained. "You're late back."

I kneeled beside her. "De Max was feeling sorry for himself. Are you all right?"

"I still have pains, low down." She placed a hand on her belly, just above her pubic bone.

"You should see a doctor."

"In the morning." Leaning her head against the wall, she took a deep breath and let it out slowly. "Was he good tonight, de Max?"

"Yes, he was good. But when I went to his dressing room afterwards he was all alone. He was drinking. He wouldn't let me go."

Claude nodded. This was a side of de Max she seemed to know.

"I made some drawings," I said.

"Show me."

I opened my sketchbook and turned the pages for her.

"There's something rather wolfish about him, isn't there," she said, "now that he's older."

"Yes," I said. "There is."

Our doctor's diagnosis was inconclusive, but Claude's stomach pains did not go away. If anything, they became more acute. No one had an explanation, though. That winter, I took her to see a surgeon Monsieur Schwob had recommended. The surgeon had been a friend of Claude's uncle, Marcel, and had also, coincidentally, studied under my father. Following a number of examinations and tests, which were carried out over a period of many months, he informed us that Claude was suffering from ovarian cysts, and that she would benefit from surgical intervention. She might also need a hysterectomy, he said. When Claude provided her father with details of the diagnosis, he became distressed, and insisted that she seek a second opinion, but the second opinion proved more or less identical. In the end, we all agreed that Marcel's friend should perform the surgery.

Arriving at Claude's bedside on the day after the operation, I saw tears in her eyes.

"They took my ovaries, my womb—everything," she said. "I will never have children."

"But you didn't want children," I said gently, "did you?"

She looked away from me, towards the window. "I don't know. I suppose not."

Whenever she talked about her childhood, she would describe it as an ordeal. She would never put anyone through something like *that*, she would say. What's more, she found the whole idea of procreation ideologically unsound. She had been impressed by Havelock Ellis's two-volume work *The Task of Social Hygiene*, in which he warned of the dangers we would face if the planet was overpopulated. She didn't necessarily want to *have* children, but she didn't want to be told that she couldn't. What had upset her, I decided, was the abrupt and brutal removal of a possibility. She couldn't stand any form of diminishment.

While in Jersey the following summer, Claude and I learned that Bob Steel had got married. Though we didn't receive a wedding invitation, two slices of cake wrapped in tissue paper and tied with pink ribbon appeared at our hotel in St. Brelade's Bay. It was an ambiguous gesture. We were being included in the event, but only at a distance. I also thought we were being warned. I saw Mrs. Steel's hand in it. The news of Bob's marriage came at a time when Claude was vulnerable—she was still recovering from her hysterectomy—and on our return to Paris she tried once again to kill herself. I had been delivering a portfolio of drawings to a local theater, and when I walked back into our apartment I found her on the floor next to the bed, her pulse weak, her breathing shallow. She was wearing a sleeveless striped top and a pair of shorts with a belt. Her toenails were silver. I lifted her and carried her down the stairs. She was a dead weight, but not heavy. Three in the afternoon. The street was quiet and warm and curiously still. Inside my head, though, things felt chaotic. Frenzied. Someone was viciously crossing out whatever had been written there. A car stopped for us, and we were driven to the nearest hospital, where doctors pumped Claude's stomach and administered some oxygen. When she regained consciousness she gave me a rueful smile, as if she had been in the know about the outcome all along. Sometimes I wondered if her attempts on her own life might not represent a convoluted form of vanity. She wanted to vanish for long enough to be missed, but she didn't want to vanish altogether. After all, if people *really* want to die, don't they jump off bridges or throw themselves in front of trains?

It was in 1926, I think, that Claude and I traveled to England, visiting London, Oxford, and Parsons Mead in Surrey, where Claude had gone to school. We spent our last weekend at the seaside, in Brighton. On the day we arrived, Claude's hair was cut short, with a side parting, and the proprietor of our hotel, a brittle but enthusiastic spinster called Miss Flett, assumed she was my son. Claude immediately slipped into the role she had been assigned, asking if the football results had come in yet.

Miss Flett turned to me. "Such a chirpy fellow—and his English! Like he was born and bred."

On our first night we found a restaurant that overlooked the beach. The rain fell steadily, and small waves collapsed against the gray-and-orange shingle. I had never seen a sea that looked quite so exhausted.

Claude consulted the menu, two frown lines between her eyebrows, then leaned back in her chair and lit a cigarette.

"I'm not hungry," she said.

"You haven't had anything all day." I shook my head. "I worry about you."

"Tobacco's a food." She blew smoke sideways and watched as it flowered against the window. "Don't make a scene. Please."

I looked away.

One of the drawbacks of traveling with Claude was that she was able to find excuses for not eating. At home in Paris, I would put a wide variety of dishes on the table. This allowed her to choose what she wanted while still feeling she was rejecting most of what was being offered. Also, I would give her a plate that was smaller than mine, which would make her think she had taken less than I had. It was sleight of hand on my part, but it worked. She would eat without realizing she was eating. When we were abroad, though, or even in a restaurant, she became too aware of the food. It reinforced her aversion, her disgust. And she could always claim—and often did—that there was nothing on the menu that appealed to her.

"You go ahead," she was saying brightly. Cigarette slanting from one corner of her mouth, she picked up the menu again. "Why don't you try the mussels? They're bound to be good."

"You're so thin," I said. "You'll waste away."

I knew from past experience that this was the wrong thing to say, but sometimes I just couldn't help myself. I had watched her dressing for dinner. Her suit trousers were falling off her hips, and her ribs stuck out below her breasts.

"Nonsense." Her chin jutted in defiance. "I'm in excellent shape."

The waiter came. I ordered the mussels.

She had always been hard on her body. *I want to change my skin,* she wrote once. *Rid myself of the old one.* That evening in Brighton, she told me she had turned her back on food when she was very young. Being at home had frightened her, she said. The time she woke in the dark to feel what she thought was rain landing on her face. Her mother bending over her. Her mother's tears. Or the time a slow black tongue of blood pushed under her bedroom door . . . She wasn't sure if she was remembering or imagining. The border between the two became so thin, like the transparent, wrinkly membrane between two layers of an onion. Starving herself seemed to simplify the world. Remove her from whatever might be happening. Also, she thought it would make her beautiful—or acceptable, at least. She thought Toinette would love her more.

"I'm sure she loved you, Claude," I said.

"Perhaps," she said. "But not in a way I understood."

We drank beer, warm and brackish, the color of tea with no milk in it. I ate the mussels, which were good, just as she had predicted. She told me not eating had seductive side effects. She liked the lightheadedness. The visions. It was like being a saint.

Listening to her, I couldn't think of anything to say that she wouldn't have an answer to. There was a moment when she brought her eyes up from the table and told me that her body was a page on which the lack of food would write its story. Her face was almost evangelical. She saw the starved version of herself as yet another incarnation, and it was obvious from the clear, steady look she gave me that she wanted me to feel proud of her.

By the time we paid the bill the rain had stopped. A black shine to the lanes. A ticking, tapping world. Claude had drunk on an empty stomach, and I had to support her as we walked back to our hotel.

Later that night, I woke suddenly. The room was cold, and light spilled from the bathroom. There was a choking sound, and then a splattering. I got out of bed and pushed the door open.

Claude looked up at me, eyes glistening with tears. "I don't feel very well."

I stayed with her until she had finished being sick. Afterwards, I cleaned the bath and washed her pajamas in the basin. Claude was asleep again by then.

Dawn. A seagull stood on the windowsill, in profile, like a famous person on a coin. Claude lay in the bed next to mine, one arm draped over her eyes.

"I think that beer was bad," she said.

I made a noncommittal sound.

She lifted her arm away from her eyes and looked at me. "What?"

"I didn't say anything."

"You're angry with me. You've got that look."

"A little. But mainly I'm tired." I rolled over, onto my side. "Let me sleep."

Why did she always insist on drinking, even though she knew she wasn't capable? Why didn't I stop her? It seemed to me that she was trying to kill herself, but couldn't decide whether to do it quickly or slowly. There were times when I wished she would get it over with. Moments later, though, I'd be on my knees, my face pressed into her belly, the belly that no longer contained a womb. *Don't leave me. Please. Don't ever leave.*

When Claude's father died, his body was shipped to Paris to be cremated, as he had requested. A few days later, we took the urn that held his ashes to the columbarium in Père-Lachaise. It was early April, but the wind had a cold metallic edge to it; I could still smell winter in the air. Shortly before his death, Monsieur Schwob had rewritten his will, and he had left his entire fortune to his second wife, my mother. Though Claude, Georges, and I would continue to receive our monthly allowances, Georges was incensed. The rift that had opened up between father and son at the time of the divorce had only deepened with the passing years, and Georges saw the new will as an insult and a violation. During the journey to the cemetery, his face was white, and I couldn't tell if it was grief or fury. Probably it was both.

Afterwards, as we left the columbarium, Georges's wife, Madeleine, fell into step with me and asked whether she could count on my support in challenging the will. Claude and I would stand to profit, she assured me. In fact, she said, we would be rich. I told her I had no intention of challenging the will. She swung round and blocked my way, and a loose strand of hair blew across her mouth, as if the wind thought she should not speak. Small sharp pimples stood out on her forehead.

"It's because Madame Malherbe is your mother," she said, "isn't it."

I refused to rise to the provocation. "The assets were Monsieur Schwob's, to bequeath as he saw fit—"

"Oh, for God's sake—"

"Also," I went on, "my loyalty is to Claude, and she respects the wishes of her father."

"Georges will never respect his father's wishes. Never." Her lips looked bloodless, numb. "The moment we get home, he will be starting legal proceedings."

Later, when I told Claude what Madeleine had said, she developed such a severe headache that she took to her bed. Though she didn't get up for almost a week she found it hard to rest. Her sleep was interrupted by nightmares, and by the wayward beating of her heart. My heart frightens me, she said. I gave her whiskey and sedatives and sat next to the bed, her hand in mine. Claude had genuine problems with her health throughout her life, but she was also a notorious hypochondriac, and it was sometimes difficult to distinguish between imagined ailments and real ones.

Now Monsieur Schwob was gone, my mother pleaded with me to return to Brittany, but I found myself making excuses. It was Claude I was thinking of. She wouldn't have been able to stomach the idea of moving back. It would have signified the closing of a circle—another kind of death. The decision haunted me, and when Claude was feeling stronger I traveled down to Nantes. Summer had come, and the streets were bright and hot, but I could smell the river in the shadows. The daughter of a bookseller, my mother had always found comfort in literature. I read to her from some of her favorite novels—Balzac mainly, and Zola—and the words often made her cry, though they were not, in themselves, particularly sad. Her stoical nature, which had seen her through the deaths of two husbands and a son, seemed to have forsaken her, and she could no longer find any hope or glitter in her life. The dark setting was all there was. Back in Paris, I would sometimes glimpse an old woman at a window high up in a building, and I would think of my mother, looking out over Place du Commerce, uncertain how to fill the hours. It would be another eight years before she died peacefully, in her sleep.

———

While I was in Nantes, with my mother, Claude shaved off all her hair and removed her eyebrows. Her hair had been cropped before, when she was studying at the Sorbonne, but this time it was more extreme. She looked like someone who had been ostracized. She looked alien. We took many photographs that year—Claude in a black swimsuit, Claude dressed as a sailor, Claude with an elongated head, like a reflection in a fairground mirror—and some of them acquired a fleeting notoriety, since they were featured in Georges Ribemont-Dessaignes's magazine, *Bifur,* and were admired by none other than Man Ray, but the images I found most powerful and unsettling were those in which she appeared as her father. We were copying a picture that had been taken in 1917, in which her father sat sideways-on to the camera, with his eyes lowered. She too sat sideways-on, with her eyes lowered. The light fell across the right half of her face in exactly the same way. She had the same sloping nose, the same bald head. The same air of resignation or acquiescence. In turning herself into her father, she was expressing the affinity she had with him and paying him a kind of homage, but she was also, paradoxically, articulating the very differences that had caused him so much anxiety and bewilderment.

Henri Michaux had been traveling in the Amazon when Claude's father died, but he came to visit us the moment he returned. Claude had met Michaux in 1925. He had read her book *Heroines,* and had admired it so much that he had written her a letter. During their first meeting, at La Rotonde, they had talked for hours, uncovering all kinds of common ground. They shared a propensity for what Michaux called "delicious isolation"; there were things they had both dispensed with, or had learned to live without. He asked her to teach him English, and she said she would. Though he disliked being photographed, he agreed to sit for her. With his dark eyes and his generous, expressive mouth, Michaux could be impassioned, mischievous, and scathing, all in the space of five minutes, and he quickly became one of the few people who was allowed to call on us without letting us know in advance.

Settling on the sofa in our drawing room with his cherrywood pipe, he told us that his whole journey had been banal and pointless. He had walked in tropical rainforests and climbed fifteen thousand feet to the volcanic crater of Atacatzho, and he had felt nothing.

He gestured at the floor beyond his feet. "I could have stared at this carpet for a year," he said, "and learned more than I learned in South America."

I smiled. Michaux specialized in a kind of quiet melodrama. That might sound like a contradiction in terms, but somehow, in Michaux, the two existed side by side.

"You heard about my father?" Claude said.

He nodded. "Very sad."

Claude drew her shawl more tightly around her shoulders, as if she were cold.

"I wish my father was dead." Michaux's fingers hovered above the pouch of tobacco at his elbow. "In fact, I wish both my parents were dead."

"Henri!" Claude said. "You can't say such things."

Lighting his pipe, Michaux sat back. He was smiling. He knew Claude well enough to realize how rare it was to elicit a conventional response. "Tell me honestly. Don't you feel liberated, now your father's gone?"

She didn't answer. She only shook her head.

"I crave that sense of liberation," he said. "I long for it."

"Are your parents really so terrible?"

"I don't usually talk about them." Michaux puffed on his pipe, sweet smoke clouding the air. "Childhood is only interesting as an idea. The reality is savage. Unbearable."

"I feel the same," Claude said. "But couldn't you tell us *something?*"

He sighed.

He had grown up in Belgium, he said, with the flat land, the north wind, and the cold. His mother was grasping and dissatisfied. She was always trying to belittle her husband, and he chose not to defend himself. Instead he would bury his head in the local paper. Life was something to be "got through," as he put it once.

"I was ashamed of them," Michaux said.

It was like being a foreigner. His parents were people whose customs and expectations baffled him. He refused to speak, or even interact. He hardly ate. When he was seven, they sent him to a boarding school. Though relieved to be away from home, he could find no peace. Revolted by the food, he wrapped it in paper and buried it outside. Much later, in Brussels, when he encountered Buddhist teachings for the first time, he instantly understood what the Buddha's closed lips signified. A kind of negation or self-sufficiency was being advocated.

"Yes," Claude said. "Exactly."

When he moved to Paris, Michaux went on, he decided to steer clear of the Surrealists. For him, automatic writing was a form of incontinence. He found it monotonous. But mainly he didn't have the energy to belong to a movement. Though Claude and I knew he had a heart condition, he liked to present his weariness as a philosophical stance. Fatigue was a valid response to modernity. It also justified his failure to participate.

During the months that followed Michaux's return to Paris, Claude saw him regularly. They both had trouble sleeping, and would often telephone each other in the middle of the night. Though he seemed unaware of his effect on her—his ironic approach to life prevented him from noticing, perhaps—he did much to anchor her at a time when she was floundering.

Robert Desnos didn't recognize me when Claude and I met him in 1929, and I decided not to mention the night I saw him perform in André Breton's apartment. I didn't want to embarrass him, nor did I want to have to describe the whole episode to Claude. She wouldn't understand why I hadn't told her at the time, and I wasn't sure I understood it either. In any case, Desnos had fallen out with Breton, and was about to be "excommunicated" by the Surrealists. I sat back and let Claude do all the talking. She was well aware of the role he had played in the founding of the movement, and she was familiar with his poetry and his ideas. She admired his work to such an extent that she sensed a kinship—a bond that was "stronger than blood," as she put it some twenty years later.

"We have so much in common," she told him on that first day.

There was something about him that triggered a combination of frankness and hyperbole in her, and I saw him smile, though it wasn't clear if he was flattered, entertained, or simply wary.

"When I read your work," she went on, "I realize that identity is something that can be consciously assembled, like a jigsaw.

From a distance, the image looks solid, whole, but that's an illusion. Up close, you can see the joins. You can see how it has been put together. How it might come apart."

"A jigsaw . . ." Robert nodded slowly.

"What excites me most, though, is how you play with gender. You demonstrate something I have believed for a long time—namely, that the two genders are contingent, and interchangeable. You're able to relinquish your masculine identity, for example, and inhabit a feminine equivalent—or sometimes you loiter in the twilight territory between the two."

"I do all that?" He was smiling again, but this time it was less guarded, more obviously affectionate.

"Yes," Claude said, "you do."

Some days later, we called on Robert at his studio on rue Blomet. It was a chilly November afternoon, the puddles on the pavements crisp with ice. Though his stove gave off almost no heat, he was elegantly dressed, in a striped shirt, a tie, and a dark jacket with wide lapels. On the peeling walls hung several works by Francis Picabia and a painting by de Chirico. I peered through the window. Below was a neglected courtyard, two discolored disks of marble adrift in a sea of weeds.

"It doesn't look like much," Robert said, appearing at my elbow, "but in the winter the snow stays whiter than anywhere else in Paris, and when the summer comes the birds sing all day long."

He went and changed the record on the gramophone.

"We're listening to Jelly Roll Morton," he said. "I listen to a lot of Fats Waller too. I have to play music nonstop or I can hear the Spaniard fighting with his mistress." He paused. "Either fighting or fucking. I'm not sure which is worse."

The Spaniard. That was how he referred to Joan Miró, who rented the studio next door. It was one of Robert's jokes. He knew perfectly well that Miró was a proud Catalan. While he was talking, my eye was drawn to the wax sculpture of a mermaid that was fixed to the wall opposite his bed. Her long hair tumbled over her shoulders and bare breasts, and her face was turned to one side, the subtle smile suggesting that she had abandoned the mundane world of Robert's studio for some deeper and more pleasurable reality. When silence fell, I asked Robert where he had bought her.

"I didn't," he told me. "She was a gift from Yvonne George."

Yvonne was a Belgian *chanteuse.* For almost two years he had been obsessed with her, but she had failed to respond to his attentions. He still found it hard to understand.

"I mean, what's wrong with me?" he said. "Am I too intelligent? Too sophisticated? Was she perhaps in awe of me?"

Claude and I were smiling.

But if Yvonne had been his great unrequited love, he went on, he had recently met a woman who he felt might be her equal. Even, possibly, her superior. Her name was Youki, which meant "pink snow" in Japanese. He had fallen under her spell the moment he met her, in La Coupole.

Claude asked if she was Japanese.

"No, she's French," Robert said. "Though she grew up in Belgium, like Yvonne."

She had just married a Japanese painter called Foujita. He wore round glasses with tortoiseshell frames and a ring in his right ear. He was much older than Youki, though he didn't look it. Josephine Baker, the dancer, had sat for him. So had Man Ray's girlfriend, Kiki of Montparnasse. Foujita didn't appear to be jealous of Robert's friendship with his wife. Quite the opposite. Not long ago, he had given them both tattoos. He had decided that Youki should have a mermaid, since that was how Robert had described her.

"What did you get?" I asked.

"A bear and a ring of stars," he said. "Ursa Major is my favorite constellation."

"But she's still with this Foujita?"

"It's not a problem. They have an open relationship." Robert paused. "I think something will happen between me and Youki. In fact, I know it will."

I looked at Claude. "I hope she doesn't find him too intelligent."

"Or too sophisticated," Claude said.

Robert laughed. "I despise you both. I never want to see you again."

An evening in March, a new decade. We were still living in the same building on rue Notre-Dame-des-Champs, but we had moved to a different apartment, where there was more space, more light. Candles burning in the silver-plated Louis XVI candlesticks. A jazz record playing on the gramophone. Champagne.

Robert came early, with Youki. Though he was approaching thirty, his smile was that of a young boy, and his eerie eyes, which reminded me of opals, were paler than ever. He had been trying to persuade Youki to leave her husband, but so far she had refused. Perhaps she enjoyed playing the two men off against each other. Perhaps she liked the attention. She was a beauty, just as Robert had said. That evening, her black dress clung to her breasts and thighs, and her lips, which were painted a deep glossy red, like Chinese lacquer, stood out against her clear white skin. Living with Foujita, though, she had become accustomed to luxury, and I wondered how Robert could possibly afford her. A few days before, I had been out walking near Parc Montsouris, and Youki had passed by in a chauffeured Delage convertible, her dark gaze sliding over me as if I were a lamppost or a tree. She had looked removed, immortal.

"I'm so sorry, darling," she said when I told her. "I just didn't see you. I'm terribly shortsighted."

"It's true," Robert said. "Half the time she has no idea who I am, even when I'm in bed with her."

The door opened behind him and Béatrice Wanger swept in with an armful of gladioli. Béatrice was an American dancer and a neighbor of ours. She would not be staying long, she told me, as she was giving a performance later, at the Théâtre Esotérique. Her stage name was Nadja, or "La Belle Nadja," and Claude and I had seen her dance on several occasions. Her slender body would be draped in flimsy scarves and veils that left little to the imagination, and her smile, which did not waver, was intended to convey a mystical or trancelike state. She was usually accompanied by a single instrument—sometimes a flute, other times a gong. I suspected Claude of having slept with Béatrice—she had taken a number of explicit photographs—but Claude had only laughed when I confronted her. Sleep with Béatrice? she said. I'd suffocate.

More guests arrived. Pierre Albert-Birot, an avant-garde theater director Claude had worked with recently, and Jacques Viot, our old friend from Nantes. Jacques had started writing screenplays, though none had been produced as yet. On their heels was Sylvia Beach, accompanied by Georges Ribemont-Dessaignes. Georges was thrilled with the collage Claude had devised for the cover of his new novel. Adrienne sent her apologies, Sylvia said.

She was in bed with the flu. Roger Gilbert-Lecomte appeared in a smoking jacket and dark glasses. Like Robert Desnos, Roger had been "excommunicated" by the Surrealists. He wasn't sure why. He had been taking morphine, he said, and hadn't slept for days. The American editor Jane Heap made a dramatic entrance in a man's cream linen suit, her lover Margaret Anderson on her arm. But it was Claude who stood out, as always. She wore an off-the-shoulder dress that was charcoal gray over her breasts and black below the waist, and her shaved head was painted gold.

The singer Georgette LeBlanc didn't like to be predictable. Instead of commenting on Claude's gold head, she wanted to know where Claude had bought the dress.

"I forget," Claude said.

Jane and Margaret came over. They ran *The Little Review*. They had been the first to publish Hemingway.

"Claude, you look spectacular," Margaret said. "Like a Buddha."

"Or something recovered from the tomb of Tutankhamun," Jane said. "One of those extraordinary artifacts."

Margaret looked at me, and then at Claude. "I hear you were interviewed by the *Chicago Tribune*."

"*Who's Who in Paris*." Claude gave her an ironic smile.

"Americans," Jane said. "What do they know?"

We all laughed.

Jacques asked Claude if she'd been writing.

She nodded. "My book's coming out in the spring."

It was a sensitive subject. Claude had been writing on and off for years, but it was only in 1926, with Adrienne's encouragement, that she had started collecting the various pieces into a book. When she finally delivered the manuscript, it wasn't at all what

Adrienne had been expecting, and she turned it down. Claude had found another publisher—eventually—but Adrienne's rejection had been a shock and an embarrassment, and relations between the two of them had cooled. I wondered if that was the real reason why Adrienne had chosen not to come.

Someone behind me said, "Isn't Georgette sleeping with that Armenian mystic?"

"Gurdjieff?"

"That's right—Gurdjieff . . ."

I moved away across the room. The air was a rich tangle of languages—English, Hebrew, Greek.

Over by the window I spoke to Kiki. Her eyelids were painted a copper color, and her blouse was unbuttoned almost to the waist. She had finished with Man Ray, she told me. She had started seeing Henri Broca, who was publishing her memoirs.

"I can hardly wait," I said.

Kiki downed the contents of her glass and went off in search of more.

I opened the window to let in some air. Dark trees, a shouted insult. Carriage wheels.

"Is that Dalí?" I heard someone say.

A dapper, narrow-shouldered man with slicked-back hair and a mustache was standing on the threshold to the room. Salvador Dalí. I had seen his show at Camille Goemans's gallery on rue de Seine towards the end of the previous year. I walked up to him and held out my hand.

"I'm so glad you could come, señor."

His huge dark eyes moved from one part of my face to another, his mustache twitching. "And you are?"

"Marcel Moore. I live here."

"Ah yes. You're one of the famous lesbians of Paris, are you not?" His remark caught me off guard. Though direct, it was playful, edged in wit.

"You're very well informed," I said.

"Of course." He stood up a little straighter, eyes widening. "I am Dalí."

"Can I get you a drink?"

"Some milk, perhaps."

I fetched him a glass of milk.

"We have many lesbians in Paris," I told him. "In fact, this room is full of them."

"I *adore* lesbians." He sent a rapid, febrile glance around the room.

"Do you live in Paris now, señor?"

"Sometimes. But I'm about to buy a house in Port Lligat, not far from Cadaqués. Do you know the area?"

"I'm afraid not."

"You must visit. I insist."

I introduced him to Sylvia and Jane, who were standing nearby. Leaving the three of them together, I went to look for Claude. She was deep in conversation with Robert Desnos and Georges Ribemont-Dessaignes. I asked if they had met Dalí.

"Not yet." Georges looked in his direction. "Did you know that Gala has left Paul? She's with Dalí now."

"That's an unlikely combination," I said.

Robert shrugged. "She's very ambitious. She must think he's going to be rich."

"See that mustache?" Georges said. "Apparently, he got the idea from Velázquez."

"Where did you get the idea for yours?" Robert asked.

I wandered out of the room and down the corridor. When no one was looking, I slipped into our bedroom and closed the door. A gray kitten was curled up at the foot of the bed, one paw over his eyes. Constant Lounsbery had arrived at our apartment with a wicker basket a few days before. After performing in three of Albert-Birot's plays in as many months, Claude's poor health had forced her to give up acting, probably for good, and Constant had thought a pet might comfort her.

"Kid," I said. "Dear Kid."

I was about to give him a stroke when the door creaked open and Claude walked in, a lit cigarette between her fingers.

"How's he settling in?" she asked.

"See for yourself," I said.

She leaned down and pressed her lips to his small striped head, then tickled him behind his ears. He yawned and stretched.

"You've really taken to him, haven't you," I said.

Straightening again, she smiled at me through the smoke spiraling upwards from her cigarette.

Later, we walked back up the corridor, back into the drawing room. Claude's aunt, Marguerite, was talking to Dalí. She was curious about the fragrance he was wearing. It had been made for him personally, he told her, in Barcelona. The principal notes were orchid, lotus wood, and amber, but he suspected that chocolate might also be involved. Claude's aunt was laughing. Chocolate, she said. Of course.

Dalí turned to me. "You have gold paint on your lips, and on your cheek." He came up close and spoke into my ear. "You have been kissing a god, perhaps."

Later still, a group of us left for the Théâtre Esotérique. As we crossed rue Mazarine, Georgette started talking about a fifteenth-century Breton song called "Gwerz Penmarc'h." In four brief stanzas, drowned sailors addressed the people of Pointe de Penmarc'h, who lit fires in their parish church and lured unsuspecting vessels onto the rocks. It was a song sung by the dead, she said. It was part lament, part curse. Somebody asked if we could hear it. Georgette began to sing. Slow, forlorn, and filled with regret, the song also had an edge of menace and defiance, as if the dead posed a threat to the living, and though it was a chilly night people stepped out onto their balconies or peered down from open windows, and when she finished applause came from all around. As we walked on, she told us she had learned the song from a lover—in Quimper, she thought, or was it Quiberon?—and that she had only slept with him once.

"Only once," Robert said, "and yet he taught you that beautiful song."

"He was lucky to have had me at all," Georgette said.

She was almost sixty—her waist had thickened, and her arms were fleshy—but I could still see the young woman she had been, impassioned and brazen, the dark hair tumbling, the sultry mouth and eyes. She had lived with Maurice Maeterlinck for almost twenty years—she had inspired many of his plays—but in the end he found her attitude to sexuality too bewildering and painful. It was known, for instance, that she went to bed with other men—with women too—and that she considered such behavior quite normal. In those days, in Paris, it sometimes seemed that women were more powerful than men.

There was a crowd outside the theater, the cold air clouded with breath and smoke. My latest poster was on display—La Belle Nadja in her veils.

Dalí was at my elbow suddenly. "Did you do this?" Up close, he smelled of old gardenias, their petals browning at the edges. There was no hint of lotus wood, or chocolate.

"I thought you left," I said.

He gave me a wide-eyed, wild look. "I left," he said, "and yet somehow I'm still here!"

I laughed. Drawing was my great love, I told him, though I wouldn't dream of comparing my draftsmanship with his.

He leaned closer to the poster, his nose an inch from the glass, his mustache tips needle-sharp. "*Té un gran talent,*" he said, reverting to his native language. "Very—how do you say—economic."

"Economical," I said. "If you mean concise, that is. Otherwise you'd be talking about money."

"I *love* to talk about money," he said.

Smiling, I took his arm. We went inside.

He had never seen Béatrice dance before, and I seemed to watch her through his eyes. She had painted her eyebrows black, her eyelids too, and her lips were so red they looked poisonous. The veils in which she had wrapped herself were even more transparent than usual; like a mist that is burned off by the early morning sun, they seemed in danger of disappearing altogether. Béatrice, I knew, saw it differently. She had told me once that she felt clothed by the gaze of the audience. She only became naked if people lost interest and looked away. No one looked away that night, least of all Dalí. There was a stillness in the house, a sense of rapture.

When I took him backstage after the show, he threw himself on the floor in front of Béatrice. She watched, one eyebrow raised, as he kissed her bare feet, first one, then the other. Upright again, he asked her where she had got such an extraordinary body.

She shrugged. "I don't know. They just gave it to me."

"I could watch you dance for an eternity." He looked beyond her, eyes staring. "No!" His forefinger lifted, perpendicular, into the air. "Longer!"

Eventually, we made our way back to the foyer, where Dalí was himself surrounded by a group of admirers, and I didn't see him again for several years, and then only from a distance.

Not long afterwards, I dreamed I had traveled to a country somewhere in Africa. It was the custom, in that place, for the king's children to be fed both by their mother and by a wet nurse. This made good sense, I thought, until I noticed that the wet nurse had only one breast, and that the other one had been cut off. The left side of her chest was flat as a man's, except for the harsh ridges of the scar, which were even darker than her skin.

"Like everybody else in the world," the king told me, "you have doubtless observed that when a baby suckles on one breast he tends to hold or fondle the other. It seems to work best that way.

"But we have discovered that if one of the wet nurse's breasts is removed babies learn to talk more quickly. They worry at the absence until they produce a word with which to question those around them—and the word they come up with is always the same."

"Really?" I said. "What's the word?"

"Apricot," he said.

An absurd dream—unnerving too—but people were always amused when I told them about it, and Michaux liked it so much that he put it in a book of his.

———

Claude's most important written work, Disavowals, was published in the spring of 1930. She had harnessed her intelligence, her poetic gift, and her talent for provocation in an attempt to jolt the literary world out of its complacency—she longed to have an *effect*—but the book was received, for the most part, with a resounding silence. She had confronted all her doubts and fears— about love, about her family, and about what she referred to as her "badly-made body"—and no one cared. She felt rage, but she also felt ashamed. She continued to go out, often dressed as a man and wearing a monocle—it was said that André Breton would leave cafés as soon as Claude arrived because he found her appearance so disturbing—and yet, at the same time, she felt the urge to hide away. There were whole weeks when she refused to leave the apartment. She wouldn't look out of the window, but kept the curtains drawn. The world had turned its back on her. It was over, even before it had begun.

Several months after publication, on a chalky, gray-white September afternoon, we went out to buy bread and flowers and some flea powder for Kid. As we passed Shakespeare & Company, Sylvia Beach's shop, she saw us through the window and insisted that we come in for a drink.

"Adrienne's here," she said, tossing the words casually over her shoulder as we followed her to the office at the back.

I felt Claude hesitate. Her book was so intimate that she had seen Adrienne's refusal to publish it as a condemnation not just of her writing but of her as a person, and they hadn't had much contact since. It was very like Sylvia to pretend not to have noticed any awkwardness.

Adrienne was sitting at an untidy desk, going through a pile of receipts, the smoke from her cigarette blue in the chill gray air. When she saw Claude in the doorway I thought I detected a flicker of concern or apprehension in her face.

"Claude!" She stood up and kissed Claude on both cheeks. "It's good to see you. Marcel, how are you?" Her necklace of heavy wooden beads knocked against my collarbone as we embraced.

"Sylvia's keeping you busy, I see," Claude said.

Adrienne smiled. "Sylvia has no interest in money. It's beneath her."

Sylvia uncorked a bottle. "Some wine, perhaps?"

Later, when we were seated, Sylvia told Claude she had seen her book in the window of a shop on rue de Clichy. Claude responded by saying that she had been overlooked by all the most important newspapers.

"They aren't interested," she said. "No one's interested."

Sylvia glanced at Adrienne, but Adrienne didn't appear to notice.

"They will be," I said. "In time."

"It's not even the kiss of death," Claude went on. "It's the kiss of utter indifference." She turned to me, cheeks flushed. "How do you know they'll be interested—*in time*?"

I drank from my glass. The wine was cold and inky.

"Well?" she said.

We were living in an era when women's voices were only just beginning to be heard, I said. It was a profound shift, and society was still struggling to adapt. But she—Claude—had treated the concept of a woman who is powerful and independent as the norm, and she had pushed that concept one stage further. Maybe people weren't ready for that. Maybe they weren't prepared to see a powerful, independent woman take herself apart in public. It was too much. It was too soon.

"Since when did you become such an expert on women?" Claude made no attempt to keep the sneer out of her voice.

I shrugged. "It's just a theory."

Sylvia reached for one of Adrienne's cigarettes and struck a match. "I think Marcel's right," she said. "You're ahead of your time, Claude. You're early."

"You're all in this together," Claude said, "trying to make me feel better about my own irrelevance."

"You're saying difficult things." Sylvia rolled the tip of her cigarette against the edge of a saucer. "Someone has to be brave enough to do that."

"Or foolish enough," Claude said. Then her defiance collapsed. "I wasn't trying to be difficult. I was trying to be beautiful." She put her hands over her face, and her shoulders began to shake. She was like a child suddenly.

"You *are* beautiful," Sylvia said. "To the people who understand these things."

"Three of you," Claude muttered. "It's hardly an audience."

"Michaux loved your book," Adrienne said.

"That makes four—or is it still three?" Claude gave Adrienne a pointed look.

We left the shop soon afterwards.

Claude would not be consoled. She stopped eating. She smoked and drank instead. She wanted to "kill her feelings," as she put it. Sleep eluded her. At night she wandered through the city, and I went with her. We met drunks and prostitutes—or sometimes, if it was late enough, we didn't meet anyone at all. Claude was reminded of Boiffard's photographs of deserted streets and doorways. The pictures were deliberately mundane, she said—they looked like pictures of nothing—but they suggested a secret life, a life hidden by time. Was that empty square the site of a forgotten catastrophe, or was it the scene of a crime that had yet to be committed? We walked for miles, often until dawn. Once, beneath a railway viaduct, we saw people fighting over a pile of old clothes. If you value something, Claude said, does that make it valuable?

She thought of Soulef, the fortune-teller, and imagining that Soulef might be able to give her some direction, or steady her at least, we traveled to Porte de Clignancourt. Almost a decade had passed, and the brick building where Claude claimed to have spent the night had been demolished. We asked everyone we came across if they knew of Soulef's whereabouts. Nobody had heard of her.

A few days later, Claude remembered Soulef's daughter. Once again, I went with her. The corner bar where she and Soulef had stopped for a glass of calvados was still there. When we walked in, an African woman of about our age was wiping the zinc counter with a rag. Her name was Eugénie. Claude began to ask her about Soulef. At first, Eugénie seemed suspicious, and would only answer in monosyllables, but then Claude told her the story of how she had spent an entire day guiding her mother through the city.

Clicking her tongue, Eugénie shook her head. "It's not the first time she's played that trick. She always did like company."

"So it's not true," Claude said, "that she needs help?"

"Not as much as she makes out." Eugénie folded the rag and draped it over a tap. "And something else: she's not my mother."

"But she said—"

"She's my aunt. At least, I think she is. It was her sister that was my mother."

"Do you know where I might find her?"

"Soulef? I haven't seen her in a year or two. But she might walk in that door at any moment."

Claude asked if they could be photographed together. Eugénie let out a short, sharp laugh, half startled, half dismissive. It would be the first time, she said, that she had stood in front of one of those machines. Claude told her the machines could give her a kind of immortality. In one hundred years, complete strangers might happen on the photograph, and they would see her exactly as she was. But she'd be gone. Long gone.

"All right." Eugénie dried her hands and came out from behind the bar.

As I took the picture, I was surprised to see an awkwardness in Claude. She looked humble, shy. Uncertain of her ground. She had laid one hand over Eugénie's forearm in a gesture that seemed familiar, almost possessive, though you might at the same time be forgiven for thinking that she was clinging to Eugénie for support. This ambiguity felt truthful. Where Claude was hunched, Eugénie stood upright, her weight evenly distributed. With one hand tucked into her jacket pocket and a piece of cloth wound round her head, she gave off a sullen nonchalance.

It was overcast when we left the bar, but as we walked down rue d'Hauteville the clouds parted and hot yellow light spilled through the gap.

"I feel better now," Claude said.

Without another word we crossed the street, moving from the shade into the sun.

In the spring of 1931, while in the bath, I found a small lump in the upper slope of my left breast. When I told Claude, she immediately assumed the worst: it was cancer, and I was going to die.

"You can't leave me." She gripped my hand so hard that she almost crushed the bones. "I have to go first. You promised, remember?"

She was referring to a late-night conversation we had had in Le Croisic when we were young. Nothing should be allowed to come between us, she had said. Not circumstances, not people either—but what to do about death? She fell silent. Through the open window I could hear boats shifting in the harbor. I have to go before you, she said at last. She looked at me. You're not saying anything. I agree, I said. As if death was something I could influence or manage. You'd let me go first? she said. You'd do that for me? Yes, I said. It wasn't because I didn't love her as much as she loved me, nor was it because I could bear the thought of her being gone. It was because she was more fragile than I was, and more vulnerable. Even at the age of twenty, I somehow knew I would find it easier to carry on alone.

Luckily, the tumor was benign, though my doctor advised me to have the breast removed, and the procedure was carried out in July. I was unprepared for the extreme discomfort that followed. For at least two months, I couldn't raise my left arm, which made simple tasks like getting dressed almost impossible. Also, I had the feeling ants were swarming just beneath my skin, a sensation caused by the severing of highly sensitive nerves. Worse still, there were moments when it seemed someone was gouging a hole in the left side of my body with a rusty knife.

It was during my convalescence that Claude recalled my dream about the woman with one breast.

"Uncanny," she said, "don't you think?"

I nodded. "I suppose so."

"I don't think you're clairvoyant, though."

"Don't you?" I watched her from the bed as she paced up and down, in the grip of an idea.

"No," she said. "We *know* ourselves—better than we think we do."

I wasn't sure she was right. My theory had always been that the dream was a comment on our relationship, but since I had yet to work out what exactly it was saying I decided not to mention it.

That year, we went to Jersey later than usual, at the end of August. We were both debilitated. Only a few weeks before, Claude had learned of the death of her mother. Georges had telephoned, informing her that Toinette had died in his apartment. He had arranged for her removal from the clinic. He had that authority, he said. He had realized that she was nearing the end, and thought it important she was with her family.

Claude stood facing the wall. "What about me? I'm not family?"

As Georges began to try to justify his behavior, she dropped the receiver and walked away, leaving it hanging from the edge of the hall table on its black cord. I picked it up and listened as Georges talked on. He had acted in their mother's interests, he was saying. He knew what was best for her. At no point did he apologize.

I didn't speak until he finished.

"Thank you for letting us know," I said.

"Suzanne—?"

I replaced the receiver.

Claude believed that Georges had deliberately kept the news from her because he wanted to punish her both for siding with their father over the divorce and for approving of his marriage to my mother. Georges had been vengeful, she said, and cruel. In 1928, she had tried to visit her mother—she hadn't seen her since our stay in Le Pradet some seventeen years before—but she had been turned away by the staff at the clinic. Georges had ensured that Toinette was concealed in death, just as she had been concealed while she was alive. There was a terrible symmetry about it. I agreed. But perhaps, in a way, I said, her mother's passing should come as a relief. The absence that had so tormented her had been one that people like Georges manipulated and controlled. It had been an absence that could be altered—though not by her. This new absence did not discriminate. It was permanent, and irrevocable. She didn't turn on me, as she had done in the past. Instead, she lit a cigarette and stared at the floor, and when she had finished that cigarette she lit another. At night, I often woke to find myself alone, Claude's half of the bed untouched. As I lay on my back, I would hear the piano. A piece I didn't recognize. Later, she told me she had written it herself. It was through music that she grieved—everybody in the building sleeping, the glimmer of white keys in the dark . . .

In Jersey, the weather was cold and wet. We wrote to Robert and Youki, asking them to join us, but Youki had already gone away on holiday, and Robert was so short of money that he had taken a job as an estate agent. The rain did not let up. We spent more time in the cinema than on the beach. We went to the new Greta Garbo film and one that starred Marlene Dietrich, but the highlight of the summer was *Monkey Business*. With their ludicrous but deft routines, the Marx Brothers inspired us to laugh at our misfortunes, and at ourselves. For them, the world was simply an excuse to wreak havoc, and there was no situation that did not have its funny side.

I think we saw the film three times.

It was through our friend Jacques Viot that Claude first met André Breton. One spring afternoon Jacques brought Breton to our apartment on rue Notre-Dame-des-Champs. Breton wore a green suit and a pair of spectacles, and he carried his famous cane on which were carved vaginas, erect penises, and slugs. Sylvia had told us that his spectacles were an affectation. The lenses were made of ordinary glass.

Things got off to an awkward start.

"I understand," Breton said in his somber, somewhat pedantic voice, "that Robert Desnos is a friend of yours."

"Yes," Claude said.

"We were also close once, but he disappointed me." Breton stuck out his lower lip. "I no longer expect anything from him."

Claude lit a cigarette. She was dressed conservatively, in a dark-blue dress and a wool beret. Her hair was short, but not cropped.

I spoke to Breton. "I read your novel. I admired it very much."

Breton inclined his enormous head in thanks, but made no comment.

Jacques leaned forwards. "Claude has also written a book."

"I've heard great things," Breton said, "though I have not, as yet, had the pleasure of reading it."

Claude took a copy from her bag and put it on the table in front of him. "A gift."

Her boldness surprised me, but if Breton was taken aback he gave no sign of it. He merely nodded and said, "How kind."

Before he left, he admired our collection of primitive and Cubist sculptures.

Not long afterwards, he invited us to the Cyrano, where he and his fellow Surrealists liked to gather for aperitifs. Since the café was next to the Moulin Rouge, and just down the street from the Cirque Medrano, it attracted an eclectic clientele. You might find yourself sitting next to a trapeze artist, a pimp, or an American. We arrived early. For almost an hour we had Breton to ourselves. He repeated a sentiment expressed in the letter he had written to Claude after their first meeting—namely, that although he didn't know what to make of her and her work, somehow her presence moved him. He believed that, in time, he would feel less disconcerted. He blamed what he called his "straightforwardness."

At five o'clock more people arrived. They ordered *oxygénés*, a drink made with white pastis. The noise level rose. A young man began to talk at the top of his voice. He was telling a story about a princess and a decommissioned submarine. He had the eyes of a stone angel in a graveyard, wide and serene, but also astonished. I asked Jacques who he was.

"That's René Crevel," he said.

René was a talented poet, Jacques told me, but he took too many drugs. Hashish, cocaine. Opium. His life was chaotic. He slept with people of both sexes. He was a member of the Communist Party and of the Surrealist movement, neither of which approved of homosexuality. He worshipped Breton, though, and followed him everywhere. Jacques paused. He had heard a rumor, he went on. He wasn't sure if it was true. When René's father hanged himself, his mother had forced him to look at the body. René was only fourteen at the time.

"He needs looking after," I said.

Jacques nodded. "I'll introduce you."

There were many conversations and encounters with Breton, and it is hard to separate them out. I remember Claude sitting close to him in a café, discussing the increase in tension between politics and art. Like everybody else, she was saying, she had joined the Association of Revolutionary Writers and Artists, the AEAR, since it was only the Communist Party that seemed prepared to oppose Hitler's fascist and xenophobic program. She was beginning to have second thoughts, though. She wished Stalin had not stripped communism of all its romantic aspects. In turning his back on libertarian aesthetics, he had betrayed the legacy of Rimbaud and Lautréamont.

Breton looked pensive.

"What's more, I'm worried by the party's attitude to freedom of speech," Claude went on. "They appear to think that everything we create should somehow reflect their ideology. I can't—and won't—accept those kinds of constraints."

"Unlike Aragon," Breton said.

Claude nodded. "A case in point."

As Claude and I both knew, Breton had fallen out with Louis Aragon, once his most intimate associate, and a real force in the Surrealist movement. Also, Aragon had started publishing poems that regurgitated Communist Party dogma. They were awful.

"Art must be free of any shackles," Claude said, "or it will die. I'm thinking of writing a defense of creativity." She paused. "Which would amount to an attack on Aragon, and on the PCF."

She was passionate that afternoon. She glowed like heated metal. Of the feelings of incompetence that had prevented her from writing for Soupault thirteen years before there was no sign. Had she finally overcome her shyness? Or was she inspired by Breton's company?

"A defense of creativity?" There was a hint of a smile on the great man's face. "I'd be interested to see that."

At around that time, Claude came home weighed down by morning editions of all the daily newspapers. Her face was troubled, pale.

"Is something wrong?" I asked.

There had been a double murder in Le Mans, she told me. Two housemaids, Christine and Léa Papin, had killed their employer, Madame Lancelin, and her daughter, Geneviève.

I asked her what had happened.

She gave me the background first. Christine and Léa came from a dirt-poor rural family, she said. Their father, a violent alcoholic, had raped their older sister, Emilia, when she was ten. Their mother blamed Emilia, and sent her to a brutal local orphanage. As a baby, Christine was sent to the same place. Léa, who was born six years later, was farmed out to a great-uncle. In time, Emilia became a nun. When Christine said she wanted to follow her sister into the church, her mother forbade it, insisting that both Christine and Léa go out to work in order to provide her with an income.

For seven years, the Lancelin family had no cause for complaint—Christine and Léa worked hard, and kept themselves to themselves—but on the night in question a power cut had plunged the house into near darkness, and something in the two young women must have snapped. When the police arrived at the house, they discovered the bodies of Madame Lancelin and her daughter on the landing, at right angles to each other, severe wounds inflicted to their heads and legs. There was an eye on the third step down from the landing. There was another eye in the hall. The carpet was drenched with blood, so much so that it gave underfoot, like moss. The youngest of the policemen was called Truth. Claude let out a laugh that was disbelieving, humorless. She had always paid great attention to names, and liked nothing better than to make them up, especially for me.

It was Truth who found the two sisters, she went on, in the attic, lying side by side in bed. Their hands and faces were scrubbed clean, as were the knife and hammer they had used as weapons. They put on matching blue kimonos, and he escorted the sisters down the stairs and out into the cold black February night, where they were photographed, their expressions shocked and masklike, their hair disheveled.

When Claude opened one of the papers and showed me the picture I was mesmerized, and it was a while before I worked out why.

"It's just like you," I said at last.

She looked startled. "What do you mean?"

The picture reminded me of Pierre Albert-Birot's production of *Barbe-Bleue*, in which Claude had played the role of Bluebeard's wife, Elle. She had worn a floor-length dress with black crosses all the way up the front of the bodice, as if she had been ripped open and then sewn back together. Her eyes were ringed in black, and her mouth was painted to look smaller than it was. A thick blond braid framed her face like a primitive hairband.

Her presence onstage was chilling, since her movements were awkward, almost mechanical, and her face remained expressionless throughout. Even at the time, I had seen the performance as a portrait of repressed emotion. Elle could not react to—or even think about—the multiple rapes and murders her husband was committing. Her blankness became a screen on which the audience could project its own ideas about what she might be feeling.

I pointed at the photograph of the two sisters. "Christine and Léa are the same. You see?"

"Yes," Claude said. "I do."

For Surrealists like Breton, the case became a cause célèbre, since they saw the crimes as an attack on bourgeois complacency, but Claude and I were far more interested in the psychological aspects. We followed the case obsessively, discussing each development, no matter how inconsequential.

The trial took place in September of that year. Though both sisters were judged to be sane, experts subsequently claimed that Christine was almost certainly a paranoid schizophrenic. It emerged in court that Christine had been responsible for the murder of Madame Lancelin, and that Léa had copied her sister by killing the daughter. Léa didn't speak except to say that she had used the knife to make "little carvings" on Geneviève's thighs, which was the site of the secret of life itself. She was asked why she believed such a thing. Christine had told her so, she said. Christine was sentenced to the guillotine. Léa received a lighter sentence—ten years' hard labor—since the jury felt she had a weak personality and had fallen under her sister's spell.

Shortly before Christine was executed, the newspapers printed something she was supposed to have said. *Sometimes I think that in former lives I was my sister's husband.* This statement echoed some of Claude's preoccupations. First of all, Christine was questioning the boundaries of her gender. In defining herself as male, she had taken on a role that was proprietorial and dominant. Secondly, she had rejected the genetic link in favor of a union that was a choice. She had *chosen* Léa. The two young women were bound together by emotion, not by blood. Since Christine and Léa were sisters, and also, it was rumored, lovers, I wondered if Claude saw them as dark parallels, nightmare versions of ourselves. The thought was disconcerting, and I kept it to myself.

In time, the case disappeared from the newspapers, but Claude's interest in mental disturbance and states of alienation did not fade. We met the poet and psychiatric doctor Gaston Ferdière, and would often attend his lectures at the Sainte-Anne hospital, with either Michaux, Breton, or René Crevel. I could never rid myself of the feeling that Claude was attracted by the very thing that had frightened or confused her as a child. After all, hospitals like these had been her mother's refuges, worlds from which she—Claude—had always been excluded. They were also places in which she might herself have ended up. What had she written once? *Madness looks at me with fixed eyes.* In visiting Sainte-Anne, I thought, she was somehow visiting herself.

Though we grew close to René, we didn't see as much of him as we would have liked, since he suffered from tuberculosis—his "dirty lungs," as he called them—and he would disappear to a sanatorium in Davos for weeks on end. In his many letters to us, he referred to it as "being imprisoned." If he wasn't undergoing treatment in Switzerland, he was usually traveling the world, but he would come and visit us the moment he returned to Paris. He would often bring Mops Sternheim-Ripper with him. She was a German-Jewish divorcee, with gleaming black hair and a slim figure. She worked in the theater, as a designer.

One night in 1934, after a month or two of silence, the couple appeared at our door while we were cooking for Henri Michaux.

"Am I interrupting?" René said.

"Of course not," Claude said. "Come in, come in."

Everyone said hello.

Claude spoke to René. "You look so well. Were you in Switzerland again?"

"I was with Dalí," he said. "In Port Lligat."

"I *love* Dalí," Claude said.

René's eyes opened wide. "You sound just like him."

He had spent three weeks in Catalunya, he told us, at the fisherman's cottage that was now Dalí's home. I remembered Dalí describing the place. *You must visit. I insist.* Later, he had written me a letter in which he told me he had bought the property from the "witch" of Cadaqués, a paranoid woman by the name of Lídia Noguer. He admired her madness, he had said. It was so individual, and so inventive. Even after the sale had gone through, he would call on her, just for the pleasure of hearing her talk.

At first, René said, he had been alone with Dalí and Gala, who was ten years older. Some people found Gala high-handed or secretive—she had what Dalí called a "wall-penetrating gaze"— but he was devoted to her, and deferred to her at every opportunity. She walked around bare-breasted, even in public, wearing nothing but a flimsy little skirt. She turned heads everywhere she went. She was a nymphomaniac. Halfway through his stay, René went on, Mops had taken the train down from Berlin. They spent the days swimming in the lagoon or lying naked among the rocks behind the house. They dined on sea urchins and champagne and sardines caught when the moon was new. Some nights they slept on the flat roof, beneath the stars.

"Dalí used to try and watch us," Mops said. "Making love."

René nodded enthusiastically. "I caught him once, peering into our bedroom. He had a special peephole."

"Dirty so-and-so," I said.

But I didn't mean it. I didn't hold Dalí's voyeurism against him. Somehow I could never hold anything against Dalí.

"Did you hear about the swans?" René asked.

We shook our heads.

Dalí owned three swans, he told us. When dusk fell, small cages would be fastened to their heads, each cage containing a lighted candle. Dalí liked to be able to watch the swans gliding across the bay while he was eating dinner.

The more René talked, the more fantastical his stories became, but he swore that every word was true.

"Usually I embellish," he said. "With Dalí, though, there is no need!"

Towards midnight, Michaux rose from the table, visibly exhausted after hours of listening.

"I'll see you out," I told him.

When we were by the front door, he leaned close to me and spoke in a low voice. "He likes to talk, doesn't he?"

I nodded. "It can be hard to get a word in edgeways."

"Hard?" Michaux said. "Impossible." He paused. "Do you remember what he said when he first walked in?"

"No, what?"

"'Am I interrupting?'"

―――――――

About a year later, on a midsummer morning, we were in a café with two Marxist friends, Néoclès Coutouzis and Lilette Richter, when we learned that René had killed himself. He had been found in his kitchen, with the oven on. He was younger than we were, only thirty-four.

Claude's face drained of blood. "Does no one recall that line in his first novel?"

We all looked at her.

"*I open the gas tap,*" she said, "*and forget to light a match.*"

Someone gasped. "He wrote that?"

"It was in *Détours,*" Claude said, "published eleven years ago."

There was a silence, then she pushed her chair back and left the table. In normal circumstances, I might have followed her, but I was thinking of my dream about the wet nurse with one breast, and how I too had appeared to be predicting my own future.

Later that day, as we walked in the Luxembourg Gardens, the weather cool and gray for June, Claude talked about René's death. She was shocked and saddened—he had been a close friend and a pure spirit—but her overriding feeling, she said, was one of envy. She was jealous of his success.

"Success?" I was momentarily bewildered. As a writer, René had been a marginal figure, at best.

"He has accomplished something I have failed to accomplish," she said. "He has shown me up for the fraud that I am."

At last I understood. "Because you haven't managed to end your life," I said.

"What else?"

"But René was never very stable—"

"And I am?"

"He didn't really have anyone."

"No one has anyone."

A dog bounded past us with a stick between its jaws. Its simple joy seemed outlandish, unachievable.

"Does our love count for nothing?" I said.

"Of course it does. But you can't weigh love against death. There are no scales for what we're talking about."

"Maybe not. But you seem to be saying that death is heavier."

"They belong to two completely different categories," she said. "They can't be compared."

She asked if I remembered the lines that had appeared in her last book. *Before being born, I was condemned. Executed in my absence.*

I nodded.

"I was referring to my father," she said.

One morning, when she returned from the dentist—she had been twelve at the time—her father had sat her down and asked her to forgive him for having brought her into the world. He saw her life as a mistake, a piece of carelessness. An abrogation of responsibility on his part. At some deep level, in a place where words could not be formed, she said, he had wished her dead. Or if not dead, unborn. Unthought of. Why? Because he didn't want her to suffer, like her mother. Because he loved her. There were tears in his eyes as he spoke. Poor father, she said, taking his big hand. Don't cry. She had been wished out of existence, and he was the one who had needed comforting! If she had been a boy, it would have been different. She didn't think he had ever lost a moment's sleep over her brother, Georges. His anxiety had been exhausting to live with. She had never been so tired as she was when she was young.

"That's why I say that nonexistence is my natural state." She looked ahead, down the long straight path. "It takes an enormous effort, sometimes, to go against all that."

I remembered the photographs in which she appeared as her father. In merging her identity with his, perhaps she had been trying to remove herself from the equation. Wipe herself out.

"Oh, Claude," I said.

The wind picked up. The leaves on a nearby plane tree shifted, and I felt something I had never felt before, the urge to do something sudden and destructive. To harm myself.

Maybe Claude sensed what I was feeling because she took my arm.

"This park is too depressing," she said. "Let's go home."

I think it was in 1936 that Claude first suggested we should move away from Paris. After spending most of the twenties on the sidelines, we had been admitted into Breton's inner circle. As paid-up members of AEAR, we were signatories to a number of high-profile protests and petitions, specifically against French imperialist policies and the rise of fascism. In 1934 Claude had published *Les paris sont ouverts*, the polemic she had promised Breton on one of their first meetings, and it had met with his enthusiastic endorsement. When Breton fell out with Georges Bataille—he was always falling out with somebody, it seemed—we helped him to form a new splinter group called Contre-Attaque. It didn't last. Nothing lasted. The movements came and went more quickly than the seasons, and the rifts between people we knew were perennial and vitriolic. Some years later, in a letter, Breton would refer to Claude as "one of the most inquiring minds of our time"—he had thought highly of *Disavowals*, the book she had given him—and he went on to regret that she seemed to "find pleasure in remaining silent," but he never realized the extent of her weariness and disillusion. If she still wrote, it was in secret, with no thought of being published. Though Paris was believed to be the center of the world, particularly for artists, and people were always congratulating themselves for being in the right place and pitying those who had the misfortune to live elsewhere, Claude was beginning to feel that something had been extinguished. This wasn't clairvoyance on her part. René's suicide was like a light going out, she told me. At the same time, she had noted the rise of right-wing factions like Croix de Feu, and the way in which anti-Semitic attitudes were once again in evidence throughout Europe. Newspapers ran articles that complained about the "swarming" Jews who were taking over the Parisian art scene, and Montparnasse was regularly demonized as an alien or "Jewish" area. Claude had already faced prejudice during her childhood, and she had no desire to face it again. What's more, her health, which had always been delicate, had been worn down by her family's endless bitter wrangling over money. She had been further weakened by surgical intervention, and by long years of starving herself, or eating poorly. Her eyesight was failing, and she was frightened that she might go blind, like her grandmother. The city drained what little energy she had. In her novel *Nightwood*, Djuna Barnes described Paris as having "the fame of a too-beautiful woman." This was a compliment, of course, but only on the surface. The word "too-beautiful" said it all. One could be overwhelmed by Paris. One could become sated. And it was hard for a city to retain that kind of allure. There was the implication that it would fade. There was that inevitability.

"I've been thinking that we should live somewhere else," Claude announced one warm May afternoon.

We were sitting in a café on Place Blanche, one that Breton frequented, though he hadn't arrived as yet.

"Where would we go?" I asked.

"We could emigrate—to Canada."

"*Canada?*"

"Why not? We have the money now."

My mother had died the month before, after a long, slow decline. As a result, we would no longer have to rely on monthly allowances. From now on, we would have complete financial independence.

Canada, though . . .

I remembered Bob enthusing about the country, and wondered if his dreams had lodged in Claude, become her own. Though she did her best to conjure up the place for me—the gritty, French-speaking cities, the wide wheat prairies, the tall blue skies—the whole idea began to seem exaggerated and absurd, and by the time Breton appeared we were both laughing at a vision of ourselves in Stetson hats and jeans.

"What's so amusing?" Breton asked as he mopped the sweat from his forehead and took his place at the table.

"Canada," I said.

The look that rose onto his face confirmed a feeling I had often had about him. For all his brilliance and authority, there was something preposterous about André Breton. No wonder Robert Desnos called him "the Pope." One couldn't help wanting to prick the bubble of his self-importance. Decades later, when I visited Paris for the last time, someone told me about Breton's trip to Mexico, when he stayed with Diego Rivera and collaborated on the famous *Manifesto for an Independent Revolutionary Art* with Rivera's house guest, Leon Trotsky. When Breton had departed, Rivera's wife, Frida Kahlo, was asked what she thought of him. "Pompous, arrogant, and boringly intellectual," she said. "I couldn't stand the old cockroach." Anyone who had spent time with Breton would know what she meant, even if they didn't agree with her.

But if not Canada, Claude said that night, then where?

It was still hot outside, and we were lying in bed with the windows open. The air stood solid and unmoving in the room.

"Do we have to leave?" I said. "I like it here."

She walked to the window, the sheet twisted round her waist and trailing behind her. She looked like a ravaged bride, her wedding dress in tatters, half torn off.

"What about Jersey?" she said.

I thought once again of Bob, though we hadn't seen or heard of him in at least ten years, not since he got married. But Claude was talking about the heat, the sea. All the summers we had spent, our bodies rocked by the waves, then drying in the sun. Our skin slowly turning brown. Cycling down green lanes, reading in the shade. The taste of farm butter, studded with tiny chips of sea salt. The goat cheese, the blackberry jam. The eggs. When we were on the island, we were accepted for who we were, she said, and no one interfered. In recent years, it was the place where we had been happiest.

"We feel at ease every time we go," she went on. "It's like one of those smooth stones you keep in your pocket because it feels so good in your hand. Also, it's positioned between France and England, without belonging to either. It's independent and awkward and oddly fierce. It's an anomaly. Like us. Why didn't we think of it before? Everything we want is there." She turned to face me. "Why are you smiling?"

I was smiling because she had said "we," even though the whole thing was so clearly her idea. I was also smiling because I could feel myself beginning to give in. It was the kind of speech I might have made. I was the practical one, the sensible one. I was the rock. Sometimes, though, just sometimes, Claude would become me and I would become her—while making love, for instance, or dancing—and it was unforced and seamless, it was comfortable, this reversing of our roles, this intermingling of our attributes and our desires. I had seen acquaintances of ours notice this capacity in us, and I had watched it arouse their jealousy, despite the fact that they were richer than we were, and more celebrated, and despite the fact that they were not, as a rule, people for whom a feeling like jealousy was either natural or valid. But they realized that they didn't have anything we wanted, and they took our self-sufficiency as a kind of rejection, or even as an expression of contempt. If money, beauty, and fame aren't coveted by the people who don't have them, they lose their value for the people who do. Perhaps that was why we had been sidelined. Since you want for nothing, the world had said, I will give you nothing. See how you like *that*. For all Claude's talk about the irrelevance of recognition and success—she maintained they were bourgeois preoccupations—she still felt she had been excluded, and that exclusion hurt. I would tell her not to listen to the world. She should only listen to herself. Easy to say, but not so easy to achieve. If we removed ourselves, it was not because we had been vanquished, but because we were complete.

"Jersey," I said at last. "It would be like being on holiday, only all the time."

She came towards me, skin gleaming in the half-dark. "So you agree with me?"

"Yes."

"You don't think we'd be playing safe?"

"Only on the surface."

She laughed. "You're more than I deserve."

I reached for her, our bodies locking into place. We would move to Jersey, with its idyllic beaches, its green gullies and ravines, its delicious isolation. Friends would visit from time to time, but we would have privacy and peace. We would live quietly, take photographs.

Love each other.

SELF-PORTRAIT IN NAZI UNIFORM

1937–1944

The moment we set foot on the island in May 1937, things seemed to spring into motion, almost as if our arrival had been anticipated, or as if we had responded to a summons. Bob Colley had taken over as proprietor of the St. Brelade's Bay Hotel—his mother had retired—and he greeted us with his customary warmth and humor. The Colleys were like family, as Claude was fond of saying, but without any of the complications or disadvantages. We had been staying at the hotel for no more than a few days when Bob approached us at breakfast. Leaning over the table, he told us in a low voice that there was a property for sale that might be of interest.

"Where is it," Claude asked, "this property?"

"That's the wonderful thing." He pointed past me, through the window. "It's just over there, on the other side of the road."

"The church?" Claude said.

"No, not the church . . ." Bob's eyes squeezed shut and his mouth opened wide and a rhythmic creaking or wheezing emerged, as if something deep inside him needed oiling. "Oh, you do make me laugh," he said when he had himself under control again. He shook his head. "It's a house," he said. "I think you should take a look."

La Rocquaise was a long three-story residence that dated from the fourteenth century, with walls built from granite and dormer windows set in a roof of reddish-orange tile. One room opened onto the next through what the estate agent called "Jersey doors," leading at last to a drawing room with a large stone fireplace that felt almost baronial. The upstairs rooms were darker and more cramped, but most of them had sea views. What made the house irresistible to us, though, was the way it turned its back on the land and gathered protectively around a garden that overlooked the beach. The tide was high that day, and the sea and sky were the same fuzzy shade of eggshell blue in the heat haze, a rocky headland framing the view to the southwest, the horizon faint as the crease in a folded sheet of writing paper. Standing on the bright grass, surrounded by dwarf palms and exotic shrubs, I felt I had been transported to Jamaica or Singapore.

"What animal is it," Claude asked, when the estate agent was out of earshot, "that uses urine to mark its territory?"

"Cats maybe," I said. "Why? Is that what you're about to do?"

"If necessary." She turned and looked up at the house. "I love this place, Suzanne. I feel it should be ours."

I felt the same.

The asking price was considerable, but we had plenty of capital at our disposal, and this, coupled with our status as honorary locals—Bob Colley's words—guaranteed that our offer was accepted. We returned to Paris at the end of the summer with the title deeds in our possession.

It was during one of Robert and Youki's famous Saturday gatherings in their apartment on rue Mazarine that we finally revealed what we were planning. That afternoon Philippe Soupault had appeared with a brace of freshly killed guinea fowl, and we had eaten at a long table, nine or ten of us, in a room with a chessboard-tile floor. After dinner, more people arrived. It was a wild fragrant October evening, low ragged clouds sliding past the rooftops, the air filled with whirling yellow leaves.

On hearing our news, Robert lowered his eyes and was silent, and I had the feeling he was discarding any reactions that might seem flippant or self-interested. Wax dripped from the tall church candle that stood between us. The black cloth that covered the table gave the glass of red wine at his elbow a vampiric look.

"You won't miss all this?" He glanced away from us, into the next room, where a bearded man in a military-style jacket was dancing a rumba with a woman half his size.

"Not really," Claude said. "But I *will* miss you."

Shortly after they met, Claude had offered to organize Robert's papers for him, as a secretary might, not, I suspected, because she needed the work, but because she was looking for an excuse to be close to him, and when she wrote to him, she often signed the letters "Love, Claude," something she didn't do with anybody else. Robert was one of the few men she felt attracted to, both mentally and physically, though she had come to realize that her feelings would never be reciprocated.

Robert was smiling, and nodding to himself. "Jersey, it's not so far."

"It isn't," Claude said, "is it."

"You probably take a train, and then another train. Then something else . . ." He fell quiet for a few moments. "Actually, where *is* Jersey?"

We all laughed.

Later, when most people were gone and we were sitting close to each other on a deep sofa, Claude asked Robert who the dancers were.

"The woman with the lovely eyes was Damia," he said. "She's a singer. She has been in films as well. The man was Ernest Hemingway."

"That was Hemingway?" I said.

He nodded. "Yes."

"I'd like to have met him," Claude said.

"Well, you'll have to come back and visit us," Robert said. "And we'll visit you too, in Jersey." He ran a hand through his swept-back hair and turned to Youki. "That's a promise, isn't it, my love."

Youki reached for her drink. "Of course."

But he didn't come, and nor did she. None of us realized, at that point, how close we were to war, or which of us it would take.

We didn't move into La Rocquaise until the following spring. Claude left it to me and our Northern Irish housekeeper, Nan, to do the unpacking. I didn't mind. It allowed me to bed myself in, to convince myself that I was somewhere I wanted to be. Slowly, we redecorated rooms, put books on shelves. Slowly, we hung the

paintings. Blue mornings, cool wood floors. Afternoons in the
garden, or by the sea. In the evenings, after a glass of whiskey on
the terrace, Claude and I would light a fire in the big room. We
were so lucky to have bought the place. It was lush and private—an
Eden with two Eves, no Adam. Sometimes we visited Brown's
Café, which was run by a widow from Manchester. Mrs. Brown
wore a long black dress with a high collar, and her features were
permanently set in a mask of disapproval. We would also meet
up with Vera, the young Englishwoman who had tried to attach
herself to us at the beginning of the twenties. Like us, she had
bought a house on the island, and though Claude had once pointed
out that she had an eager quality that seemed to invite cruelty, a
remark I remembered every time I saw her, a friendship had gradually grown up between us. That year Claude began to call me
Suzanne again, as she had when we first met. I had always signed
my work "Marcel Moore" or "Moore," but the name had fallen
away towards the end of the twenties, when I stopped drawing.
My middle name was Alberte, after my father, and some local
people called me Bertie. Claude found this highly entertaining. She said it made her feel as though she was living with an
English gentleman. She rechristened our house La Ferme sans
Nom—The Farm without a Name—since its previous existence
was no longer relevant. We needed a blank slate, she told me, on
which we could write our own history. It was also a homage to
the house with the black chandelier, where we had found refuge
when we were young.

I went to bed earlier than I had in Paris. I got up earlier too.
In the summer I often swam at dawn, when the sea itself seemed
only half awake. Claude kept different hours. She wrote at night,
or read, or played her beautiful Pleyel, which had been shipped to

the island along with everything else we owned. She would come to bed at four or five in the morning, still trembling at the feelings she had found inside herself, feelings she hadn't known were there. Sometimes she would wake me and we'd make love. Her body cool, mine warm. Daybreak gradually revealing us to each other, as if love brought light. We were like a photograph developing. Later, while Claude was sleeping, I would have breakfast, my hair damp from my first swim of the day, the prickle of salt on my skin. Black coffee, fresh bread. The doors and windows open, and shadows angling across the garden. The house motionless and quiet, only the soft jolt of Kid throwing himself down in a patch of sunlight and the steady breathing of the waves.

Later still, I would hear the bus arrive from town.

On mainland Europe things were volatile. The French government had resigned, leaving no one to oppose Hitler's annexation of Austria.

"What if the Nazis look westwards?" Claude said one day. "If they threaten France, we might have to consider leaving."

My response was immediate and fierce. It had taken years for us to think of a place where we could be happy, and I couldn't believe she wanted to throw it all away. La Ferme sans Nom was our fortress and our sanctuary, I told her, and I would never leave.

"If you really think it's dangerous," I went on, "then you should go. I'll wait here till you return."

She let the subject drop.

That summer Nan departed for Canada, where she would be starting a new life with her second husband. Before she left, she suggested that her daughter, Edna, should take over from her. Edna, who was twenty-two, had been working at the lunatic asylum in St. Helier, as a nurse. She was a bundle of contradictions—loyal, reckless, impudent, and kind—and she liked to drink to excess, but we warmed to her liveliness and took her on. She would be with us for almost ten years.

In late August, when the first storm blew in, we found that the house was protected by the headland and by the concrete pier that reached sideways into the bay. We stood at the bottom of the garden and watched huge waves curl from right to left and thump against the hard sand farther down the beach, spray catapulting into the air and resolving itself into an eerie, drifting mist.

"You see?" I had to shout to make myself heard. "We're safe here."

The next morning, the lawn was crusted with salt, each blade of grass edged in white and oddly crisp. We walked on it barefoot, as children might. It was a new beginning, a second innocence. We were both already in our forties, but we felt ageless. Blessed.

In November, only a few months after we moved in, Michaux came to visit. We caught a bus to St. Helier and met him off the boat. He appeared on the walkway in a brown jacket and pale trousers, a leather suitcase in his hand. As if in answer to his wishes, his parents had died in 1929, and within a couple of weeks of each other too, and he had been traveling ever since—to India, China, Japan, North Africa. In the harsh winter sunlight his high forehead and dark eyes stood out. We hadn't seen him for at least a year, and he looked more vulnerable than I remembered.

That month, he had exhibited at the Galerie Pierre on rue des Beaux-Arts, and had been described in the press as "poet turned painter," and less flatteringly as "the bizarre Michaux." Exhausted and contemplative, he was glad to be away from it all,

he said, in what he only half-jokingly called our "little paradise."
Over dinner we asked about his alleged transformation. What
did it feel like? We were eager to find out.

"You and half Paris . . ."

His voice was jaded and sardonic, but we knew he was pleased
we had asked. In an attempt to explain, he read us an excerpt
from "Painting," an article he had written. *The word-factory dis-*
appears . . . You locate the world through another window. Like a
child, you have to learn to walk. You don't know a thing . . . New
problems. New temptations.

Claude admired his clarity, but he was frowning.

"Words are a compromise forced on us by reality," he said.
"When we put something into words, we break faith with an inner
communication that transcends language." He took out his cherrywood pipe and turned it in his hands. "Words are approximate.
The more capable a writer is, the less approximate they are, but
there will always be a gap. Always. It's unbridgeable."

Sipping her whiskey, Claude said nothing.

"That's why I love the dictionary," he went on. "The words
are in their virgin state—pristine and immaculate. They have yet
to be corrupted or enslaved by being placed next to other words."
He paused again. "The dictionary is pure. It's the only true book."

Claude smiled. "The bizarre Michaux."

He let out a soft but corrosive laugh, then shook himself, like
a yacht changing tack. "What about you, Claude? Have you been
writing?"

"Not a thing," she said. "Well, some music . . ."

"You have your piano here?"

"In the next room." She crushed out her cigarette. "It's exactly
as you say. New problems, new temptations."

There were our photographs, though, which Michaux admired, and Claude had also been making small figures that were part sculpture, part collage, which she showed him later that evening.

"How strange," he said, "that we should both be moving in the same direction . . ."

He talked about the difference between reading a text and looking at an image. In a book, he said, the path was already laid out. It was a gradual, linear experience, and he had begun to find it laborious, even dictatorial. With a painting, there was no one single trajectory. You saw the whole thing at once. You were free to choose. As he bent over one of Claude's photographs to illustrate his point, his shoulder almost touching hers, I thought about the many levels on which they appeared to coincide. Michaux had told Claude, in strictest confidence, that his mother had not wanted him. *I would have preferred it if you'd never been born*, she had said to him when he was nine. Like Claude, Michaux had been wished out of existence. They were both rejected children. Claude had sworn me to secrecy on the subject, since Michaux was intensely private, and tended not to reveal too much about himself. His relationships had always been a mystery to us. A source of fascination too. When Claude and I first met him, it seemed to us that he operated in a different dimension, where sex had no place, but over the years he had proved us wrong. There had been a woman in Montevideo, for instance—a poet called Susana—and he had also become involved with Marie-Louise, the wife of our friend Gaston Ferdière.

One evening, when Michaux had settled in, Claude asked if he was seeing anyone.

"Seeing anyone?" Both eyebrows raised, he tinkered with his pipe, pretending not to understand the question.

"Are you in love with someone?"

"Ah. Well." He sipped from his glass of lemonade. He didn't touch wine or spirits. He had experimented with various substances, usually while abroad, but he believed alcohol was hazardous. "It's quite complicated," he said at last.

"We have all night," Claude said.

He sighed. "There's Marie-Louise, of course . . ."

Some years before, in the mid-thirties, we had introduced Gaston and Marie-Louise to Michaux at a dinner in our apartment on rue Notre-Dame-des-Champs. To our astonishment, Michaux and Marie-Louise fell for each other. We had never imagined that such a thing might happen.

"How *is* Marie-Louise?" Claude asked.

Michaux knocked the dead ash out of his pipe. "I'm hoping she will come to Brazil with me next year."

I looked at the floor. In the spring of 1937 Michaux had tried to bring his affair with Marie-Louise to an end, not because he didn't love her, but because he felt his freedom was being compromised. She promptly swallowed half a bottle of barbiturates. Michaux found her in time—he had saved her life—but Gaston had been furious with him. The situation was certainly "quite complicated."

"What drew you to her in the first place?" Claude asked.

Michaux peered into the corner of the room, as if Marie-Louise was standing in the shadows and he was trying to make her out. "Her legs are very elegant," he said. "When she dances, she tends to bite her bottom lip."

Claude said she hadn't noticed that.

A few weeks after the dinner party, Michaux told us, he had been in a club in Montparnasse when Gaston and Marie-Louise walked in. He was sitting in a booth. They didn't notice him—at least, not at first.

"Did you dance with her that night?" Claude asked.

He shook his head. "She danced. I watched her dance. I think she knew I was watching. There were moments when I felt she was dancing for me."

"But Gaston was there," Claude said.

"He was watching her as well." Michaux opened his pouch of tobacco and started to refill his pipe. "He looked dispirited."

"Perhaps he sensed he was losing her . . ."

Michaux tried to affect his usual diffidence, but I saw a flicker of excitement in his face, and longing.

"You make her sound exotic," Claude said, "like someone we have never met, but should." She gave me a wink, then turned to Michaux. "We might have to lure her away from you. Enlighten her."

"Show her the true path," I said.

"The true path?" Michaux reached nervously for his lemonade.

"*We all remember Helen*," Claude said, "*who left her family / Her child, and royal husband / To take a stranger's hand / Her beauty had no equal / But bowed to love's command.*"

Claude's face was glowing. She liked to say she didn't need anyone apart from me, but she often burned more brightly if we had company, especially if it was one of our old friends from Paris.

Michaux lit his pipe. "I think I should warn Marie-Louise about you two."

"I wouldn't if I were you," Claude said. "It will only make her curious." She paused. "Anyway, she already knows the worst."

"Who wrote those lines?" Michaux asked.

"Sappho," Claude said.

Michaux smiled. "I should have guessed."

Later in Michaux's visit, the conversation turned to politics, as it was bound to, perhaps, given the times. He was concerned about the effect Hitler's policies might have on us.

"I'm thinking of leaving France," he said. "You should too. It's not just the chaos and destruction war will bring. It's Hitler's attitude to anyone who's Jewish."

"Charles-Henri Barbier is worried too," Claude said. "He wrote me a letter." She paused. "Our housekeeper, Nan, has moved to Canada."

"Sensible," Michaux said.

I spoke to Michaux. "You don't think we'll be safe?"

"If Paris falls, these islands will fall too." He paused. "At the very least, consider the idea."

"We *have* considered it," I said. "We're staying."

Michaux glanced at Claude.

"If we left," she told him, "I would feel I was deserting. Didn't I teach you that English phrase about the rats and the sinking ship?"

"The only part of the phrase that feels relevant," Michaux said, "is the part about the sinking ship. If Germany attacks, France will sink—and you'll sink with it."

Michaux's vehemence surprised me. It was testament to the strength of his feelings for us, I thought, and I was touched.

But he was still wrangling with Claude.

"—and actually, it's your precious England I was thinking of. You've always liked the place. Why wouldn't you think of going there?"

"Hitler probably has designs on England too," she said. "I'm not sure we'd be any safer. Besides, you can't defeat the Nazis by running away."

"Ah, so you intend to *defeat* the Nazis. I'm sorry. I hadn't realized." Michaux had an ironic smile on his face, but his fingers were trembling as he filled his pipe.

It went on for hours, with Michaux cajoling us, and reasoning with us, and even, finally, pleading, but Claude and I remained calm throughout, and stubborn. No ground was given on either side.

Not long after midnight Claude left the room. Had she decided to go to bed? Surely not. It was too early. Michaux turned to me as he had turned to me so many times that evening, either to put forward a new argument or to communicate the extent of his despair, and claimed, mischievously, that since Claude had beaten a retreat he had triumphed—over her, at least.

"I'm not sure," I said, "that you should see it as a retreat."

I was right.

Michaux and I had forgotten all about Claude, and were once again discussing the likelihood of war, when a figure appeared in the shadows at the far end of the room. We held our breath, transfixed, as Claude stepped forwards in a brown shirt, breeches, and a pair of tall black riding boots. Her hair was damped down and plastered across her forehead, and a small rectangular mustache adorned her upper lip. Round her right bicep was an armband with a swastika on it. Coming to a halt in the middle of the room, she clasped both elbows, just as Hitler did during his most important speeches.

"Our belief in Germany is unshakable," she said, her voice dramatic and guttural, but also quavery with emotion, "and our will is overwhelming, and when will and belief combine so powerfully, then not even the *heavens* can deny you—"

Michaux turned to me. "My God, for a moment I really thought it was him."

Claude brought her heels together with a loud click and lifted her right arm into the air. "*Sieg heil.*"

I went to fetch the camera.

Michaux didn't bring the subject up again, though he did refer to it indirectly, on his last evening.

"I've stopped using white backgrounds," he announced suddenly, at dinner. "I'm using black instead. Or sometimes darkest blue. It represents the night, of course—the night I feel all around me . . ."

Claude and I said nothing.

"The night," he continued. "It's where the mystery comes from—and the vagueness." He paused. "The monsters too." He put his pipe on the table and looked down at his hands. "I'm weak," he said, "and frightened. But most of all I'm tired."

"They're your strengths," Claude said. "You've made virtues of them all."

He shook his head. "I have no backbone, no moral fiber. I'm the kind of person who will go to any lengths to save his own skin."

Claude gave him a long look, but once again she didn't speak.

"I admire you both," he said.

The next day, we stood on the quay in St. Helier and said our goodbyes.

"It has been lovely having you here," Claude said. "Will you come and visit us again?"

"Of course I will." Michaux's face was angled away from us, his eyes fixed on the glittering semicircle of St. Aubin's Bay.

He didn't, though.

We never saw Michaux again.

A few photographs remain, some taken in our garden, others in the ruins at Grosnez, but Michaux is always a distant figure, and on his own, or if Claude is in the picture with him, as sometimes happens, there's always a gap between them, a gap I hadn't noticed at the time. I remembered his characterization of words in the dictionary, and how he felt they were pure and free because they had yet to be attached to any other words, but he didn't give off an air of purity and freedom. He seemed lonely. Unengaged. Could that be another way of looking at the dictionary?

Only a few months later, Jacqueline Lamba came to stay. Breton had fallen in love with Jacqueline in the early thirties. At the time, she had been performing naked in a tank of water at a nightclub called the Coliséum. When I met her not long afterwards, all we talked about was the recent art exhibitions she had seen. I asked her if she painted. She said she did, then added, drily, that Breton preferred to think of her as a mermaid. Something about her delivery reminded me of Carole Lombard, the American *comédienne,* and I told her so. Lombard was one of her idols, she said. She had such deadpan wit, such timing. She's not bad-looking either, I said. Jacqueline laughed at that.

She had brought her three-year-old daughter, Aube, with her, but Breton had remained behind. When she arrived, I was

shocked by how worn she looked, not at all her usual glamorous self. She was recovering from bronchitis, she told us, which
was true, though it wasn't long before she confessed that she and
Breton had not been getting on. The sunlight and saltwater did her
good, and she soon regained her strength. I was relieved Breton
hadn't come, since I didn't think he would have understood our
new and seemingly limited existence, and I couldn't have endured
the look of baffled distaste that always rose on to his face when he
was confronted by a situation or a remark that made no sense to
him, a look he was usually unable—or unwilling—to disguise.
After Claude's initial meeting with Breton, she had fallen under
his spell, and despite his views—he found homosexuality repulsive, but was titillated by the idea of a lesbian—she would refer to
him all the time, so much so that I used to tease her. Now, though,
as spring came to the island, she fell for Breton's wife, with her
swept-back golden hair, her one-liners, and her two-piece eau-de-
nil bathing costume, the latest in Paris fashion.

Of all the pictures that Claude took during the six weeks Jacqueline stayed with us there is one that stands out from the rest. A
bronzed Jacqueline is shown from the waist up, with pale stripes
undulating across her skin, as though she is under the sea and the
midday sun is striking down through the clear water. A wide ribbon or sash circles her neck and hangs down, partially obscuring
her right breast. Her eyes are closed, and her expression is calm
and faintly dismissive, with just the hint of a smile or a sneer on
her perfect lips. She looks less like a human being than a goddess.
She appears to inhabit a world that is inaccessible to mere mortals.

The first time I saw the photograph, an unexpected surge
of jealousy went through me. That Claude should take such a
picture of another woman, even if she was a friend of ours. That

she should capture her beauty with such sensuality and precision. The image was unquestionably erotic—it spoke of the laziness of summer, and the dark urgency of lust—and there was a part of me that resented that, though I would never have admitted it. The more I turned it over in my mind, however, the more I began to see that there might be other, less obvious interpretations, meanings Claude might not have intended, and might still in fact be unaware of. I remembered standing at a downstairs window. Claude sat on the lawn, her legs folded sideways, her weight propped on one arm. Jacqueline and Aube were nearby, playing with a ball. When I noticed the expression on Claude's face, the hair prickled at the back of my neck. At first I thought she was envious, but then I realized it was more like a kind of craving. Craving for what, though? It wasn't that she wished she could sleep with Jacqueline—not, at least, in that moment—nor did I think she was wishing she had a child of her own. No, she was watching the scene *through a child's eyes*. She didn't *want* Aube. She wanted to *be* Aube. The next time I looked at the photograph I saw it as a portrait taken by somebody who longed for the impossible. Claude, the adoring child, and Jacqueline, the mother. Imperious, alluring. Out of reach.

The dark time came, as Michaux had predicted. During the months following Britain's declaration of war against Germany, we kept a close eye on developments in countries like Poland, Denmark, and Norway, and were left in no doubt as to both the scale of Hitler's ambition and the might of his armed forces. We knew the Germans were coming. It was just a matter of when. In the last decade of his life, Monsieur Schwob had constantly written editorials that warned readers of "the German threat." *He was right*, Claude would murmur as she pored over the newspaper. *He was so right.*

That winter was bitterly cold. In January a dusting of snow lay on the ground, the crust glittering in the sun like granulated sugar. The island had never looked more beautiful. After lunch Claude would retire to an upstairs bedroom, draw the curtains, and sit in the gloom for hours, tuning in to broadcasts from the BBC. Sometimes she spent whole nights there too, and when she reappeared she would give me the latest bulletins—Polish Jews had been ordered to wear Star of David armbands, Chamberlain had resigned. She came to me once at dawn and told me that Mussolini had met Hitler at the Brenner Pass, and that Italy would be entering the war. Her eyes were dull and listless. Her hands were trembling.

"This isn't good for you," I said.

She laughed a short, sardonic laugh. "It's war," she said. "It isn't good for anyone."

Though Claude had resisted Michaux's arguments at the end of 1938, she began to talk once again about the possibility of leaving. She ruled out a return to Paris: we would be too exposed—and besides, most of our friends had already scattered, some to the south of France, others overseas. We could move to New York, though, as Breton had—or there was always Quebec or Montreal . . . We circled the subject night after night, but I refused to change my mind, and in the end she decided to stay put. She didn't want to be parted from me, of course, but there was something else. The idea that she would be allowing the Nazis to determine her future. The idea of being driven out—of *fleeing*. That went against the grain.

———

On a warm, drowsy afternoon at the beginning of June 1940, Claude and I had an unforeseen encounter. We had been for a swim at Beauport, and were returning by way of La Route des Champs, a road that curved back down the hill, past the house where the rector lived. Claude picked wildflowers as we went. She had an idea for a new series of photographs that didn't feature her at all. They would be interiors, she said. Still lifes. As we came out onto La Marquanderie, we noticed a group of men standing outside the St. Brelade's Bay Hotel. They were drinking beer and talking in loud voices. Their laughter was loud too, and abrupt, almost like shouting. Probably they were locals, from the farms up on La Moye. Farm people often drank at the hotel bar. There was nowhere else for miles around. As we approached, one of the men detached himself from the rest and stood in front of us. He looked at Claude, then at the flowers.

"Those for me?" He grinned. Though his feet were planted wide apart, he was swaying a little from the waist up.

"Bob?" Claude said. "Is that you?"

"It's me all right." He drank from his pint. "I heard you were living here."

The other men had stopped talking. Bob was aware that they were listening, and it seemed to make him bolder, more confrontational.

"You bought the big house," he said. "That must have set you back a bit."

"We're very happy here," Claude said.

"You never married, then?"

Claude looked past him, along the road, as if she was waiting for a bus. Bob kept his eyes on her for a while longer, then turned to me.

"Suzanne," he said. "You were always hanging about—always there . . ."

There was a domineering edge to his voice that I couldn't remember hearing before. The years must have changed him—or perhaps it was just the alcohol.

Claude came to my rescue. "You're well, though, Bob?"

"Never better," he said.

He drained his pint, and for a moment he was all unshaven throat and chin. Then his face came back down. He wiped his mouth on his sleeve.

"Well, it was nice seeing you." Claude took my arm.

Bob's mood shifted again, and he became jovial, almost clownlike. Stepping back, he lifted an imaginary hat and sketched a bow. One of the men behind him laughed.

"Nice seeing you too," Bob said.

We moved past him, towards our house.

Once inside, I asked Claude if she was all right.

"I'm fine," she said.

She laid the wildflowers on the hall table.

"He looked so much older . . ." She went to the mirror and studied herself.

"Did you ever find out who he got married to?" I asked.

"Some local girl," she said. "I forget her name."

Even if she knew the girl's name, she would never admit to remembering it.

"He was very drunk," she said.

"Yes, he was."

"So uncouth." She gave a little shudder. "I don't know what I ever saw in him."

"I know exactly what you saw," I said.

She glanced at me in the mirror, startled, but I was already turning away.

On July 1, three days after the bombing raid that had caught us unawares, a small group of German officers landed at the airport, and by the end of that week several hundred troops were billeted on the island, including dozens of Luftwaffe pilots. These young men might be losing the Battle of Britain, but they didn't seem in any doubt about the eventual outcome of the war, and they were a constant presence in St. Helier in their immaculate gray uniforms, drinking coffee, having their hair cut and their nails manicured, and buying gifts for their loved ones. If they were full of themselves, they were also courteous, stepping off the pavement to let women pass and greeting everyone they came across, not at all the monsters people had been expecting. As early as the first week of August, dances were organized in two or three of the more exclusive hotels. Rumbas were played, and foxtrots. Viennese waltzes.

According to the guidelines laid down by the Bailiff, we were supposed to maintain "correct relations" with the invaders, but where did correct relations end and fraternization begin? From the outset, Claude and I took a hard line. If a German soldier spoke to us, we would ignore him, and Claude, being Claude, usually went further.

"Why won't you talk to me?" a soldier asked as we were crossing Royal Square during the first month of the occupation.

"Because you shouldn't be here," Claude said in a clear voice. "Because we despise you."

The soldier looked down at his boots.

I admired her integrity, I told her afterwards, her courage too, but I felt compelled to caution her. If she persisted with that sort of behavior she would be arrested. Claude shrugged and said she didn't care.

Later, I learned that the Germans had a name for people like us, who refused to acknowledge their presence. They called us "ghosts." How intriguing, I thought, that they should think to turn things around like that. We were treating them as though they didn't exist, and yet somehow we were the ones who had become invisible.

One hot night I was woken by the tapping of a typewriter. I glanced at the clock. Ten past two. Putting on my dressing gown, I stood at the window. It was high tide. The air was heavy with the smell of jasmine, and the sea had the consistency of oil. The typing stopped. Through the wall I heard Claude murmur something to herself and laugh.

I walked into the next room, my feet cooled by the bare boards. Claude was sitting in front of her black Underwood. Except for the silk scarf tied around her head and the Moroccan slippers on her feet she was naked, though a pale-green robe was draped over the back of her chair. Lying on the desk, next to the typewriter, was a revolver I had never seen before. Claude's brown skin gleamed in the lamplight. So did the barrel of the gun. Only a few days earlier, the German authorities had issued an order in the *Evening Post*, demanding that all weapons be handed in. Claude had obviously paid no attention.

"Where did that come from?" I asked.

Claude glanced at me across one shoulder. "I thought you were sleeping."

"You woke me up."

"Just as well. We need to talk." Claude drew her robe around her and lit a cigarette, then she went to the open window and looked out into the night. "The Nazis must be resisted at all costs, on ideological grounds. We're agreed on that, aren't we."

Folding my arms, I leaned against the wall. "Of course."

"It's not enough just to ignore them when we pass them on the street. We need to do more."

"For example?"

"Did you hear about the dentist?"

Apparently, there was a man in St. Helier—a dental surgeon—who had been attacking members of the Gestapo when they were walking back to their barracks late at night. He would surprise them in dark alleys, she said, and knock them out cold. In his youth, he had been a welterweight boxing champion.

"You made that up," I said.

She tapped some ash into the ivy that grew around the window. "It's true."

"So you want to start attacking the Nazis," I said, "with your bare fists?"

She smiled. "You sounded like your brother then. That's the kind of thing he used to say."

"What are you proposing, Claude?"

Her eyes drifted towards the gun.

"You're not serious," I said.

"It belonged to my father."

"Does it work?"

She shrugged. "There's no reason to think it wouldn't."

I walked over and picked up the gun. It was lighter than I had expected, and the wooden grip felt comfortable, as though it had been made with my hand in mind. I wondered if that inbuilt seductive appeal was part of the design.

"It's a Ruby," Claude said. "Standard issue for the French military during the last war." She crushed out her cigarette and took the gun from me, her forefinger curling around the trigger. "It holds nine rounds. That ought to be enough, don't you think?"

"For what?"

As I was well aware, she said, the Nazis had commandeered the northeast corner of the churchyard for their own dead soldiers. Two days earlier, while I was shopping in St. Helier, she had watched from an upstairs window as a funeral took place. When the staff cars arrived, they were carrying the most important Nazi dignitaries on the island, including Gussek, the *Kommandant*. They parked by the entrance to the churchyard, right opposite the door that led to our garden. They looked so nonchalant, she said. So utterly at ease. You would never have guessed they were fighting a war, or that they were on enemy territory.

"What struck me forcibly," she went on, "was the fact that they appeared to take their security for granted. In that moment, despite their armor-plated cars and their automatic weapons, they suddenly seemed vulnerable in a way I couldn't have predicted or imagined." She put the revolver back on the desk and reached for her packet of Craven A's. "That was when I had the idea."

"I know what you're going to say."

She lit a cigarette. "It would be so easy."

"You don't know how to shoot."

"I could learn."

I looked at her. "You could learn."

"Yes," she said. "I could."

Later that same day, Claude and I set off along the road that led east, towards Le Frêt. We were making for the woods on the headland, where we would have some privacy. It was late August. The sky had clouded over, and the air felt dense, electric. I hoped no one stopped us. It would be hard to explain why we were carrying a loaded revolver and an empty shoe box.

I was still trying to dissuade Claude, even as we walked, but she was in the grip of a scenario she had already spent a lot of time imagining. When the day came, she told me, she would pretend to be a widow visiting her husband's grave. She would wear black, perhaps even a hat with a veil. Circling the house, she would make her way slowly and painfully along the road towards the church-yard. She would be carrying a prop of some sort—flowers, or a prayer book.

Picture it, she said. The entrance to the churchyard, the parked cars with their Nazi pennants, the officers standing in groups in the winter sunlight, their greatcoats draped over their shoulders, talking and smoking . . . Since they only had eyes for the blond-haired beauties of the island, they would be unlikely to pay any attention to the old crone who was approaching. When she passed behind the Kommandant, she would take out her revolver and fire several shots at close range. The sharp shocked smell of cordite, Gussek's body lying facedown on the tarmac . . .

I sighed, then shivered.

"Don't you see how clever it is?" she went on. "The death I'll be dressed for isn't the death of my husband, a death that happened in the past. After all, there *is* no husband. I'll be dressed for the death that is *about to happen*. My widow's weeds are for my enemy. My flowers are for him." She paused. "Perhaps I'll even toss them onto his dead body, as one might toss flowers onto a coffin once it has been lowered into the ground."

"No, Claude," I said. "I won't let you do it."

"Think of how it will reverberate. The head of the occupying forces shot dead—and by a woman! They'll probably discuss it on the BBC."

"No."

"What's wrong? You see a flaw?" She had a look on her face that I had seen many times: the confidence—no, arrogance—of someone who felt not only justified but unassailable.

"You don't know how to use a gun."

"That's why we're going to the woods—for a bit of target practice. It can't be that difficult."

When we reached the top of the hill we turned off the road and followed a track that led towards the headland. Since leaving the bay, we had passed nobody. We'd not been seen. At first there was heather on either side of us, but soon the trees closed over our heads. Oak, sweet chestnut. Pine. We followed a narrow path that curved down into a gully. All the sound drained out of the world. I couldn't even hear the sea. There was only the rustle of our shoes in the undergrowth.

Once at the bottom, we found an area of level ground, the sky blocked out by overhanging foliage.

"This is as good a place as any," I said.

I set the shoe box on a fallen tree trunk and stood back. Claude aimed the gun. There was a crack, and her arm jerked sideways and upwards. A bird took off, wings clattering. Claude tried to hide her look of shock. The shoe box was still intact.

"Where did the bullet go?" she asked.

"I didn't see."

"I think I hurt my shoulder."

She took a step closer and pointed the gun at the shoe box. It seemed impossible that she could miss. She fired again. This time I saw something fly through the air. A piece of bark had been gouged from a nearby tree, a streak of white appearing on the trunk.

"Am I getting closer?" she asked.

"I'm not sure. Maybe."

Another shot, and then another. I walked over and checked the shoe box. Not a mark on it. The gun had jammed. Claude dropped it on the ground and bent over, holding her wrist. Pain tightened her mouth. I picked up the gun. The barrel was hot to the touch.

"I think you should forget it," I said.

She gave me a fierce look, her body in a kind of crouch, like a vulture interrupted while feasting on a carcass.

"Well, you're not exactly a crack shot," I said, "are you."

"Maybe if I keep practicing . . ."

But I could tell from her voice that she no longer had the stomach for it.

I put the gun in my pocket and retrieved the shoe box and started back up the path. At the top of the slope I stopped. Claude was still standing where I had left her.

"Aren't you coming?" I said.

Nursing her right wrist in her left hand, she began to climb the slope. Neither of us spoke.

"It's probably just as well," I said when we reached the road again. "I understand the attraction of a single dramatic act, but there are other considerations."

Claude was listening, head lowered.

"Think of how it would rebound on the local population," I went on. "It's not just you who would be punished. The Nazis would become vengeful, draconian. There might even be random executions." I paused. "What I'm saying is, it would be selfish on your part."

Claude placed a cigarette between her lips, but seemed to be having trouble lighting it. In the end, I had to light it for her.

"Thank you," she said.

She still hadn't looked at me.

It was then that I heard the rumble of an engine. In the distance I could see a dark-green German army truck laboring up the hill towards us in low gear. I took the gun from my pocket and dropped it in the ditch. We walked on, towards our house. As the truck passed by, one of the soldiers waved at us. Claude had averted her gaze, and didn't notice. I gave him a curt nod. Once the truck had vanished round the bend, I went back for the gun. Claude stayed where she was, smoking.

"This isn't about you," I said when I returned. "This is about everybody who lives on the island."

"In your opinion, then," Claude said slowly, "it would be better if I didn't kill the Kommandant."

I looked at her, and she looked at me, and suddenly her face crumpled. She was laughing. To the second German army truck that passed us a few moments later, we were just two harmless old women, sharing a joke.

Little did they know.

———

That autumn, while we were out looking for blackberries, Claude noticed a cigarette packet lying at the edge of the road. It was green, with a number 5 in the middle. She bent down and picked the packet up. ECKSTEIN. A German brand. This made sense, since we were about a mile inland from where we lived, on one of the roads that connected the airport with St. Helier. Claude wrote on the packet in red ink and put it back on the grass verge. The words were in German. *Sieg? Nein. Krieg ohne Ende.* Victory? No. War without end. I asked her what she was doing.

"I'm giving the Germans something to think about," she said.

Unable to sleep the night before, she had been flicking through an old issue of the satirical monthly *Le Crapouillot* that focused on Germany when something in the text jumped out at her. *Schrecken ohne Ende, oder Ende mit Schrecken.* Terror without end, or an end to terror. The sentence seemed to resonate with our current predicament, she said. This was the choice we faced. This was the dilemma. She thought they were the kind of words that might prove useful in our propaganda campaign.

Our propaganda campaign.

I stared at her.

"Well, it's better than shooting someone, isn't it," she said.

On every piece of packaging she came across that afternoon, she wrote the same words, or a variation on those words. Sometimes it was "War without end," sometimes simply "Never-ending."

One morning shortly afterwards, I found her at the kitchen table, spooning jam onto a crust of bread. Next to her plate was a small black notebook, held open with a rubber band. Once I was sitting down, she told me she was thinking of walking along the main road again, only this time she would be actively looking for pieces of litter on which something might be written. She had prepared a few slogans while I was asleep. She gave me a cool, measured look. She seemed to think I had been shirking my duties.

"I'll come with you," I said.

"I thought you disapproved."

"I didn't say I disapproved. I just can't see what good it will do." I poured myself some coffee and reached for the bread. "Anyway, I don't want you going alone."

"I'm not a child."

I sipped my coffee and said nothing.

"All right," she said. "You can come. It might look less suspicious if there are two of us."

She took a bite of bread and jam and pushed her notebook across the table. On the right-hand page I saw the following:

Who has the right to sacrifice an entire nation to save a government?

Why lay down your life for a lost cause?

Hitler doesn't care if you live or die.

"These aren't bad," I said, "but they'll have to be translated into German."

"That's where you come in," she said.

As a child, I'd had governesses from Alsace, and I had learned to speak German even before I could speak French. Though I was no longer fluent, I still had a reasonable command of the language.

"Ah," I said, "so you do need me after all . . ."

Claude placed her hand on mine. "I'll always need you."

———

As Claude had suggested, the aim was to give the Germans
something to think about, and it sprang from a shared belief that
by no means all the soldiers who wore a German uniform were
Nazis. They might simply, and unthinkingly, have obeyed Hitler's
call to arms. They might be patriots who believed it their duty
to serve their country's leader. They might never have paused
to consider the rights and wrongs of the war in which they had
become embroiled. And even if they *did* have Nazi sympathies,
their allegiance might not stand up to scrutiny. It could be eroded,
perhaps, or even dismantled. We liked to think that beneath
every Nazi there was an ordinary decent human being, and if we
could appeal to that human being, if we could present him with
arguments that were sufficiently convincing, we might be able to
change his mind.

After a week or two of leaving inflammatory messages by the
side of the main road, we became bolder and more ambitious.
Sickened by what Radio Paris was broadcasting—the station was
no more than a mouthpiece for Goebbels and his cronies—we
decided to set up a news service of our own. Since Claude's English
was better than mine, it was her job to tune in to the BBC, especially to the broadcasts of the self-styled "Colonel Britton." She
would jot down any information or ideas that she thought might
be of use to us and then convert them into a more digestible or
entertaining form. Sometimes she wrote a fable, sometimes a
poem. Sometimes it was a snatch of dialogue, like an excerpt from
a play. I would translate whatever she gave me. I would often add
an illustration, too—Göring with a napkin tucked into his collar,
devouring a plate of German pilots, or Hitler with his right arm
in a sling, unable to salute. Later, while I slept, Claude would
type the pieces up, using carbon paper to produce as many as a

dozen copies, and varying her typing style in an attempt to give the impression that we were not just two people, but an entire movement. We tried to make our leaflets look as if they came from somebody worth listening to. We wanted them to feel personal, like a voice whispering in your ear. Like a conscience.

In the early days of our campaign, we went for two or three long walks a week, gathering berries or mushrooms or even, sometimes, cigarette butts—supplies of tobacco on the island were already running low—and depositing our leaflets as we went. If there was a Nazi funeral in the graveyard next to our house, I would keep watch from an upstairs window while Claude slipped out of the side door and dropped subversive material into the staff cars parked outside the church. Once, I looked beyond her, over the wall, and saw the new Kommandant, Josias Erbprinz zu Waldeck und Pyrmont, standing at the graveside of a fallen soldier, his hands clasped behind his back. It was strange to think that, but for me, he also might be dead.

"What if they suspect us?" I said to Claude. "We live so close."

"They won't," she said. "No one living this close would dare to behave so recklessly. No one would be that stupid."

On Saturdays, we traveled into St. Helier. Giving priority to areas that were popular with German troops, we deposited our leaflets in outdoor locations—on walls, in letter boxes, under doormats. We dressed as ordinary countrywomen, in raincoats, headscarves, and Wellingtons. Wary of leaving any fingerprints, we always wore gloves. By the autumn of 1941, each of our leaflets had the words *Bitte verbreiten*—Please distribute—printed in the bottom right-hand corner. Like a newspaper, we wanted as big a circulation as possible.

As the months went by, we discovered ways of widening our reach. We realized that if we hid a leaflet in a German vehicle it was unlikely to be discovered until the truck or car was in another part of the island altogether. The same technique could be applied to individual German soldiers. In restaurants and cafés, I became adept at secreting leaflets in their coats, their knapsacks, or even in their boots. Claude was astonished at my nerve. I had clearly missed my vocation, she told me. I should have been a pickpocket.

It was generally Claude who thought up the text, but sometimes I surprised her. One morning, when she woke, I handed her a scrap of paper on which I had transcribed the following:

Jesus is big—but Hitler is bigger
Jesus laid down his life for people
But people lay down their lives for Hitler

"This is excellent," Claude said. "And I know just what to do with it."

Once I had produced a number of placards, the Gothic characters executed in the red, black, and gold of the German national flag, we left them in prominent positions in the entrances to all the churches that were frequented by the occupying forces. Later, we learned that some German soldiers had taken our piece of provocation at face value, believing it to have been issued by the Nazi high command. In a church in St. Helier, an SS officer had marched up the nave, escorted by soldiers armed with machine guns, and proudly nailed one of our placards to the pulpit. Members of the local congregation were scandalized, and the Kommandant had to intervene. Claude and I were delighted with the outcome. If nothing else, we were spreading confusion and disorder.

———

That summer, our housekeeper Edna married a local man called George, and they moved in with us. Though George was a great help, particularly with the heavier jobs, life became more complicated. We could only work on our campaign during the small hours, after the newlyweds had gone to bed. It was imperative they didn't know what we were up to—for their own safety and for ours. Edna was famous for her indiscretion, not least when she had been drinking—and she was always drinking. We adored her wayward and irrepressible spirit, but she was not to be trusted with a secret. During the occupation, you didn't tell anybody anything, not even those closest to you. Not unless you couldn't avoid it.

If our privacy had already to some extent been compromised by the presence of Edna and George, worse was yet to come. In October of that year, a German officer knocked on our front door. He was seeking lodgings for a number of horses, and for the men who looked after them. Edna tried to persuade him to commandeer one of the many evacuated houses in the area, but he claimed they were all taken. Besides, it was obvious that we had plenty of room. As we showed him round, he was politeness itself, asking if he might perhaps use the small bedroom and bathroom at the top of the main staircase. We could hardly say no.

Given almost no time to prepare, we moved into the rooms next to the kitchen, at the east end of the house, taking the blankets, the curtains, and the electric radiator with us. We hid anything that might make our unwelcome guests more comfortable. We carried our valuable books and artworks up to the attic and locked the door, but we had to leave our furniture and carpets where they were. The officer returned. The soldiers in his charge were billeted in the entry hall, and the horses, four of them, were stabled in the garage, though they were always escaping, and were often to be found in our garden, devouring the plants.

"I never thought we'd end up actually *living* with the Nazis," Claude muttered on the day of their arrival.

I shrugged. "Maybe it will concentrate our minds. Give our propaganda a new edge."

Claude gave me one of her disparaging looks. "Mine didn't need concentrating."

"In any case," I went on, "I'm sure it's only a temporary measure."

It was seven months before they left.

One bitter evening, as we huddled by the electric heater, Claude suggested that we leave some leaflets in the St. Brelade's Bay Hotel, which the Germans had also requisitioned. They were using the hotel as a *Soldatenheim*—partly a barracks and partly a place of relaxation—and late at night we could often hear the soldiers shouting and singing.

"But it's so close," I said.

"You said that about the staff cars outside the church. The same argument applies." Claude saw that I wasn't convinced. "Anyway, this time you're coming too."

She would take care of distribution, she told me, while I distracted any German soldiers who happened to be on duty.

I looked at her. "How am I supposed to do that?"

I should ask them questions, she said, and appear not to understand the answers I was given. I might even seem to be

having trouble grasping the idea that the island had been occupied. It might be useful if I pretended to be a little slow.

"In that case," I said, "perhaps you should be the decoy."

She sighed.

Obviously, I was free to improvise, she told me later, but under
no circumstances was I to let it be known that I spoke German.
She began to tremble. As I knew full well, all German speakers
were supposed to have reported to the authorities, yet another
order we had failed to observe.

"If you're nervous," I said, "we can always postpone it."

She looked affronted. "I'm not nervous."

"You're shaking."

"That's excitement."

I remembered how she had trembled once when I touched her
on a winter evening in Nantes. My fingers on her neck, under her
hair. Little earthquakes happening inside her. I had asked her if
she was all right. She murmured something I didn't catch.

The pools of lamplight on the towpath, and us between them,
in the darkness. The black of the canal—

"Suzanne?"

Claude was leaning forwards in her chair. She wanted to know
if I was ready.

"Yes," I said.

"We need a name," Claude said.

We were lying in bed, a gale blowing outside, the glass panes
creaking in their lead frames. It was the winter of 1941, the coldest
in fifty years, and rationing had been extended to bread and fuel.

"Our leaflets would be more effective if they were signed," she went on. "Not by us, obviously, but by someone. We need to invent a persona."

"A German persona," I said.

"Yes. But I don't think an ordinary person will work. There would be no mystery, no tension. We want something that appears to undermine them from within."

"A soldier—"

"Yes."

The space between us seemed to tighten.

"He should be anonymous," I said, "like those soldiers who die in battle, but whose bodies are never identified . . ."

The messages would appear to be coming from one of their own, a man who had lost faith in the regime. Or perhaps he was one of the fallen, and realized that he had thrown away his life. Perhaps he was a kind of ghost . . . I thought of the house we were living in—La Ferme sans Nom—and my heart leapt.

"We should call him 'The Soldier without a Name,'" I said. "Is that mysterious enough for you?"

I felt Claude go still. "He could be alive," she said, "and stationed on the island—or else he could be dead, one of the futile dead, a voice speaking from the dark, beyond the grave . . ."

"Exactly what I was thinking."

She turned to me and kissed me. "You're brilliant."

A burst of laughter came from the other end of the house, where our German lodgers were entertaining some of their friends.

The more I thought about it, the more layers of ambiguity emerged. The name could refer to an *actual* soldier, or to somebody who *saw* himself as a soldier, somebody who was fighting for a cause. Either way, it would have a destabilizing effect. What's more, it would conceal our gender. No one looking at the word "soldier" would think of a woman.

I lay back on my pillow.

Fear flickered through me, fast and reptilian, like the tail of a rat or a lizard vanishing into a hole in the ground.

There was the feeling, at the outset, that the German troops who occupied the island were gentlemen—people often referred to them, euphemistically, as "visitors"—and that the stories about brutal behavior elsewhere in the theater of war were exaggerated and unfair. Once, in St. Helier, I passed an old couple sitting on a bench. They're not so bad, the Germans, I heard the woman say. It was a convenient and self-serving belief, since it allowed local people to "carry on as normal." There were many who felt justified in cooperating with the Germans, and even, eventually, in working for them. Why not? They paid good wages. By the same token, resistance became problematic, since there was nothing to resist except the idea of occupation itself. But then, in early 1942, the Germans revealed a darker side.

One bright winter morning, Claude and I were returning from a rare trip into St. Helier when a sharp stink pushed through the bus windows, even though they were closed. I could smell urine and feces, and also something pungent and strangely interior that reminded me of the infestation of mice our housekeeper Nan had to deal with when we first moved into La Ferme sans Nom. The bus slowed until it was barely moving. On the road ahead of us was what appeared to be a long line of prisoners of war. When the guards became aware of the bus, they began to drive the prisoners into the ditch, hitting them with rifle butts and wooden truncheons and sometimes with their fists. The bus edged forwards. Some of the prisoners were adults, but others were boys of no more than twelve or thirteen. It was hard to tell their ages, since they were all so emaciated. One man wore a woman's dress and a pair of pajama bottoms. His feet were bleeding. He had no shoes. Another wore a jacket with nothing underneath. His ribs stood out like the ribs on a stray dog. One man with a dark bruise on his cheek looked straight at me through the window, his gaze so vacant that I felt I existed in a different dimension. My life, though perfectly ordinary, and happening only a few feet from his, was one he could no longer hope for, or even imagine. I glanced at Claude. All the color had drained from her face.

"Disgusting," she said.

As the bus moved on, towards St. Brelade, a conversation started up among the passengers. Who were those people? What were they doing on the island? A man who worked in the harbor master's office told us they were part of a new slave-labor force. Most of them were Russians, he said, captured on the eastern front. Some were Spaniards, rounded up in the south of France after fleeing Franco. The slave labor would be used to build anti-tank walls and gun emplacements. Cement was being imported in huge quantities. You could see it if you went down to the docks. The Germans had coined a new word to describe Hitler's obsession with the Channel Islands. *Inselwahn.* Island madness. Apparently, Hitler believed Jersey and Guernsey were of vital strategic importance if an invasion of England was to be attempted.

Several days later, Claude and I caught the bus back to St. Helier. Rain was beating on the roof, and all the windows had steamed up. I wiped a hole in the condensation and peered out. In the pockets of Claude's Burberry coat were copies of our latest

tract. I had drawn a starving Russian prisoner being beaten by
an SS guard. I had given the guard the head of a donkey. *If you
treat human beings like animals*, the caption read, *you forfeit your
humanity*. Still outraged by what we had witnessed, Claude had
talked me into something I felt we might regret. During the past
few months, we had devised and perfected a kind of double act.
On entering the *Soldatenheim* in St. Brelade's Bay, for instance,
I had asked the officer on duty a series of simpleminded questions, while Claude, whose role it was to appear irritable or bored,
had wandered away from me, into the hall. Though I had been
unnerved by the soldiers playing Ping-Pong in an adjoining room,
the tapping of the white ball on the dark-green surface of the table
seeming to replicate the irregular, light bouncing of my heart,
Claude had succeeded in offloading all the leaflets she had brought
with her, some in greatcoat pockets, others between the pages of
magazines. This time, though, she had chosen Silvertide, a private
house that had been requisitioned by the *Geheime Feldpolizei*, the
secret military police. It was almost certainly the most dangerous
building on the island.

By the time we stepped out of the bus in St. Helier, the rain
had eased. We hurried through the wet streets to Havre des Pas.
Silvertide was a long white two-story house, the French windows
on the first floor giving onto an ornate balcony that ran all the way
along the front. As we started up the path to the main entrance, we
passed two German officers. They were discussing a girl they had
met at a dance. One of them described the girl as "very willing,"
a phrase that was accompanied by knowing laughter.

The hallway had a tiled floor, and smelled of stale cigar smoke
and damp cloth. A soldier was sitting behind a desk, like a receptionist in a hotel. He looked up as we approached. He wore rimless

glasses, and his mouth was like a paper cut. Something seemed to uncoil low down in my belly. I asked if he spoke French.

"A little," he said.

I used a similar strategy to the one I had used in the *Soldatenheim*, pretending that I didn't fully understand the curfew.

The soldier looked impatient. "The curfew has been in place for eighteen months already."

"Has it?" I said. "I live in the far west of the island, far from everything, and I don't read the newspapers."

"It's not so big, the island."

"Probably if you come from the mainland it feels small, but not if you have lived here for most of your life." I was aware of Claude moving away from me. "Where are you from?"

"Cologne."

"You have a wonderful cathedral."

"Yes." Lowering his eyes, he adjusted the position of some forms. "The curfew is very straightforward. Everybody must be home by ten o'clock at night."

"But someone told me you changed the clocks . . ."

"It's one hour later than it used to be, so ten o'clock is actually nine."

I frowned. "Ten o'clock is actually nine. I see."

"There are only two exceptions to the rule—Christmas Eve and New Year's Eve." He glanced up at me again. "There has to be some fun, don't you think, even during a war?"

"Fun?" I said. "Yes. Of course." I remembered the officers we had passed on the way in. "Do you have a girlfriend on the island?"

"A girlfriend?" Suddenly he was flustered. "No—"

"It's so exciting for the young women, all you glamorous foreigners arriving."

"They find it exciting?"

"Think about their lives before," I said. "This is an island. There are not so many choices." I leaned closer, as if to impart a secret. "Your uniforms have made a great impression."

The soldier took off his glasses and began to polish them. He was young, in his early twenties, and though his lips were thin his eyes were earnest, almost kind.

A door opened and closed behind me, and I heard crisp footsteps on the tiled floor. I looked over my shoulder. A German officer in a black leather jacket stood in front of Claude, who was by the coat rack.

"What are you doing here?" He spoke English, but with an American accent.

"I'm waiting for my sister," Claude said.

"Your sister?"

"She's over there." Claude pointed to me. "She had some questions."

He held out a hand. "Papers."

Claude took out her identity card and gave it to the officer. He scanned the card.

"Schwob," he said.

"It's a German name," she said calmly. "It was given to people who lived in Swabia."

He stared at her, then turned and moved towards me. The leather jacket, the square jaw. The American accent. He reminded me of a gangster from the movies, and I wondered if this was a look he had cultivated.

"I'm Wolf of the Gestapo," he said. "You have questions?"

"I'm sorry, but my English is not so good. This man is helping me." I indicated the soldier behind the desk.

The soldier told Wolf he had been explaining how the curfew worked. He said I was a simpleminded woman from some far corner of the island. *Simpleminded*. I smiled to myself. The soldier had been completely taken in by my performance.

Wolf was eyeing me coldly. "This is not a place where you come for information. There are other places for such things."

"I'm very sorry," I said.

"You should not be here, not unless you've been arrested. Do you want to be arrested?"

I shook my head.

"Then get out," he said. "Now."

Once we had left Silvertide, I told Claude we had been lucky not to be detained.

Claude looked straight ahead. "It was worth it."

The rain had stopped, and a light breeze was blowing. In the harbor the boats rocked on the dull green water.

"*Wolf of the Gestapo*," she said. "Who does he think he is?"

We were crouching by the fire in the big room, our knees almost touching, no lights on. Upstairs, George and Edna were asleep. As for the Germans, they had finally moved out, taking their horses with them. It was a cold clear night, and the full moon laid gray shapes on the floor by the window.

"What if we get caught?" Claude said.

She looked feverish, the skin under her eyes moist and livid, like leaves trapped beneath a stone. She had told me she had a temperature. Also, she had run out of English cigarettes. She was smoking a cheap French brand that hurt her throat.

"We won't," I said, "not if we're careful."

"But what if we are?"

We had heard that "antifascist enemies of the Third Reich," as they were known, were being sent to a camp in France where they were beheaded with an ax, and though the rumors were unsubstantiated it was clear that executions had been taking place. It was also clear that we fell into the category of "antifascist enemies." We were in breach of all manner of Nazi regulations. Since the ban on radios, more than ten thousand sets had been handed in. We had surrendered two radios of our own, but we had kept a third, which we hid in the sideboard, under a pile of napkins. Weapons were banned as well—obviously—and yet we had held on to Claude's revolver. What's more, I had failed to report my knowledge of German to the authorities. That was another offense. There was also the fact that Claude appeared as "Lucie Schwob" in the official records. Strictly speaking, she wasn't a Jew—she had only two Jewish grandparents, and they were on her father's side—but "Wolf of the Gestapo," as we had mockingly taken to calling him, had remarked on her name, and sooner or later, I felt, she would begin to attract attention, especially since orders restricting the movement and behavior of Jews had been proliferating in the last few months. Finally—and this rendered our other crimes more or less irrelevant—there was our propaganda campaign. We had started using a more elaborate signature—*Der Soldat ohne Namen und sein Kameraden*—which suggested a growing network of resistance and dissent, and our leaflets were beginning to find their way to every corner of the island. Though the network existed only in our imaginations, we hoped it might constitute a reality for the Nazi high command.

"We need to be prepared for the worst," Claude said, "don't you think?" She was scratching her left arm, her nails leaving grazes on the pale skin. Shadows leapt and shifted on her face.

"Don't worry," I said. "I've already thought about it."

"You have?"

"Kid would have to be put down. He's old. We couldn't leave him to fend for himself."

"I don't want to think about that."

"Edna would take him to the vet. Or George—"

Claude was still scratching.

"In any case," I said, "I'll make sure we're ready."

"But how?" She fumbled for a cigarette.

"It's better you don't know."

"You'll take care of it, though? You promise?"

"I promise."

"So if we lose, we win," she said in a low voice.

She wasn't stupid. She knew that our illegal activities might put us in a position where the only option would be to take our own lives, and she had just realized that I was willing to go with her. She would be able to die without having to abandon me. It had always been a dream of hers that we might leave together, like guests who had wearied of a party. We would slip away unnoticed, climb into a waiting car. Off we would go, into the dark . . . Angry with myself for having allowed our conversation to drift so close to one of her obsessions, I threw a handful of twigs onto the fire. Sparks burst upwards, scarlet against the blackened brick. It occurred to me that she might be hoping we would be discovered. She might *want* to be caught. Then she would have the perfect excuse. Perhaps that was why she had changed her mind about leaving the island, and why she had seemed so excited on the night the Nazis bombed St. Helier. All her brave talk about defeating fascism . . . This wasn't about ideology or principles. This was nothing more than an elaborately conceived suicide pact. I felt she had outmaneuvered me, and I took a certain pleasure in making the case for our survival.

"I'll see that we're prepared," I said, "but I don't think it will be necessary."

"You don't?" The note of disappointment in her voice seemed to prove my theory.

"No one will suspect us. Why would they?"

We had always kept ourselves to ourselves, I told her. Apart from the Colleys and the Steel family, local people knew virtually nothing about us. We were two French sisters who lived in the house next to the church. We wore men's clothes and took our cat for walks along the beach.

"They think we're bohemian," I said. "A bit deranged."

"That's how they see us?"

"Honestly, Claude. You live in a world of your own."

There was an imperceptible shift, and another Claude emerged, withering and haughty. "Is there another world? I hadn't realized."

I rose to my feet. "I'll see if there's more wood."

Instead of making for the garage, though, I stood on the lawn and stared up into the sky. Huge clouds hung about, their edges silvered by the moon. Away from the fire, I felt the rawness of the night. I walked over to the new concrete wall that stood between the end of our garden and the beach. Earlier that year, in February, half a dozen German army trucks had parked on the slipway. We watched from an upstairs window as slave workers unloaded sack after sack of cement. They resembled the men we had seen from the bus—starved, unshaven, dressed in rags. Through Edna, we learned that the entire length of the bay was to be fortified. Claude paced up and down, her arms folded tightly across her chest. The bastards, she said. They're going to spoil our view. At least we still have somewhere to live, I said. We knew of several people who had received requisition orders, and had been forcibly ejected from their homes. Bastards, she said again. The wall took three months to build. The slave workers, who were mostly from Spain and Eastern Europe, were always collapsing, or being beaten, but we didn't dare to intervene. All we could do was slip them items of food or clothing when the guards weren't looking. I remember only one moment of light relief. That spring, Claude came downstairs with something bunched up in her hand. What have you got there? I asked. Something for the workers, she told me. She showed me two pairs of fine wool socks. That time Michaux visited, she said, before the war. He left them behind. She gave me a sly grin. Do you think he'll mind?

I climbed the ladder we had placed against the wall and stood on the top, looking out over the beach. A recent storm had tossed a quantity of seaweed up onto the sand, where it lay in black uneven rows, like scribbled instructions in a language I couldn't decipher. My smile faded. Was it true, what I had said to Claude? Would we continue to outwit the Nazis? There were times when the whole thing felt like a parlor game, something we had dreamt up for our own amusement, to stave off the boredom and frustration of the war. It felt so innocent and playful that it was hard to believe we were breaking the law. We were taking such big risks, though, day after day. It would be a miracle if we got away with it.

Before dawn one morning, I left Claude sleeping and went downstairs. No one else was up. In the kitchen Kid pushed his small striped head against my leg. I picked him up and kissed him.

"Kikou," I whispered. "How are you, Kikou?"

His head smelled faintly of burnt coffee, as always. After I had fed him, I walked outside. It was a crisp January day, the sky turning gray above Le Frêt.

I left the garden by the side door and crossed the slipway. The sea was sluggish, as if it too had been asleep. Once in the church-yard, I picked my way through the graves and went out through the gate behind the Fishermen's Chapel. Instead of climbing through the trees, I took the path that led to the groyne or jetty that extended sideways into the bay.

Stepping down onto the concrete, I noticed a pale object in the water on the side that faced the open sea. At first I assumed it was debris—a container of some kind, a piece of torn canvas—but as I drew closer I realized I was looking at the body of a woman. She was floating face down, and she wasn't moving. A deep, dark laceration curved down her back, between her shoulder blades, and another ran across her thigh, just above the knee. Her hair, which was dyed a bright peroxide blond, flared out around her head like a ragged halo. I thought briefly of Ophelia, though this woman was no longer young.

I looked over my shoulder. No one about.

Not wanting to leave the dead woman where she was in case something happened to her while I was gone, I took off my espa-drilles, my jacket, and my trousers and climbed backwards down a rusty ladder. I swam every day for most of the year, though rarely in the winter, and the water I lowered myself into was so cold that it chased the air from my lungs. There was an eerie, dull silence now I was on the side of the jetty that faced the ocean, and I felt a stab of fear I could not explain. It was as if the woman was a lure, and I had put myself in danger.

I reached for her shoulder. Her flesh was lard white and resilient, but also slippery. Gripping her high up on her arm, I began to steer her towards the end of the jetty. Strands of her long hair wrapped themselves across my mouth. I couldn't see her face. It was beneath the surface. Though it seemed likely she had been dead for several hours, I kept feeling that she was trying to communicate with me. I felt she might come alive. Lift her head and look at me, her eyes bleached and empty. Pushing the thought away, I kicked hard. The wide arc of the bay came into view.

Once we were clear of the jetty, the current took hold. It was dragging us sideways, towards the east end of the bay, and I had to fight to stay on course for the beach below our house. By the time I reached the shallows, the muscles in my arms were aching, and I was breathing hard. About fifty yards away, a woman in an overcoat was walking on the sand. I stood up and waved.

"Can you help?" I called out.

The woman came over and stood at the edge of the sea with her hands on her hips. It was Constance, the adopted daughter of Mrs. Brown, who ran the café at the far end of the beach. Constance was a strong swimmer, and was known to have saved more than two dozen people using equipment she had herself invented. I noticed her glance at my shirt, which had stuck to the flat place where my left breast used to be.

"Is she dead?" Constance asked.

I looked down at the body that was bumping gently, almost affectionately, against my leg. "Yes."

Taking off her coat and shoes, Constance helped me haul the woman out of the water and up onto the sand. We turned her onto her back, and I saw her face for the first time. Her eyes had a glazed or puzzled look, as if she had just been told a joke she didn't understand. She had a scar on the right side of her belly, where her appendix had been removed. Her lips were a strange dark mauve.

Constance asked who the woman was.

"I've never seen her before," I said. "She was on the other side of the jetty. I thought I should bring her in." I began to shiver.

"You did the right thing." Constance picked up her coat and draped it over the woman's face and body. "I'll stay here. You go and get warm—and telephone the authorities."

I returned half an hour later, with Claude, Edna, and George. I had brought Constance a blanket, but she said she didn't need it. Bending, Edna lifted the coat and peered at the woman's face.

"I've seen her in town," she said. "She's a prostitute."

Claude spoke to Constance. "Do you think she might have killed herself?"

Constance shook her head. "People don't come to St. Brelade to kill themselves. If they drown on this beach, it's usually because they don't know what they're doing."

Not long afterwards, an ambulance drove down the slipway and out across the firm, damp sand.

It was a few days before I heard the story. Edna was right. The dead woman was a prostitute who had been working in St. Helier. The year before, the German authorities had opened a brothel in the Hotel Victor Hugo, and a number of women had been brought over from mainland France, principally from Normandy. It had not been a success. Perhaps the women were lacking in youth or charm—most of them were over thirty, and some were almost fifty—or perhaps the German soldiers preferred to find girlfriends on the island. Whatever the reason, business was so slow that the establishment was closed down in late November, and the German authorities arranged for the women to be returned to the mainland on a freighter captained by a Dutchman. There were two hundred German troops on board as well. After departing from St. Helier in a dense fog, the ship ran aground on the rocks off Noirmont Point. Most of the passengers drowned. The bodies of thirty-six Germans were recovered from the sea, and they were buried in the cemetery next to our house, but the authorities denied the existence of any prostitutes.

I never did learn the woman's name.

A couple of months later, when Claude and I called in at our tobacconist in St. Helier to buy cigarette papers, we found the woman who ran the place talking to a gray-haired man in a fawn-colored Crombie. We waited patiently as he railed against "the filthy foreigners" who had arrived in such great numbers. At first I assumed he was referring to the occupying forces—there were twenty thousand German troops on the island at the time, one for every two members of the local population—but as the conversation continued it became clear that it was the slave workers that had upset him.

"They're riddled with disease," he said. "Typhoid, tuberculosis, dysentery—there's no telling what you might catch."

"Most of them are criminals, apparently," the woman said.

The man nodded. "Some are homosexuals too. They were in Russian prisons before the Germans brought them here."

"My neighbor caught one of them in her garden, stealing—"

"Typical."

I could feel Claude's outrage building and put a hand on her arm to restrain her, but it was too late.

"You're repellent," she said, "both of you."

The shopkeeper lowered her eyes, and the old man's cheeks reddened, as though he had been slapped.

"Now look here—"

"Those people are innocent," Claude said. "It's the Nazis who are the criminals."

"You'll get us into trouble," the old man said, "talking like that—"

"And as for you two," Claude went on, "you're even worse than the Nazis. At least they have the courage of their own convictions." She turned towards the door, then stopped, one hand on the doorknob. "I won't be shopping here again."

"You're not welcome here," the old man said.

The woman still hadn't spoken.

We left the shop, Claude slamming the door behind us.

I approved of the stand she had made. How could I not? Too many people on the island thought that if the slave workers were mistreated it was because they had done something to deserve it. Nevertheless, I thought her outburst ill-advised. It was a bad time to be making enemies. The Germans had been offering rewards to informers, and there were always those who were prepared to turn in their neighbors in exchange for extra food rations or a cash payment. Some betrayed out of a sense of self-righteousness or self-interest: they believed that if you resisted the Germans you were breaking the law. Others exploited the situation to settle old scores. With one phone call, you could ruin someone's life while at the same time bettering your own.

Outside, on the pavement, I put an arm round Claude's shoulders, and we set off for the bus station. It was a mild April day, all bustling clouds and splashes of sunlight, but her face was pinched, as if with cold. I decided not to mention my misgivings. There wasn't any point.

At that time, George was working at the *Soldatenheim* as a cook. In principle we disapproved, but there were distinct advantages. Sometimes he was able to smuggle food out of the kitchens, and we would feast on luxuries like cake and cheese. As a rule, though, all we had to eat was turnip soup or dandelion soup or soup made using weeds. Even Kid ate soup. We became inventive. I blackened slivers of root vegetable in the oven and ground them into a powder. When added to boiling water, this provided us with a decent substitute for coffee. Edna managed to extract flour from potatoes, and also, being Edna, alcohol. Once, I went out hunting with a butterfly net and caught a sparrow. Claude made sardonic jokes about a Sunday roast. Since we had a large garden we were luckier than most, but we still grew weak from lack of nutrition. If I made the slightest effort—if I swept the floor, or mowed the lawn—I would break out in a sweat that smelled oddly bitter, like the sap of plants. If we didn't wear belts our trousers fell down, as though we were in a Charlie Chaplin film. That winter, we only had electricity for two or three hours a day, and not at all at night, and hunger gouged at us, keen as a knife. Even Claude suffered, since she seemed to have had more of an appetite since the arrival of the Nazis. We often went to bed for twelve or fourteen hours at a stretch, curled round our empty stomachs. There was no wood left; it was the only way of keeping warm. We drifted in and out of consciousness. If we talked, we talked about the past. *Do you remember the evening in Shakespeare & Company, when Joyce read from* Ulysses? *Do you remember his voice, so light and reedy, hardly a breath between the*

words? What words, though. What words . . . And what about the
time we saw Josephine Baker at the Folies Bergère? She had noth-
ing on except a few pink feathers. We were sitting so close that her
sweat landed on our clothes. Remember? The past: it was hard to
believe that any of it had happened. Dalí, and Breton, and Kiki
singing pornographic love songs to Man Ray. The psychoanalyst,
Lacan, forever running off with other people's wives. The night we
watched Murnau's *Nosferatu* with Charles-Henri Barbier. What
had Barbier said afterwards that made us laugh so much? *You should*
have auditioned, Claude. You might have got the part. Jacques Viot
making films of his own, Desnos broadcasting on the radio. Even
our recent visitors, Michaux and Jacqueline—even those last golden
days before the war . . .

  With our energy at a low ebb and so many other people either
passing through the house or living there, it was proving hard to
sustain our campaign of propaganda. We had to be more circum-
spect than ever. Claude still spent hours listening to the BBC,
and the news was heartening—the siege of Leningrad, the Allied
bombing of Leipzig and Berlin—but perhaps the most hard-
hitting leaflet we produced that winter was something we dreamed
up ourselves. While walking through St. Helier, we had noticed
that all the German soldiers we saw were either very young or
middle-aged. The contrast with the troops who had arrived at the
beginning of the occupation could not have been more marked.
On a sheet of unlined writing paper I drew a baby in a cot and
an old man leaning on a stick. Above my drawing, we printed the
following words in big block capitals:

NEW RECRUITS TO THE GERMAN ARMY
(EVERYBODY ELSE IS DEAD)

———

One morning in December 1943, I opened the front door to let Kid out and saw Jean, my brother, standing on the lawn. He was looking this way and that, as if highly entertained by his surroundings. As if the garden—or the world—was somehow ludicrous. He was in uniform, but his feet were bare. His heels were blistered, mauve against the snow. His mouth leaked smoke, like a gun that had just been fired. I remembered how every letter he had written from the trenches had begun with the words *I'm fine.*

"Where are your boots?" I asked.

He laughed, as though I had said something typically naive. His foolish sister.

I asked if he would like to come inside and warm himself. Perhaps I could light a fire. Make some tea. He looked up at the house, his hands searching his pockets. He found a cigarette and struck a match. A flare of orange in the milky air. He bent his head into the flame. Straightening again, he shook the match and dropped it on the ground.

"There was a man with half his head blown off," he said. "He screamed all night—just screamed and screamed. Then, at four in the morning, the screaming stopped.

"He wasn't dead, not quite. I bent close to him, my ear near his mouth. He was whispering the same words, over and over. *Nice watercress, tuppence a bunch . . . Nice watercress, tuppence a bunch . . .*"

"Is there nothing I can offer you?" I said.

He was fiddling with the button on his jacket, which was still loose. "You never understood what we went through," he said.

"You never stopped to think. The rats, the mud, the gas, the lice, the rain—"

"Jean," I said, "why don't you come inside? I could sew that button on for you."

He glanced at his watch. "I should be going."

I moved towards him, but he began to cough. A stream of blood spilled from between his lips. Red all down the front of his uniform, red that quickly blackened. Red holes in the snow.

The cigarette still burning between his fingers.

Winter eased. Claude and I were sitting on the terrace one afternoon, our faces tilted to catch the last rays of the sun, when a low whistle came from the east side of the garden, where the shade was deepest. The postman's son stepped out from the cover of the bushes. He looked furtive and tense, his head drawn down between his shoulders. Behind him was a scrawny man in clothes that were too small for him, his wrists protruding from his sleeves, his trousers stopping halfway down his calves. There were scratches on his face and hands. The postman's son told us the man's name was Pyotr—Peter—and that he had escaped from a slave-labor camp. He and his parents had been sheltering Peter for the last few weeks, he said, but Peter had been spotted by the neighbors, and it had become too risky.

"We'd be happy to look after him," I said.

Claude was nodding. "Of course."

Thanking us, the postman's son shook the Russian's hand and slipped back into the shadows.

We took Peter into the kitchen and gave him a cup of my ersatz coffee and some potato flavored with salt. He ate slowly, but cleaned his plate. He spoke a few words of French and English, and filled in the gaps with sign language.

I offered to wash his clothes. He seemed alarmed. What would he wear instead?

"We'll give you new clothes," Claude said.

He looked at me, and then at Claude. "Women's clothes?"

Claude shook her head. "Men's clothes. We wear men's clothes."

"You wear men's clothes?"

"Yes." Claude paused. "Why? Would you prefer women's clothes?"

"No, no." He held up his hands, palms facing out, as if to ward something off. "Men's clothes good. Very good." We all began to laugh.

"A man borrowing clothes from a woman who just happens to wear men's clothes," Claude said later. "It's like something out of Shakespeare."

While Peter was with us, we asked him about the camp where he had been interned. It was in the northwest of the island, he said. He didn't know its name. The prisoners were expected to work for twelve to fourteen hours a day, summer and winter, with almost nothing to eat. They hauled bags of cement. They dug tunnels. They moved earth and stones. If they stopped working for even a moment, they were beaten. The coffee they were given in the morning was like gray water. Lunch was soup. More water, with bits of turnip floating in it. The same in the evening. In desperation, some prisoners ate wild berries. They died of poisoning. Others prized limpets off the rocks and ate them raw. When they lay down at night, they fell asleep in seconds. It was the sleep of the dead. Every other Sunday they had a day off, but there was no food at all. If you didn't work, the Germans said, you didn't eat. But he had heard that conditions were far worse on Alderney. Terrible things were happening there. Really terrible.

Peter's pronunciation of "Alderney" was so unusual that we thought he must be referring to a work camp on the mainland—or even, perhaps, in Russia—but after questioning him further we realized he was talking about a neighboring island, no more than a mile or two away.

He had met a man from Kiev, he said. The Ukrainian had been a circus strongman before the war, and also, ironically, a prison guard, but he had trembled as he told Peter about Sylt, the camp on Alderney where he had been held for seven months. When they arrived, the Ukrainian said, they were told that none of them would leave the camp alive. His clothes were made from discarded cement sacks. Shirt, trousers—even shoes. He used a cement sack as a blanket too. He slept in cement dust—it was softer than the wooden planks—but his skin blistered and turned raw. The filthy rags he wore were crawling with vermin. He could have scooped handfuls of lice from under his armpits or from his groin. Rats ran over his body while he slept. They ate the lips, ears, and noses of men who didn't last the night. When men died, the Ukrainian said, they were dumped in the sea. No funeral, no burial. Not even any prayers. Just thrown away, like rubbish. Sometimes they washed up on the beach a few days later. Prisoners were ordered to carry them up onto the cliff and toss them back into the waves. The bodies often came apart in their hands. One man was crucified for eating an apple. As dusk fell, the guards nailed him to a gate and hurled buckets of cold water at him. It was December. He died before morning.

I thought of the drowned woman I had brought back to the shore, and of all the other women whose bodies had not been recovered, and I imagined how the bones of a Russian prisoner of war might even now be knocking against those of a French prostitute—a sad, surreal union on the seabed . . .

Claude spoke to Peter. "This is true?"

"He swore it was true." Peter struck his chest with the side of his right fist. "All of it."

His broken French and English only added to the vividness and horror. Perhaps, in any case, when asked to describe the things he had either witnessed or been told about, normal language was found wanting. In the face of such atrocities, words simply fell apart, like the bodies of the dead.

It was in the spring of 1944 that rumors began to circulate. We heard that German soldiers were not only deserting but committing suicide, and there was a sense, possibly for the first time, that Germany might not win the war. We weren't out of danger, though. Not yet. In March, Claude received a letter from the Nazi high command, demanding that she report to Silvertide. I told her it was almost certainly routine, but all kinds of sinister scenarios whirled through my head.

When the day came, Claude wore the outfit she had devised for the assassination of the Kommandant. She rubbed face powder into her hair to make it gray and put on an austere black dress and a black hat with a veil, completing the look with a walking stick and a pair of spectacles. If she appeared as an old woman in poor health, she reasoned, the Germans would be less likely to treat her as suspicious.

"I want you to stay here," she said. "We can't have them suspecting you as well.

She wouldn't listen to any of my arguments.

By the time the taxi arrived, she was in character, her back hunched, her hands gripping the curved handle of her cane.

I wished her luck, then sat on a deck chair with a blanket over my knees, trying not to think. A rotten smell hung in the air. The deep trench between the wall at the end of our garden and the wall the Germans had built was clogged with seaweed, dead leaves, and stagnant water. In a month or two there would be mosquitoes.

The sun came out. Went in again. Seagulls circled overhead. Once in a while, I stood up and stretched my legs.

Three hours later, a car pulled up outside, and I hurried out to the road. Claude emerged, blinking, as if she had just been released from a dark room. I asked her what had happened.

"Not here," she said.

When we were inside, she told me she had been questioned by the head of the *Geheime Feldpolizei*.

"Wolf of the Gestapo?" I said.

"No," she said. "His name was Bode."

Bode was a stocky middle-aged man with a thick neck and thick lips. The expression on his face was stern, as if he sensed insubordination or impertinence. There had been another officer in the room, a corporal with hideous ears. His name was Erich.

"Hideous ears?" I said.

She nodded. "They were fleshy and—I don't know—*convoluted*. I imagined his own ears had been removed and replaced with ears taken from an animal—a pig, say, or a baby elephant."

"How repulsive."

"Oddly enough, he was quite intelligent," she said. "He asked me about the island's history."

She was beginning to tell Erich about the passage graves, which dated from Neolithic times, when Bode interrupted. They weren't there to talk about the Neolithic times, he snapped. They had more pressing business. His priority, it seemed—and the reason for the summons—was to establish whether or not she was a Jew. She elaborated on the story she had told Wolf of the Gestapo the last time she was in the building. She said the name Schwob originated in southern Germany in the Middle Ages, and that it had been given to people who came from Swabia.

"What's this?" Bode said. "Another history lesson?"

Adopting the naive approach I had employed on previous occasions, she asked why he wanted to know if she was Jewish. He told her he was following guidelines that came from higher up. Much higher up. Perhaps she had failed to notice, he said, but a series of orders had been issued in the *Evening Post*, restricting the activities of any Jews who lived on the island. All Jewish identity cards were now stamped with a red *J*, he went on, and businesses that were Jewish were marked as such. Furthermore, Jews were forbidden from entering shops except in the afternoons, between the hours of three and four. They were also banned from public buildings such as theaters, cinemas, and libraries. This was an attempt, he said, to legislate against contamination. At times, it was almost as if he had intuited her heritage and her beliefs, and was trying to provoke her, trying to elicit an incriminating reaction or response. As a result of the measures he had introduced, he said, several Jews had taken their own lives. He smiled and sat back.

"Well," Claude said, "I suppose it saves you the trouble."

"I couldn't have put it better myself." Bode's smile lasted, but his eyes were appraising, cold. "That will be all—for now."

Claude was elated by her performance—she had fooled the head of the Gestapo—but the effort had exhausted her.

She slept for the rest of the day.

Three months later, in the middle of June, I stood on the beach below the house, drying myself after an evening swim. The tide was out, the sea a flat, metallic blue. As I toweled my hair, I heard what sounded like a muffled drumbeat. A man on a black horse was riding in my direction. Farther out than I was, where the sand was wet, he was wearing nothing but a pair of swimming trunks. His body was thickset, deeply tanned. The horse's hooves flung arcs of spray into the air. As he rode past me, at a distance of twenty yards, he took one hand off the reins and waved. Did I wave back? I'm not sure. I recognized him, though. He was Baron von Aufsess, the new civil administrator. I had seen him once before, in Royal Square, lounging on the backseat of a chauffeured car, and Edna, the source of all gossip, had told me that he had a suite of private rooms in St. Helier where he drank champagne and liqueurs and courted svelte young women from the island. Claude referred to him, in English, as "Baron von Abscess." I watched as he swung round and galloped east again, towards Le Frêt, the last of the day's sun on his back.

Earlier that month, the Allies had launched an assault on Saint-Malo, which lay due south of us, no more than fifteen miles away. In bed at night we heard the dull boom of shells. There were orange flickers in the distance, and in the morning smears of black smoke showed on the horizon, like scuff marks on a skirting board. After fierce fighting, the town had fallen, and from that day on the twenty thousand German troops on Jersey were cut off, with no means of escape. The baron must have known the war was lost, and that it was only a matter of time before he would have to contemplate surrender. In the circumstances, it was tempting to view his dash across the firm dark sand as arrogance, but I saw something else in it, something that was more deserving of sympathy or understanding—a willingness to give in to a fleeting exhilaration, a few sublime moments of thoughtlessness. That, I imagined, was why he had waved.

On returning to the house, I found Claude in the big room, where she and Peter were cleaning the chimney. I told her about my sighting of the baron. Dusting the soot off her hands, she looked distinctly unimpressed. There had been something poignant about it, I said, trying to explain. Something very human. I actually *felt* for him.

Her lips twisted. "Do you know what that horse is called?"

I told her I had no idea.

"Satan," she said.

It was six days after my birthday, and we were halfway through our evening meal, a thin wheat-and-turnip gruel, when there was a banging at the door, such a banging that the windows rattled in their frames. I looked at Claude. She was motionless, her hands closed into fists on the edge of the table, her eyes slanting across the room. The knocking came again, even louder than before.

When I opened the door, there were five Nazi officers on the flagstones, their faces exhibiting a sullen, brute determination, a kind of boredom. Or perhaps they were listless with hunger, as we were. The German army was short of provisions too.

"Suzanne Malherbe?"

The officer who had spoken had blank eyes and a big bald head. The look on his face was one of disdain or disgust, as if he had just bitten into something that tasted bad.

"Yes," I said. "Who are you?"

"Colonel Bode. *Geheime Feldpolizei*."

This was the man who had questioned Claude back in the spring.

"Step aside," he said.

He pushed past me. The others followed. The shoulder of one man caught the barometer that hung in the hall, almost dislodging it. In that moment, I realized that the typewriter we used for all our tracts and leaflets was on the desk in Claude's study, in full view. We hadn't had time to put anything away. Before I turned back into the house, I noticed that one of the officers was standing on the lawn, facing the sea. He was wearing a long black leather coat. Wolf of the Gestapo.

When Claude saw the Germans she ran towards the stairs, but one of them caught her by the arm and pushed her down into a chair.

"You're too late," she said. "You've already lost the war."

"Search the house," Bode said in a soft voice. He might almost have been talking to himself.

"I can show you where everything is," I said. "Then you won't have to look."

"*Ruhe*," he said. Quiet.

Wolf appeared in the doorway. His dark eyes rested on me for a few moments, then drifted across the room.

I heard the crash and thump of boots as the soldiers moved about above my head. Drawers were opened. Cupboards too.

Something fell over. Something broke. They *wanted* to search the house. They liked going through other people's things.

As Wolf moved towards a framed photograph of Jacqueline Lamba, I glimpsed a movement in the garden. Peter was crossing the lawn, dressed in one of George's jackets and a pair of wool trousers I had bought on rue du Faubourg Saint-Honoré in 1931. I watched as he clambered up onto the anti-tank wall and disappeared over the top. After he had been with us for about a month, he had come to us one evening and wrapped his thin arms around us and kissed our hands. He had told us he would never forget what we had done for him. We were angels, he said. We belonged in heaven. We don't believe in heaven, Claude had told him. He smiled. I also don't believe, he said. In truth, we were the ones who were filled with gratitude. He had done more for us, we felt, than we had done for him. At a time when we were beginning to lose strength and weary of our struggles, he had turned up at our door and told us stories. With his mangled French and his made-up sign language, he had dispelled our disillusion. He had given us back the very thing we valued most in ourselves. Our conviction. Our resolve.

I faced back into the room. Kid had leapt onto the table and was finishing my soup. I glanced at Claude. She was still slumped in her chair. Her eyes were closed.

Turning away from the picture of Jacqueline, Wolf looked at Claude, and then at me. "I've seen you two before."

I shrugged.

Kid was still lapping up the soup with his rough pink tongue.

When Wolf's three colleagues reappeared, they were carrying Claude's typewriter, the radio, my German dictionary, and an assortment of the empty cigarette packets we used as containers for our smaller leaflets. They had found Claude's gun as well.

Opening her eyes, Claude spoke to Bode. "This has nothing to do with my sister. I was the one who listened to the radio. I wrote the leaflets, and was responsible for their distribution." She rose to her feet. "What's more I lied to you three months ago. I'm Jewish—"

"Claude," I said.

"Outside," Bode said. "Both of you."

I addressed him in German for the first time. "Excuse me, Herr Oberst, but would you allow me to fetch my sister's medication?"

His dull eyes seemed to animate at the sound of his own language. It was as if I had brought him back from somewhere far away.

"What medication?"

"She has a heart condition," I said. "Without her pills, she'll become seriously ill. She might even die."

"Where are they?"

"In the bathroom."

He jerked his head sideways. "*Schnell.*" Be quick.

Wolf spoke to another officer. "Lohse? Go with her."

Lohse had the amiable, inoffensive face of a greengrocer. I could see him with an apron round his middle, weighing onions. As he followed me up the stairs, I asked him what he thought of Jersey.

"It's not so bad," he said.

"Better than the Russian front," I said, "in any case."

"I have a brother there."

"You must be very worried."

"Yes."

I was talking to calm my nerves, and to normalize the situation. I needed to think clearly. At the top of the stairs I looked towards our bedroom. Furniture had been upended, and the floor was a slew of pictures, clothes, and papers.

Lohse nudged me in the back. "Keep going."

He waited by the bathroom door while I opened the medicine cabinet above the sink and took out a dark-blue glass bottle labeled Milk of Magnesia. I had lied to Bode. Claude's health might be fragile, but there was nothing wrong with her heart. The bottle contained a barbiturate called Gardénal, which I had been stock-piling against precisely this eventuality. Though I wasn't supersti-tious, I had sometimes thought that being prepared might prevent disaster. Like an insurance policy. But here we were, about to be arrested . . . Heat prickled across my scalp, and the wall began to swell. I leaned on the sink, my head lowered.

Lohse asked what I was doing.

"Sorry," I said. "I feel dizzy."

"Please hurry."

When we reached the ground floor, Bode's eyes fixed on the blue glass bottle. "Let me see." Taking the bottle from me, he opened it and peered inside. "A heart condition, you said?"

My own heart quiet, like a clock stopped by a catastrophe.

"Yes," I said.

He looked straight at me, his gaze disdainful as before. I didn't look away. At last, he screwed the top on to the bottle and gave it back to me. I thanked him. Claude had once told me I was like a statue, but it was only years later that I had asked her what she meant. You present a solid surface, she said. You're hard to read. Bode had just proved her right.

Out on the road two cars and an army truck were waiting. A light rain was falling, and the sea was flat. There was no sign of Peter. I was glad he had escaped, and hoped he would find shelter.

As Claude and I were marched towards the truck, I stopped and took her in my arms.

"I love you," I whispered.

She pulled me closer. "I love you too."

To my surprise, none of the Germans interfered.

We climbed into the back of the truck and sat next to each other, my right shoulder up against the cold metal of the cab. The roof was green canvas, as were the walls. Two officers sat farther down, next to the tailgate. They faced each other, rifles upright between their knees.

The truck shook itself and moved away, the engine raucous, the canvas all around us flapping. We passed the hotel, then the garage. Then the post office. Our house disappeared from view. We passed Mrs. Brown's café. We were leaving everything behind. If I tried to think ahead, my brain seized up. In my right hand was the blue glass bottle. I would have to choose the moment carefully.

As the truck climbed the hill to Route des Genets, Claude turned to me. "I'm sorry, Suzanne."

I looked at her. "What for?"

"It was all my fault."

"Don't be stupid. We were in this together, from the beginning."

"But it was my idea."

I looked beyond her, beyond the soldiers. The road was like a thread, a clue, something that fed out behind us so we could find our way back to the world we knew and loved. Would we find our way back, though? I couldn't imagine it.

"It was selfish of me," Claude went on. "I'm self-destructive— and now I have destroyed you too."

"I would rather be destroyed by you," I said, "than by anybody else."

We were somewhere above St. Aubin. Trees closed over our heads, forming a green tunnel.

"I'm not afraid," she said. "Are you?"

"If I'm honest, yes."

"Suzanne." She turned to me again and held me. I could feel her arms around me, arms I might never feel again.

"Are you crying?" she asked.

I couldn't answer. My throat was raw, and full of obstacles.

"You never cry," she said. "It must be bad if you're crying. It must be really bad."

"It's the thought of not being with you," I said, my voice jerky, thin. "It's the thought of all this coming to an end."

"Have I been good to you?"

"Yes."

"I haven't tortured you too much?"

I smiled through my tears. "Not too much, no. Just a little."

"There. That's more like you." She stroked my hair, over and over, the way a mother might. "I was difficult, though, sometimes . . ."

"Sometimes. But you were also astonishing." I looked into her eyes. "We're doing it, then?"

"Yes. We can't let them have any power over us. That would be unthinkable." She glanced at the two soldiers. "Also, I'm nearly fifty. You're fifty-two. It's not as if we haven't lived." Her face emptied. She was somewhere else. I wondered if she was thinking about the people she had never been allowed to love.

"And me?" I said. "Was I enough for you?"

She smiled. "It's true what I told my father all those years ago. You were my salvation."

This was something she felt deeply, and often needed to reiterate, and I thought of the unlikely marriage that had made sisters of us. My mother's gift to Claude's father had been calmness and consistency, qualities he must have craved. Perhaps my gift to Claude had not been so dissimilar.

"Do you believe me?" she asked.

"Yes, of course."

When the soldiers weren't looking, she kissed me on the lips. Her tongue tasted of zinc or iron. This was panic's residue. That mad moment when she fled towards the stairs.

"I do have one regret," she said. "I'm sorry we won't see the Nazis lose the war."

One of the soldiers' heads jerked in our direction. *"Nicht reden."* No talking. I noticed his ears, which were unusually large and fleshy. Was this Erich, the young officer who had been so curious about the island's history?

We passed the brick Martello tower in Beaumont. The sky was overcast. Gray sea showed between the houses. In ten minutes we would reach St. Helier, and it would be too late. I glanced at the two Germans. They were watching the coast road unwind behind us. One of them—Erich—seemed on the verge of sleep, his chin falling forwards, onto his chest. Shielded by Claude, I opened the bottle and tipped the pills onto my palm. We were to take half each. I passed Claude her share.

"Is something wrong?" she asked.

"No," I said. "Nothing's wrong."

She began to swallow the pills. I did the same. The Germans were still staring at the road and didn't notice.

WICKED WHITE

1944–1945

The truck turned in through the gates of the prison on Gloucester Street and came to a halt in a small courtyard of blackened brick. *Is something wrong?* Looking at my share of the pills, I had had sudden qualms about the dose. Twenty tablets would probably be sufficient for Claude—she was much more slightly built than I was—but I suspected I might need something to help me finish the job. Climbing down out of the truck, I kept my eyes open for anything that might serve as a blade. When I saw a shattered roof tile lying at the base of a wall I bent down, pretending to tie my shoelace. I waited until the Germans looked away, then I pocketed the fragment with the sharpest edge.

We were escorted into a starkly lit room filled with military personnel and prison guards. Bode began to issue orders. I didn't listen. We sat on hard chairs against the wall. It was hot in the room. Claude's eyes closed, and she started to fall sideways. I had to hold her up. A guard pulled my arm from around Claude's shoulders and told her to sit up straight. No longer supported, she slid onto the floor.

"*Aufstehen!*" the guard shouted. Stand up.

Claude failed to react.

Wolf came over. "What's happening here?"

"I think she fainted," I said in German.

Looking down at Claude, Wolf kicked her shoulder. She murmured, but didn't move. He kicked her again. This time his boot caught her forehead.

"Stop that," I said.

"You don't give the orders round here." Wolf spoke to a nearby guard. "Put her in a cell."

The guard led me down a dim gray corridor. I couldn't seem to draw any air into my lungs. We climbed a flight of stairs, and then another. My legs grew heavy. My head seemed to have floated free. I thought of a child holding a balloon, then letting go. The balloon drifting up into the sky. From far away came the jingling of keys. A door opened, and I was shoved into a small dark room. It was a kind of luxury to sink down onto the pallet bed. The door clanged shut, a key turned in the lock.

I closed my eyes.

I was lying on my stomach, one arm beneath me. There was a smear of vomit on the mattress. I was still alive. And Claude? My vision was blurred, and the inside of my head felt soft, like mud at the bottom of a pond. Claude was weaker than I was, and she had lost consciousness before me. She must be dead—surely . . . The thought was bland. It had no force.

I wondered how much time had passed.

I turned my head. The mud slid sideways. There was a small window high above me, very little light. I tried to sit up. My skull seemed to split in two, the pain so abrupt and vicious that I couldn't move. I felt I had gone deaf. The headache stopped me hearing.

Sometime later, I remembered my hidden weapon. I pushed the sharp edge against my wrist and dragged it sideways, hard as I could. There was a shriek. I knew it was me, but it seemed to come from somewhere else, somewhere outside my body. Outside the room.

Then nothing.

To my left was a huge, high wall. I couldn't see over it. Curving off into the distance, it was a screen of pastel colors. Mauve and tangerine and gray. The pink of artificial limbs. A sickly pale green. There was no landscape, just an empty plain. Ground like powder. Dust. What was the wall made of? It looked solid, but behaved as liquid does. A smooth, dense liquid, like oil or soup. The colors kept undulating, pushing against each other, without ever mingling or forming new colors. I felt nauseous, and there was a steady buzzing sound, like an insect. A machine. My body was supported, but not defined, distinct. I would have given anything not to be looking at that wall, but I couldn't seem to turn away. Wherever I looked it was always there.

I rose to the surface, my left arm throbbing. A white wall circled me, its eyes on me. It was a different room. A sink stood near the bed. The pallet I was lying on was covered with dark stains. My clothes as well. There was a bandage round my wrist. My head had been cut into two sections which had then been crudely fitted back together. When I thought about the join I coughed and almost vomited.

A nurse bent over me. I tried to speak.

My sister . . .

The words wouldn't come out. My voice had rusted solid.

A few days after my second failed suicide attempt, I was taken to Silvertide to be interrogated. It was Bode, the head of the *Geheime Feldpolizei*, who was seated behind the desk. The man with the greengrocer's face—Lohse—stood by the window. I had not heard any news of Claude, and assumed that she was dead.

When Bode looked up from the file he was studying, his eyes moved from my face to my wrist. "You didn't do a very good job, did you."

Since he had spoken to me in German, I replied in German. "It would seem not."

"Your sister also failed."

"She's alive?" My heart was beating so hard that there was a strange, transparent pulsing in my vision. I was desperate to find out how she was, but I couldn't afford to reveal my true feelings. If I showed concern, or even curiosity, it would weaken my position.

"Yes," Bode said, "though she has kidney problems. Uremia." He consulted his dossier again. "There is, however, nothing wrong with her heart."

"No."

Without opening his mouth, he ran his tongue over his front teeth, as if to cleanse them of an unpleasant taste. "You think you can fool us."

I kept silent.

"You're lucky," he said, "you and your sister."

Once again, I chose not to speak.

"If you had not attempted suicide," he went on, "you would probably have been transported to the camp in Aurigny, on the mainland—and from there to another destination, farther east . . ."

His words had an understated menace that I didn't understand.

"As it is, you missed the last shipment of prisoners to France, and there won't be any more." He sat back. "If you hadn't tried to kill yourselves, you wouldn't have survived. Amusing, no?"

I looked at the documents on the desk, each one stamped with a German eagle. I looked at the drab yellow walls and at Lohse, still standing by the window, and then I looked at Bode, his lips thick and contemptuous, his bald head like an egg laid by a dinosaur.

"Perhaps I didn't survive," I said. "Perhaps I'm already dead, and in a kind of hell."

Bode eyed me with an interest that seemed genuine, then returned to his dossier. For the next half hour he went through my personal details while a clerk typed my answers. When he had all the information he needed, he asked how long I had worked for the Resistance.

"I didn't work for the Resistance," I said. "I didn't work for anyone."

He leaned forwards. "You expect me to believe that you produced and distributed all those leaflets by yourselves?"

"It's the truth."

He looked at me steadily, but said nothing. It was the pro-
nounced arches of his nostrils, I realized, that made him look
disdainful.

"We acted alone," I said.

"You and your sister?"

"Yes."

Still staring at me, Bode tapped the blade of a letter opener
against his thumbnail. My eyes drifted to the window. The room
overlooked the sea. A gull flew past, white against the low dark
clouds. I remembered how we had painted the German words for
DOWN WITH WAR on coins and left them lying in an amusement
arcade where German soldiers liked to go. It had been Claude's
idea to use Wicked White, a nail varnish by Peggy Sage. Such
a perfect name for what we're up to, she said. White because we
have right on our side—and wicked? Well, that's obviously ironic.

Lohse broke the silence. "You don't deny that you dissemi-
nated propaganda?"

"No."

"How long did you do it for?"

"About four years."

"Ever since we occupied the island?"

"Yes." I thought back to the empty packet of German cigarettes that Claude had found by the main road. "It began as a
small thing. A gesture, really. Then it grew."

"How did it grow?" Bode asked. "I'm curious."

"We devoted a lot of time to it. We did very little else." I
paused. "I don't think we've ever been so busy."

"I find it astonishing," he said, "that you got away with it for
so long."

"We also found it astonishing."

His lips tightened. Looking past me, he addressed the guard. "Take her back to her cell."

I was held on the top floor of C block, which had once been the women's wing. The chief jailer, a slight man, and his much larger second in command both went by the name of Heinrich. We called them Little Heinrich and Big Heinrich. The other guards were Otto and Ludwig. It was several days before I learned that Claude was farther down the corridor. Since there was an empty cell between us, and also a windowless room that used to be a library, and since the walls were made of granite, it would not be possible, Little Heinrich told me, for us to speak to each other. Sharing the floor with us were several German soldiers who had attempted either to desert or to mutiny. It seemed an oversight on the part of the authorities that we were being held in the same building as men who our propaganda had been aimed at, men who might even have been influenced by what we produced. Also in C block were half a dozen young people from the island—Belza Turner, for instance, who had tried to sail to France with plans detailing the German fortifications, and Peter Gray, not even seventeen, who had been found with a cache of guns and ammunition. Though we were old enough to be their parents, and from a different culture, there was, from the beginning, a real sense of solidarity. These were people we felt for and sympathized with, people we understood.

Of the guards on my floor, Otto was the most approachable. He had a big, awkward body, and when he smiled I could see the spaces between his teeth. He could have played the ogre in a

pantomime. "Gut morning," he would say, attempting English
—until he realized I spoke German.

Once, when he opened the door of my cell to check on me, I
asked him how Claude was.

"Still weak," he said.

"Could you give her a message for me?"

He pressed his lips together and slowly shook his head. "It's
against regulations."

"What if it was just a few words?"

"Like what?"

"Tell her I'm in good health. Tell her I love her."

"Perhaps. But I can't promise." He took a step backwards
and peered down the corridor. "She's always writing, your sister."

"She has writing materials?"

Otto nodded. "She uses toilet paper from the guards' room.
The Russian cleaners steal it for her." Even though he was himself
a guard, Otto was smiling.

I asked him what she was writing.

"Some kind of diary or testament." He massaged the back of
his neck with one hand. "She thinks you will both be executed."

"She told you that?"

"She used signs. She doesn't speak German, not like you."

"And you, Otto?" I said. "What do you think?"

He shrugged.

"That's not very reassuring," I said.

"I have no power here." His eyebrows lifted, and he held his
arms away from his sides. "If it was up to me—" Embarrassed
suddenly, he backed out of my cell.

"Thank you for your kindness," I said.

His face seemed to wobble, like a drop of rain just before it spills from a leaf, then he closed the door and turned the key.

As August wore on, the interrogations began to blur, one into another. Sometimes Bode was alone, or sometimes he had one of his colleagues with him—the ingratiating Lohse, or Erich with his bestial ears, or Wolf of the Gestapo, vain and sadistic, a Nazi version of Al Capone. But Bode himself was always behind everything, always in charge. On one occasion, I was pushed, blinking, into his office. Bright sunlight burst through the window. I had become accustomed to the darkness of my cell—we prisoners called them "coffins"—and even though they had driven me across town, from Gloucester Street to Havre des Pas, my eyes didn't seem to have adjusted.

Looking up from his paperwork, Bode remarked on the beauty of the day. He felt like a fraud, he told me. He wasn't at war. How could he be, in this idyllic place? He rose to his feet and paced up and down, hands clasped behind his back. He was beginning to understand why Jersey was such a popular holiday destination. He was only sorry that his wife and children couldn't join him.

"*Come to Sunny Jersey,*" he said in English, quoting the headline from an advertisement. He laughed, then switched back into German. "Is that why you live here, for the climate?"

"Are we going to talk about the weather?" I said. "I thought that was an English obsession."

He stared at me across one shoulder. "You really are a very difficult woman."

Returning to his desk, he produced a small tin that I recognized. He must have stolen it on the day of our arrest—or subsequently, perhaps, since I was sure they would have searched the house a second time. He opened the lid, took out a pinch of tobacco, and began to roll a cigarette. It was his way of reminding me that my home was in the hands of strangers. His way of pointing out how little power I had. He looked at me as he moistened the narrow strip of glue on the rolling paper with the tip of his tongue. I was careful not to react.

Smiling, he lit the cigarette and leaned back in his chair. "There's an aspect to this affair which I don't understand . . ."

A fly was circling his bald head, and I found myself on the verge of a dangerous hilarity. I had to cough to keep myself from laughing. He asked if I was troubled by the smoke.

"It's nothing, just a cold." I gestured vaguely. "The cells . . ."

He nodded, then inhaled.

"You owned an illegal radio," he said. "You listened to the BBC. You translated British propaganda into German. All this I understand. What I don't understand is your approach. The poems, the drawings—the rhymes . . ." His thick lips twitched. It was a smile of sorts.

"We're artists."

Even as I spoke, I felt it was a lie. I found myself doubting the life I had lived prior to my imprisonment. The glitter and glamour of Paris—it was fantasy, or wishful thinking. Even more recent memories seemed exotic, overblown. Swimming in the bay at dawn, sunbathing in the garden. The smell of Claude's skin. The taste of her . . . Did any of it happen? Surely not. There was only this questioning, this smell of damp. This loneliness.

"Artists?" Bode looked curious, but also skeptical.

"Before the war," I said, "Paris was full of artists."

"You lived in Paris?"

"Yes."

He stubbed out his cigarette and consulted a document. "It says here that you've lived on Jersey for thirty years."

"Not true."

"Should I have heard of you?"

"I designed handbills and posters for a theater in Montparnasse. I did illustrations for magazines. I illustrated books as well. I wasn't famous, though." I paused. "Claude was much better known than I was."

"Claude?"

"Lucie. My sister."

Watching me, Bode tapped a pen against his thumb, something he did when he was deep in thought, or when he was suspicious.

"You don't look very much alike." His eyes were cold suddenly, and abrasive, like bits of gravel.

"We're not related by blood," I said. "We're stepsisters. Her father married my mother."

"Really?" His voice had softened, but it wasn't gentle. "What are the chances of that?"

Panic passed across my head like heat. I had talked too much. I had given myself and Claude away. In an attempt to distract him, I spoke again. In as calm a voice as I could muster, a voice that verged on the seductive, I said, "Wasn't there something you wanted me to help you with?"

"You *have* helped me."

"I don't see how."

"The creativity—I understand it now." He shook his head. "So clever of the Resistance, to think of recruiting artists . . ."

I sighed.

Calling for a guard, Bode closed the file that lay in front of him. He would see me in a day or two, he said. He advised me to use the time to search my memory. If I didn't offer him some credible explanation, things would become difficult for me. For my sister too.

I asked if she was strong enough to be interrogated.

"We have already spoken to her," he said, "at length. She's stronger than she looks."

"But hasn't she told you exactly what I've been telling you?"

"Your stories are remarkably consistent." He sat back, hands folded snugly over his potbelly. "You're extremely well trained, both of you. It will be hard to break you down."

What was the truth for me was a highly polished fabrication for him, and I wasn't sure there was anything I could say that would convince him otherwise.

It was only when the Russians who emptied our slops agreed to deliver notes in secret that Claude and I were finally able to communicate, but for the first few weeks of our imprisonment we had no contact at all, and every time I asked Otto whether he had passed on any of my messages he became evasive or noncommittal. One night, when the building had fallen quiet, I decided to sing "Petit chagrin" in the hope that Claude might hear me and be comforted. *Les mots les plus tendres jamais / Ne diront combien je t'aimais* . . . Even the most tender words could never

/ Let you know how much I loved you . . . As I sang, I thought I felt the silence in the jail deepen, and I was certain that she was listening.

I had sung "Petit chagrin" before—to Madame Schwob, when we stayed at Le Pradet in 1911. As I sang the song again, more than thirty years later, in the darkness of a prison cell, I remembered how Claude had woken me one morning, just after dawn, her forefinger upright against her lips. She took my hand and led me through the silent house and out into the grounds. Pines and oaks stood about, motionless and black, the hills behind them smoky, mauve. There were five palm trees on the property, she had told me, each one planted for a different child. I followed her along a path that would take us to the beach. The grass was wet with dew. Her bare legs shone. A cock crowed in a farmyard on the edge of the village. When we reached the cliff we sat in the shade of an umbrella pine, the dry earth carpeted with needles, the blue sea glittering below. I remembered how Claude turned to me, her face close to mine, and how, at that same moment, a middle-aged man with a butterfly net came up the path towards us. He stopped and showed us what he had caught that morning. He was a friend of Claude's grandmother. Years later, Claude told me that when the man with the butterfly net appeared she had been about to kiss me. I hoped she could hear me singing, and hoped too that she was thinking of that morning in the south of France when we almost kissed for the first time.

I was being interrogated by Bode one September evening when the door opened and a guard led Claude into the room. Behind her was Wolf of the Gestapo, in the black leather coat he liked to wear. The guard pushed Claude towards the only empty chair. She had aged since the day of our arrest—the skin around her eyes was puffy, and her cheeks had slackened—and yet something inside her seemed to have intensified or grown in strength, and I remembered the evening of the bombing raid, and how elated she had been. *We're going to be tested.*

She was staring at my wrist. "What happened?"

I shrugged. "An accident."

"She tried to kill herself," said Wolf of the Gestapo, in English.

Claude didn't look at him, only at me. "Is that true?"

"I thought you were dead," I said.

"Quiet," Bode said.

He had a list of names, which he wanted us to listen to. If we were familiar with any of the names, we were to let him know.

Claude raised an eyebrow, but said nothing.

As Bode began to run through the names, all of them French, Wolf of the Gestapo watched us closely. He was hoping, I imagined, for a physical reaction, an involuntary flicker of recognition. My gaze drifted back to Bode. His dome-shaped head, the thick lips that peeled back from his teeth. *The master race.* How was it possible for these people to look in the mirror and believe such a thing about themselves? I was dumbfounded by the power of the spell that Hitler had cast over them.

Bode was still running through his list. It was meaningless. Absurd. There came a point where I was tempted to "recognize" one of the names, if only to bring an end to the charade. But the respite would only have been temporary. They would have wanted descriptions, addresses—codes. And besides, I would have been putting someone's life at risk . . .

At last Bode stopped. "None of the names mean anything to you?"

Claude stifled a yawn.

"We have already told you many times," I said. "We worked alone."

"In detective fiction," Claude said, "this is what they call an open-and-shut case. You caught us and we confessed. You should be satisfied."

Wolf of the Gestapo spoke to Bode, but I didn't hear what he said because Claude had touched my hand and was addressing me in French. "What do you think of our accommodation?"

Something leapt in me at the feel of her hand on mine. I had been starved of her.

"Our accommodation?" I said. "It's not bad, I suppose."

"My room is extremely comfortable."

"So's mine, actually. And the view is wonderful."

"No complaints?"

"None at all."

"The staff are very helpful, aren't they."

I smiled.

"You know something?" she said. "I think it might be the best hotel on the—"

Bode brought the flat of his hand down on the surface of the table, making me jump. The desk lamp flickered, but stayed on.

"*Genug*," he said in a strangled voice. Enough.

We were returned to our cells.

Alone again, I thought how unusual it was for Bode to lose his temper. But then the joint interrogation had not been a success. From that moment on he kept us apart, hoping he might be able to play us off against each other, and also, I think, because he realized that separation would be, in itself, a form of torture. It wasn't until a few days later that I understood why he might have been so out of sorts. In a brief exchange with Joe Mière, a local man who was being held in a cell near mine, I learned that Bode had a girlfriend in St. Helier, a dance teacher called Miss Lillicrap, and that somebody had found out about the relationship, and had painted the front of her house with tar.

In early October I was taken to a small room in the basement of Silvertide. The walls were gray, and the floor was bare concrete, and apart from a metal chair and a metal table there was no furniture. A single window gave on to a grim gray corridor. The smell of bleach didn't quite conceal the smell of something human, something rusty. Blood, I thought, or fear.

I had been waiting for no more than a few minutes when a young officer appeared. He wasn't someone I had seen before. I would have remembered. He was enormous, like one of the Raymond brothers, the muscles in his upper arms and thighs outlined by a uniform he had long since outgrown. His face was all harsh planes, his cheekbones clenched like fists under the skin, his forehead broad but dented at the temples. His eyes were slits. His lips were wet. He placed both hands flat on the table and looked right at me.

"I need names," he said.

When he leaned over me, he made the room feel so cramped that I could hardly breathe. I felt like a character from *Alice in Wonderland*. Where was the pill that would reduce him to his normal size?

"Tell me the names."

I wondered how many local women had swooned over his remarkable physique. I wondered how many he had slept with. I had a sudden nightmare vision of an island overrun by the young man's bastard progeny—giant children with narrow eyes and moist red mouths.

He was still leaning over the table. "I need the names of the people who recruited you."

"No one recruited me."

"Who did you work for? Who did you report to?"

"Nobody. We worked alone."

"Two old women like you?" He straightened up and shook his head.

"It's not about age," I said. "It's about intelligence."

I didn't see his hand move. All of a sudden, though, my left ear was burning. He stood back, folding his arms. He had put very little of his strength into the blow, but my whole head buzzed.

"Give me the names of your superiors," he said.

He asked the same question over and over. He had the infinite patience of the truly unimaginative.

"Let's look at things the other way round . . ." I could hardly hear myself above the crackling in my head, which was like a kind of interference. "Why on earth would the Resistance hire a useless old woman like me? It just doesn't make sense."

He watched me carefully, as if he suspected I was playing a trick on him. The transparency of the look told me how inexperienced he was. What had his life been like before? I could see him tramping through flat fields with a knapsack and a loaded gun, a brace of rabbits with bloodied heads lolling in one fist. The evening would find him in a hostelry with other brawny, raw-boned

men, a mustache of beer foam on his upper lip. Could his crudity
be part of Bode's strategy? Maybe Bode was trying to drive me
to distraction. Maybe he was trying to *bore* me into a confession.

"Names," the young man said.

As I looked at him, things around me began to swim and
buckle. I coughed twice, and nearly vomited. "Can I go back to
my cell?"

"After you've given me the names."

"I don't have any names," I muttered. "I wish I did."

"Why are you protecting them? What have they done for
you?" He was still standing in the middle of the room with folded
arms. "They've done nothing for you. You owe them nothing." He
came forwards again, in the grip of a strange exhilaration. "They
don't give a shit about you. You're dead to them. It's almost as if
you never existed."

I looked up at him, surprised. This was considerably more
interesting than his previous line of questioning. He had surprised
himself, perhaps. But I was tired. So tired.

"This is going nowhere," I said.

Swooping down, he seized my jaw. His thumb dug into one of
my cheeks, his fingers into the other. He was so close that I could
see the sleep in the corner of his eye.

"Aren't you scared?" he said.

I struggled to speak. "Yes," I said. "All the time."

Wrong-footed, he stepped away from me, head lowered. I
sensed that his thoughts were elsewhere. *What shall I eat tonight?
How much shall I drink? Who shall I fuck?*

The door opened and Bode walked in. He asked the young
man if he had made any progress.

"Not really, Herr Oberst," the young man said. "She refuses to cooperate."

"She's very stubborn." Bode looked down at me, and I felt him select a weapon. "Perhaps," he said at last, "you'll have more joy with the other one."

I kept my eyes on the table. I would not plead on Claude's behalf. I would not give him that satisfaction.

"I've been observing you. You know what I see?"

Once again I had been transported to Silvertide, only this time I was back on the first floor, and it was Wolf of the Gestapo who was sitting behind the desk.

"Where's the colonel?" I asked.

"That's no business of yours." Wolf lit a cigarette and leaned back in the chair, watching me through the smoke. His lips were crumpled. Thin. "Do you know what I see when I look at you?"

I sighed. "Not really."

"Pride," he said.

I felt my insides twist. My stomach had been upset by the watery soup they had been feeding me.

"Your pride's misplaced, though." Wolf stood up and walked over to the window. His black leather jacket creaked as he lifted his cigarette towards his mouth. "You may have had some small significance when you lived in Paris, but you're nothing now. You no longer count." He gave me a long hard look, over his shoulder. "All those people you used to know—they've forgotten you. You're worthless. Disposable."

I kept quiet.

"You've only got one breast," he went on. "You're not even a proper woman."

"Apricot," I said.

"What?"

"Nothing."

"How old are you? Sixty?" This time he didn't wait for an answer. "You have nothing to look forward to. Only pain, perhaps. The body breaking down. Then death."

My stomach twisted again, so sharply that I let out a gasp. Wolf didn't appear to notice.

"I need the lavatory—"

He talked over me. "If you were to cooperate we might be lenient. We might let you and your sister share a cell. We might even send you back to that nice house of yours—"

My legs were suddenly warm, then cool. A foul smell lifted into the room. Wolf stared at me in horror, one arm over his mouth and nose.

"It's not because I'm afraid of you," I said.

Our trial took place in the middle of November. Not long after dawn, I was led down the stairs and out into the prison yard. It was cold in the shade, but the sky was a hard, pure blue. I drew the crisp air deep into my lungs. Our guilt was not in doubt. What would they do, though? Would they decide to make an example of us? Since the fall of Saint-Malo, all the shipping links to the mainland had been cut, but they could always fly us to Berlin and carry out our executions there. I couldn't imagine what the future held. Still, at least all the uncertainty would be coming to an end.

Claude was already in the car, sitting upright, her face white and tense, her hair scraped back from her forehead and smoothed down flat. As I climbed in, I thought I felt something ease in her. I took her hand. Her fingers closed round mine. Neither of us spoke.

We were driven past Parade Gardens and along Rouge Bouillon to an address on Lower King's Cliff. The car pulled in to the curb, and soldiers escorted us through the back door of a building and up a flight of stairs. The courtroom was heated, and sunlight slanted through the three tall windows that overlooked the street. We were shown to two upholstered chairs. They faced a long table that was covered with green baize.

Claude leaned close. "Front row seats!" she whispered.

I couldn't help but smile. "I've missed you."

She let out a sigh. "This is blissful, isn't it? The armchairs, the central heating—a chauffeured car to bring us here . . ."

The three judges sitting at the table wore military uniforms, and were flanked by the prosecutor and the defense counsel. Behind them, on the wall, was a portrait of Hitler. On the other walls were watercolor views of somewhere that resembled Switzerland. In front of the five men, on the green baize, was a seemingly random assortment of items. Among them I could make out several things that belonged to us—Claude's gun, her typewriter, the Kodak camera, several piles of leaflets, and the radio. Claude was just murmuring that it looked like a jumble sale when one of the judges, a Colonel Sarmsen, silenced her by bringing down his gavel.

The trial began.

From the outset the judges appeared uneasy and irascible, perhaps because they found themselves in an awkward predicament. After all, France had already been liberated, and Germany itself was under threat. Early on, Sarmsen accused us of breaking all their regulations.

"All of them," I said, "except the ones that didn't bother us."

Claude laughed.

Sarmsen brought the gavel down again.

The prosecutor was in a permanent state of outrage, his complexion so ruddy that there were moments when I feared for his health. He could not have had a stronger case. An initial search of the house had turned up a wealth of evidence. In addition, he had our confessions, since we had never denied our guilt. As if all that wasn't enough, he attempted to smear our characters still further by referring to the "pornographic material" discovered in our house during the days following our arrest. There were various photographs of sadomasochistic practices, he claimed. One of the accused—Miss Schwob—appeared naked in several of the photographs, sometimes with a head that had been shaved. These obscene items confirmed the authorities' suspicions, he said. We were, quite simply, "the worst kind of Jews." I let out a stifled snort of derision. The Nazis hadn't *had* any suspicions. That was why our activities had gone undetected for so long. What's more, I wasn't Jewish. Not even Claude could properly be called a Jew, since her mother was a Catholic. I glanced at our defense counsel, a fidgety man with the narrow jaw and bristly side whiskers of a rat, but he failed to object to any of these characterizations. He wouldn't even meet my eye. It was clear that he had no interest in securing an acquittal.

The aforementioned items had been seized, the prosecutor informed us, and would be summarily disposed of. I felt no embarrassment, no shame. If the Germans felt the need to destroy the images, it was because something in themselves had already been destroyed. It was because they were, themselves, obscene. All the same, I was saddened by the loss. I glanced at Claude. She was staring straight ahead, chin raised. As the prosecutor continued to build his case, various witnesses were called, including Bode. At one point, I caught our counsel giving us a look of sly satisfaction. It struck me that he was as hostile as the prosecution, if not more so, and I interrupted the proceedings to register a complaint. My remarks were noted, but no action was taken.

We had not employed any violence, Sarmsen said in his summing-up, but that didn't mean the verdict should be lenient. Contrary to popular belief, the use of what he called "spiritual weapons" constituted a more serious crime than the use of weapons that were real. The effect of bombs and bullets could be readily assessed, he said. With words, however, there was no telling how much damage they might do.

"Extraordinary," Claude whispered. "He actually said something that made sense."

Though Sarmsen's remarks didn't augur well for our sentencing, Claude didn't care. Unlike most prisoners who appear in the dock, she *wanted* to be found guilty. It was important to her that our campaign was acknowledged and recorded, otherwise it would all have been in vain. At the same time, and even more importantly, it would expose the Nazis to embarrassment and ridicule. If any of those involved kept diaries, I doubted they would mention the trial. The entries for that day would focus on the weather—glorious—or perhaps November 16 would be left blank.

While the judges deliberated, we drank a delicious ersatz coffee called *Malt Kneipp* from porcelain cups in an adjoining room. Three hours later, Sarmsen delivered the verdict. Since we had spread propaganda designed to jeopardize the Nazi war effort and—worse still—since we had tried both to incite mutiny and to encourage assassination attempts on high-ranking officers, we were to receive the death sentence. Though I had feared these words might be coming, I felt nothing. There was a sheet of glass between me and the men sitting at the table. I had to strain to hear what was being said. It was like the pinched, almost comical voice that comes out of a receiver when you hold it away from your ear. We were also sentenced to six years' hard labor, Sarmsen went on, and a further nine months in prison, for possession of firearms, a camera, and a radio.

"Do we have to do the six years and nine months *before* we're shot?" Claude asked.

I smiled.

Sarmsen's face stiffened—he knew he was being mocked—but he kept his voice level. "The death sentence takes precedence."

Claude thanked him for the clarification.

If we would like to appeal against the sentence, he went on, there were documents we would be required to sign. As he reached for the relevant papers, I looked at Claude. She shook her head.

"No," I said. "No appeal."

Sarmsen gaped at us, his arm still outstretched.

Since the day of our arrest, the Nazis had found it hard to accept that we were responsible for a four-year campaign of subversion, but once we were in front of them, in court, they could no longer ignore the fact. They had been outwitted by two middle-aged Frenchwomen, and it seemed likely that the harsh sentences they had handed down were a direct conse-quence of their discomfort. In finding us guilty, though, they were admitting their own incompetence. I think that explained

Claude's air of triumph that day. I felt triumphant too, though it rapidly ebbed away when Sarmsen told us that we would be held in separate cells until such time as our death sentences could be carried out.

"And when will that be exactly?" Claude asked.

Sarmsen told her that it was none of her concern.

"The date of my death is none of my concern?" Claude said. "That's hilarious."

Sarmsen spoke to the guards. "Take them away."

In that moment, I realized that I might never see Claude again. They say a heart breaks, but it doesn't. It goes on working, mute and stubborn as a mule. I stared at the floor.

"Suzanne?"

I looked up, blinking back the tears.

Claude was smiling at me. "I heard you singing, in the middle of the night. About three weeks ago."

"It was for you."

"I know. I loved it. And, once, I thought I heard you laughing . . ."

"Did you?"

"Maybe I imagined it. Or maybe it was a memory. Your laughter, though—I think it's the most wonderful sound in the world."

As she was led to the door, she glanced over her shoulder and gave me a bright look. Then she was gone.

During the days that followed, as I lay curled up on my hard bed wrapped in all the clothes I owned, my insides tightened like a small cold fist. Something in me had been dismantled or removed. Resilience, perhaps. Or hope. I remembered Wolf of the Gestapo's words. *You have nothing to look forward to.* Maybe it was as simple as that.

Whenever I closed my eyes I found myself thinking of the party we had given at the very beginning of the thirties. I saw Dalí in his tight-fitting suit and his starched collar—in those days he used to dress like a clerk—and I remembered how he told me I had gold paint on my lips and on my cheek. *You have been kissing a god, perhaps.* I remembered him talking about the fisherman's cottage he was on the point of buying. *Do you know Cadaqués? No? Then you must come and stay. I insist!* Somehow the invitation, which we had never taken up, and René's description of his time in Spain became entangled in my mind, and it seemed to me that Claude and I had been there too. I could see the shack with its white walls, a wooden table by the shore. I could see the swans. We swam as soon as we woke up. It was an inlet, a kind of lagoon, protected from the waves and currents farther out by the jagged, brooding island of Sa Farnera. At dawn, the water was cool and lazy, the color of lead. Later, it turned a silky pale blue. We ate fried perch with fennel and ham sliced thin as onion skin, and went for long walks on the rugged, rust-brown land behind the house. We visited the huge, contorted rock that inspired Dalí to paint *The Great Masturbator.* We took dozens of intimate photographs, all of which would have been burned by the Nazis. Some nights it was so hot that we slept on a flat roof, under the stars . . . Did Dalí spy on us while we were making love? Almost certainly. We didn't care.

I returned again and again to that landscape, which I had never seen. The simple wooden table by the water, the harsh brown ridge behind. The three swans floating, candlelit. A feeling of wonder and well-being as we sat in the deep blue dusk and listened to stories about Lídia Noguer, the paranoid woman who had owned the house before, and her two sons, the fishermen, both of whom had ended their days in an asylum in Girona . . . This fantasy that felt like a memory wasn't something I would ever have expected, but I didn't seem to have a choice. It just kept coming to me, unsolicited, as if the cinema inside my head could only play one film. We had always imagined we would visit Dalí at some point. Somehow we didn't manage it. He became too famous, perhaps. Too sought after. As time went on, Gala took more and more control of his life, and she had no interest in us. Probably we weren't famous enough ourselves . . .

On waking, either from a shallow sleep or from a daydream—there was very little difference between the two—I would feel pleasure spiral through me, like smoke lifting from a cigarette, curiosity as well, but then I would realize where I was, and the curiosity and pleasure I had felt would be extinguished, and a dark, cold dread would take their place.

Each silence was the silence that precedes a death sentence.

Each footstep was the footstep of an executioner.

Not long after New Year I was woken in the night by the sound of someone crying. In the cell next to mine was a German soldier who had been found guilty of desertion. I had seen him only once, as I was escorted down the corridor, and there had been no chance to speak to him, but Little Heinrich had told me that his name was Siegfried. Heinrich had also told me, in a whisper, that he sympathized. He too had lost faith in the Nazi cause, and longed for an Allied victory. Standing on my bed, I directed my voice towards the air vent high up in the wall.

"Can you hear me?" I said in German.

The crying stopped, but he didn't reply. Perhaps he was embarrassed.

"Would you like to talk?" I said. "It might make you feel better."

"Did I wake you?" he said.

I told him not to worry about that. Since the verdict, I had only slept in fits and starts.

"They told me I will be shot tomorrow," he said. "In the morning."

"Don't think about tomorrow," I said. "Think about yesterday, and the day before that. Think about what you did, which was so brave."

"No one thinks I was brave."

"I do—and I'll tell other people too. I'll make sure they know your name."

"You're the Frenchwoman, aren't you."

"One of them."

"You have also been sentenced to death."

"Yes."

"If you've also been sentenced to death, you won't have so long to tell people what I did."

I smiled. "Good point."

"Your German's excellent," he said.

I told him I had spoken German all my life, but I had never thought it would come in so useful, or that it would bring about my downfall. I said I had no regrets. I would do the same again.

Siegfried was silent for a while.

"Perhaps I would also do the same again," he said eventually.

"How old are you?"

"Twenty-five."

"I don't have a son," I said. "I don't know what that's like. But if I did have a son, I would hope that he would be like you. Someone who wasn't afraid to stand up for his principles. Someone I could be proud of."

"I don't think my mother will be very proud of me."

"How would you know?"

"She'll see me as a traitor and a coward. That's what people will be saying in the village I come from."

"If that's how she sees you, then she's blind," I said. "It's not her fault. Most of the people in your country have been blinded by the events of the last few years. That was Hitler's great achievement, to rob an entire nation of its sight. If the German people had been seeing clearly, they would never have followed him, or even obeyed him. But you, you're seeing clearly."

On the other side of the wall the silence seemed to have grown much more intense.

"It's your clear sight that upsets them," I went on. "It's because your eyes are open, and theirs are not. That's why they say bad things about you, Siegfried—*if* they say bad things. That is your name, isn't it?"

"Yes," he said.

"You don't mind if I call you that?"

"Of course not. What should I call you?"

"Suzanne."

"It's good of you to talk to me, Suzanne."

"I would put my arms around you if I could. I would comfort you."

"That's what you're doing—with your voice." He paused. "Please don't stop."

I talked to Siegfried for half the night. I tried to be the mother he deserved. This is why I learned the German language, I thought. It was for this. Later, when I ran out of things to say, I sang to him, as I had sung a few months before, for Claude. I sang "Le coeur du poète" and "Fermons nos rideaux" and "Quand les lilas refleuriront." My voice was old and weak, and I doubted he could understand any of the words, but none of that mattered. Though I didn't hear anything from him I kept on singing, just in case he still happened to be listening.

At first light, footsteps came up the corridor and stopped outside his cell. A key turned in the lock. The door scraped open. I called out to Siegfried, telling him I was proud of him, and that I would always remember him. He didn't answer. The door slammed shut, the footsteps faded.

Though I lay quite still, I never heard the firing squad.

They must have shot him somewhere else.

On a February evening, my cell door was unlocked and Little Heinrich appeared, with Koppelmann, the prison governor.

"*Aufstehen,*" Heinrich said, then moved aside.

Reluctantly, I stood.

Koppelmann stepped into the room and briskly rubbed his hands together. "Cold in here."

I said nothing.

Bending down, he tested my pallet with the flat of his hand, as if he were checking into a hotel. Was this curiosity or sarcasm? With the Nazi high command, you could never be sure.

"I have some news," he said.

I waited at the end of the bed, my hands by my sides, my nails pushed fiercely into my palms.

"Your death sentence has been commuted to life imprisonment," he went on. "It seems you won't be executed after all."

"Why's that?" I said.

Koppelmann seemed baffled by my response. "Aren't you pleased?"

"*Pleased?*"

Ever since the trial, I had been living in a state of trepidation. Three months of thinking that I might be shot at any moment. But not knowing which moment. Never knowing. Three months of trying not to think. And now someone was standing in front of me and telling me that none of it was true—and I was supposed to be *pleased?* Besides, I wasn't sure if I believed him. What if this was another of their sadistic games?

Koppelmann was still staring at me. "I'm beginning to understand why Bode was so frustrated. You're quite impossible."

"And my sister's sentence?"

"It has also been commuted." He stepped over to the wall and examined the damp plaster. "You will be allowed to share a cell."

Something burst through me, then slowly dropped and faded, like fireworks falling into a dark sea. I stared at my hands—the small red crescents in my palms.

Koppelmann was watching me over his shoulder. "You're pleased about that at least."

I said nothing.

He still hadn't answered my question, and he wouldn't, and I thought I knew why. He couldn't bring himself to admit that if our sentences were being commuted it was out of weakness.

The war was as good as lost, and the Nazis didn't want it to be known that they had executed two old women. They were feeling apprehensive. They were playing safe. Could Koppelmann read my thoughts? Perhaps. Because he gave a small disgusted shake of his head and then turned on his heel and left.

It was almost two weeks before Claude and I were reunited, long enough for me to wonder if the governor had changed his mind. But he hadn't. When my cell door opened and Claude appeared, I took her in my arms and held her, and I remember nothing except her yellow jacket, which was too close for me to focus on, and the tapping of her heart against my chest, and I thought of the time I called at the apartment on Place du Commerce, the time she ran down the hall and hurled herself at me with such force that she almost knocked me off my feet, her slender arms around my neck, her hot voice in my ear. *I love you, I love you, I love you . . .*

THE WRONG SHOES
FOR A FIRE

1945–1954

When we were released from prison, just fifteen minutes before Churchill's broadcast to mark VE Day, I stayed behind and talked to Otto and Little Heinrich, who had been good to us, but Claude rushed out into the town. On her return, she told me she had struggled to feel any true exhilaration or relief. She felt she was imitating a feeling that ought to have been flooding through her. It had certainly been flooding through the crowds she had mingled with in Royal Square. She had seen a pink hawthorn tree, and it was everything that she was not, its double blossoms seeming to explode in front of her, ecstatic. She sank onto the curb. Began to cry. Something had been given back to us, but at the same time something had been taken, and the sense of loss was more immediate, and more acute. It was as if we had come to rely on the presence of an enemy, and without it there was nothing left to hold us up, nothing we could define ourselves against. Once freedom had been tampered with, she said, it wasn't so easy to reassemble.

Our friend Vera had arranged for us to stay in a house belonging to English people who had abandoned the island in 1940. In an attempt to make us "feel at home," she had brought a few things from St. Brelade's Bay, things Edna had saved from our house before the Nazis raided it—some glass ornaments, an antique chest, and a book of poems by Robert Desnos. Vera was a kind person, but her kindness could feel like an imposition, since she tended to offer services we hadn't asked for and didn't need. What's more, she had converted to Catholicism, and was evangelical about her new religion. Though Claude doubted she would be able to stomach the arrangement for longer than a night or two—she had taken to referring to Vera, rather caustically, as "Faith"—we set off for the house in the late afternoon, pushing a wooden handcart that contained our Red Cross parcels and various personal possessions. We were grimy and flea-bitten, and looking forward to our first hot bath in many months.

Not long after leaving the prison, we saw the woman from the tobacconist walking towards us. This was on Union Street, near the Parish Hall. When the woman caught sight of us she came to a standstill, and one of her hands flew up to her mouth. Then she turned and ran. As she fled down the nearest sidestreet, something bulky tumbled from her pocket. I called after her, but she kept running. She didn't even glance over her shoulder. In the bright sunlight, her crumpled shadow slid along the white brick wall beside her, like a crude evocation of her shock, her shame.

"Her face," I said. "Did you see?"

Claude nodded. "It was green."

I crossed the street. The woman had dropped her purse. Inside, among other things, was her identity card, some loose change, and a photo of a plain young girl with pigtails.

"What shall we do with this?" I asked Claude.

She shrugged. "Hand it in, I suppose."

Outside the police station, she took out a pencil and a small piece of paper. Leaning on a low wall, she scribbled a few words on the paper and slipped it into the woman's purse, next to the photo of the girl.

The officer on duty asked if we wanted to leave our names. After all, he said, moistening his lips, there might be a reward.

Claude told him we weren't interested in rewards.

His smile was sudden and benign. "Well," he said, "it's someone's lucky day, isn't it."

Later, I asked Claude what she had written.

"How much did they pay you?" she said.

We had often suspected someone of betraying us, but we had never been able to work out who it was.

Now we knew.

We stood on the road outside our house. A still blue afternoon, the sun hot against my hair. The fractured metal glitter of the sea. There were fortifications all along the coast, more conspicuous than I remembered, and more ugly. I thought of the slave workers who had lost their lives—some had been buried in the very structures they had been forced to build, if the rumors were to be believed—but nobody was talking about the slave workers, or about the Jews, or about brave people like the Reverend Cohu and Mrs. Gould, who had been deported and were probably now dead. The island had been liberated, and the most important thing, everyone kept saying, was to "get back to normal."

Earlier that day, I had spoken to Edna on the telephone. I had told her we were coming to St. Brelade's Bay. She warned me that the house was in a state. I asked about Kid. She'd had him put down by the vet, she said, not long after we were arrested. If she hadn't done it, the poor thing would have starved—or else the Germans would have killed him. I heard crying in the background. Edna had had a second child while we were in prison. When the phone call was over, I told Claude what I had learned.

"No," she said. "No, no . . ."

I followed her down the slipway and through the door that led into the garden. Everywhere I looked, I saw evidence of the Germans. There were bullet casings in the flower beds and boot marks on the lawn and, worst of all, the concrete wall was still there, crude and blatant, blocking our view of the bay. Claude stood on the terrace, near the front door, and called for Kid, the single syllable lifting plaintively towards the end. She had always believed their lives were intertwined. It was as though he was her shadow or her spirit—the embodiment of some treasured, hidden part of her. If she summoned him, he would hear her. He would come. It was a warm day, and she wore a Burberry raincoat over an elaborate jacket and a pair of trousers cut in the style of jodhpurs. She was sweating.

I asked whether she wanted me to take her coat.

"No," she said again, more sharply.

One by one, she checked the sun traps Kid had always favored—the stone porch, the south-facing windowsills, the roof of the shed.

"Claude," I said, "he's not here."

"Be quiet."

Under the bright fall of light I saw how imprisonment had altered her. She seemed fragile and querulous. Her mouth had lost its youthful certainty.

"He's dead," I said. "Edna—"

She came at me with her fists raised. "Shut up, shut *up*—"

I gripped her wrists to stop her hitting me, then pulled her close and held her until all the fight had gone out of her. He had had a long and happy life, I told her. It would have been cruel to leave him on his own, with no one to care for him.

She pushed back from me. "He's dead." She stared down at the grass, mouth trembling, hands fidgeting in her coat pockets. "I loved him so much."

"I know you did."

I took her in my arms again. She wouldn't hold me, or even move.

The wall at the end of the garden blurred. The smell of hot grass was heady, almost sickening.

"I know you loved him," I said. "I loved him too."

Her body began to shake. She seemed to have forfeited all the power and defiance she had showed during the trial, and I worried that the months in Gloucester Street—especially the months she had spent alone—might have broken her. I closed my eyes and held her tight, my cheek against her hair.

"My little bird," I murmured.

Though we knew the house would have been plundered, not just by the occupying forces but by local opportunists and thieves, we weren't prepared for the scale of the devastation that awaited

us. Much of our furniture had been stolen. Many of our books
and artworks too. Almost all my drawings. Electrical wiring had
been ripped out of the walls. Floorboards had been prized loose.
Edna had told me that German soldiers had been in to clean the
day before—the smell of bleach was so fierce that it burned my
nostrils—but when I opened a cupboard in the drawing room it was
full of everything that had been swept up: torn and crumpled photographs, shards of glass, dried mud. We moved from one room to
the next in silence, like ghosts of ourselves. The sense of emptiness
kept growing. They had taken all the beds except the one where
George and Edna slept. They had taken the curtains, the towels,
the sheets, the lamps, the keys. They had taken the light switches
and the doorknobs. They had even removed the locks.

"There's nothing left," Claude said. "It's just a shell." She
stood in front of her Pleyel, hands clenched into fists against her
thighs. The piano, miraculously, was still there, though someone
had spilled a drink over the keyboard, staining the white keys a
sticky pink. "It's like a rape."

"We still have the most valuable thing of all," I said.

"Our lives. I know." Her voice was dry, sardonic.

She played a chord that jarred the air. The piano needed
tuning.

"Don't worry, my love," I said. "I'll have the whole place
cleaned and painted. I'll make it beautiful again, just like before.
I'll even do something about that wall. In the meantime we'll
stay in a hotel."

My promise felt hollow, rash. What were we going to do for
money? All our assets were in France, and it seemed likely they
would be tied up for years to come. I wasn't even sure how we
would live from day to day.

Later, as I followed Claude out of the house, she came to a halt. "Do you have the camera?"

I nodded. "Yes."

Knowing our Kodak had been seized by the Nazis, Vera had lent us hers.

"Could you take a picture?" she said.

"Of course. Where?"

"Here. In the doorway."

I positioned myself on the terrace with my back to the light and looked into the viewfinder.

"Wait," she said.

She reached into her pocket and took out the metal eagle a German prisoner called Niedermayer had given her as a memento. She brought it up to her mouth and gripped it between her teeth.

I clicked the shutter.

Some weeks later, when the film came back from the developers, the image disappointed me. At first glance, it had none of the drama or daring of the photographs we had taken before the war. Claude was wearing her pale raincoat, and a headscarf was knotted loosely beneath her chin. She had thrust one hand into the pocket of her jodhpurs. Behind her was the front door, which stood half open. Beyond that, the darkness of the interior. Her body cast a thin rind of shadow onto the door's curved stone surround. There were also shadows on her shoulder, and on the hem of her coat, and the shapes reminded me of butterflies. Black butterflies. She had Niedermayer's insignia between her teeth, of course, but in the end it was just a photograph of a woman standing outside a house . . . Then I looked more closely at the expression on her face. She was giving off an unexpected confidence, a kind of optimism, something I hadn't noticed at the time. This was so unlike her that my breath caught in my throat. What lay behind this latest incarnation? Was she celebrating the defeat of our enemy? Presumably. But she also appeared to have been influenced by *Blood and Sand*, a Rudolph Valentino film that had featured a woman dancing with a rose between her teeth. Was she alluding to our love, which had endured in spite of all that we had been through? It seemed too obvious—too simple. There was something I had failed to understand.

It was only years later, when I moved to a different house, that the deeper meaning came to me. As I stood at my bedroom window, watching a stray cat pick its way through my rockery, I thought of Kid. Always a skillful and determined hunter, he would often appear at our front door with the body of his latest victim wedged between his jaws. In the photograph, Claude might well have been referring to both our triumph and our reunion, but she was also paying homage to a member of our family who had not survived. The picture was a performance, as all our pictures were. She wasn't just a Resistance heroine, showing off a trophy from the battle. She was a cat on a doorstep with a mouse.

Towards the end of June, while Claude and I were having breakfast at the Casa Marina, a hotel in St. Helier, I was called to the telephone. The *Jersey Weekly Post* was on the line.

"Is that Miss Schwob?" the journalist said when I picked up the receiver.

"This is Miss Malherbe. Her sister."

"Good." He told me he had been trying to track us down for weeks. He wanted to write a piece for the newspaper. His voice was eager, resonant.

"A piece?" I said.

"An article that covers your experiences during the war."

Claude and I had already been approached by the *Daily Herald*, an English newspaper, and by an American magazine, and Claude had agreed to both the interviews on one condition: I had to do most of the talking. When I asked her why, she told me she wanted our achievements conveyed in simple language, and she thought I would be more direct and less distracting. She was always so perceptive about the newspapers—how powerful they were, and how they lent themselves to all manner of distortion. In that sense, she was her father's daughter.

"One moment." I put down the phone and walked back to the breakfast room. Claude looked up. "Somebody from the *Post* would like to talk to us," I told her.

"About time," she said.

The journalist came to our hotel that same day, in the afternoon. He was younger than I had imagined, with thinning dark hair, and he wore a brown suit that was loose on him. Probably it had belonged to someone else. He began by asking what our crime had been.

"Interesting word," I said. "Not one I would have used."

Claude sat back with her legs crossed, as if she was being treated to an evening at the theater.

I told the journalist about our propaganda campaign, and about our refusal to comply with many of the Nazis' regulations. I told him about our day in court as well. After I had relayed what Claude had said to Sarmsen about our sentencing, I looked across at her and we began to laugh. Our lightheartedness seemed to take the journalist by surprise.

He was curious to know what prison had been like.

I talked about how we were kept apart for the first seven months, and how grateful we were to the other prisoners, who had done so much to lift our spirits. I said we had some very pleasant memories from our stay on Gloucester Street. Once again, the journalist looked startled. I explained that we had made good friends, and mentioned a few of them by name—Hugh Le Cloche, Micky Neil, Evelyn Janrin, Belza Turner, and "the Dynamite Boys," Arnold Bennett and Peter Gray. These young people from the island were heroes, Claude said, interrupting, and we were hoping to keep in touch with them.

The journalist leaned forwards. "How did the Germans treat you?"

"Not badly," I said.

I focused on examples of their foolishness, describing how Bode and Wolf of the Gestapo had clung to the belief that we were part of some far-flung and highly sophisticated network. I also mentioned a conversation I'd had with Lohse in which he had tried to ingratiate himself by telling me how much he hated fighting his "cousins," the English, only to realize, too late, that I was French. When he told me that he also hated fighting the French—you're my cousins too, he said—I asked him if there was anyone he was fighting who he was *not* related to.

The journalist grinned, then glanced at his notepad. "Is it true your house was ransacked?"

I told him many of our most valuable possessions had gone missing. We had lost artworks by Max Ernst, Joan Miró, and Frédéric Delanglade, and limited editions of books by Louis Aragon and Lise Deharme. We had lost the Louis XV furniture we had inherited from our parents. We had even lost some of our clothes. Still, we didn't regret anything that we had done. We would do it all over again. Our only sadness was that our cat had to be destroyed, and that our housekeeper, Edna, and her husband had been imprisoned, even though they were both entirely innocent.

After two hours the journalist stood up and shook our hands. He told us it had been a privilege to meet us.

The following weekend I bought a copy of the *Post*. The article about us took up most of the front page. SENTENCED TO DEATH BY ISLAND NAZIS, the headline said. And underneath, in smaller type: *The Story of Two Gallant Frenchwomen*. I took the newspaper back to the hotel and showed it to Claude, who was sunbathing on the terrace. She began to read. After only a few moments she lowered the paper and started laughing.

"Have you read it?" she asked me.

I said I had.

"Didn't you notice?"

She pointed at the middle of the front page. Inserted into a paragraph that described our interrogations by the Gestapo was a small advertisement that led with the words NON-STOP RELIEF *from* PILES.

She started to read out loud from the advertisement. "Germaloids will completely banish your fear of the daily bowel action—"

"Claude," I said.

Still grinning, she put the paper down.

"Well," she said after a while, "it certainly puts our heroic activities into perspective."

Later that summer, after we had moved back into La Ferme sans Nom, the Bailiff of Jersey telephoned to ask us over for drinks. I thanked him for the kind invitation, but said Claude and I no longer found social occasions comfortable, and that I hoped he would understand if we declined. This wasn't a social occasion, he told me gently. It would be a quiet evening—just him, his wife Babs, and us. Aware that he had pleaded our case with the Nazi high command, and that his intervention had probably helped to save our lives, we felt obliged, in the end, to accept.

When the day came there was a cloudburst, though by the time we arrived at the Bailiff's house in the hills above St. Aubin the storm had moved on. Stepping out of the taxi, I heard a grumble of thunder out over the sea. There was the smell of the warm road cooling, and the trunks of trees gleamed from the recent rain. The Bailiff's wife, Mrs. Coutanche, met us at the door. She told us she was disappointed by the weather. She had been planning on sitting in the garden. It was her husband's passion, she said. He had been gardening on the day the Germans landed. Weeding, in fact. When they came to the house he had greeted them in a crumpled sports coat and a pair of torn gray flannels.

She showed us into the drawing room, where Mr. Coutanche was crouching beside a cocktail cabinet in a dark-blue pinstripe suit. I had only ever seen him from a distance, speaking from a balcony in Royal Square on Liberation Day. Up close, he had a square forehead and melancholy eyes. On the sideboard was a small bowl of crisps.

Usually his butler, Coleman, served the drinks, Coutanche told us, but Coleman was in England, seeing relatives, so he would have to do the honors himself. He hoped he wasn't going to poison us all. His wife's laughter felt dutiful, and her eyes glittered with a strange, unsteady light.

When Coutanche had handed us whiskey-and-sodas and toasted our bravery, I thanked him for all the efforts he had made

on our behalf. If it were not for him, I said, we might not be here
at all. He responded by saying that he had only done what any
Bailiff would have done.

"Crisps, anyone?" Mrs. Coutanche held out the bowl.

Once seated, Claude asked Coutanche about the difficulty of
mediating between the occupying forces and the local population.
She was broaching a delicate subject—some thought the authorities in Jersey had bent over backwards to appease the Nazis—but
Coutanche simply told her he had always been guided by what was
best for the people in his charge. It was a politician's answer, and
I knew Claude would think he was sidestepping the controversial
issue she was trying to address. During the occupation, Claude and
I had been in the minority. Most people had cooperated with the
Nazis, either by looking the other way or by pretending not to notice
what was happening, and this mild form of collaboration had been
seen as acceptable, or even necessary. Those who had gone so far as
to work for the Nazis resented people like us, since our activities had
heightened the tension and threatened, at times, to disrupt the status quo. Once the war was over, the guilt felt by these collaborators
transformed itself into a self-serving brand of optimism. The past
was the past, they would say. Water under the bridge. Anything
that made them feel ill at ease—and that included so-called acts of
heroism—was blotted out or buried, but there had, nonetheless,
been reprisals against those who had consorted with the enemy,
the most vicious being reserved for women who had granted sexual
favors in return for preferential treatment. One woman was pinned
to a tree with nails through the palms of her hands. Another had
a petrol-soaked rag stuffed between her legs and was taunted with
a match. It was rumored that the most flagrant collaborators were
to be removed from the island by British Intelligence in order to

defuse the situation, and Coutanche would know all about this. If he was wary, that perhaps was why.

Before Claude could press him further, I told him about a walk that she and I had taken through St. Helier not long after liberation. As we reached the harbor, two British fighter planes flew overhead, the sound so abrupt and guttural that we didn't hear it so much as feel it, inside our bodies. Moments later, they flew past again, almost scraping the rooftops. A young man in a patched gray suit and clumsy Red Cross boots was standing near us with tears spilling from his eyes. He put both hands over his face, but couldn't stop crying.

I turned to Claude. "Do you remember?"

"I gave him a hug," she said. "I hugged you too."

Coutanche cleared his throat. "It has been an emotional time—for all of us . . ."

In the silence that followed, Claude asked if she could use the WC. Mrs. Coutanche showed her the way. While they were out of the room, the Bailiff rose to his feet and switched on a large brown Bakelite radio.

"Some music, perhaps," he said.

By the time his wife walked back into the room, the radio had warmed up, and a dance band was playing. The blare of saxophones and trumpets, the jaunty, light-fingered rhythm of the drums.

The lush swoop of strings.

Mrs. Coutanche asked about our house. I told her it had been looted and vandalized, and that I had spent all summer trying to restore some order. I had even hired a couple of local men to remove a section of the concrete wall which the Germans had built at the end of our garden. At least we had our view of the bay again, I said. We had also traveled from one end of the island to the other in a car belonging to a doctor friend of ours, trying to recover our stolen possessions.

"Any success?" Mrs. Coutanche asked.

I told her about an afternoon in late August. Claude and I had been in Grouville, on the trail of a missing Max Ernst collage, when we saw a woman strolling along the seafront in one of Claude's favorite coats. When we challenged the woman, she claimed the coat was hers. It was a gift. Claude wanted to know which Nazi officer had given it to her.

"A fair question," Coutanche said.

"The woman was furious," I told him. "She gave Claude a push, and Claude tripped and fell."

I had helped Claude to her feet. She was shaken, pale. You know what? Claude said to the woman. Keep the bloody coat. I will, the woman said. People on the promenade were staring. Claude let me lead her away, but we had only walked a few steps when she jerked her arm out of my grip and turned around. She had just remembered the word the islanders used for women who had fraternized with German officers. Jerrybag, she said. Then she said it again. Louder. So everyone could hear.

Mrs. Coutanche shook her head and looked at the floor.

"And the Max Ernst piece?" Coutanche asked.

"It was a false lead. I don't think we'll ever see it again." I suddenly realized that ten minutes had gone by, and Claude had not returned. "I should check on my sister," I said. "She's not been well."

As I climbed the stairs, I wondered how long the Bailiff and his wife expected us to stay.

I knocked on the bathroom door. "Claude? Are you all right?"

"Nearly finished," she said.

Back in the drawing room, I said that Claude would be down soon. We sat with our drinks and listened as the band played a foxtrot. Mrs. Coutanche stood up and opened a window. Cool night air drifted in. Her husband had crossed his legs, and his right foot moved in time with the music.

As the foxtrot ended and applause burst through the room, Claude appeared in the doorway. She had shaved off both her eyebrows.

"Oh," Mrs. Coutanche said. "Well." She turned to her husband and smiled brightly. She was attempting to laugh the whole thing off, but she was uncertain of her ground. I sensed that she might even be frightened. I glanced at Claude. She gave me a little shrug.

"Would anybody like a top-up?" Coutanche said. "I think I could do with one."

"Thank you," I said.

Claude, too, held out her glass.

A new dance number began as Coutanche mixed the drinks. His wife's smile had faded, and she was examining one of her rings.

"When Herodotus traveled to Egypt in the fifth century BC," Claude said, once Coutanche had handed us fresh drinks, "one of the aspects of society that most fascinated him was its attitude to cats." She sipped her whiskey. "This is excellent."

Coutanche gave her a salute that looked vaguely nautical. Was he drunk?

"Cats protected the grain stores from mice and rats," Claude went on. "They also killed snakes. Tomb wall paintings show that Egyptians took cats hunting with them in the marshes. If there had been no cats, the people would probably have starved."

"I didn't know that," Mrs. Coutanche said.

Claude lit a cigarette. "In the temple of Beni Hasan, which was dedicated to the feline goddess Pahket, a cemetery was found. There was a layer of mummified cats beneath the ground—thousands of them. Some had gilded faces. Pots of milk had been buried with them. Vermin too. Provisions for the afterlife. Cats weren't just loved. They were revered." She tapped half an inch of ash into a nearby ashtray. "When a cat died, the people it belonged to would go into mourning, as if they had lost a relative. All the members of that particular family would shave off their eyebrows."

I turned to the Bailiff and his wife. "Our cat was put down while we were in prison—"

"His name was Kid," Claude said. "I named him after Captain Kidd, a pirate my uncle wrote about in one of his biographical fictions."

Coutanche leaned forwards in his chair. "When you came back from the bathroom, I knew your appearance had altered in some way, but I couldn't for the life of me work out how." His gaze darted from Claude's face to mine and back again. "I looked and looked, and I simply couldn't see what was different—and then, suddenly, I could. Peculiar, don't you think?"

"It's not the first time it has happened," I said.

Mrs. Coutanche steered a bright, seemingly disdainful glance in my direction. "Why? Have you lost a cat before?"

Everybody stared at her, even her husband. Lowering her eyes, she scrutinized her drink.

Coutanche began to talk about Egypt, which was a country he seemed to have read about, and which was, therefore, a subject on which he could hold forth at some length, and the matter of

Claude's bizarre behavior was glossed over and pushed into the background, but never, I felt, entirely forgotten.

Within a few days of his appointment to the parish of St. Brelade, the new rector called on us. When I answered the door, he was standing on the terrace, the glory of the garden behind him like a kind of halo. He had a confident, almost condescending manner, as if his presence in our house was a rare honor. Being well connected was clearly important to him, since he managed to mention several members of the island's aristocracy before I could even show him into the drawing room.

"I'm told you live here with your sister," he said when he was seated with a cup of tea.

"Yes. She's upstairs, working."

"Close-knit families: the cornerstone of any decent society."

"I'm not sure we provide much of a cornerstone," I said.

He received my words thoughtfully, and with a certain gravity, as if I were confiding in him, or confessing. Though this felt presumptuous and I objected to it, I found myself elaborating.

"We tend to keep ourselves to ourselves. We're very private." I paused, and then, to my surprise, went further still. "We live differently to others."

"You weren't always private—during the war, for instance . . ."

"I'm not sure who you've been talking to."

"Am I wrong?"

"It was our privacy that was the secret of our success," I told him. "If we hadn't kept ourselves to ourselves, if we hadn't been something of a mystery, the authorities would have suspected us much sooner."

The rector looked towards the window. He seemed to decide the subject was controversial, and that he had pursued it as far as he could. His wrists, I noticed, were covered with silky black hairs.

He was about to speak again when the door opened and Claude appeared, a cigarette between her lips. The skin under her eyes was dark, as if colored in with ink, and the thinness of her neck made her head look big. It wasn't just the months in prison that had undermined her, though for someone with Claude's fragile constitution that might, in itself, have been enough. She had also lost some of those who were closest to her. Béatrice Wanger had died in New York, of lung cancer. Lilette Richter had died too, after suffering months of chronic stomach pain. And Robert Desnos was missing, believed dead. Towards the end of the war he had been arrested by the Nazis and sent to a camp. We had no details. All we knew was that he had not returned. As for the friends who had survived, they seemed to have stopped writing to her. She was lonely, she had told me. She was ill with loneliness. Not so long ago, an abscess on her kidney had almost killed her. She had started to talk about moving back to Paris.

The rector stood. When they had shaken hands, Claude took up a position by the fireplace, one elbow resting on the mantelpiece, her right ankle crossed over her left. Though what she was wearing was understated—a white cable-knit sweater, loose trousers of gray serge, and a laborer's cloth cap—the rector didn't seem to know where to look. It was still unusual, at that time, for a woman to be seen in trousers.

"I've always been fascinated by your profession," Claude said.

The rector adjusted his black robes. "I prefer to think of it as a calling. A vocation."

"I like to think that I was called too," Claude said.

"Though not to the Church . . ."

"No." Claude stubbed out her cigarette. "I have to say, I expected more of the Church during the war." The rector's eyes followed her from the fireplace to the open window. "I've read the Bible—as much, at least, as I could stand—and I seem to remember there being a great deal of talk about charity. About looking after those who are less fortunate than ourselves."

The rector nodded. "'And whosoever hath this world's good, and seeth his brother have need, and shutteth up his compassion from him, how dwelleth the love of God in him?' 1 John 3:17."

"Very good," Claude said, almost as if he were a pupil in a class she was teaching. "But the Jews were in need, and so were the Russian slave workers, and the Church did absolutely nothing."

"I wasn't here during the war."

"That's beside the point. Jews were persecuted, then deported. Slave workers were routinely brutalized, starved, and killed. All of this in plain sight. And the Church made no attempt to stand up for them." She fingered the ivy that grew around the window. "The Church passed by on the other side, so to speak."

The rector lowered his eyes, but not, I thought, out of shame or regret.

"Actually, that's not quite accurate," Claude said. "There was one man—one *Christian*." She gave the word a sardonic twist. "Canon Cohu. Have you heard of him?"

"I know the name."

"Clifford Cohu. He was born in Guernsey, but spent most of his adult life in England. He returned to the Channel Islands just before war broke out. By then he was in his fifties. When the occupation began, he spoke out against the Nazis, both from his pulpit and on the streets. In 1943, he was sentenced to eighteen months' imprisonment for spreading 'anti-German news.' He was sent to Saarbrücken, then to a camp near Frankfurt, where he was kept in solitary confinement. In 1944, he was transferred to Zöschen. He was singled out for special treatment by the SS guards because they saw him as English. He was severely beaten. He died in September of that year, aged sixty."

"It's a terrible story," the rector said.

"Yes, it is."

He watched Claude as she walked back to the fireplace and lit another cigarette. "Can we expect to see you in church?"

She gave him a long, cool look, the blue smoke rising past her face. "Unlikely."

"We're Marxists," I said.

"I see. Well." He glanced at his watch, then stood up and turned to me. "Thank you for the tea."

"You're leaving?" Claude said.

He nodded. "I have other people to call on. Other parishioners."

"Was I too hard on him?" Claude asked me after I had showed him out.

"Perhaps," I said.

"He seemed oddly aggressive. He kept staring at me." She paused. "Do you think he was attracted to me?"

"Only if he likes boys."

She laughed and threw her cigarette into the grate.

I woke at dawn to see that Claude's side of the bed was undisturbed. It didn't worry me. Since our time in prison, she was troubled more than ever by insomnia. Also, she spent most of the day in bed, either resting or working on her account of our wartime activities. In the small hours she would play the piano. Through a thin layer of sleep I would often hear the sparse, silvery notes of a piece by Erik Satie, or a Chopin nocturne, more melancholy, and more liquid. I walked along the landing to her study. The room was empty. A copy of *Fleurs du mal* lay open on her desk, flakes of ash scattered across its pages.

I went downstairs. On the kitchen table was a jug of lilac stems and a blue bowl crowded with dusty green plums. There was no sign of Claude there either, though the coffeepot on the stove was warm. I opened the door and stepped outside. The lawn glistened. It was one of those late summer days that begins with a low-level shifting mist and the smell of dew-soaked vegetation. I moved towards the part of the garden that overlooked the graveyard. Beyond the church, just visible among the trees, was the house where the rector lived. A gull wheeled, screeching, overhead.

Then I saw her.

She was wandering among the tombs in a gauzy transparent garment that resembled a nightgown. On her head was a white leather flying helmet. Her feet were bare. Since the clothes she was wearing were pale, there were moments when she blended with the mist and almost disappeared. Following the rector's visit, we had speculated as to his secret predilections, and Claude liked to refer to the speed with which he had retreated, as if he feared that she might lead him from the path of righteousness. I wondered if her early morning excursion to the churchyard in that revealing outfit wasn't partly intended as an assault on what she perceived as his resolve—or was she dancing for La Belle Nadja, our dead friend?

A movement to my right distracted me. A girl stood at the top of the slipway. She had blond hair and wore a simple yellow sundress. I didn't recognize her. Like me, she had noticed Claude, though she was staring, wide-eyed and open-mouthed. Perhaps she took Claude for a ghost. Deep in a kind of reverie, Claude remained oblivious, her right hand floating in the air above a nearby grave. The girl shook herself and hurried down the slip-way, glancing over her shoulder as if she was anxious that she might be followed. Once on the beach, she stopped to undo her sandals, hooked a finger through the straps, and then ran on.

Sometime in the late forties, Claude received a shipment of fabric from a haberdashery in Paris. Inspired by eighteenth-century English silk merchants, Claude had been planning to line the walls of the room that she retired to when she couldn't sleep. She had based the design on the paper that had covered our bedroom walls in rue Notre-Dame-des-Champs—a dusting of small stars on a ground of midnight blue—and had been eagerly awaiting the delivery. I helped her lift the cylindrical package onto the kitchen table. As we removed the brown paper wrapping and unrolled the bolt of cloth, my elbow caught the handle of the coffeepot and coffee splashed onto the silk.

"It's ruined." Claude's voice was eerily matter-of-fact. "The whole thing's ruined."

"It's only the edge," I told her. "I can easily—"

"You ruined it." Her face drained of color, and her hands clenched into fists, the knuckles white. "It's no use to me now. I might as well throw it out."

She began to hurl insults at me. I was careless and stupid. I had no feeling for fine things. My hands were ugly. I was shocked into stillness by this onslaught, and this stillness seemed to infuriate her even more. I was vulgar. Wooden. I was a drone. I couldn't bear to see her succeed at anything. I wanted to undermine her. Destroy her.

I backed away and left the room. My head filled with a kind of tangling or static. I felt close to madness then. I knew what it was. No thoughts, just knots and noise. I found myself outside, in the garden. I had no idea where I was going. A place where I couldn't hear her voice, I suppose.

"You think you can just walk away?"

It was evening, the sky above the sea already darkening, but flecked with bright-brown filaments, like threads of saffron. The inside of my head felt swollen, queasy. Numb. Was this the end of everything?

Claude stood behind me. She was like a piece of paper curling in the heart of a blaze. "You think you can walk away from me and things will be all right?"

Niké, Kid's replacement, fled across the lawn.

"You're frightening the cat," I said.

"You're talking about the *cat*? Listen to yourself. You're ridiculous. Pathetic."

She came at me so fast, and with such venom. I had no time to think. If I answered back, it fueled her rage. If I kept quiet, she thought I was being dismissive, or critical, or even—and this was worse—indifferent, and she became more furious still. But if you can't speak, and you can't not speak, what are you meant to do? There's no third place.

I reached the bottom of the garden. Intent on concealing or disguising the German wall, Claude had planted ivy, honeysuckle, and tall green ferns, and we would often sit facing each other in the carved-out gap, with our backs supported and our legs stretched out. It had become a place where we read books or took the sun. I leaned on the rough concrete and laid my forehead on my arms. Behind me, Claude was still raging.

"Oh, so *you're* the one who's suffering. *Poor Suzanne*—"

I decided to make one last attempt.

"I'm sorry," I said. "It was an accident."

"And I'm supposed to forgive you, am I, just like that?" She hit me in the lower back. The pain was a bright flash, a picture taken in the darkness of my body.

Though I was doubled over, I managed to grab her by the wrist.

She struggled to free herself. "Get *off.*"

"Stop it!" I shouted. "Shut up. Go back inside."

She suddenly went slack. I let go of her. She walked back across the lawn, her head lowered. The sky's orange filaments had faded. A door slammed deep inside the house. There was poison in her blood, and I didn't have the antidote. All I could do for her was stay. Not go.

Later, I found her curled up naked on our bed. Dim light from the window traced the curve of her right hip. She lay quite still, but there was no peace in the room. A force field flickered round her body, a muted crackle or sizzle, as if she was not a woman but an electric fence. I stood near the door, unsure if I should approach her.

"Are you all right?" she murmured.

I sat on the edge of the bed.

Shifting her position, she put her arms round me, her breath feathery against my neck. Her skin was cool.

"I don't remember what happened," she said. "I don't remember what I did."

"You don't want to know."

"It was that bad?"

"Yes."

"I said terrible things . . ."

"Yes."

"I'm sorry."

She had molded herself against me, as if to remove all the distance and tension that had come between us. Her arms circled my belly, and she had pressed her face into the space between my shoulder blades. I could feel an area of heat where she was breathing into my shirt.

There were things I couldn't bring myself to tell her.

You hit me.

"I'm sorry," she said again. "I don't know what I'd do without you."

Sometimes the person you're closest to is the one you understand the least. Sometimes, when you're that close, everything just blurs.

Or were things clearer than they had ever been?

She lay beside me, fast asleep, her face turned away from me, towards the window. The summer of 1949. Four years since our release, and time enough to have made the house our own again. Time enough, also, to have resigned ourselves to our many losses. It was hard to believe the war was over. It was equally hard to believe that it had ever happened. The truth lay in the gap between the two, perhaps, a gap in which I sometimes felt that Claude had become marooned.

Though she was brown from our many afternoons on the beach or in the garden, a white band ran up over her shoulder, the ghostly afterimage of the bathing suit she wore if we were in a public place, and the space behind her ear, that subtle curve of bone, was also pale. Traces of lipstick clung to one corner of her mouth, and her hair, which stood out against the whiteness of the pillow, hesitated between blond and gray. A pulse tapped in the thin skin of her neck.

My little bird.

I kissed the outer edge of her right eye. "I love you," I murmured. "I always will."

She brushed at her face as if a fly had landed there. I stroked her hair, then lay with my cheek against her naked back. Outside, there was no wind. Behind her breathing I could hear the breathing of the sea.

I dozed.

"Fire," she said.

She was lying on her back, one forearm draped over her eyes. I waited to see what she would say next.

"A small house by the water," she said. "The roar of the flames, the swans taking off—and Dalí with the wrong shoes on."

I leaned up on one elbow. "The wrong shoes?"

"The wrong shoes for a fire." Though her eyes were covered, I could see her mouth. She was smiling. "Gold high heels."

On waking, Claude would often speak directly from her dreams. Like the Surrealists, she believed dreams had a way of throwing light on the fundamental questions of our daily lives. Sometimes it was an image, sometimes a line of dialogue. Sometimes it was just an atmosphere. She said the photographs we took together came from dreams. The photographs *were* dreams. Attempts to capture or decode her volatile and fluctuating self. Attempts at the impossible, in other words, for even as the shutter clicked she was beginning to change into someone else. Some*thing* else. Michaux had told her once that the self wasn't one thing, but many. Nothing was fixed or stable. To be was to become. He liked to claim that he had multiple selves trapped inside his body. It was one of the causes of his great fatigue.

Claude asked if I remembered what René Crevel had said about Dalí's bedroom.

"Yes," I said. "He had a mirror on the wall that was angled towards the window. It was so he could lie in bed and watch the sun come up."

"That wasn't the reason."

She told me that Dalí wanted to wake up every morning with his face bathed in sunlight, illuminated and golden, like a mythical creature. Like a hero. Like a god.

"The mirror wasn't there to help him see the sun," she said. "It was there to help the sun see him."

I smiled. Dalí's imagination was unguarded, free of all restraints and inhibitions. He was like a child, demanding and perverse—the absolute center of his world.

"You think he still lives in the madwoman's cottage?" Claude asked.

"When he's not traveling the world," I said, "being lionized."

"He deserves it. His work's astonishing."

"I used to think about that place when I was in my cell. I thought about it all the time. I'm not sure why."

"The things we could have done," Claude said, "but didn't . . ." Her arm was still draped over her eyes. "What's the weather like?"

I got out of bed and walked to the window. "Sunny. Cool, though."

"Maybe we should take some photographs today."

"Maybe."

As I crossed the room, still thinking of the fire, the frantic beating of swans' wings, the gold high heels, I suddenly remembered what had happened to Marie-Louise. During the war she had finally left Gaston, her husband, and had married Henri Michaux. One evening, though, her nightgown had caught fire. The burns had been so severe that she had died. On reaching the door, I stopped and looked at Claude.

"Do you think you were dreaming about Marie-Louise?"

"No," Claude said, her face in profile. "I was dreaming about my mother."

Those bright, brittle years after the war. They seemed ethereal, even at the time. We should rightfully have been dead, both of us, and yet there we were, back in our house, and still together. We were like cats, Claude told me, with our nine lives . . .

Who was it who said that at every moment we stand on the edge of eternity? I don't remember. But that was how it felt to live with her.

That was how it felt from the beginning.

Something woke me. A subtle shift in the air. I could smell whiskey and cigarette smoke, and something cold was being held against my throat. Claude was bending over me, her head close to mine.

"Don't move," she said.

Her face was stiff, her eyes glittering through peepholes in her skin. What had she written once? *Under this mask, another mask.*

And then another. I will never finish removing all the masks. The ceiling above her tilted at an angle, like a ship's deck in heavy seas.

"What are you doing?" I said.

"Be careful." Her voice was tender, dreamy. "This knife is sharp. I sharpened it."

Perhaps that was the noise that had woken me—Claude crouching at the kitchen table with a knife in one hand and a whetstone in the other.

"I had a revelation," she said. "If I kill you, I will be free to die."

She had been prevented from taking her own life by the fact of my existence. She couldn't bring herself to leave me. If she killed me first, though, she would be removing all the obstacles. It was entirely logical, a brilliant resolution of her dilemma. So what could I say that would dissuade her? I swallowed, the tendons in my neck pushing cautiously against the blade.

"Claude?"

"What?"

"I love you."

"I love you too." Her voice was drowsy, drugged.

"Do you?"

"Of course I do," she said. "Very much."

The gulf between her words and the knife was a wide one, and I didn't know if I could close it.

"Will you come for a walk?" I said.

"Now?" She looked towards the window. Moonlight on the ivy, a lick of silver on the black.

"Walking at night," I said. "There's nothing better."

Though she didn't seem sure how to respond, I felt the blade leave my throat. I remained where I was, on my back, the ghost of the knife still with me, a cold line on my skin.

Keep talking. Don't give her time to think.

"Hand in hand through the darkness," I said, "the night wind on our faces, and in our hair—"

"You're trying to trick me."

Claude was clever. Even this new, twisted version of Claude was clever. I had found a way of speaking to her, though. It was a matter of stalling her. Deflecting her. I had to insert doubts and possibilities into her thinking, like slack into a rope.

"A little walk," I said. "After that, you can do what you want."

"All right." She put the knife down on the bedside table, where it caught the light, like a thin spill of water. "Will I need shoes?"

"Yes, you will."

She followed me downstairs, mute but powerful. Once in the hall, I found a pair of Wellingtons for her, then I helped her into a coat. She was docile, but the Claude I knew was still concealed. I opened the front door. A shoulder of air pushed past me, the smell of grass and brine. My plan was a simple one. We would keep walking until whatever it was that had possessed her had been worn down or driven out.

We left the garden and crossed the slipway, Niké running ahead of us. Everything was restless—the plants, the trees, the sea. Our end of the bay was sheltered by the pier, but farther down the beach huge waves hurled themselves against the sand with the deep dull sound of thunder. We entered the churchyard. Lights showed in the windows of the manor house. The rector was still awake. We skirted the Fishermen's Chapel and passed through the wicket gate. I looked behind me. Niké was sitting upright on a grave, watching us. She had reached the limits of her territory.

Above Beauport beach I stopped to rest. The sky was full of ragged clouds, a blurred half-moon dropping in the west. Below us was the field of bracken where we used to lie on hot days when we were in our twenties. We had made love in that bracken. But this was a different Claude, a Claude I hardly recognized. I asked her if she was all right. The soaring of the wind and the rush of waves against the rocks were so loud that I had to shout. She nodded. On her face was a look of uncertainty, as if she no longer knew what we were doing, or how it had begun. Perhaps the spell was losing its grip. I couldn't risk turning back, though, not until she was herself again. But what if that didn't happen? What if the woman I loved had disappeared forever? What if the madness that had fixed her with its eyes was real? I had to push that prospect to the darkest corner of my mind.

"Come on," I said.

Beyond Beauport beach, the path climbed upwards again, following the coast with all its intricate coves and inlets. There was less cover now, there were fewer trees. Only rugged heath-land, coarse grass. A few hundred yards offshore was a rash of small, protruding rocks known as Les Kaines, though I couldn't see them in the dark. It was in my mind to walk to the lighthouse at Corbières, or even to the long, west-facing beach at St. Ouen, where the waves would roll in unimpeded from the open sea, enormous and deafening, but as the path rounded a splintered crag we were met by the full force of the wind, and it almost knocked me off my feet.

Claude tugged at my sleeve. "Shouldn't we go back?"

The woman who had been intent on killing me had given way to someone else, someone who was younger and more fearful. If I had asked her about what had happened in the bedroom, I doubt she would have understood, or even remembered. But I had to make quite sure.

"Not yet," I said. "It's such a beautiful night."

I walked on.

Later, as we paused for breath above the jagged, hostile shore at Fiquet Bay, Claude wrapped her arms around herself and stared out towards the invisible horizon. "How far are we going?"

"Not far."

"I'm really tired."

"Just a little farther," I said. "Soon it will be dawn."

At the beginning of the fifties, Claude became obsessed by the idea of moving. She claimed the island was too crowded, and that she was starved of intellectual stimulation, but I sensed that the quest for privacy and peace, once so important to her, had begun to seem perverse, if not dangerous. Perhaps, after all, she had some memory of the night she held a knife against my throat, that long walk in the wind . . .

By early 1953, her plans to visit Paris had taken shape. Jean Schuster wanted to meet her, she told me—Schuster had become the leader of the Surrealist movement, and was seeking her involvement—but I knew she would also be searching for somewhere to live. I had become resigned to the move. If nothing else, it would solve our financial problems.

Claude left in June and was gone for a fortnight.

When she returned, she talked too fast, her sentences tumbling over one another, as they used to when she was young. At first she had stayed at the Hôtel Le Royal. After a few days, though, she had moved to the Lutetia, which was quieter. She had looked at several apartments in Vavin, but hadn't seen anything she liked. Though most of the shops and restaurants we had frequented were still open, the area felt unfamiliar. The war had driven a wedge between the present and the past. Not long after arriving in the city, she managed to track down André Breton.

I asked her how he was.

"I don't want to talk about it," she said.

That evening, we walked along the beach to the Café des Amis. When we had ordered our drinks, I asked once again about the meeting with Breton. According to Claude, he had spent most of the time talking about his new wife, Elisa.

"Is that his third wife or his fourth?" I said. "I've completely lost count."

"His third."

"He has never been short of women, has he? Simone, Colette—Jacqueline—"

"You don't have to list them all," Claude snapped.

When we were first drawn into Breton's orbit, I thought I had sensed a longing in Claude. It wasn't something she ever expressed in words, but it had showed, I felt, in the way her gaze would linger on him when he appeared with somebody new. It was almost as if she was silently pleading. *Can't I be with you too—at least for a short time? Can't I be one of the many? Am I not even good enough for that?* Were I to have put it to her, though, she would have denied it. Had I imagined her interest in him?

"Whenever we talk about Breton," I said, "you lose your sense of humor. Why is that?"

"Why is it that you're always talking about him? Could it be that you're jealous?"

I looked down at my hands. *Was* I jealous? Could one be jealous of a possibility, something that had never even happened?

"You're always so measured," Claude said. "So faithful. Fidelity is cowardice at some level, don't you think? A fear of truly risking yourself—of finding out who you are, or who you might become . . ."

We were sitting at a table in the corner, and no one was listening. All the same, I lowered my voice. "I *have* risked myself—by being with you. I've risked everything to be with you."

Claude shook her head. "You're limited."

"The way I love you isn't limited. It's anything but that."

"But it's always me, just me. I carry your love around with me like a weight. Like a handicap. Because it's never in doubt. It's so—I don't know—unquestioning. It's a habit. It's as far as you can go."

I'd had enough.

"And you," I said, no longer bothering to keep my voice down, "you who are so *unpredictable*—or so you'd have us believe—are unbelievably predictable in this. I knew what mood you'd be in when you came back from seeing him. I knew what effect he would have on you. Perhaps, in the end, *you're* the one who's limited." I took a breath. "Perhaps *you're* the coward."

I worried she might lose her temper. Instead, something inside her appeared to unfurl.

"You're remarkable, Suzanne," she said.

She reached across the table for my hand, but I pulled it away. I wanted to hold on to my anger. Outside, it was dark.

"Really," she said. "You are."

The following day, at breakfast, Claude admitted she had felt apprehensive about the meeting with Breton—"unhorsed," as she put it—and that when she sat down at his table he gave off an air of disappointment, as if she didn't quite live up to his expectations, as if he had remembered her differently. He seemed baffled, even affronted, by her lack of productivity, insisting that she must write, and referring more than once to her silence, which he found "profligate." In her letters, she had told him about our campaign against the Nazis, and about the months we had spent in prison, but the subject appeared to make him uncomfortable, and he avoided it. Their conversation veered from the bizarre to the inconsequential. He talked about a fire that had broken out in his building, and described how he had run down the stairs and out onto the street in his pajamas, clutching a tribal mask under one arm and *The Child's Brain*, a painting by de Chirico, under the other. He told the story with great solemnity, and also with a sense of outrage. That something like that should happen to *him*. To her consternation, Claude felt she might be about to laugh. She excused herself and left the table. Perhaps she didn't know him as well as she had thought, or perhaps too many years had passed. In any case, the whole thing had been a disaster.

By the time she returned from the powder room, Breton had lapsed into a kind of melancholy. He mentioned the recent deaths of several close friends—Paul Éluard, Jindřich Heisler, Pierre Mabille—none of whom, he said, had even reached the age of sixty.

"And Desnos?" Claude said. "Do you know what happened to him?"

Breton shook his head. "People think he died in a camp. It seemed he was a member of a Resistance group called Agir."

He didn't know much more than she did. After all, he had been away, in America.

"You heard that I got married," he said.

Claude nodded. "It must be exhausting to have to explain yourself all over again. I admire your energy."

"With Elisa," Breton said, "it wasn't so exhausting . . ."

Claude had to sit and listen as he sang the praises of his new wife, who was a polyglot and a pianist, and who spoke French with an accent that he found "exotic." She had grown up in Chile, he said. Her father was a diplomat. He had been attracted by the look of sadness on her face. In the summer of 1943, her only child, Ximena, had drowned during a boating trip in Massachusetts. Elisa had subsequently attempted suicide. Four months later, just before Christmas, he had met her at a restaurant in Manhattan. *I was attracted by the look of sadness on her face . . .* Once again, Claude felt impossibly torn between boredom and hilarity, but she was rescued by the arrival of the Czech artist, Toyen.

The next day, Breton wrote to Claude, apologizing for having been distracted and inattentive. He had been preoccupied with a forthcoming trip to the United States, he said. He hoped they would see each other again before too long. Claude was touched by his readiness to accept responsibility for any awkwardness. In retrospect, she felt embarrassed by her own behavior, which had been inappropriate. Still, if his letter was to be believed, he hadn't noticed, and for that she was grateful.

"Did I tell you I saw Youki?"

Towards the end of her two weeks in Paris, Claude told me, she had met Youki in the Café de Flore. When she walked in, Youki was sitting with her back to the window, in a black velvet jacket and a pair of sunglasses. She was still beautiful, though her looks had coarsened and her voice was huskier. She told Claude about a recent affair she'd had—a South American poker player, weekends in Monte Carlo—but Claude kept thinking about Robert and as soon as the story came to an end she asked about him.

Youki lowered her eyes and crushed out her cigarette. "Robert," she said. "It's all anyone wants to talk about."

"I'd like to know what happened," Claude said.

Youki looked away from her, towards the door. Now her face was in profile, Claude could see behind her sunglasses. Her eyes were puffy, dry.

Claude leaned across the table and put a hand on Youki's hand. "You have to tell me. I loved him too."

Youki sighed.

In a voice that was rough-edged and sour, she said she had been the last to know that Robert was working for the Resistance. He hadn't trusted her enough to tell her. Though Claude tried to look sympathetic, she didn't blame him. Youki would never have intended to give Robert away, but like Edna, our old housekeeper, she became wildly indiscreet when she was drinking. No secret was ever safe with her.

The first she knew of his involvement, she said, was when the telephone rang on the morning of February 22, 1944. It was a woman who worked at *Aujourd'hui,* a newspaper Robert had been writing for. She wanted to warn him that Gestapo agents were looking for him. There had been ample time for Robert to escape, Youki said, but he had been hiding the son of her dressmaker above a false ceiling in the kitchen, and he wanted to make sure that the young man wasn't caught. He had also been unwilling to leave her on her own. If he fled, she might be arrested in his place, and rumor had it that women were being tortured in an anonymous building on rue Lauriston. He was still hesitating when there was a loud knocking on the door. The three Gestapo agents who entered were in plain clothes, and were led by an officer with bright blond hair. After only a few minutes, they found a piece of paper hidden in the binding of a book. On it were written a number of names and addresses. Robert tried to pretend it was a list of his contacts in the world of publishing. He was a journalist, he said. A poet too. The fair-haired officer smiled sadly, as if Robert's failure to lie successfully had disappointed him. Youki began to cry. Before Robert was led away, he handed her his favorite Parker pen. Keep it safe for me, my darling, he called out as the Gestapo escorted him down the stairs.

He was taken to Fresnes prison on the outskirts of Paris, and then to Royallieu, a transit camp near Compiègne. Youki's first care package contained clothing, shoes, a hat, some cutlery, a pouch of tobacco, and a pipe. She also included fresh fruit, half a chicken in aspic, tins of sardines and tuna, and jars of mustard, jam, and honey. The German soldier who delivered the package joked that Robert's wife must be divorcing him, since she appeared to have sent him all his worldly possessions. All my worldly possessions? Robert laughed. These are just the basics. Another package followed shortly afterwards, filled with champagne, cigarettes, sausages, eau de cologne, port, chocolate, and three kilos of bread, which she had secured using fake bread tickets that she had forged herself. When she visited Robert a few weeks after his arrest, he was wearing the leather jacket and khaki trousers she had sent. He looked wonderful, she thought.

She reached under her dark glasses and wiped her eyes.

On her return to Paris, she tried to plead Robert's case with the Gestapo, and might have succeeded, had it not been for the intervention of a right-wing journalist called Laubreaux, a man Robert despised and had once insulted. Laubreaux told Gestapo agents that Robert posed a threat, and they believed him. Her request for Robert's release was rejected.

Following a tip-off that he was about to be deported to a labor camp, Youki once again traveled down to Compiègne. She arrived in time to see a long line of prisoners being marched towards the railway station. She couldn't reach Robert to hand over the cigarettes she had brought, but he waved at her and called out that he would be back soon, and that she should not forget to give his love to all their friends. He boarded a train to Auschwitz-Birkenau, where he received a second tattoo. This time it was a number. 185443.

After a couple of months he was transported to Buchenwald. His courage and his sense of humor lifted the spirits of everyone around him. When it was rumored he might be moving again, east this time, to Flossenbürg, he smiled and said he was happy to be led by his destiny. He wanted to see "as many camps as possible."

"That sounds just like him," Claude said.

From that point on, Youki went on, the information became more sketchy. From Flossenbürg, Robert was transferred to Flöha on the German-Czech border, where he and his fellow prisoners were housed in a disused textile factory. He threw soup in a guard's face and was subjected to a vicious beating. His glasses were destroyed. In the spring of 1945, having survived a three-week death march, he arrived at Terezín. On the day the camp was liberated, a soldier photographed a group of prisoners in striped clothing sitting on the ground. One of the men was caught in profile, his head resting against the shoulder of a bald man in a dark coat. He bore a close resemblance to Robert. If indeed it was Robert, it was the last picture ever taken of him. Weakened by dysentery and a high fever, he contracted typhus. He died on June 8, just a month after the Germans surrendered.

Claude asked Youki if she had seen the photograph.

Youki nodded.

"How did he look?" Claude asked.

"How do you think he looked?"

Youki was silent for a long time, smoking and staring out of the window.

"He looked exhausted and frightened," she said at last. "He looked like someone who was about to be hit."

Claude lowered her head.

"I always wondered who the bald man was," Youki went on. "Was he a stranger, someone who just happened to be sitting next to Robert when the photograph was taken, or was he a friend? Did he live or die? What was his name?" Tears ran from beneath her dark glasses. "I'm sorry." She took off the glasses and dabbed her eyes.

Claude walked round the table and bent over her and held her in her arms. Youki stared straight ahead. A couple sitting nearby looked at them, then looked away.

"I wrote him a letter," Youki said. "This was in July 1945."

She promised she would devote the rest of her life to him. She would help him to forget the nightmare of the last fifteen months. She sent him a kiss "as big as the Eiffel Tower." Before she could post the letter, though, a friend called and told her Robert was dead. She still had the letter, she said. She couldn't bring herself to throw it away. She didn't know why.

Three months later, at nine in the morning, her doorbell rang. A man in a shabby raincoat was standing in the stairwell. He was from the French embassy in Prague. His name was Lacombe.

Once she had invited him in, he presented her with a cocktail shaker containing Robert's ashes. The cocktail shaker had been his idea, he said. He had bought it himself. The embassy had been unable to afford an urn. He'd had it engraved with Robert's name and dates. He seemed listless and distracted, as if he had drunk too much the night before. Not knowing what to do with the cocktail shaker, she placed it on the mantelpiece, between a pair of silk stockings and a jar of cold cream. The man from the embassy nodded, as if she had unwittingly obeyed some arcane ritual or law. He left soon afterwards.

Later, as they stood on the pavement, saying goodbye, Youki told Claude that when the camp at Terezín was liberated Robert had been offered a lift to Paris, but he had turned it down. He had lost a box in which he kept his valuables—a novel he had started, the letters she had written to him, some poems by a friend. It was while he was looking for the box that he caught typhus. If only he had forgotten about the stupid box. If only he had just come home. Youki began to cry again.

Turning to me, Claude asked what I thought about the story of the box.

"It doesn't make any sense," I said. "How could he go looking for a box if he had dysentery and a fever?"

Youki had implied that Robert's failure to return from Czechoslovakia had been a matter of choice. He had been thinking of himself when he should have been thinking of her. In dying, he had betrayed her, and yet, as Claude and I both knew, he had loved her more than anything. But it was like Youki, I thought, to have manipulated the facts in such a way as to allow her to feel wounded. There was something about this aspect of her character that reminded me of Claude.

"What is it?" Claude asked.

She had caught me looking at her quizzically.

I shook my head. "Nothing."

That autumn, Claude began to struggle for breath. She spent more and more time upstairs in a darkened room, the windows closed, the curtains drawn. The stale air rattled in and out of her lungs. She would hardly eat. Her breastbone showed through her skin. She felt there were two of her, she said, one of whom was drowning inside the other. We wouldn't be moving to Paris, I realized. We wouldn't be moving anywhere at all.

An impatient edge crept into even the most ordinary conversations. Afterwards, she would apologize, but the pattern would repeat itself. Her behavior became moody and erratic, as if she were going through a second adolescence, and I began to feel like the mother of a sullen and precocious child. We no longer slept together. Instead, we turned into the sisters that people had always taken us for. Yet, in some ways, we were closer than ever . . . Is physical love bound to decay, just as everything in the physical world decays? Is it natural for love to change and deepen into something that feels almost spiritual? Had I altered, or had she?

When Edna left, after ten years of working for us, it took me a long time to find a new housekeeper, but in the end I settled on Lucille, a young woman who had been recommended by Bob Colley, and also by Mr. Gibau-Ratel, who ran the post office. She was tiny, less than five feet tall—she seemed dwarfed by our Jersey doorways—but she was honest and industrious, and I liked the inscrutability of her wide blue-gray eyes. She had been with us for only a few months when she approached me one morning and asked if she could clean Claude's room.

"You don't need to ask," I said.

"She told me to go away." Lucille's wide eyes grew wider still. "She swore at me."

"I'm sorry, Lucille. She's not been herself."

Lucille bit her bottom lip.

"I'll have a word with her," I said.

I went upstairs and opened the door to Claude's room. As usual, the windows were shut and the curtains were closed, even though it was in the seventies outside. The only light came from a lamp on her bedside table. The air felt still, almost solid.

"Claude?"

She was sitting in bed with a pen in her hand, a sheet of paper propped on her knees. Ever since the late forties, she had been writing letters—to Charles-Henri Barbier, to Jean Schuster, to Gaston Ferdière. Some of them stretched to twenty or thirty pages. Her eyesight had deteriorated to such an extent that her face would hover an inch or two above the pen, and her handwriting was shaky, as if she were on a train or in a moving car. She didn't show me the letters, but once, as I straightened the blanket that covered her, I caught a glimpse of a single, short sentence. *J'éteins la lampe.* I switch off the light. Its meaning was clear. She was preparing for the end.

"Lucille needs to clean your room," I said.

She glanced at me, her face afloat in the half-light but tremulous, in danger of sinking below the surface, into the dark. "Some other time, perhaps."

"You always say that." I looked around. Clothes heaped on the floor, crumpled paper. Dust. "It's dirty in here."

"I don't want to be seen by anyone," she said. "Not like this."

I sat on the end of her bed and stared at the wall, which was lined with the star-flecked, dark-blue silk she had ordered from Paris. The names she had hurled at me that day—in the kitchen first, then later, in the garden . . . Though she appeared not to remember what had happened, I had been unable to forget. Some things, once said out loud, seem to live on in the mind, with no dulling of their effect. *Vulgar, wooden—ugly* . . . I scrutinized the silk, my eyes moving methodically from one section to the next. There was no sign of spilled coffee, no hint of a stain.

"Can't you do it?" Claude said.

There was a new noise, she told me. She could hear it every time she took a breath. It was like old brass wheels turning. Creaking, but also grinding. Sometimes it was almost musical.

I called the ambulance.

Claude was taken to St. Helier, and I traveled with her. She gripped my hand with what felt like the last of her strength. Her voice was weak. I had to put my ear to her mouth to hear what she was saying. Her breath smelled metallic, as if her gums had started bleeding, and her eyes looked milky, veiled. Once in a while, though, her gaze would sharpen, and I could see that she was well aware of what was happening, and that she hated it. During the first few hours in the hospital, I suddenly understood why our imprisonment on Gloucester Street had been so difficult for her. It wasn't the lack of light or the constant hunger or the cold. It wasn't the way we were kept apart, in different cells, or even the death sentence that hung over us. It was the fact that she had forfeited control. The idea that she might be treated *just like everybody else* represented an assault on her belief that she should be free to create and define herself, with no interference and no limitations. It unmade what she had worked so hard to make—the constantly shifting construct that was herself.

For the next five days I hardly left her side. There were moments when she was awake and lucid, and I did my best to think of subjects that might entertain her. I told her that Édouard de Max had kissed me once. She wanted to know when.

"The night I saw him in the Georges Rivollet play," I said. "You weren't feeling well. I went by myself."

"You came home very late."

"You remember?"

"Yes."

"I was drawing him," I said.

"Did you make love?"

"No. But he tried to force himself on me." I paused. "He said I had nobility."

"Cheeky sod."

I smiled.

"Anything else," she whispered, "that you would like to confess?"

My smile lasted a few seconds longer, then I began to cry. Claude didn't notice. She had fallen asleep again.

Once, in the middle of the night, I left the room to stretch my legs. The hospital corridor reached away into the distance, deserted and immaculate, its floor glossy as a sheet of glass. At the far end, a nurse in a white hat sat in the light of a bare bulb.

When I returned, Claude's breathing was fast and shallow, and her head had lifted off the pillow.

"It's all right, my love," I said. "I'm here."

Her hand lay in mine, brittle and weightless as the skeleton of a bird's wing. Time became an element. Something we were floating in.

Sixty years.

It was a wonder she had lasted as long as she had. I remembered my father telling me about his favorite dish, glass eels. Born five thousand miles away, in the Sargasso Sea, they swam north through the Atlantic, only to be caught by French fishermen, in the waters of the Loire. He wasn't sure if they were transparent when they set out on their journey, or if they shed color as they went. It was hard to believe that such a delicate creature could travel so far. It was a kind of miracle.

There was a moment when Claude's eyes opened wide, astounded.

"Natural causes," she whispered.

A dry husk of a sound came from the back of her throat. Her last laugh. The irony of the manner of her death had not escaped her.

Just before dawn, on the morning of December 8, she began to murmur. Her voice was so faint that I couldn't make out any of the words. I leaned close to her. A sweet dense smell, like compost, or rotting hay.

Her lips moved again. "Lady Noggs . . ."

In the early twenties she had called me Lady Noggs, one of the many nicknames she had given me over the years. *Lady Noggs* was a silent film we watched when we first moved to Paris. At the time, we had been convinced that Joan Morgan, the actress who played the heroine, was homosexual. Morgan had never admitted it, of course. But she had never married either.

While a nurse gave Claude a bed bath I turned my eyes to the window. A rooftop, a gull. A pill-white sky.

The day was ordinary. Cruel.

There are people who claim you can see souls leave the bodies of the dead. They talk about a field of energy that hovers in the air above a corpse. They say it has a shape, a color. I don't know about any of that. When Claude stopped breathing, not long after the bath, I felt something go—but not from her, from me. Can the love somebody has for you be tangible like that, there one moment, gone the next? Does it take up space inside you? And when it evaporates, does it leave a gap where it once was?

Against the crisp whiteness of the pillow Claude had a jaundiced look, but the wrinkles at the corners of her eyes and mouth had been smoothed away. She seemed younger, less troubled. I placed a hand on her forehead. It was cool and damp, not like skin at all.

Death.

A loss of control, an end to flexibility and change. The assumption of a final form.

Everything that she did not believe in.

It was a February afternoon, and I was sitting in the garden wrapped in a blanket, the sea rustling beyond the wall, the air a smoky blue that felt autumnal. The rector had come by earlier. He regretted not having visited Claude in hospital, he told me. He hadn't known she was so ill. As I told you the first time we met, I said, we're private people. That may be, he countered, but you're still my flock. He paused. Perhaps I could have offered her some comfort. If you had appeared at the hospital, I said, she would probably have asked you to leave. I imagined Claude aiming a trembling forefinger at the door. *Get out.* The rector adjusted the glasses on his nose. And you? he said. Are you in need of any comfort? I think it's too late for that, I said. He nodded slowly. After a long silence, he began to recite a poem. *Our two souls therefore, which are one / Though I must go, endure not yet / A breach, but an expansion / Like gold to aery thinness beat.* The English was difficult for me to understand, and I asked him to repeat the lines. When he had finished a second time, I thanked him. That was beautiful, I said. John Donne, he said. Then he gave me his blessing and left.

A gust of wind turned the pages of my newspaper, and I glanced up. Claude's face lifted through the leaves of a nearby rhododendron bush like wreckage surfacing. Her eyes were closed, then open. She was smiling. Something cold crawled up my spine, into my hair. I couldn't speak. In her arms were the kinds of flowers she used to arrange throughout the house, sometimes in such abundance that it began to feel like a mausoleum—dahlias with white fringes to their deep pink petals, blood-black tulips, and dwarf gladioli, their scarlet shameless against the darkness of the evergreens. A question rose into my mind and floated there. *Why didn't you come before?* After all, the cemetery where she was buried was only a short walk away.

She was dressed in the raincoat and headscarf she had worn on the day I photographed her with the German eagle between her teeth. This wrong-footed me. In death, I had imagined she would be flamboyant, as she had been in life, but she appeared to have stopped caring—or perhaps it was a form of tact. She had been trying not to startle me. She had wanted to be recognizable for once . . . I still couldn't think of anything to say. Nor, it seemed, could she. Her smile was benign and wistful, in keeping with the mystery of the world beyond the grave, and it made me feel like a novice. Like someone who embarks on a journey without the proper knowledge or equipment. She had often made me feel like that. It was the fineness of her mind. Not her erudition, though that had a similar effect. The mind itself. The instrument. She *thought* like no one else.

Finally, I spoke. I'm not sure what I said. Something banal, no doubt. Something ridiculous. She turned her face away and sighed and sank back into the bush. She left no trace of herself in the foliage, not even a ripple to suggest that she had passed that way. Had I disappointed her? If I had kept silent, would she have stayed? I put my paper down, and the loneliness that gaped in front of me, like the entrance to a dark, damp cave, was worse than anything I had experienced since the day she died.

Three weeks later, she came to me again. This time she was naked. She was young too, much younger than before. I almost didn't dare to look. I was in an outbuilding we had always called the garage, though we had never owned a car. Thinking I might start drawing again, thinking it might fill my time, I had removed everything except a wooden chair and a door that rested on a pair of trestles. She sat sideways-on to me, on the dirt floor, her thighs pulled up against her chest, her hands clasping her ankles. The sun angled down from a high window, a thick beam of light that reached across her body, making her look insubstantial, only half there. Such a delicate thing, in any case, with hardly any flesh on her, and me in my ugly glasses and my sweater with the holes in the elbows, old enough to be her grandmother.

She behaved as she used to behave when I was photographing her. There was no communication—or rather, the communication was unspoken, based on familiarity and intuition. She knew I would know what to do. Every few minutes she would alter her position, like a model in a life drawing class, revealing nothing but a quarter of her face, or sometimes half, the loose curve of her spine, and the tighter curves of calf, thigh, shoulder, ear, but no disclosure of her breasts or sex, and everything in the garage motionless except for the dust whirling in silent fury inside the shaft of light, and her ribs, which rose and fell, a shell appearing and disappearing beneath her skin as the air went in and out of her, the breathing of the dead . . .

Hairs rose all along my arms.

Afterwards, I wondered what would have happened if I had fetched the camera and taken a picture. Would it have showed rough walls, a floor of beaten earth, the sunlight reaching diagonally across the frame? Or would I have captured, magically, the suggestion of a figure, the subtle but electric outline of a girl—the last faint trace of a great love?

I had thought that if I stayed on in La Ferme sans Nom I would find some measure of consolation, and that memories of the time Claude and I had spent there would sustain me, but my life felt hollow, desolate. My heart wasn't broken so much as missing. I had nothing left with which to feel. We had been together for more than forty years. If I was in a dark mood, she would lead me out of it. If I gave off light, she basked in it. Reflected it. In her absence, though, everything I did exploded outwards, hurtling away from me, vanishing into a kind of infinity. Nothing came back. I felt frictionless, too thinly spread.

I contacted an estate agent in St. Helier and instructed him to put La Ferme sans Nom on the market, then I began to go through the For Sale advertisements in the *Evening Post*. I didn't have much money at my disposal. After the war, Claude and I had remortgaged the house, otherwise we wouldn't have been able to survive. Luckily, though, my needs were modest. I had been looking for several weeks when I found something on the promenade in Beaumont. A solid, unshowy house with pale-yellow walls, Carola stood at the far end of a row of seaside villas, on a narrow strip of land between the coast road and the beach. Though the front door opened on to the road, the real front was at the rear, where the windows took in the whole wide sweep of St. Aubin's Bay, with nothing in the way except a low wall and two stunted cordylines. It felt to me as if the house had turned its back on the land; all it had time for was the water and the sky. Inside, it was just as contrary, since the two bedrooms and the bathroom were on the ground floor, off the hall. If you wanted the kitchen or the lounge, you had to climb the stairs. My desk was in the lounge, in front of a window that overlooked the road. Not long after moving in, I decided to paint the glass. I chose a cool pale green—like ferns. The light passed through it, but people in the houses opposite could no longer see in. It gave me the privacy I had become accustomed to, the privacy I couldn't live without. At the other end of the lounge was a picture window with a view over the bay. A balcony ran along the back of the house, and a wrought-iron staircase curved down into an unassuming rectangle of garden. Lucille, who had agreed to carry on cleaning for me, even though her journey would be much longer, called it "an upside-down house." Claude wouldn't have understood my choice—aesthetically, Carola had little to recommend it—but she wasn't the one who had lived on, alone.

Six months went by.

On a warm evening, as I was changing my bed, the sheet
billowing out over the mattress, a movement beyond the open window caught my eye. The sheet dropped through the air to reveal
Claude posing on the garden wall. Facing east, she was dressed
in a piece of gauzy fabric she had secured with a thin leather belt.
On her head was the flying helmet. It was the outfit she had worn
once before, in the graveyard next to our old house, at dawn.

"What are you doing, you fool?" I murmured. "People will
see you."

I shook my head.

Half an hour later, when I looked up from the kitchen sink, I
saw her reflected in the black glass of the window. I cried out, and
the plate I had been holding slipped from my hands and shattered
on the floor. Slowly, I turned round. She was up against the wall,
where the calendar was, in a sand-colored shift and a pair of dark
glasses. Her feet didn't reach the ground. It was like looking at a
coat hanging on a hook.

I spoke without thinking, my hands blurred with soapsuds.
"You can't do this any more. You have to stop."

She stared at the floor, as if ashamed. This was unlike her. If I
was ever critical, she always fought back, usually with a few carefully chosen and lacerating words that put me in my place. This
new passivity—this *obedience*—felt unnatural. Wrong. What if
she had come for my sake, though? What if she was worried about
me, and wanted to make sure I was all right?

"I'm sorry if I shouted," I said. "I love you."

She didn't lift her eyes to mine, but seemed to radiate a powerful new stillness.

"You can leave now," I said. "Really. You can rest." I wiped
my hands on my apron. "I'll be fine."

AFTERLIFE

When I moved to Beaumont, I was moving to a place where no one knew me. At that time, I still had good days, when I was not in pain, and I would go for walks, sometimes along the promenade, where the railway line that linked St. Helier to Corbières used to run—it had been dismantled just before the war—or sometimes along the coast road, past the shops and the Martello tower, and on towards the little harbor at St. Aubin. I always took my camera with me, especially in winter. I photographed the wide deserted bay, the brooding cloud-filled skies. The empty sea. In truth, I no longer had a subject. My subject had been taken from me. My *love* had been taken from me. Or perhaps that was my subject. Perhaps I was trying to capture what was left after the justification for a photograph had been removed. Background, distance. A lack of focus. I remembered the picture I almost took in the garage at La Rocquaise, the horizon much closer suddenly, the solitude more personal, and more explicit . . . I wasn't sure my photography had any merit. It was just a habit—a reflex. My heart wasn't in it.

Sometimes, in the quiet of the day, I stopped at the Foresters Arms for a brandy. I was terse and laconic, as I had always been in public, and my appearance, which I thought of as forbidding— glasses with thick lenses, short gray hair—tended to put people off. Since I dressed in trousers and smoked a pipe I was often mistaken for a man. I had the feeling, as I sipped my drink or knocked my pipe against the edge of the ashtray, that I wasn't living but waiting, though if you had asked me what I was waiting for I wouldn't have been able to tell you. Or perhaps I would have told you that I was waiting for the life I had already lived. Does that make sense? My life had begun again, but it was also over. This didn't sadden me. Instead, there was a calmness, a settling. A lessening—or removal—of expectation. I took the days as they came, and was grateful for simple gifts, like the color of the evening sky or a letter from a friend.

Towards sunset on a raw, cloudy day—I suppose it was October or November—I was passing the Foresters Arms, on my way home from a walk, when the door in the lower ground floor opened and a young man ran up a flight of steps and out onto the pavement. On seeing me, he stopped and called out.

"Miss Suzanne?"

He had a good-humored face and tousled dark-blond hair, and his easy familiarity led me to think he had a few pints inside him. He had used my first name, though. Did I know him?

"It's me," he said. "Alan."

"Alan . . ." The name felt slow and blurred on my tongue, like ice cream melting.

"You really don't remember?" He wasn't insulted, only amused. His teeth gave off a dull white gleam.

"My memory isn't so good these days," I said.

"I knew you when you were in the big house, with your sister." He shifted from one foot to the other. "I'm sorry she passed away."

"You heard about that?"

He nodded. "Someone told me." A car flashed by. As the headlights moved over his face, it seemed to widen. "I saw her sunbathing once—with nothing on . . ."

He didn't seem in the least inhibited, and I wasn't sure it was just the alcohol. He was naturally carefree. It was a rare quality. Attractive too. When I first heard him call my name I'd had the urge to hurry away, but now, suddenly, I found myself wanting to prolong the encounter. I was lonely, I realized—there were whole days when I didn't speak to anyone—and this insight cut me to the marrow like a gust of bitter wind. There was no self-pity, only a sense of isolation. That dark, damp cave again.

"She loved the sun," I said. "She—"

"She wasn't embarrassed at all." His words tumbled over mine. "I was the one who was embarrassed. I didn't know where to look. I was only about ten." He grinned.

As we stood there by the traffic lights I thought I could see him at the back door of what he called "the big house," a boy in shorts, his hair much blonder, almost white.

"You had a bicycle with red mudguards," I said.

"That's right. I did." He was grinning again. "I knew you'd remember."

"You delivered the groceries sometimes."

"The post too, for a while. You used to come to the door, both of you at the same time. Always the two of you, never just one. As if you did everything together." He paused. "You would offer me a drink of something—lemonade, usually—and sometimes a biscuit, or a piece of cake. Once, at Christmas, you gave me half a crown."

"Was that a lot?"

"Oh yes. Yes, it was. Even rich people only gave me a shilling."

I smiled.

"You know what people called you, here on the island?" he said. "'The French Ladies.'"

"I expect they had other names for us as well."

He laughed. "They weren't being unpleasant. It was just that you were different. Not what they were used to." He looked past me, up the street.

Not wanting to lose him just yet, I thought of a question. "What do you do now, for a living?"

"I work as a plumber. I do a bit of gardening and decorating too." He produced a card and handed it to me. "If you ever need any work done, or even odd jobs around the house—anything at all. My rates are very reasonable."

I looked down at the card, which was dog-eared and creased. *Alan Seznec. Plumber & Handyman.*

"I should be going," he said. "Nice to see you, Miss Suzanne."

"Nice to see you too."

He hurried off along the street, his shirt untucked, his hair glinting in the dim light of the streetlamps.

One bright spring morning I caught the bus into St. Helier, thinking I would buy fresh fish and courgettes for supper. I was in the middle of town, just round the corner from the market, when I saw a woman walking towards me. I had seen her last on the day I was released from prison. Back then, she had fled. This time, though, the sun was in her eyes, and she didn't notice me until it was too late—or perhaps it was only when I was standing right in front of her, not moving, that she realized who I was. After all, many years had passed, and I had changed. So, too, had she. Her hair, once black, was whitish yellow, like the coat on a zoo-kept polar bear, and there were patches of dry skin on her face.

She looked at me, then looked away, teeth gritted. "Oh God . . ."

It was as if she thought I had engineered the encounter. As if *I* were the guilty party. The tormentor. I let out a soft yet bitter laugh. I had always found it savagely ironic that Claude and I, both passionate smokers, had been betrayed by a tobacconist.

"I feel awful," the woman said. "I should never have—"

"Should never have what?" I said.

She glanced at a man who had just emerged from a nearby café. Was she hoping to be rescued, or worried about being overheard?

"I had no choice," she said. "It was the Germans. They came into my shop—"

She took a step closer, one hand gripping the other, and began to talk about the brands of cigarettes and rolling papers we used to buy, and how the Germans wanted to know who the customers were for those particular items. They kept asking the same questions, she said. They threatened to close down her business. I shook my head. It wasn't good enough. She could have claimed that the items the Germans were asking about were popular. She could have claimed that almost every smoker on the island had bought them at one time or another. But she had been too stupid, or too frightened. Or perhaps, still smarting from Claude's insults, she had seen it as an opportunity to take revenge on us. To put us in our place.

"They already knew who you were," she was saying. "Someone told them. All I had to do was point you out . . ."

I stared at her. "You pointed us out?"

She nodded.

"Like this?" I stepped back and aimed a finger at her.

"Yes."

A gust of wind swept in off the sea and circled us, muscular and questing, like a shark drawn by the stink of blood.

"Do you know what happened," I asked the woman, "when my sister and I were arrested by the Nazis?" I said.

"What happened?" the woman asked in a faint voice, almost a whisper.

"We tried to kill ourselves."

She attempted to push past me, but I caught hold of her arm.

"We took pills," I went on, "but there weren't enough. I tried to cut my wrist. I didn't have a knife, though. All I had was a piece of broken tile." I rolled up my left sleeve and showed her the scar. "I made a mess of it, as you can see."

The woman stared at my wrist, her head lowered, her center parting white as bacon fat.

I rolled down my sleeve again, then looked past her, up the street. A man was lifting a cardboard box from the back of a red car. A cat sunned itself on a low brick wall.

"I don't know." I shook my head again, this time at the absurdity of it all. "Maybe we were reckless," I said, "or arrogant. Maybe we brought it on ourselves—"

"No, no," the woman said, talking over me. "I should never have done what I did. It was terrible. I'm sorry."

"All right." There was nothing left to say.

I let go of her arm.

"Thank you," she said.

She looked at me quickly, then hurried past me and was gone.

I often thought of Alan Seznec, but it was only when my kitchen sink became blocked that it occurred to me to call him. He arrived on the same day, in a white van. As he lay on the floor, beneath the sink, I asked him about his life. He had grown up on a potato farm in St. Brelade, he said, a mile or two inland from the bay. He was the youngest of three, the only boy. I asked if he knew the Raymond brothers. He nodded. One of them broke his father's nose. In books they say that when someone hits you you see stars, his father had told him, but when one of the Raymond brothers hits you it's not stars you see, it's a whole bloody galaxy. He grinned. His father had died when he was twelve, he went on, and his mother's brother took over the running of the farm. His uncle wasn't suited to the work. There were arguments. His mother sold up, and they moved to a house on the edge of St. Helier. He didn't like being in town, and did poorly at school. He left when he was fifteen and joined the merchant navy. It was a tradition on Jersey, he said, to go to sea. These days, he rented a flat on the east side of St. Helier. It wasn't much, only three rooms, but he was happy enough.

"What about relationships?" I said. "Are you in love with someone?"

He looked at me quickly from the shadows beneath the sink. He had a girlfriend, he told me. Her name was Leslie. She worked as a receptionist in one of the big hotels. They had been together for seven years.

"It's good you've lasted so long," I said.

"You think so?"

"I was with Claude for more than forty years, and she could still surprise me, even towards the end."

"So you weren't just sisters, then?"

"No."

He nodded to himself. "That's what I heard."

I had thought he might be shocked by what I had told him. Instead, I was the one who was shocked. "Did *everybody* know?"

"Not everybody. Just a few people in St. Brelade."

We were sisters by marriage, I said, not by blood. There was nothing incestuous about it. That *would* have been scandalous.

"It's not as rare as you might think," he said. "Not round here."

We smiled at each other and then fell quiet.

I moved to the cooker. "It's a mistake to think that a long relationship is boring. The longer you're with someone, the more mysterious they become." I lit the gas. Blue flames licked round the burnt base of the coffeepot. "We went through a lot, Claude and I, but sometimes I felt I didn't know her at all. Sometimes I felt I knew her best right at the beginning, when we first met . . ."

Claude.

A leaking around my heart. Was it really ten years since she had gone? My throat tightened. I lifted two mugs down from the cupboard. One of them said I LOVE JERSEY. A present from Lucille.

Alan was on his feet again, and running cold water into the sink to test the flow.

"Is it true that you were sentenced to death by the Nazis?" he asked.

"Yes, it's true."

"What was that like?"

I thought back to my cell—the black iron door, the bitter cold, the lack of light, the fleas . . .

"I was always frightened of the dawn," I said. "That was when the executions happened. Sometimes I heard the shooting from where I lay. It sounded like fireworks." I carried the mugs and the coffeepot over to the table. "If you were given breakfast, you knew you weren't going to be shot. Not that day, anyway. They wouldn't waste a bowl of turnip scrapings on people they were going to execute. Some mornings I was so frightened I couldn't eat, even though I was starving. I just sat on my bed and trembled. Other mornings I thought, *Kill me, just kill me. Get it over with.* The fear attaches itself to all your thoughts. If you try and remove the fear, it can take part of you with it, the way the skin on an orange sometimes clings so tightly to the fruit that some of the flesh comes away when it's peeled." I looked at Alan, who was staring at the floor, his thumbs hooked into the pockets of his jeans. "Even now, I wake up scared. Then I feel the blankets over me, and I hear the sea outside, and I realize everything's all right—though Claude's no longer here, of course . . ."

"Did you receive any kind of honor for what you did?"

"They gave us something called a Silver Medal," I said. "Since Jersey was outside French territory, we weren't eligible for anything else."

This had irritated Claude intensely. During the course of her life she had, at one time or another, rebelled against almost everything she had been given—her family, her race, her gender, her body, even her name—and she tended to resist all forms of recognition, viewing them as attempts to co-opt or label her, but she thought that if we had been awarded a more prestigious accolade—the Legion of Honor, for example—at least it would have come in useful in the political arena, since her name would have carried more weight when she signed left-wing declarations and petitions. The Silver Medal, though? That wasn't any use at all.

"Can I see it?" Alan said.

"It's just a piece of paper," I said. "If you want the actual medal, you have to go to a special shop in Paris and buy it. We never bothered to do that." I paused, then smiled. "Claude was always rather rude about it—until she found out Picasso had got one too . . ."

"My life's so ordinary." Alan sounded wistful.

"No one's life is ordinary." I looked past him, at the sink. "Have you finished?"

He nodded. "Yes. All done."

"Have a seat."

I poured him a cup of coffee. As we sat in silence at the kitchen table, I had the strange but vivid feeling that we had lived together for a long time. It wasn't a feeling I could explain. A fly bounced against the window. The clock ticked on the wall.

"I think you and Claude should be celebrated," Alan said after a while. "There should be a statue—some kind of monument . . ."

"What would we be doing? Sunbathing with no clothes on?"

"I'm serious," he said, though he was laughing.

Producing a packet of tobacco and some rolling papers, he asked if he could smoke.

"Only if I can have one too," I said.

"Of course."

I fetched a saucer.

He rolled two cigarettes and passed one to me, then struck a match. I bent into the flame. I hadn't smoked a cigarette in years.

"During the war," I said, "when we couldn't get hold of cigarettes, Claude used to make them herself."

"Really? Out of what?"

"Rose petals, fennel. Leaves from our cherry tree." I drew the smoke deep into my lungs. "She would dry the ingredients in the sun—roast them, if you like—then season them with cloves or mint or the juice from poppies."

"How did they taste?"

"Not entirely pleasant. Bitter. Our tongues would turn black." I inhaled again. "Not as good as this."

"And the effect?"

"Rather strange. Dreamy. We would drift."

"It was the poppies, maybe . . ."

"Maybe."

Smiling, he sat back. "You're quite something, Miss Suzanne. You really are."

"To look at me, you'd never know."

He watched me across the table, his head at a slight angle. He hadn't understood.

"When you're old," I said, "no one can ever imagine what you were like when you were young. It's as though you've always been old—or as though you've lived two different lives, one of which seems made up and overblown, hard to believe. It will happen to you as well, of course, in time. But you probably don't know what I'm talking about, do you?"

He was still watching me. His smile was calm, affectionate.

I put my cigarette butt on the saucer and reached for my purse. "How much do I owe you?"

"Nothing," he said.

"Alan, really—"

"Not a thing. I was in the area anyway, and it was just a simple blockage." Leaning forwards, he stubbed out his rollup. "If you're ever stuck, or you need someone to run an errand, you can always call me."

"Thank you. That's very kind."

I looked down at the table, hoping he hadn't noticed the tears in my eyes. I didn't want to embarrass him.

At the end of the sixties I received a telegram from Charles-Henri Barbier. He had business in Jersey, he said, and he was wondering if we might meet. Charles-Henri had left for Australia in 1928, returning to his native Switzerland not long before the war, but Claude and I had kept in touch with him by letter. Once, he sent us photographs of Andratx, a tiny seaside town on the island of Majorca. You should go there, he told us, before the rest of the world discovers it. After Claude's death, I began to receive post-cards from wherever he happened to be—Oslo, New York, Lagos, Bombay, Interlaken. It seemed I was often in his thoughts, and I wasn't sure what I had done to warrant that.

When the day came, he picked me up from my house and took me to his hotel for tea. As we sat across from each other, he looked at me with a halting, almost wounded expression.

"You look the same," he said.

"No, I don't," I said. "And nor do you."

He smiled.

"Forgive me," I said. "That was a bit abrupt. I'm no longer used to company."

"You always were abrupt, actually. Forthright, anyway. It's something I remember about you." He reached for his cup of tea. "I used to admire you for it."

"People thought I was rude."

"Perhaps." He shrugged. "Now we're the age we are, though, and time is limited, it seems like a considerate approach, if that doesn't sound too paradoxical."

The thought that I might, over the years, have grown into myself had never occurred to me before. I liked the idea of directness as a response to aging. It upended the usual wisdoms, that engagement with old people was a long-winded, repetitive affair.

"Where's Gertrude?" I asked.

Gertrude Agelasto was his wife. They had married in Australia, only a year after he arrived.

"She's out buying presents for the children," he said. "She'll join us later."

He had four children, I remembered, one of whom he had named Lucette, as a kind of homage to Claude.

"Will you be in Jersey long?" I asked.

"We leave tomorrow."

He had lost some of his hair, and his eyelids drooped at the outer edges, which gave him an air of disappointment and fatigue that was probably misleading. He liked to take his time, even with something as mundane as stirring a spoonful of sugar into a cup of tea. I felt a smile ease onto my face. He had always been attentive.

"Claude wrote to me," he said.

In the early fifties, especially, he had received several letters from her. He remembered being struck by how long and detailed they were.

I nodded. "I think she knew she was dying."

"I wish I could have come to the funeral. I was at a conference that week, in Africa."

I told him he hadn't missed much. It had been an understated affair—a few local people, a distant relation of Claude's from

France. Our old housekeeper, Edna, got drunk at the wake. The weather had been cold and wet.

"I can't believe she's gone," Charles-Henri said. "She was still so young."

"Sixty," I said.

"Was it suicide?" He too, it seemed, could be direct. "When I first knew her, I felt she wasn't long for this world. A cliché, I know, but I'm not sure how else to phrase it." He took a sip of tea. "It's as if what was level ground for most of us was a steep slope for her."

"Yes, that's how it was," I said. "But she didn't kill herself. It was her lungs. An embolism, then heart failure. She had all kinds of health problems towards the end."

"Her path was very singular. She didn't like to expose herself to the approval of others."

"That's well put—and true. Even my approval wasn't always welcome." I paused, thinking back. "She had a great capacity for admiration, though. She loved nothing better than admiring people."

His careful, wounded look returned. "It must have been difficult for you, the last fifteen years."

"I live quietly. I see almost no one."

"You have no friends?"

"There's Lucille, who comes to clean—she's been with me for years—and then there's Alan. He's a plumber by trade, but sometimes he does my shopping for me, or fetches my prescriptions."

"A cleaner and a plumber . . ." Charles-Henri gave me a look that was quizzical, incredulous. I suppose he expected me to have befriended intellectuals.

"They're good people," I said.

"I'm sure."

He stared out of the window. In the hotel car park, a man was loading a suitcase into a car, his wife looking on, and I felt a sudden, overwhelming melancholy. Time taken up with menial tasks, things coming to an end. I shifted in my chair.

"What about you?" I said. "Have you been happy?"

He smiled. "Always the easy questions."

"Well?"

"I have been fortunate."

His marriage had lasted, he said, unlike the marriages of so many people he knew, and he had four daughters, all wonderful in different ways.

"And your work?"

In his work he had also been lucky, he said. His job at Coop Suisse had been stimulating; he had traveled all over the world. More recently, he had been given a position at UNESCO. Everything he had studied as a young man had come in useful—law, philosophy, linguistics . . .

"I read something about you," I said, "in a newspaper."

"Really?" He looked at me indulgently.

"The journalist said he had spent years looking for defects in your character. He hadn't been able to find a single one."

"It's true. I'm perfect." Charles-Henri smiled and shook his head.

"I hope he's not boring you, Suzanne . . ."

We hadn't noticed Gertrude approaching, but there she was, with her lopsided smile, laden down with shopping bags.

Later, she took a photograph of us, Charles-Henri with his arm around my shoulders, and when they sent me the picture I was surprised at how accurately it captured us both. Though Charles-Henri was looking into the lens, he seemed aware of me.

He was full of affection and solicitude. As for me, I faced the camera in my plaid shirt and my swagger coat, uncompromising, resolute. I could have been standing in that conservatory on my own.

Afterwards, he walked me out onto the street. I said I would catch a bus back to Beaumont, but he told me I would do nothing of the sort. I would take a taxi, he said. He would pay.

"Are you all right for money?" His collapsing eyelids added to the impression of concern.

"Yes. Thanks to you."

Not long after Claude's death, I had written to Charles-Henri, asking if he could intervene on my behalf with the *Office des Changes*, since they wouldn't allow me access to my funds. He had spoken to his son-in-law, who was a banker in Paris. Things had become easier after that.

Charles-Henri took my arm. "There's really nothing you need?"

"My needs are dwindling," I said. "Soon they will be nonexistent."

He gave me a quick, sharp look. "You're not thinking of doing something rash, I hope."

"Rash? Since when have I been rash?"

I hadn't answered the question, and he knew it, but he didn't press me further. Instead, he waved down a passing taxi.

"Did you ever go to Andratx," he asked, "you and Claude?"

"We talked about it a lot, but we never quite got round to it. Our health always got in the way."

"That's a pity." He leaned down and kissed me on both cheeks. "Goodbye, Suzanne. Be well."

"Goodbye."

He helped me into the taxi, then stood on the pavement, with one hand raised, until I turned the corner.

On a wet, windswept day in the spring of 1970, I received an invitation to Alan's wedding, which was taking place in August. I propped the card against a vase of flowers in the hall. The silver bells above the names of Leslie's parents glinted in the bleak March light. August, I thought. How carelessly young people treat the future, as though it were an infinite resource!

The last time I had seen Alan, in September, he had done my weekly shopping for me. Once we had put the groceries away, I offered him a beer. I always kept a few bottles in the door of the fridge, in case he called round. It was a warm evening, and we took our drinks out onto the balcony.

"Did you ever love a man?" he asked.

"Goodness," I said. "Where did that come from?"

He grinned. "You don't have to answer, not if you don't want to."

"No, it's all right. You surprised me, that's all." I considered his question. "Actually, Claude was the one who tended to fall in love with men—though I'm not sure 'fall in love' is the right verb."

"Were you jealous?"

"Sometimes." I shifted on my chair. The arthritis in my knees was troubling me. "It was my own fault, though, in a way."

"Really?"

When Claude and I fell for each other, I told him, it was the first time that she felt acknowledged. It was as if I was the first person ever to have *seen* her. In one of the many paradoxes and ironies that characterized our life together, my love for her freed her to pursue other more conventional entanglements, the very entanglements that might endanger it.

I talked about Bob Steel, and about Breton.

"You couldn't imagine two men who were more different," I said, "but Bob was more of a threat."

Alan wanted to know why.

Claude was young when they met, I explained, only twenty-one, and he was even younger. They quickly became close. I didn't think they ever slept together, but he satisfied something in her. It had to do with how he looked at her. Who he allowed her to be. It lasted for a long time.

"What upset me most," I went on, "was the fact that she was flirting with the kind of life that she had persuaded me to turn my back on. It seemed perverse. Almost cruel."

"How did it end?" Alan asked.

"I ended it. I did something I'm not proud of." I sipped my beer, thinking back to the morning when I sat with Mrs. Steel, shelling peas. "I don't think it would have worked, anyway—not in the long run . . ."

"Not like it did with you."

I thought about that for a moment, then I nodded and said, "Not like it did with me."

"You still haven't answered my question."

"The answer's no."

I told him that what had happened to me when I met Claude had been so powerful that nothing that came afterwards could match up to it.

"You're lucky if that happens once in your life. You don't expect it to happen twice." I looked at Alan, the last of the sun on his face. "How was it with Leslie?"

He picked at the peeling label on his beer bottle. He seemed younger than thirty-two. "It wasn't as dramatic as that."

"Perhaps one day I will meet her," I said.

He smiled. "I'm sure you will."

Six months had gone by since that evening.

I reached for the telephone and dialed his number. As always, he answered almost immediately. I thanked him for the invitation, and said I was very happy for him.

"And you'll come?" He sounded apprehensive. He knew I hardly ever went out.

"Of course. It was so thoughtful of you to ask me."

"Well, we're old friends, aren't we. It wouldn't be the same without you there."

"No, there'd be one less person."

He laughed.

On the day of the wedding, I spent all morning trying to think of good excuses not to go. Apart from anything else, I had no decent clothes; I had given them away when I moved to Beaumont. I remembered how Charles-Henri's eye had lingered on the shabby coat I had worn when I met him, though he was too much of a gentleman to mention it. Perhaps if I sat at the back no one would notice me, and when the service was over I would be able to leave without drawing attention to myself. As I approached the church, however, a young man walked up to me. He was an usher, he said. Taking my arm, he led me down the aisle to the second pew from the front.

"There must be some mistake," I said. "I'm not a member of the family."

"You're Madame Malherbe?"

"Yes."

"There's no mistake. It was Alan's wish."

The last time I had set foot in a church, for Claude's funeral, I had almost been sick, and the spillage of lurid green and yellow light through the stained-glass windows and the stuffy, ornate smell of incense brought the nausea back again. I lowered my head, hoping that people would think I was praying. Finally, I was able to look up, and Alan, who was already waiting by the altar, glanced over his shoulder and gave me a smile.

When Leslie walked up the aisle on her father's arm a few moments later, she also smiled at me. I don't think she knew who I was; she was merely including me in her happiness. She had brown eyes and long brown hair, and her teeth were slightly crooked. She looked like somebody who found pleasure in simple things. If my intuition was correct, this was a great gift, one from which Alan could only benefit.

After the service, as I was about to slip away, another young man came up to me and introduced himself. He was Alan's cousin, Edward. Most of the guests were walking to the wedding reception, he said, but the hotel was more than a mile away and he was wondering if I might like a lift. I could hardly say no.

At the reception I drank two glasses of champagne, and when the music began and the bride and groom took to the floor for the first dance I found myself thinking of a dinner Claude and I had given at our apartment on rue Notre-Dame-des-Champs. Youki had married Foujita not long before, and Robert was desolate, his pale eyes paler than usual, as though he had been crying. She should have married me, he kept saying. It should have been me. You don't need to be married, Claude told him, just as we don't need to be married. We're above all that. Beyond it. She had been speaking for both of us—for all of us, perhaps—but there had been a part of me that was unconvinced, and hadn't wanted to be included . . . Later that evening, Youki arrived. She was drunk, and on her own. I sat on the sofa with her, and she began to tell me about Foujita. She had fallen for him the moment she saw him. His black hair cut in a straight line above his eyebrows, his horn-rimmed spectacles. His funny little voice. He came from a samurai family. Did I know that? I nodded. He had almost no hair on his body, she said. His chest was smooth as a boy's. The first time they made love she felt she was lying on a flat roof with a hot wind blowing over her. He had a presence, and yet somehow he wasn't there. Robert appeared and sat on the arm of the sofa. He wanted to know what we were talking about. Youki smiled up at him. You, of course, she said. And he believed her. Two years later, Foujita left for Japan without even saying goodbye to Youki—he had met another woman—and all Robert's dreams came true.

As Alan swept Leslie across the dance floor—other couples were beginning to join them—I regretted that Claude and I had never had a simple, sentimental day, a day when we were celebrated by all the people who were closest to us. Instead, we had made a virtue of being unique and hidden. Since we were excluded, we became exclusive.

"You look sad."

Alan stood in front of me in his black tailcoat and his striped gray trousers.

"Perhaps I shouldn't have come," I said. "I spend so much time on my own these days. I have forgotten how to behave in public."

"You're doing fine. I was just worried you might be lonely."

"You can't worry about me, Alan, not today." I gestured at his clothes. "Look at you, though. You look wonderful."

He grinned. "Do you think it fits? I hired it from that place near Royal Square."

"It's perfect."

"I would have liked to dance with you, Miss Suzanne, but I don't suppose that's possible."

"I would have liked that too."

"Are you in pain?"

"It's not too bad. But I don't think I'll be dancing."

"Well." He looked at his feet, then at me again. "Thanks so much for coming, anyway."

"It wouldn't have been the same without me."

"That's right," he said. "There would have been one less person."

We smiled at each other.

When I returned to Beaumont that evening I stood in the hall, my coat still buttoned. I felt none of the relief I usually felt when I got home. The silence in the house seemed unnatural, forlorn. It took me a long time to adjust.

About a fortnight after the wedding, Alan appeared unexpectedly. I had taken tablets for my arthritis, but they had had almost no effect, and I wasn't able to climb the stairs. Once I had showed him into my ground-floor bedroom, and we were standing by the window, he held out the check I had sent him in the post. "I can't accept this."

"Why ever not?" I said. "It's a wedding present."

"It's too much."

I had written the check in the hope that it might bring them happiness—or if not happiness, opportunity. I didn't need the money myself. I no longer had any use for it.

He tried to press the check into my hand, but I refused to take it.

"Alan, I *want* you to have the money. If you don't feel you can spend it now, put it in the bank. It will come in useful later—if you need a mortgage, or if you have children."

He looked down at the check. "You're sure?"

"I'm sure."

Stepping towards me, he put his arms round me, and I smelled sea salt, paint, and something sweet, like straw. I felt the tears coming.

No one had held me in almost twenty years.

READING PALMS

1972

I sit at my desk, in front of the green window. A Friday morning in February. Outside, the traffic rushes by. Sometimes I sense Lucille behind me in the doorway, looking in. The first time she saw my painted window, her nose wrinkled up. Like an aquarium, she said. I told her I was thinking of a wood, in summer. She shrugged as if to say it wasn't worth discussing. Not many words ever pass between us—she follows the same routine as always, and picks up her money from the table in the hall—though I know she likes to hear me talking French. She speaks Jèrriais, a version of the Norman language that is native to the island, but is beginning to die out.

The pains return, a stabbing sensation low down, in my pelvis.

"Miss Suzanne?" Lucille is calling up the stairs. "I'm off now."

Trying to keep my voice strong and level, I call out goodbye. The front door opens and closes.

She's gone.

I get to my feet and make my way down to the hall. My legs are stiff and sore, and it takes me several minutes to negotiate the stairs. The telephone crouches on a small round table under the mirror. Picking up the receiver, I dial the surgery. I ask Dr. Brown's secretary if he can make a house call. I tell her I have gastric problems. She says it's his half-day, and that he's not available. He could probably call by in the morning, though.

I thank her and put down the receiver.

Back upstairs, I sit at my kitchen table with a cup of tea. The window frames a square of dull gray sky. Rain hides the sea. The radio is on, the volume turned down low. Nixon has left for China. In Britain, the miners' strike is causing blackouts and power cuts. The wind is from the northeast, and the hours of sunshine forecast are nil. I glance at the calendar. Lucille isn't due again till Tuesday, and the doctor won't be here until morning. I'm seventy-nine years old. Perhaps this is the moment I've been waiting for. Perhaps, at long last, the time has come.

I sip my tea.

When Dr. Brown arrives tomorrow he'll ring the doorbell, but I won't answer. He'll ring again. Still no reply. Perhaps he'll step back and look up at the house. I have seen people do that. Then he'll ring for a third time, more insistently. When nobody comes he'll walk round to the back. My bedroom curtains will be closed. Scaling the garden wall, he'll knock on the window. *Madame Malherbe? Madame Malherbe!* After failing to elicit a response, he'll climb the spiral staircase and try the door that leads to the kitchen, where I'm sitting now. It will be locked. He'll peer through the window. There won't be any sign of me. Eventually, he'll cross the road and walk into the hotel and ask if he can use

the telephone. He'll call the fire brigade, who will break down
my front door. He'll find me lying on my bed. When he puts his
fingers to my neck to feel for a pulse he'll realize that I'm dead.
I don't know what will happen after that. It's possible that I've
already imagined too much.

I switch off the radio.

I didn't expect my final moments to be so ordinary, so calm. I
can't hear the fridge or the clock, only the tapping of my ancient,
stubborn heart. The place where my left breast used to be is aching. It's lucky I don't have a cat. If I did, I'd have to find a home
for it. Who would I ask? Alan? No, it would be too much of an
imposition—and anyway, he might become suspicious . . . At the
very least, I would have to fill a number of bowls with food and
water, just in case the doctor doesn't come. I remember how Kid
used to sit in doorways and stare at me, the tip of his striped tail
curled neatly round his two front paws. If he saw me put down
several bowls at once, he would know something wasn't right.
Cats always know. I remember how the top of his head smelled
of burnt coffee, and how I didn't have the chance to say goodbye.

Something about the rain reminds me of touching, or being
touched. The gentleness, the repetition. I lean my forehead against
the big, cold pane of glass. Outside, the gray is giving way to black.
It seems an age since I saw sunlight. And suddenly the dream I
had the night before comes back to me. It was the early fifties,
and I was with Lucie—I think of her as Lucie now, as I did at the
beginning—and we had traveled to Andratx, the little seaside
place Charles-Henri always talked about. We arrived on a bus
from Palma in the late afternoon, children running alongside,

their arms and foreheads varnished by the heat. I thought of
something Dalí said. *To look is to invent.* The one-story villa
we had rented was in the hills above the town. We followed the
owner up the steps that led to the front door, lemon trees growing
in narrow terraces on either side. Lucie had to stop halfway to
catch her breath. The house smelled of the wood fires people lit
in the evenings. There were terra-cotta tiles on the floor, and the
whitewashed walls were smeared with small brown streaks and
splashes where mosquitoes had been killed. The Bakelite radio
was tuned to a station that played opera. The heat was fierce but
the house was cool.

That evening we took chairs out onto the terrace. I opened
a bottle of white wine and emptied black olives into a bowl. The
whole town was arranged below us, a jumble of flat rooftops, shut-
tered windows, and small backyards hung with vines or washing.
People had just woken from their siestas. A man in a pale singlet
appeared on a balcony. He yawned and scratched his belly, then lit
a cigarette, the blue of the smoke he exhaled lost against the blue
of the harbor. Somewhere a motorcycle growled and snapped. The
restaurants on the waterfront would soon be opening. Since the
sun set behind the house, the part of the terrace that was closest
to the front wall was already in shadow. A ginger cat sprawled on
the tiles near our feet. Lucie had christened him Cooper, after
a brand of marmalade she used to eat in England when she was
young. We sat in a strip of gold that narrowed as we talked.

Lucie let out a sigh of pleasure. "Why didn't we think of doing
this before?"

"We were happy where we were."

"But couldn't our happiness have been moved from place to
place," she said, "like furniture?"

I smiled.

A fishing boat eased round the headland, a thin dark flap opening in the water behind it. The muffled chug of its engine carried through the stillness. The sun was warm on my shoulders and on the back of my head.

"My hands look old." Lucie was holding them out in front of her, palms facing down.

"Oh, stop it," I said.

But she insisted. "They're the hands of an old woman."

"I have held those hands," I said, "and kissed those hands. I've felt those hands in my hair and on my body. They've touched every inch of me. They're part of me and known to me, but somehow they're also new. They're always new. It takes a long time for all that to happen." I looked out over the town again. "They're the age they are."

She turned her head towards me and for a few long seconds she didn't speak. The dark glasses she was wearing were large and opaque, and enclosed her eyes completely.

"My philosopher," she said at last.

"You always mock me."

"It's affectionate." She reached across and took my hand. "I'm glad we came. I don't have long."

My throat began to ache. "You don't know that."

"There's no point fooling ourselves."

Lucie's kidneys were failing, and the doctors had told us that nothing could be done. Her eyes had grown paler. The skin had loosened around her jaw. She had lost a lot of weight, but her ankles had swollen. White marks showed in the pink of her fingernails. I had lived with the possibility of her death for more than forty years, a death that would come about because she was careless

with her life. Her desire to be with me could never quite outweigh
her desperation to be gone. I tended to push that knowledge to
the very edges of my mind, where I could no longer see it, but
she seemed determined, with the last of her strength, to drag it
out into the light.

"What will I do without you?" I murmured, in my dream.
What *have* I done?

Deprived of her company, I have deprived myself of all company. I have lived like a recluse, seeing only the people I need
to see—the doctor, the postman, the newsagent. Charles-Henri
commented on my lack of friends, and later, when his wife arrived,
he talked about my anonymity. Not only had I not been celebrated
for what I had done during the war, he told her. No one even knew
who I was! I thought he was exaggerating, but his disbelief seemed
genuine, and I felt obliged to offer him some kind of explanation.
Lucie and I had always guarded our privacy, I told him, from the
moment we first moved to Jersey. Since her death I had lived even
more quietly, if that was possible. It was all my fault, I said. I had
brought obscurity upon myself.

I fill a glass with whiskey and switch on the radio. The news is
just starting. Nixon has landed in Hawaii. In my bedroom are the
barbiturates I was prescribed on my last visit to Paris. This time,
I know that taking too many pills is as ineffective as taking too
few, and I have worked out the optimum dose, based on my weight
and tolerance. This time, there will be no awakenings, and no
mistakes. It seems a final irony that Lucie, the would-be suicide,
died naturally, while I, the one who devoted myself to keeping
her alive, have decided to kill myself. I remember the late-night

conversation in Le Croisic when we were young. The glitter of
her eyes, the darkness of her arms and hands. The fishing boats
beyond the open window. You'd let me go first? she said. You'd do
that for me? And I said yes. Even at the age of twenty, I somehow
knew that I would be better equipped to face life on my own—and
I have been proved right, I suppose, though it has not been much
of a life . . . Stepping into the lounge, I reach for the manuscript
of *Confidences au miroir*, a work she never completed, and turn
to one of the pages where I appear. *I see her eyes, the color of the
weather. I see her little teeth, white petals. No tension in her lips.
The eternal snow of her shoulders* . . . I move round the room, pull-
ing plugs out of the wall, then I pour more whiskey into my glass
and go downstairs. As I look at myself in the hall mirror—the
gray hair flat against my skull, the thick-rimmed glasses, the wide,
implacable mouth—I wonder if it could possibly be me who Lucie
was referring to. *White petals, eternal snow* . . . It seems beyond
belief that I could ever have been seen that way—by anyone . . .

The pains come back, stiletto-sharp. I clutch at the place and
murmur something. They will probably say I took my life "while
of unsound mind," but my mind is the only sound thing I have
left. It's my body that is unsound. My knees, my hips. My pelvis.
Leaving the curtains open, I lie down on my bed. Rain still falling,
dusk falling too . . .

I switch off the light.

Life was simple in my dream. At dawn, we walked on the sloping land behind the house, the sun yet to rise above the ridge, the
air musty with wild herbs. Later, on the terrace, we breakfasted
on black coffee and local fruit—cherries, oranges, green figs. We
swam in the sea and lay in the sun. We read books. The heavy
heat softened our Atlantic hearts. I photographed the villa and

its terraces, the distant mountains, the thin stray dog that moped about at the foot of the steps, but Lucie, at her insistence, remained outside the frame. My pictures were scenic but empty. When the sun dropped behind the hills, we dined in a restaurant that overlooked the harbor. The wooden tables were painted a dusty pale blue, and hurricane lamps hung from a vine-covered pergola above our heads. The owner had hair that clung to his skull in tight white curls. His resemblance to a sheep was quite uncanny. When the meal was over, he treated us to slices of almond cake made by his wife, and glasses of a brown liqueur. I leaned close to Lucie. After this, I said, it will be impossible to eat anywhere else.

I get up and look out of the window. The rain is falling harder, and there are no breaks in the cloud. I have the feeling it will rain all night. I return to my bed and start to take the pills. I realize I have left the back door open. It doesn't matter. I'm not likely to have any visitors between now and tomorrow morning. I reach for my whiskey, the glass almost empty. Things will be easier when I am gone. It's not that I believe in a world beyond this one, or that I have hopes of seeing Lucie again, wonderful as that would be. No, the comfort lies elsewhere. Once dead, I will no longer be aware of being without her. That's why the past eighteen years have been so difficult. It's not true what they say. Time heals nothing.

"You were everything to me," I say out loud, "whether you liked it or not. There was never anyone but you."

My voice doesn't sound like mine. Are the pills beginning to take effect?

In the dream, as we sipped our liqueurs, Lucie told me she missed Robert.

"Desnos?" I said.

"Yes."

I began to recite one of his poems, the poem he had written for the singer, Yvonne George, his unrequited love. *"Never anyone but you will put her hand on my forehead over my eyes / Never anyone but you and I renounce lying and unfaithfulness—"* I broke off and looked at Lucie. "I've forgotten what comes next."

"You may cut the rope of this anchored ship," she said.

There were tears in her eyes. Mine too.

In the late 1950s I traveled to Paris. I had heard that Youki was still living on rue Mazarine, and prompted by Lucie's account of their meeting a few years before I decided to call on her. Though it was early evening when I reached her building, the air was stifling. I stood in the shadow, staring up at her apartment. All the shutters were closed. It would be just my luck, I thought, if she had gone away. I began to climb the stairs. Several times I had to stop and rest. The building was quiet and cool—people at the seaside, or lying in darkened rooms. At last I reached the floor where Youki lived. I rang the bell and waited. I was about to turn away, disappointed, when the door opened and Youki's face appeared.

"Suzanne! Good God, is that you?"

In the twenty years since I had seen her last she had grown much heavier. Her neck was thick, and deep curving folds ran from the sides of her nose down to her jaw. In her right hand she was holding a black fan. It was gloomier in the apartment than it was on the stairwell, and I followed her through a kind of twilight, the silver patches on her kimono floating ahead of me, disembodied, the rest of her invisible. She had closed the shutters against the heat, she said. The heat had been frightful.

She led me into a room I didn't remember, a small lamp burning in one corner. She was having gin, she said. I asked for water.

When she returned with the water, she told me she had been devastated by the news of Claude's death. There was nobody like Claude, she said. It was so dark that I could only see her properly when she struck a match and leaned into the flame to light a cigarette. I felt she was using the heat as an excuse, and that she always kept the shutters closed, no matter what the weather was like. She didn't want to be seen. I asked about her life. She mentioned a few friends, people whose names I only dimly recalled, or didn't recognize at all. There was no talk, this time, of affairs. She didn't seem remotely curious about me. We no longer had much in common, perhaps. Everything that had bound us together—Lucie, Robert, youth itself—was gone. We were two people struggling to remember why we knew each other, and there were long silences filled only by the creaking of her fan and the crackle of her cigarette as she inhaled. It had been wrong of me to come, I decided, and I was about to take my leave when she began to tell me about a Czechoslovakian doctor who had called on her.

"He turned up unannounced," she said, "like you."

He told her he had sought her out because he had known Robert. She asked him in. He had thin hair and hollow cheeks, and his ill-fitting suit looked decades old. Her first thought was that he wanted something—money probably—and she wished she had closed the door in his face, but after a few minutes she noticed a sort of distance in his eyes, as if he were focusing on another, more rarefied world, one to which she had no access. He didn't show the slightest interest in her or her surroundings. He wasn't envious of what she had, or even aware of it. She felt insulted by his all-encompassing indifference. He wouldn't accept anything, not even water.

"So what did he want?" I asked.

Youki reached for her gin. "He wanted to tell me a story."

While in Auschwitz—or it might have been Birkenau, she couldn't quite remember—the doctor, then a medical student, had found himself caught up in a straggling group of prisoners who were being herded towards a low brick building. At the time, he had no idea that the building housed a gas chamber. He didn't even ask himself where he might be going. He was too exhausted and too ravenous to think at all. He was simply putting one foot in front of the other. Doing what he was told. In front of him was a man wearing spectacles and a dark wool cape. He had heard the man speaking French. A dull rain fell, and the mud was ankle-deep. The sky above was thick and gray. It was impossible in that place to believe that there might be another kind of weather—sunshine, for example . . .

Less than a hundred yards from the brick building, the Frenchman became animated and jumped sideways, out of line. As a rule, this would have earned him a blow from a rifle butt or a casual bullet in the back of his head, but none of the guards reacted. It was the sheer unlikeliness of what was happening that wrong-footed them, perhaps. You can induce a kind of paralysis in people, the doctor said, if you're sufficiently original.

The Frenchman seized a young woman's hand and began to tell her fortune. I see a long, contented life, he said, with many children and grandchildren. The woman thanked him and bent her head and drank the rain from the palm of her own hand. What about me? cried a man who was shivering nearby. What will happen to me? He was in his late forties, and dressed in rags. The Frenchman studied the lines on the man's hand. I see a fire burning in a hearth, he said, and the love of a good woman. I see a peaceful old age. *And me? What about me?* Prisoners crowded round, eager to discover what lay in store for them. In every case, the reading was positive. A windfall here, a new job there, but always happiness and love and children, many children. Longevity too. That above all else. The guards stood about, uncertain what to do. Though they all had guns, they seemed disarmed. The sky still overcast, the rain still coming down . . .

Youki asked what happened next.

The guards marched all the prisoners back to their huts, the doctor told her. The Frenchman was Robert, of course, and he saved a great number of lives that day.

Including yours, Youki said.

The doctor swallowed. Including mine, he said. And then again, more quietly, Including mine.

I drank some water.

Youki lit a cigarette and looked away from me, into the room. "I no longer want to think about that time. I'm sick of it."

I was struck by the change in her. The numb heaviness, the disgust. The apathy. It was hard to believe that people like Picasso and Hemingway had passed through these dim rooms, that we had talked and laughed and danced, often until dawn—Robert, Lucie, me, and her . . .

I left shortly afterwards.

The heat was still oppressive, though the sky had faded from fierce blue to a gentle, gritty violet, and the street was no longer divided into areas of stark light and shade. Glancing at the closed shutters high in the building, I felt a tightening in my throat. I knew I would never see Youki again.

You may cut the rope of this anchored ship . . .

The last bright fragments of my dream.

It was hard to leave Majorca. When the taxi pulled up outside the villa, its silver bumper bleary with pale-brown dust, Lucie and I were sitting on the terrace with our luggage. Our ginger cat didn't appear, but the thin stray dog was sniffing round the gate. The driver carried our cases down to the car, and we followed him, but when we reached the bottom of the steps Lucie told me she had forgotten something, and she turned back. The sun was high and hot, and everything was still. The shadows were so black that it looked as if pieces had gone missing from the world. I remember watching Lucie climb the tiled steps and pass through the doorway into the darkness of the house, but I don't remember her coming out again, though I suppose she must have, and I don't remember what it was that she forgot. I only remember the steps up to the open door. The stillness of noon, and the keen smell of the lemon trees. The driver whistling a tune I didn't know.

Lucy Schwob and Suzanne Malherbe

ACKNOWLEDGMENTS

During the course of writing this novel, I tried to read everything that might be relevant, but no book was more useful than François Leperlier's masterly biography, *Claude Cahun: L'Exotisme intérieur*. I owe a huge debt of gratitude to François, not only for his written work but also for allowing me access to his archive and for answering my endless questions, both in person and via e-mail. I would also like to thank François's partner, Christine Texier, for her hospitality during my stay in Conches-en-Ouche. Heartfelt thanks go to one of Jersey's treasures, Bob Le Sueur, for showing me round the island, for drawing my attention to various aspects of its history, and for introducing me to some of the people mentioned below. There were many, in the end, who helped: David Austen, Norma di Bernardo, Louise Downie and everyone at the Jersey Heritage Trust, Bob le Neveu, Alan le Rossignol, Diana Martland, Rod

McLoughlin, P. F. Misson (the Deputy Viscount of Jersey), Maureen and David Ratel, Lucille Renouf, and Derek Villette. Thanks to all of you. On the editing front, I was fortunate to have three such incisive early readers: Judith Gurewich, Katharine Norbury, and Peter Straus. Their insights were invaluable. I'm also indebted to James Gurbutt for continuing to have faith in me, to Sarah Castleton for her rare sensibility and her perceptiveness, and to Alexandra Poreda, for her sharp and focused late reading of the manuscript. My copyeditors, Yvonne E. Cárdenas and Tamsin Shelton, were, as always, wonderfully meticulous. I count myself lucky to be published by Other Press, its independent and single-minded vision epitomized by everyone who works there, above all by its creator and guiding light, Judith Gurewich. I know of no other editor who devotes so much time and energy to making a book as good as it can be. I should also mention the Society of Authors in London. The generous Travelling Scholarship I received in 2015 enabled me to make a much-needed second visit to the Channel Islands. Finally, I'm grateful to those closest to me—Katharine Norbury and Eva Rae Thomson—for their inspiration, their humor, and their love. *Never anyone but you.*

RUPERT THOMSON is the author of nine highly
acclaimed novels, including *Katherine Carlyle;
Secrecy; The Insult*, which was short-listed for
the Guardian Fiction Prize and selected by
David Bowie as one of his 100 Must-Read Books
of All Time; *The Book of Revelation*, which was
made into a feature film by Ana Kokkinos; and
Death of a Murderer, which was short-listed for
the Costa Novel of the Year Award. His memoir,
This Party's Got to Stop, was named Writers'
Guild Non-Fiction Book of the Year. He lives
in London.

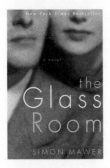

Additionally recommended:

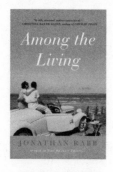

AMONG THE LIVING by Jonathan Rabb

A moving novel about a Holocaust survivor's journey back to a new normal in 1940s Savannah, during the last gasp of the Jim Crow era.

"Jonathan Rabb is one of my favorite writers, a highly gifted heart-wise storyteller if ever there was one. What a powerful, moving book." —David McCullough, Pulitzer Prize and National Book Award–winning author

NVK by Temple Drake

Set in the otherworldly megalopolis that is today's Shanghai, *NVK* blends the gothic, the erotic, and the supernatural as it charts an intense and dangerous affair.

"[A] supercharged, genre-mixing first novel." —BBC, Ten Books to Read in November

"An atmospheric and evocative tale buoyed by a sensual affair . . . a compelling read." —*Booklist*

PAIN by Zeruya Shalev
WINNER OF THE JAN MICHALSKI PRIZE

A powerful, astute novel that exposes how old passions can return, testing our capacity to make choices about what is most essential in life.

"[A] riveting exploration of family, sex, and motherhood." —*New York Times Book Review*

"Always incisive on the complexities of family and relationship dynamics . . . Shalev plunges the reader into a whirlwind story of impossible choices." —*The Guardian*

◨ OTHER PRESS

www.otherpress.com